EXECUTION

A Harry Tate Thriller

When a Russian hit team catches up with Roman Tobinskiy, political opponent of Moscow and former FSB colleague of Alexander Litvinenko, it's an easy kill; he's lying helpless in a hospital bed. They realise too late that in an adjacent room is Clare Jardine, ex-MI6 officer, recovering from wounds while saving Harry Tate's life.

EXECUTION

A Harry Tate Thriller

Adrian Magson

Severn House Large Print
London & New York

This first large print edition published 2014
in Great Britain and the USA by
SEVERN HOUSE PUBLISHERS LTD of
19 Cedar Road, Sutton, Surrey, England, SM2 5DA.
First world regular print edition published 2013 by
Severn House Publishers Ltd., London and New York.

British Library Cataloguing in Publication Data

Magson, Adrian author.
 Execution. -- Large print edition.~ -- (The Harry Tate
 thrillers ; 5)
 1. Tate, Harry (Fictitious character)--Fiction.
 2. Suspense fiction. 3. Large type books.
 I. Title II. Series
 823.9'2-dc23

 ISBN-13: 9780727896728

Severn House Publishers support the Forest Stewardship Council™
[FSC™], the leading international forest certification organisation. All
our titles that are printed on FSC certified paper carry the FSC logo.

MIX
Paper from
responsible sources
FSC® C013056

Printed and bound in Great Britain by
TJ International, Padstow, Cornwall.

For Ann, as always. Harry's biggest fan.

With thanks to Edwin and Kate, and the team at Severn House, for working the magic that makes this a book. To David Headley, my agent, whose input and support is invaluable during the writing process and beyond. To K and E, who have to remain nameless. And to all the readers out there who make this worth doing.

ONE

She awoke to the scuff of leather shoes in the corridor. Eyes dragged open, gummy with sleep, then closed again, a reflex action. Easy does it. Relax. You're safe.

She froze as a random thought wormed slowly through her befuddled mind. *The nurses don't wear leather shoes.* She was familiar enough with the hurried tread of the consultants, or the heavier, measured stroll of the security guards. So who?

Outsiders. Not good.

She willed her breathing to remain steady. Not easy with a hole in her side. She focussed instead on the air around her, going over the small details to get her brain working. She'd been shot. She was in a hospital. King's College, south London – the Major Trauma Centre, they had told her. She kept forgetting that bit. Stuff seemed to leak out of her head all the time like water from a holed bucket.

She concentrated. It was night, she was certain; at a guess, two a.m. There wasn't the hum of daytime activity, the rush of feet, the voices; nor the beep of electronics signifying seconds to someone's total blackness and a bed left empty. Wakefulness brought a throb in her temples and a woozy feeling from the drugs, and the stickiness between her shoulder blades from lying in the overheated, cloying atmosphere for too long. There was a tightness across her middle and the tug of plaster against skin, still tender and sore.

So who was out there? And why now?

The door to her room whispered open. Soft footsteps approached the bed, accompanied by a man's nasal breathing. Her body shrieked with a sense of vulnerability but she remained still. It wasn't hard – she'd had a lot of practice in this place; using it to distance herself as much from the probing of questions as of fingers, of their barely restrained curiosity about what had brought a civilian woman here with a gunshot wound.

A ghost of warm peppermint fanned her cheek. Along with it came the tangy smell of damp clothing. It made a change from the sickly aroma of anaesthetics and cleaning fluids. Must be raining outside. God, what she wouldn't give for a walk in the rain and a lungful of fresh air. And a Starbucks to go. With a double shot.

Some hope.

She tensed as the man leaned further over her. She didn't need to open her eyes to see him. Normal times, she'd have reacted by kicking back the covers and planting her foot in his face for invading her space. Watched him fall and lie still, before stepping over him and kicking him in the balls for good measure.

But these weren't normal times.

'She awake?' A whisper from over by the door. A second man, the accent rough.

10

The peppermint smell receded. 'I don't think so.' The air around her shifted and she sensed the man move to the foot of the bed, heard the clank of the clipboard being lifted.

'What's her problem?'

'She has a gunshot wound to the abdomen. Not pleasant.' This man sounded more educated.

'So she's army.'

The clank of the clipboard being replaced. 'It doesn't say. Most of them are, here. Who cares? She's out of it, so not our problem.'

Footsteps moving away. The door closed and she once more felt the emptiness of space. They had gone.

She continued to remain still, fighting against the temptation to open her eyes. A minute ticked by in silence. Two. Three. Then the door huffed, as she knew it would.

Heavy breathing. They were back.

'Well?' The one with the rough accent.

A long pause, then: 'She hasn't moved. Come on, let's get this done.'

'What if she hears us?'

'Then we'll have to finish what the bullet started, won't we?'

'We could save the bother – do it now.'

'No. There's no time. The guard might come back.' A pause, then a whisper, very close: 'You are lucky, Miss Jardine, whoever you are.'

The soft tread of footsteps moving away.

Lucky? Why am I lucky? Where the hell are the security guard and nurses?

She followed the men's progress, visualising a mental picture although she'd never seen anything of the corridor outside. You don't, when you've been gut-shot, see much of anything beyond the chaotic inner world that is the shock and pain and confusion of memories, some imagined, some real. All the rest is a blur of vague faces and ceiling lights.

The men didn't go far. Next door or across the way, she couldn't be certain. The corridor ended there. Two other rooms, two other patients. No, wait. Next door had gone not long after dark. Rushed to theatre in a controlled scramble of feet and wheels and clanking equipment.

They hadn't come back.

If it was across the way, she knew who they were going to see.

Knew what they were going to do.

Because like the patient in that room, who had gabbled on almost non-stop since his arrival two days ago, including shouting his name several times, the two men had been speaking Russian. And suddenly the mush of details sloshing around in her brain was starting to make sense.

She understood Russian. And from what the man across the way had been saying over and over again, between bouts of silence, there was only one reason for these two men to be right here, right now, in the middle of the night, when the security guard was away, probably on a fag break.

They were going to kill him.

And if they found out who *she* was – and what she had once been – she would be next.

So much for being lucky.

TWO

In a luxury Mayfair office rented by a holding company registered in the Cayman Islands, three men watched as a female technician swept the room they were in with an electronic counter-measures device. The building was checked regularly, but today was deemed especially important in view of the matter under discussion. The fact that this office was held under a blanket of cover names, and that there were no regular staff, led to a clear understanding by all who stepped foot in the building that what was discussed here stayed in the minds of those present and was never confirmed on paper or digitally recorded.

It was especially important to the three men now here, as none had been recorded entering the UK under their real names, and they would have no contact with their official embassy.

The technician finished and packed away her probe and monitor and pronounced the room clean. When she had gone, the three men sat down at a central table and opened small bottles of apple juice.

'Report,' said one of them, glancing impatiently at his watch. His thoughts were clear: it was not yet eight in the morning and his day was going to be busy.

In his sixties, he wore a grey suit and crisp white shirt, the image of a successful business-man. However, he was anything but. His name was Sergei Gorelkin. Once a senior officer in the Russian Federal Security Service (FSB), succes-sors to the old and much feared KGB, he still held the rank of colonel, although his position of Honorary Deputy in the Division for the Defence of the Constitution carried far more weight than that of any military officer.

'The assignment was completed without a hitch.' It was about as much report as Gorelkin would require, and the speaker, Fyodor Votru-khin, who held the rank of lieutenant, crunched on an Extra Strong Mint and waited for the signal to continue. A long-time member of the elite Special Purpose Centre of the FSB, Votru-khin was tall and lean, with the dark looks of a Georgian. He seemed at ease in the plush sur-roundings of the leased office, but after their journey here from Moscow and their activities of a few hours ago, he was looking tired.

Gorelkin nodded and sipped his apple juice, rolling it around his mouth before swallowing. 'Good. Glad to hear it, lieutenant.' He eyed the third man, who so far had said nothing. 'Is that your summary also, sergeant?'

Sergeant Leonid Serkhov blinked in surprise. It wasn't often that he was called on to speak, although every member of the Special Purpose Centre was aware that he or she was expected to have an opinion if asked. But this was unusual. For a start, it was Colonel Gorelkin doing the asking; and he hadn't got them here just to congratulate them on a job well done. There had to be another reason.

'Yes, sir,' he replied, flicking a nervous glance at Votrukhin. Stocky and heavy across the shoulders, with receding hair and high cheekbones, Serkhov looked as if he might be in danger of breaking something if he moved too quickly, and kept stretching his chin to ease the stiff collar of his shirt.

'Interesting. So neither of you had any concerns about the woman?'

'Woman?' Lieutenant Votrukhin lifted an eyebrow, and looked suddenly rather uneasy.

'Yes. There was a woman patient in the room next to the subject.' He waited a few heartbeats before adding, 'Or have I been misinformed?'

'No. No, that's correct.' Votrukhin cleared his throat and threw a warning glance at Serkhov. But the sergeant was staring resolutely straight ahead, the message patently clear: you're on your own with this one.

'She was unconscious or in heavy sleep,' the lieutenant continued. He didn't bother wondering how Gorelkin knew about the woman. The colonel was former old-style KGB, and those people had eyes everywhere and double-checked everything and everyone. He probably checked up on his own wife if he had one. 'We didn't think she presented a threat, so we left her alone. In any case, we had little time to do anything other than what we were there for. The security guard was incompetent, but he stayed on the move.' He rolled a fragment of mint across his

15

mouth but didn't bite into it.

'You took a close look at her, of course?' Gorelkin studied the juice bottle as he spoke. It was a trick he'd perfected over the years, feigning an interest in some inanimate object while asking questions, to make others think he was merely going through the motions. It was rarely the case.

'Yes. She was out of it. She'd been gut-shot, according to her notes. I checked the face. There wasn't a flicker, so we got on with the job.'

'Serkhov?'

The sergeant shrugged, and instantly wished he hadn't. Shrugs in the SPC were not well received. It was seen as demonstrating a lack of commitment. He said quickly, 'I, uh, was by the door, watching the corridor. But from where I was, she didn't move a muscle. Like the lieutenant says, she was out of it.'

The bottle went down on the polished table with a firm tap, and Gorelkin looked at them each in turn. 'If she was out of it, gentlemen,' he said softly, 'perhaps you could explain why, just five minutes after you exited the target building, a woman was seen walking down the stairs from that floor and leaving the building through a rear door used only by staff? Why, the following morning, the room where you had seen the supposedly unconscious or sleeping woman, was empty, and her clothes gone?'

Neither man spoke. They had messed up. Gorelkin wouldn't have been this specific if he didn't have the facts. And now they had to wait to hear what he was going to say. From long

16

experience with others who'd failed in the centre, they knew it wouldn't be pleasant. Gorelkin was every bit the old-style *apparatchik*, but in modern clothing. Scratch the surface of his kind, and there was cold, hard steel underneath. If the current administration ever turned itself back beneath the true cloak of communism, as many wanted, Gorelkin would roll with it as easily as changing his underwear, and emerge victorious.

But the expected firestorm didn't come.

'You can count yourselves lucky,' the colonel muttered coldly, 'that right now I don't have the luxury of replacing you and sending you back to whatever shit-hole regiments you came from. If I did, you'd be on the next plane out!' He emphasised the final word by slapping a hand down on the table top. The bottle jumped, then toppled and rolled towards the edge.

Votrukhin reached out instinctively and grabbed it. Placed it carefully back where it had come from.

'What should we do?' he asked. As the senior man, it was down to him to take the lead. Even if it meant sticking his neck out for Gorelkin to take off his head.

'What do you think you'll do – you find her!' Gorelkin snapped. 'She's a threat we can't ignore. She can't have vanished completely.'

'She was probably just military,' Serkhov put in with unusual bravado. 'A female grunt wounded in Afghanistan like the others in that unit. Why would she be a threat?'

'Think about it, Serkhov.' Gorelkin's voice

could have sliced marble. 'A woman recovering from being shot in the stomach. That's a nasty wound for anyone. But in the middle of the night, the same night you two turn up, she gets up from her bed and walks out of the hospital, taking whatever clothes she had with her. Now that's not normal "grunt" behaviour. Something scared her enough to get out of there – and she had the balls and toughness to get up and walk. What do you think made her do that, huh?'

'She heard us,' Serkhov replied, his tone subdued. He threw an accusing look at Lieutenant Votrukhin, a reminder that he'd urged the lieutenant that she should be taken care of, and he'd been ignored.

'Of course she heard you. I presume you spoke in Russian?'

Their silence confirmed it. He nodded. 'As I thought. Which means she probably understood every word you said. And if this wounded trooper understood *you*, what does that lead you to conclude?'

'She would have heard and understood what the target said, too,' said Votrukhin softly. Both men had received a thorough briefing on arriving in the UK. It had begun with details of the target's shooting by another member of the centre flown over to deal with Tobinskiy in the coastal town of Brighton in southern England. That operative had since left the country. The decision, they had been informed, had been made at the highest level to activate a second team to finish the job, and Votrukhin and Serkhov had been assigned that task. The reason

18

given for the urgency was that the target had been transferred to a specialist hospital in London, and had been heard raving aloud under the regime of drugs he was under. The conclusion was that the risk of anybody working on the unit comprehending what he was saying was moderate to high.

And clearly somebody had.

'It's a big city,' Serkhov put in. 'It would help if we knew something about her ... where she comes from, that kind of stuff. I didn't even see what she looked like.'

'I'm dealing with that. You'll have the information as soon as I can get it.'

'From the embassy?'

'No. Not from the embassy.' Gorelkin paused, then said, 'This mission is running under *chyornyiy* rules; you know what that means, but I'll repeat them in case you've forgotten. You are to have no contact with the embassy or any of our residents or other assets. You understand?' Both men nodded. 'You pass all requests and operational decisions through me. You need something, I will get it for you, including information, money, papers or equipment. You get caught and we do not know you. I will make all efforts to extricate you, but you know that might not be possible for some time. Understood?'

The two men exchanged a brief look, then nodded. They had heard of *chyornyiy* or black rules operations before, but had never worked under them.

'Don't they have next-of-kin details on the hospital database?' asked Votrukhin. He wanted

19

to get this business over and done with.

'No. That unit lists patients' names only. The British Ministry of Defence placed an embargo on any personal information of wounded military personnel being available in case of targeting by the press or extremists. This woman was listed simply as Clare Jardine. I'll run it through our database but I don't expect it to turn up much. I'll have to get it another way.'

'How?' Serkhov queried.

'I'm not sure,' Gorelkin admitted, his anger subsiding quickly as he considered the action to be taken. He reached in his pocket and took out a Blackberry. 'But I think I know of a man who can help us.'

THREE

In a stripped-out three-storey building off Belgrave Road in Pimlico, Clare Jardine came awake in a rush, reaching for the elbow crutch. She bit back on a yelp as her stomach muscles protested. Too quick, instincts overcoming caution. She waited for the pain to recede while assessing what had woken her in the first place, mentally gathering herself for flight.

The noise came again: it was the clatter of a rubbish skip out in the street, followed by a man swearing. She lay back. Normal everyday sounds. No threat. Not yet, anyway.

Above her head the high ceiling showed yellowed mouldings and a tracer work of fine cracks spread throughout the plaster. Bare wiring hung down from the central fitting, plaited and sheathed in fabric instead of the modern plastic coating. She shivered at the chill in the atmosphere. Like the rest of the building, the room was bare, ready for gutting and renovation. Only the two thin mattresses on the bare floorboards showed that anyone was using it, a low-quality squat in a high-society street.

But for now it was salvation. Of a sort.

She allowed the events of the night before to reel through her mind. After dressing hastily in her laundered clothes, and a T-shirt to replace the blouse ruined by the shooting, she had left the trauma centre and lost herself in the darkened streets of Camberwell. She'd headed north on Denmark Hill towards Newington and Southwark. It was an area one of her MI6 instructors had referred to only half-jokingly as bandit country, but going round it would have taken too long. Going south or east was too open; west or north-west would take her too close to Vauxhall Cross and the network of cameras around the building she had once called work: the headquarters of SIS – the Secret Intelligence Service or MI6.

Progress had been slow, keeping one eye open for cameras, the other for obstacles at ground level. Instinct had made her scoop up the discarded aluminium crutch in the stairwell of the hospital, which had helped. Aware that the two men who had entered her room might return and come after her, she'd forced herself to put as much distance between them as possible. But she was still weak after her enforced inactivity, especially in the legs, and bouts of dizziness made the street lights swim in front of her eyes, forcing her to rest up when it got too bad.

Twice she'd spotted the approach of police patrol cars and scurried out of sight just in time, losing herself in the shadows. They looked like standard night-time patrols, but a lone woman might be enough to attract a bored policeman's curiosity. She had been trained to lie for England, but had no rational explanation for being out by herself, or why she was walking in obvious pain. And with her wallet holding cash, ID and credit cards all locked up in the hospital for safe-keeping, not being able to prove who she was would be a step too far.

A couple of drunks had appeared out of an alleyway near the Elephant and Castle station, buttoning their flies. They had eyed her with eager, if unsteady interest, and she'd hurried on, leaving them behind. But at the next convenient doorway she'd studied the crutch. It was light-weight, made of aluminium, with a plastic grip and a cuff for the arm and a rubber ferrule on the end. She'd ripped off the ferrule and stamped hard on the aluminium tip, squashing it into a sharp edge.

Now it was a weapon. She wouldn't last long swinging it, but a look at the tip might put off all but the most determined of attackers. The rubber ferrule was no longer a perfect fit, but it would do. An SIS instruction drilled into the class had been a simple one: having a weapon didn't mean you had to use it. But the value of the increased confidence for a field operative, especially in hostile territory, was immense.

Although she had no easy access to a phone, she had racked her brains for someone to contact. But whatever the gunshot had done to her stomach had also blitzed her memory bank; she couldn't recall a single name or number of anybody she knew. At first she had panicked, staring out at the street in dread. What if she never regained her memory? How would she survive?

But she had forced herself to calm down and think logically. It was what she'd been trained to do in moments of high stress. Things weren't so bad, because she wasn't totally blank. She'd instinctively remembered the location of the SIS building, and the direction to take for South-wark; and she'd recognised the fact that the two mystery visitors to the unit had been speaking Russian ... and that one of them had wanted to deal with her, the words uttered with all the emotion of ordering a takeaway.

'We could save the bother – do it now.'

She shivered at the memory, hating knowing how vulnerable she'd felt right then; acknow-ledging that there wasn't a thing she could have done to stop them.

The rest of the journey to the river had been a blank, constantly dodging the most obvious street cameras, other pedestrians, cars and well-lit areas. But she had made it.

And now she was here.

She flinched as the door to her temporary refuge inched open, and lifted the crutch in readiness. A girl's head popped into view. Orange hair with yellow streaks, face piercings and black lipstick. The body followed, tall and lean. Torn denims and Doc Martens. Her name was ... Maisy? Mitzi? She couldn't remember. Only that she had met her near Charing Cross after crossing the river, sipping soup from a paper cup. She had blagged a cup for herself, then a room here for the night.

She relaxed again.

'Time to go,' said Mitzi. The German accent was strong with an American inflection. 'Are you OK?'

Clare nodded and got to her feet, using the crutch to steady herself. 'I'm good, thanks.' Although Mitzi hadn't asked, Clare had hinted at a broken rib from a mugging while dossing in south London. It happened all the time out there. 'I appreciate the help.'

'My pleasure. We have decided to move north – to Bayswater. I hear there's a place just come up with easy access and no work going on.' She was in the company of three others, friends from university, all squatting wherever they could. It was fun, for them; something to pass a few weeks in the city before heading back home to Berlin or wherever.

But not for Clare. 'I'll pass, thanks. Things to do.' She stretched cautiously, feeling the tug of her stomach muscles and a slight pain where the bullet had gone in. It was better than it had been, but not yet ready for taking on an assault course.

24

Mitzi nodded. 'There's a Starbucks down the street. Pauli is doing the early shift. If we go now, he'll give us breakfast and coffee.'

Pauli. Mitzi's sort-of-boyfriend. Skeletal, moustache, studious type.

'Yes, why not?' She needed food, anyway. And some thinking time. After eating, she'd find a place to sit and work up a plan.

If only she could come up with a name.

FOUR

To Harry Tate, the Major Trauma Centre at London's King's College Hospital in Camberwell looked no different than on previous visits. It was nearly five p.m. on a normal weekday – or, at least, a normal weekday for those not confined here by circumstances outside their control. Yet as he walked through the main entrance, there was a discernible air of unease about the place, as if its pulse was beating a shade faster than normal.

A security guard at the entrance watched him check in at the unit's main desk, and another nodded as he crossed the floor to the stairs. Both men had the ex-forces look about them, with that born-in-uniform appearance it's hard to lose. Harry made his way up two floors to where another guard was sitting behind another desk. Also ex-military, this one was younger and

25

looked edgy. He jumped to his feet at the sound of footsteps, straightening his jacket.

Along the corridor, two men in suits were talking in subdued tones. Beyond them was a line of red-and-white chequered tape strung between weighted plastic bollards. The men looked towards Harry then turned and walked away.

He gave the guard the patient's name and showed his MI5 pass. It was out of date, but he doubted the guard would notice. None of his colleagues had.

The man consulted a list on the table and nodded. 'I'll have to ask you to stay inside the tape, sir. And don't go anywhere but the room you're visiting.'

'Fine. What's going on?'

'I can't say, sir. Thank you.' He handed over a visitor's badge on a clip, his face carefully blank. 'If you'd return that before you leave?'

Harry walked down the corridor, forced by the tape to stick to the right-hand side. Turned the corner and saw the two men just disappearing into a room on the left down at the end. The tape ended there, secured to a hook in the wall. A bundle of bed linen lay crumpled on the floor just outside.

As the door closed, he caught a glimpse of another man inside, and heard the rumble of voices followed by the flash of a camera.

He shrugged and stopped outside the room where a former MI6 officer named Clare Jardine was recovering from a wound to the stomach. She'd been shot saving his life, although he doubted that had been her real intention. Even

26

so, he figured he owed her the occasional visit, whether she liked it or not. The last one had been about ten days ago, before setting off on another assignment. She hadn't been pleased to see him. Prickly by instinct and nature, it was what he'd come to expect of her.

He pushed open the door.

The room was empty.

He walked back out to the nurses' station. There was nobody in sight save for an Asian man mopping the floor and humming. He continued on to the desk down the corridor.

The guard shook his head. 'Sorry, sir. I don't have anything to do with patient movements. Maybe she's been discharged.'

'She couldn't have been; she's not well enough.'

'Like I said, sir, I wouldn't know. You'll have to check downstairs in Admin.'

Harry looked back down the corridor, at the tape strung between the bollards. 'She wasn't caught up with what's going on here, was she? Those men and the tape ... something happened. Was she part of it?'

'I can't say, sir.' He held out his hand for the visitor's badge.

But Harry hadn't finished. He turned and walked back towards Clare's room.

'Sir?' The guard's voice echoed after him. 'Can you come back, please?'

Harry ignored him. Pushed open the door and stepped inside, closing it behind him. If the guard got really excited, he had only a few seconds before help came.

The bed had been stripped, leaving no sign that it had been occupied recently. Neither was there any of the usual monitoring equipment that seemed to be in every room here, and which he'd seen on previous visits.

He crossed quickly to the bed and checked under the mattress. He wasn't sure what he expected to find, but he was being driven by instinct. Something had taken Clare Jardine out of this room, he was certain of it; what it was he had no idea. But part of his former job with MI5 had involved tracing missing persons. Looking for the smallest clues left behind by their passing was as instinctive as breathing.

Nothing under the bed. He checked the wardrobe, a slim, utilitarian model. Nothing there. The bedside cabinet was open and empty. On his last visit it had contained a plastic powder compact in a shocking shade of pink. It had been an ironic gift from Rik Ferris, his colleague and also a former MI5 officer. It was an acknowledgement of the fact that Clare had used a knife blade concealed inside a metal compact and saved their lives from the Bosnian gunman who had shot her. Clare liked cold steel.

The irony was that she didn't do pink – and she didn't do plastic. Neither had she any love or respect for Rik Ferris. It was a chemical thing. In spite of that, she had kept the compact. The fact that it was gone told him that she had left of her own free will.

The door burst open and the security guard came barrelling in. Behind him another man

28

loomed in the corridor, bigger and meaner. Neither looked ready to take no for an answer.

'I think you'd better leave, sir,' the first guard said, and held the door open wide. He was breathing heavily. 'Otherwise we call the police.'

Harry walked past him and out into the corridor, just as the door across the way opened and a head popped out. It was one of the men in suits he'd seen earlier. He eyed Harry, then the guards, assessing details, before retreating inside without speaking.

Harry walked back downstairs, shepherded by the bigger guard, and explained his problem to an admin assistant on the front desk. She tapped her keyboard, checked a couple of screens, then looked at him with an air of studied patience.

'Well, her name's on the list. Are you sure you went to the right room?'

'Yes. I've been here three – no, four times. Upstairs, turn the corner, second room from the end on the right.' He jerked a thumb at the guard. 'He can tell you.'

He received a doubting look and a shrug in return. 'Well, I can only go by what it says here. Sorry.' She turned back to her work.

'Can I talk to the nurses on duty while she was here? They'll confirm it.'

The assistant shook her head. 'That's not allowed.'

Harry took out his card. 'In that case, let me speak to your supervisor.'

The assistant took the card, and without looking at it stood up and walked away, her back rigid. She returned moments later with a large man in a smart suit and rimless glasses, checking his watch with a faint scowl of impatience.

'Mr Randolph's the unit manager,' the receptionist announced, and disappeared behind her monitor with a smug smile.

'Can I help?' Randolph glanced at the card. 'Mr Tate.'

'Did she explain the problem?'

'Uh, no. What's your query?'

'My query,' Harry replied patiently, taking back his card, 'is that a patient I've been visiting is no longer upstairs in the trauma ward. Jardine C. – female.'

'Really?' Another scowl, this one at the assistant. He shuffled behind the desk and tapped the keyboard. More taps and huffing, watched by the assistant who yawned and stared balefully at Harry. 'She was here, you say?'

'Yes. About ten days ago when I last saw her. The nurses on duty then will remember.'

'That won't be any help, I'm afraid.' Randolph seemed relieved to have found another hurdle to throw in his way. 'Following a review of resources, most of the staff from two weeks ago have been rotated to other duties.'

'So that's it? You lose a patient and can't tell me anything?'

Randolph stretched his chin out and sniffed. 'It's not that simple, sir – and we don't actually "lose" patients here. I'm sure there's an explanation. Have you checked the ... uh, patient's home address? Maybe she discharged herself.'

'With a gunshot wound to the stomach?'

Harry's voice dropped to a dangerous level. 'Are you serious?'

The guard clamped a heavy hand on Harry's shoulder. 'Excuse me, sir.'

Harry turned and looked him in the eye. It was enough to make the man back off.

Randolph, the seasoned bureaucrat, interjected quickly. 'Mr Tate, there are hundreds of patients passing through this hospital at any one time. Perhaps you should address your concerns to the appropriate authorities.'

'Authorities? What the hell does that mean? You're in charge – so I'm asking you.'

'That unit – the one upstairs – is, strictly speaking, under the control of the Ministry of Defence. Because the patients are nearly all military, the consultants and staff have specialist responsibilities. We merely supply a service.' He looked rather pleased with that summary and glanced again at his watch. 'Look, I must go – I have a staff meeting waiting.'

Harry recognised the dead hand of officialdom guiding the man's attitude. He wasn't going to get anywhere here. Better to go higher up, to someone who might know something. The one person who knew Clare Jardine's background.

Richard Ballatyne.

FIVE

'You haven't been in touch.' Richard Ballatyne's tone was as neutral as his grey two-piece suit, befitting his position as a head of operations in the Secret Intelligence Service, known otherwise as MI6. He eased himself down on the bench alongside Harry with a sigh and took off his glasses, rubbing his face.

'No need, was there?' Harry shifted over to give him room and watched as the intelligence officer's suited minder strolled past a few feet away. The man was new to Harry, albeit a clone of the previous hard-case, with a suitably square chin and watchful eyes. Ballatyne must have worn out the old one. Another man, slightly younger, in jeans and a soft jacket, with the sloppy appearance of a street rat, lounged on a bench twenty yards away. Who'd have thought, Harry pondered; MI6, equal opportunity employers. He knew their presence wasn't Ballatyne's choice, but since his predecessor had died at the hand of a rogue former special forces soldier, extra measures had been introduced by his superiors.

'True enough. That was good work in Kosovo. Messy but ... useful.' He was referring to an assignment Harry and Rik had undertaken for the UN, weeding out an assassin tracking down personnel suspected of being guilty of rape several years ago in the beleaguered region. They had also succeeded in unmasking the guilty rapist, the shock waves of which were no doubt still rattling the innermost ranks of the UN in New York, but unknown by the world at large.

'We try to please.'

They were seated in Victoria Embankment Gardens, a stone's throw from the Thames and the steady roar of morning traffic along the Embankment. It was one of two preferred meeting places for Ballatyne, the other being an Italian restaurant in Wigmore Street that Harry had never seen open for business.

'They've chopped the trees back since our last chat,' Ballatyne commented, nodding towards the clear view of the London Eye turning lazily across the river. 'Pity. I liked them in full leaf. It's like sitting in a goldfish bowl now.'

'Your choice, coming here,' Harry pointed out. 'You could always invite me to your office and show me your certificates.'

Ballatyne grunted. They both knew that wasn't going to happen. Ever since being placed on a hit list by his former boss, rogue MI5 Operations Director George Paulton, and narrowly escaping with his life, Harry had been let go by the security agency. It had been more out of embarrassment than any doubts about his character or loyalty. Ballatyne, however, had shown few qualms about using his skills, although it would probably never include being allowed inside the hallowed portals of SIS headquarters.

33

'So what's the big flap?' Ballatyne asked, brushing a stray hair from his immaculate suit. 'I was out of the country until yesterday evening, and dropped at least three active files and a second permanent under-secretary from the MOD because of your call.'

'I hope he was worth it.'

'She, actually. And yes, it was. The woman's a professional tick, like most of her kind, but we can't always choose the people we get to work with, can we? Now, spill.'

Harry took a deep breath and said, 'Clare Jardine.'

Ballatyne muttered an obscenity. 'What about her?'

Harry stared at him. He'd rarely heard Ballatyne swear, but this had been uttered with unreserved sincerity. 'Did I say something wrong?'

'We'll see. What's she done now?'

'That's what I'm asking you.'

Ballatyne looked pained. 'Please, Harry – I don't have time for riddles.'

'She's gone. Disappeared.'

'She can't have.'

'She has. I went to see her yesterday afternoon. She was there ten days ago, but now she isn't. There were security guards and suits in the place, and lots of safety tape. Something was going on. Is it anything your lot would know about?'

'Come off it, Harry. We might not be your favourite people, but we're not responsible for every bad deed in the world. Anyway, Jardine's off our hands, you know that.' Harry must have looked doubtful, because he added heavily, 'In official Six jargon, she is no longer a person of interest.'

'So you didn't discover a secondary beef with her?'

'You mean other than her having knocked off an MI6 deputy director just down the river? No. In view of what you described, we did as you asked and dropped all charges. I gave you my word, although God help you, I hope that's not about to come back and bite me on the arse.'

Harry sat back, confused. Ballatyne sounded sincere. Clare Jardine, like Harry and several other security service personnel, had been on a hit list when their presence in a shared outstation code-named Red Station in Georgia had been threatened with being overrun by Russian forces. Without official sanction or knowledge, Harry's boss, Paulton, and Sir Anthony Bellingham, Deputy Director (Operations) of MI6, had issued a termination order on them. Only Harry, Clare and an MI5 IT wizard named Rik Ferris had returned unscathed. Since then, Harry and Rik had worked together in the private sector as security consultants and tracers, tracking down missing persons of significance, often for Ballatyne.

Clare Jardine, in disgrace after being caught on the wrong end of an MI6 honey-trap, had dropped out of sight, resentful and full of anger, but only after disposing of Bellingham with a knife blade concealed inside a powder compact. Since then, Harry hadn't seen her until shortly before she was shot.

'You know why I asked you to arrange the

treatment.'

'I know – she saved your life and Ferris's.'

'And Jean's.'

'Of course. How is Jean?'

'She's fine.' Jean Fleming, a tall, willowy red-head, widow of an army officer and owner of an upmarket flower shop in Fulham. Very nearly a victim of a Bosnian kidnap attempt, she had been saved by Clare's intervention.

'And the Boy Wonder – Ferris? Not hacking into our networks, I hope.'

'He's not. Is there anyone else you'd like to ask after?'

Ballatyne grinned. 'No, that's my lot. Just showing corporate concern, that's all. We've had training in staff relations. It brings out our feminine side, apparently.'

'Poor sod. So you really know nothing about Clare?'

'No. But I'll ask around. Why are you still bothered? I didn't think you two were buddies.'

'We're not. But I owe her.'

Ballatyne grunted. 'You thought we'd wait for the dust to settle, then lift her and bang her up in a maximum security cell, is that it?'

'It had crossed my mind. It's what you wanted to do originally.'

'True enough, at first. But believe it or not, I do like to keep my word, once I've given it.' He smiled without humour. 'Although I can't speak for others in this business.' He got to his feet, shaking out his cuffs. 'Leave it with me, Harry. I'll call you.'

Harry watched him walk away, shadowed by

36

his two minders. He turned as Rik Ferris ambled up and stood beside him drinking a smoothie through a straw. Dressed in jeans and a loose shirt, his noticeably spiky hair covered with a beanie hat, he looked like an escapee from an all-night rave.

'What did he have to say for himself?' Rik asked around a hollow sucking noise.

'He had absolutely no idea what I was talking about.'

'Serious?'

'Serious. Either that or he's taken acting lessons since we last met.' Harry shook his head and stood up.

'You think something spooked her?'

'Or somebody. Maybe she thought they were still coming for her, in spite of Ballatyne's promise. She's pretty messed up. She took the compact, by the way.'

'Really? Christ, she must be in a bad way.' He sounded dismissive, but had a wry grin on his face.

They walked in silence for a while, Harry chewing over what Ballatyne had said. Or not said. Something serious had been going on at the hospital yesterday. He'd been involved in enough security operations himself to recognise the atmosphere of tension. But if Ballatyne knew anything, he was playing his cards close to his chest. He sighed. It was probably nothing to do with Clare, but he felt concerned. The least he could do was find out where she'd gone.

'I never thought I'd say this, but I want you to do something totally illegal,' he told Rik, and

37

started walking towards the underground station.

'Would this have anything to do with getting into official prison records and seeing if one Jardine C. has been transferred to a secure medical unit somewhere? Only I'm not sure in all conscience that I could do that.'

'You'd better. If you don't, I'll ring your mother and tell her what a bad boy you've been.'

'Gotcha.' Rik slam-dunked the empty bottle into a rubbish bin. His mother, with whom he was close, believed he was an ordinary office worker, the most dangerous aspect of his work being the occasional paper cut. He didn't like to give her cause for concern by telling her what he really did for a living.

SIX

British Airways flight 779 from Stockholm touched down at Heathrow's terminal five under a cloudy sky with a puff of tyre smoke and a gentle lurch to starboard. After two hours and ten minutes in the air, some through an uncomfortable stretch of turbulence, the landing received a scattered round of applause from some thirty relieved business delegates returning from a three-day IT conference in Sweden. Most of them had been drinking liberally since leaving Arlanda, taking advantage of the drinks on offer

after the eye-watering prices they had encountered in the Swedish capital.

As the seat belt sign went off, the occupant of
seat 33A undid his buckle and allowed himself to
be hustled off the aircraft, shoulder to shoulder
with two corporate managers somewhat the
worse for wear and loudly genial as they leaned
on him for support. He had introduced himself as
Peter Collins, owner of a small computer con-
sultancy in Birmingham, and they had pressed
their business cards on him before engaging
eagerly in a solid bout of drinking and exchanging anecdotes about the parlous state of the
industry.

Collins wasn't interested in their backgrounds
or opinions, and they were soon in no state to
remember what little he had revealed to them of
himself. And although he appeared to be match-
ing them drink for drink, and his manner becoming just as unfocussed, in reality he spent most of
the flight slipping the contents of his miniatures
into their glasses, which accounted for their
rapid state of intoxication.

Inside the terminal building, faced with this
noisy but good-natured group of travellers, all
holding British passports, the over-stretched
immigration desk personnel gave scant attention
to all but the most obvious queries. Peter Collins looked very much like his companions: a
middle-aged businessman on the tail end of a
business trip and a 30,000-feet bender. What
wasn't apparent was that the recent addition of a
slim-line beard had altered his face just suf-
ficiently to make it appear rounder than it really

was, and a pair of heavy framed glasses reduced the amount of detail on offer, something he had worked hard to achieve with minimum effort.

With a nod from the immigration officer, he was through and away, slipping through the baggage hall and neatly shedding his two companions as they went hurriedly in search of the toilets.

Had they been watching him rather than focussing on their bladders, they might have noticed that he had also shed the unsteady gait he'd adopted while leaving the aircraft.

Collins timed his entry into the arrivals area among another group of travellers, this time in close conversation with a middle-aged florist from Oslo. She understood very little of what he was saying, but he seemed pleasant enough, adding an early frisson of excitement to her holiday.

The usual meeters and greeters were there in twin lines, studying faces and holding aloft the customary pieces of paper or name cards as he walked out onto the concourse. Collins didn't bother checking for security watchers; he knew they'd be there somewhere. Probably junior staffers gaining valuable on-the-spot 'training', with no real idea of what they were supposed to be looking for. When he saw his name on a small hand-held whiteboard, he veered off from the florist with a brief smile and followed the greeter across the concourse to a waiting car outside.

Once in the back seat, he took off the glasses, which were pinching the bridge of his nose, and scratched vigorously at his beard. It wasn't the

40

first time he'd grown one in the course of his lengthy career, or worn the heavy frames. In a career which had often taken him into dangerous situations, subtle changes of appearance were all that had stood between success and failure, freedom or captivity. Facial hair was something to which he'd never become accustomed, but right now, back in the UK, where being spotted would mean his chances of surviving longer than a few days would be unlikely, it was a discomfort worth enduring.

'Take me to the Rivoli at the Ritz,' he told the driver expansively.

It had been too long since his last visit, and he was about ready to kill for a decent cocktail. Besides, this evening was likely to be the only quiet time he was going to get for a while, if experience told him anything. Following a call out of the blue from a person he thought he'd heard the last of, he now had a job to do. It was a reminder from his past that he could have done without, but there were some people you simply could not turn down. He didn't yet know precisely what the man wanted – he had been very cagey on the phone – but the fact that the man had called him was reason enough to risk everything by coming back to London, somewhere he hadn't expected to be for a long time.

Whatever the job, he sensed that it would mean calling in a big favour or two of old acquaintances. He still had one or two here, people he could rely on ... or put pressure on. Either way, first he'd need to brush the dust off his old trade craft and make contact with a man who owed him.

He put it to the back of his mind. First, a drink or two, followed by a decent dinner. He couldn't accomplish anything until tomorrow, anyway. By early morning he would know more about the job. Then he could get to work.

SEVEN

In a room on the second-floor of the SIS Head-quarters building, a hastily-convened meeting was underway. Darkness had blanketed the river outside, producing a glittering row of lights from the embankment on the far side and the occa-sional running lights of a craft on the water. But nobody in the room had eyes for the scenery; they had seen the view from this floor too often in the past to be intrigued anymore. Most wanted the business over and done with so that they could go home. It had already been a long day.

'It has been confirmed,' Richard Ballatyne announced, at a nod from a man chairing the meeting, 'that Roman Tobinskiy was found dead in his room at King's College Hospital the night before last.'

The five men and one woman around the con-ference table with him were silent. Most looked surprised by the news. There had been no need to explain who Tobinskiy was, since they were all well-acquainted with his history.

Roman Vladimirovich Tobinskiy was a former FSB officer who, like his friend and former colleague Alexander Litvinenko, had grown disenchanted with the Russian security agency and the government's alleged involvement in violence against its own people for political gain. After following Litvinenko's move out of the FSB and into exile abroad, Tobinskiy had dropped out of sight, fearing reprisals against him by his former masters. His concerns had not been ill-founded; in November 2006, Litvinenko, who had become an open critic of the Russian government and President Putin in books and the media, had fallen ill in London and later died. The cause was diagnosed as severe radiation poisoning by an isotope, Polonium 210, administered, it was reported, in a cup of tea. It had caused a worldwide scandal and once more highlighted the deadly reputation the Russian specialist security agencies had of following their enemies and dissidents abroad and silencing them.

Nothing had been heard of Tobinskiy other than a brief report that he had allegedly voiced his suspicions through a media mouthpiece that the FSB had acted on orders from the Kremlin to silence critics such as Litvinenko and himself. His precise whereabouts had been unknown for some years, although many suspected he had been in hiding in the United States.

The first to venture a question was the man at the head of the table. Deputy Director of MI6, Sir Callum Fitzgerald, waved a slim mobile phone in the air. 'What was the cause of death?'

'We're awaiting the results of tests. Early indications suggest it was a heart attack brought on by complications from gunshot injuries received several days ago.'

'You called this meeting, Richard,' Fitzgerald said, 'as you have every right to do. For that reason and by your tone, are we to assume that you don't believe it was a heart attack?'

'In view of the dead man's history, sir, no. I don't.'

It wasn't the main reason Ballatyne had called for the meeting; Tobinskiy dying anywhere in the world would have been suspicious enough for anyone. But the fact that he was in London and clearly under official protection of some kind at the time of his death was something that needed airing. And Fitzgerald had just done what he'd been hoping, which was to ask the right question.

'How is it we didn't hear about Tobinskiy's presence here until now?'

'Deliberate cut-outs,' Ballatyne responded simply. 'Left hand knowing he was there, forgot to tell right hand when and why.' He kept his face neutral, but his tone was clearly angry. 'His gunshot injuries weren't considered life-threatening, but he was placed in the Major Trauma Centre at King's by the Russian desk, something they hadn't got round to telling the rest of us.' He turned his attention on the one person who hadn't seemed surprised by the news of Tobinskiy's death, a woman at the far end of the table.

A blonde with large, frameless glasses and an intense, studied air about her, Candida Deane

44

was deputy director of the Russian Desk, standing in for the director who was recovering from a lengthy illness.

If Ballatyne felt any reservations about turning on a colleague, he didn't show it. Like everyone else, he'd been caught on the hop by this development, revealed only when he enquired into the disappearance of Clare Jardine with the hospital authorities. The idea that she had been lying in a room next to a staunch Russian opponent of Vladimir Putin – an opponent known to have been on a search-and-kill list by the Russian FSB for some years – had come as a shock. Now he wanted some answers and he was going to push until he got them.

Not that it would help Tobinskiy any.

'There was no need to copy other sections on the detail, that's why,' Deane replied crisply, her glasses flashing. Her voice carried a distinctly south London edge, considered by detractors to be a sign of the new tide of 'talent' being flushed through the Service as the reliance on the old Oxbridge source of recruiting was losing ground. She didn't believe in making friends and was known to have her eye on one of the top jobs in the Service. Her uncompromising demeanour showed her intentions for all to see, and she didn't care who knew it. 'He had to be kept safe while he recovered. We took the decision to keep it strictly in-section only.' She stared coolly at Ballatyne, daring him to challenge her.

'Safe from what?' Fitzgerald's voice was calm, almost bored, but there was no mistaking the look in his eye; given the high-profile nature of

45

the dead man and the potential repercussions, he too, wanted answers.

Deane shifted in her seat. 'Tobinskiy was caught up in a shooting in a Brighton nightclub a week ago. According to witnesses the shooter walked straight up to him and shouted something in an east-European language before opening fire. It wasn't the first time there had been trouble with Lithuanians or Albanians in the local drugs trade, so it was written up by the police as another gang-related hit.'

'What happened to the shooter?'

'He got away. The injured man was taken to the Royal Sussex. He had no ID on him, but one of my officers heard about it and recognised him. We got him out of there immediately.'

'And hid him among wounded military personnel?' Fitzgerald looked puzzled, although whether it was at Tobinskiy's final refuge or what an officer of MI6 was doing in the Royal Sussex Hospital at the time wasn't clear. 'Was that wise?'

Deane flushed. 'It seemed a good idea at the time and I stand by it.'

'He wasn't that well concealed, was he?' commented a man with a bushy head of hair. His name was Andrews and he headed up the internal security section. 'Somebody found him. If you'd let us know, we could have looked after him properly.'

'There wasn't time. We had one extra man on duty. Placing too much security on that unit would have attracted media attention. They already keep a watch to see who goes in there, hoping for some Special Forces personnel to put under the microscope. The duty guard must have wandered off.' She looked at Ballatyne. 'In any case, there has already been a precedent for stowing non-military patients in that unit by members of this Service. Isn't that right?'

All eyes swivelled like spectators at a tennis match towards this new focus of attention, and Ballatyne silently cursed the woman to hell and back for her indiscretion. But it was too late now; in defending herself, she had effectively swung the spotlight his way.

'You had better explain,' said Fitzgerald with a sigh, flicking a finger towards the red light on the digital unit in the ceiling. 'For the record.'

Ballatyne did so with reluctance. Words uttered here without great care could sometimes prove fatal for a career, often long after the event. 'It's correct that another patient in the unit was a former Six officer named Clare Jardine. She was shot and wounded during an operation against the organisation known as the Protectory. The man responsible was a Bosnian named Milan Zubac, one of their enforcers. As you may recall, they were preying on deserters from the army, looking for information to sell to the highest bidder, before killing off the people concerned.'

'Yes, we know who they were,' said Deane aggressively. 'But if memory serves me well, hadn't Jardine already been dismissed from the Service after murdering one of our own officers?' She frowned dramatically at the ceiling. 'Let me see ... Sir Anthony Bellingham, wasn't

47

it? Stabbed just along the embankment from here, if memory serves me right. How the hell she wasn't locked up in a maximum security cell for a hundred years is beyond me.'

The silence in the room told its own tale, and Ballatyne felt his gut sink. They all remembered Bellingham. What some chose to forget, however, was his involvement in creating a covert dumping ground outpost in Georgia, code-named Red Station. It had not been an auspicious time for MI5 or MI6, and the echoes were still rattling around the corridors of both organisations.

'The case against Jardine was never proved,' he said calmly, relieved that Deane wouldn't be aware of the initial reason for Clare Jardine's loss of position in Six: a messy honey-trap operation that had gone badly wrong in all sorts of ways. Those details had been stamped on at a higher security level than Deane was able to access, but revealing them would only have detracted from anything he might say in Jardine's favour. 'What is important to remember,' he continued quickly, as she made to interject, 'is that Jardine was shot and seriously wounded while saving the lives of two of our people. I considered that sufficient reason to argue in favour of treatment in a secure unit like the MTC at King's.' He glanced at Fitzgerald. 'Others agreed with me.'

'Maybe so. But it still remains to see which side she's on,' Deane muttered sourly, sensing a temporary defeat.

Fitzgerald tapped the table with his mobile,

effectively cutting off further argument. There was silence in the room for a few moments, then he said, 'I suggest that in view of Tobinskiy's ... chequered history and the known threats against him, we wait for the results of the tests and decide on our next course of action from there. If the suspicions we probably all harbour are correct and his death came about through the intervention of those chasing him, then it needs very careful handling.' He frowned and looked at Deane. 'As well as an immediate investigation into how his presence there became known.' He turned his gaze on Ballatyne. 'As a matter of interest, where is Jardine now?'

Ballatyne kept his face under control to avoid looking at Deane. 'I wish I knew. She walked out of the unit last night and hasn't been seen since.'

As he spoke, he was aware of Deane smiling maliciously in the background.

'It was nothing to do with us,' she put in bluntly. 'Bit of a coincidence, though, isn't it – her going missing like that immediately after a Russian dissident dies.'

Ballatyne said nothing. There was nothing he could say in response to the loaded inference that she had dropped into the room; that the unexplained death of a Russian in hiding, and the disappearance from the same location of a rogue former MI6 officer could only mean one thing: Jardine must have been instrumental in his death.

EIGHT

'I don't know if Jardine's got herself involved in something, but you'd better find her before somebody else does. The dogs are being let out.'

Ballatyne didn't wait for Harry to sit down, but spoke urgently. He was seated at a rear corner table in Richoux's restaurant along Piccadilly, across from the Burlington Arcade. For once his minders were nowhere in sight, although Harry guessed they wouldn't be far away.

He looked around at the gilded interior of the restaurant and said, 'A move up in the world from Wigmore Street, I see. Is that promotion?'

Ballatyne grunted. 'It's closed for renovations. I got tired of the décor.' He nodded at the coffee pot. 'Help yourself.'

Harry shook his head. 'Not for me. What did you find out?' It was barely eight in the morning and he'd already had his quota by the time Ballatyne's call had come in, suggesting the meeting. He'd sounded stressed, cutting the connection immediately.

'Jardine's gone on the lam. She walked out of the hospital in the middle of the night without telling anybody, dressed pretty much in the clothes she arrived in. Silly girl's going to kill herself if someone doesn't get to her first.' He frowned. 'I spoke to the consultants. You've no idea what hoops I had to jump through to do that. Anybody would think I'd asked for the Queen's medical history, not that of a former employee. Anyway, upshot is, she was very lucky. The bullet slipped by any critical organs, so no life-threatening damage was done. But she's going to be on a boring diet for a long, long time. And no strenuous exercise.'

Harry nodded. It confirmed what one of the nurses had told him. Fortunately, Jardine was a born fighter and made of tough stuff, which had helped.

'What happened to make her leave?'

Ballatyne sighed. 'There's only one reason. A bloody sound one for her, too. She might have a hole in her but she hasn't lost her instincts. Have you heard of a man named Tobinskiy?'

'No. Should I?'

Ballatyne explained briefly about the Russian and his connection with Litvinenko, and how a section of MI6 had confined him to King's College Hospital for his own protection. 'It didn't work too well – he was found dead in his bed two days ago.'

'Did they check the radiation levels?' It was a reference to Litvinenko's death.

'First thing they did. No more ticks than you'd get off your grandma's second-hand wristwatch. The Russian desk people are now pedalling fast beneath the surface to protect themselves. Fact is, there are those in the know about Russian affairs who think Tobinskiy might have been the primary target in 2006, and Litvinenko happened to get in the way.' He shrugged. 'Not that it makes much difference; the Kremlin was undoubtedly going after both of them, anyway. The Brighton shooting confirms that.'

'I take it they didn't get the shooter?'

'No. Probably back in Moscow the following morning; one of their wet job specialists.' He dropped a black-and-white photo on the table. 'Tobinskiy's on the left.' It showed two men in uniform, grinning into the camera. One he recognised immediately from press photos. It was Alexander Litvinenko, former FSB officer and later journalist, broadcaster and stated enemy of his former employers. He'd never seen the other man before. The photo was grainy and dated and, Harry guessed, probably taken from official files. Both men looked healthy, happy and full of life, and so similar in appearance they could have been brothers.

'To answer your question, we still don't know what caused Tobinskiy's death. But it certainly wasn't through falling out of bed.'

'A hit.'

'Bloody certain of it. Finishing what they started. His wounds wouldn't have killed him; he was over the worst, apparently, although he was carrying a fever and rambling quite a bit, according to reports. Kept waking other patients with his shouting.' He stared up at the ornate décor. 'Unfortunately, there are those among my esteemed colleagues who have conveniently jumped on the idea that Jardine being on-site at the time, as it were, means she must be in league with Vladimir's boys and girls. They know she went rogue in the first place, although not the details, ergo two and two makes five. Her going after Bellingham didn't help. Vanishing on the same night Tobinskiy gets bumped off has just about put the ribbon on the cake.'

'That's crazy. She wasn't in a fit state to kill a fly.'

'You know that and I know it. But she was clearly fit enough to get out of bed and disappear. She's got no money or cards, though; her stuff's still in the hospital lock-up.'

'That won't stop her.' Clare Jardine was a trained survivor; somehow she would find the means to keep her head above water. 'Could she have been taken?' It wasn't beyond the bounds of reason, although why the killers would do so was a puzzle. Lifting somebody from the hospital and taking them out into the street presented risks, even at the dead of night.

'I don't know. It doesn't fit, somehow. Look at it from the other side's point of view and you'd make the same assumption – that she bugged out under her own steam.' He shrugged. 'Whatever. We need to find her. Correction – *you* need to find her. If she's out there too long, she'll get scooped up. I'd rather that didn't happen.'

Harry felt a needle of cynicism. 'You're all at it, aren't you? Secrets within secrets. Who are you protecting?'

Ballatyne brushed the comment aside. 'I'm not. Unlike the others, I cleared Jardine's treatment in that unit with higher authorities. But placing a targeted Russian – and a former FSB man at that – in the same hospital was certifiably

53

insane.'

'Are you worried about her safety?' Harry knew what Clare was capable of. 'She's no school kid. And she stayed under cover perfectly fine before she got herself shot.'

'As you say, that was before she got shot and because she wasn't important enough for us to go looking seriously. Now she's walking wounded and it does matter, because on the one hand she's a useful scapegoat in the event of an enquiry, and on the other they'll want to stop her blabbing about what she saw or heard.' He looked sombre. 'I mean it, Harry; our people aren't going to mess about. They'll put some sub-contract ex-military attack dogs from one of the more iffy agencies on her trail until they get her. And if the people who knocked off Tobinskiy are still out there and looking to do the same, she's as good as stuffed.'

'Russians, you mean.'

'Who else? Nobody else cared about him. I don't have a line on who they are because it doesn't really matter. But I'll bet they've got the FSB oath of allegiance tattooed inside their eyelids.'

'Why should they care about Clare? If it was a Moscow hit team they'll be long gone by now.'

'Maybe. Thing is, she might have heard something, put two and two together. And after the Litvinenko scandal, the last thing Moscow needs is someone leaping out of the woodwork proving they're a ruthless bunch of bastards who'd murder a helpless man in his hospital bed to stop him talking.'

Harry pushed his coffee away. He had a feeling Ballatyne was being unusually frank about Clare. Rik had already come up against one brick wall on the HM Prison Service transfers database, but was currently trying other ways in. Unless her name had been deliberately kept off any official list, she must have gone to ground for her own reasons.

'So you want me to find her?'

'No. I don't.'

Harry was surprised. 'Then what are we doing here?'

'We're not. We didn't speak, you haven't seen me.' He swept a hand out. 'None of this took place. If you say it did, I'll have you taken out and shot.'

It explained the absent minders. Ballatyne was being very discreet.

'So this is off the books?'

'So far off, it's on the other side of nowhere.' Ballatyne looked grim. 'I'm not kidding, Harry. You and I don't know each other.' He held out his hand. 'Give me your mobile.'

Harry did so, and Ballatyne keyed in a number and handed it back.

'That's how you contact me, but by text message only. It's an untraceable number. If you need to speak, say so and I'll call you back as soon as I can.'

Harry stared at him. He had never known Ballatyne to be so cautious before. Whatever was worrying the MI6 man had to be internal – something that he couldn't talk about. Whatever it was, to be using 'black' phones and numbers,

55

it was serious.

'Find Jardine and make it toot-bloody-sweet,' Ballatyne concluded. 'If only to prove I wasn't wrong in putting her in that hospital in the first place. I'll work out a way of paying reasonable expenses, but it'll be right under the counter, so keep the costs down.'

Harry nodded. 'In that case I'll start here and now. First off, I'd like some clear photos from her personnel file, in case we need to show them around.'

'Agreed. What else?'

'Her home address. I doubt she'll go back there, but it's a start.'

'You'd be wasting your time. She sold her flat through a solicitor after the Georgia business; took the money in cash and went underground.'

'I'd still like the details.'

'Why – because of friends, drinking buddies, the man at the corner shop remembering her for her cheery hello? That's a hell of a reach.' When Harry said nothing, he sighed. 'Fair enough. You know best. And I owe you that, I suppose. What else?'

'CCTV in the hospital?'

'I've asked, but they're playing silly buggers, citing invasion of privacy. It might take time, so work on the basis that you'll have to do without.'

Harry frowned. 'It's a murder enquiry at the very least. Doesn't that trump those issues?'

'I thought so, too. But our legal brains say because of other personnel being treated there, it's rather delicate.' Ballatyne pulled a sour face. 'Bloody silly if you ask me, but there you go. Is that it?'

'Who were her buddies around the water cooler at Vauxhall Cross? You know she had some.'

Ballatyne looked wary. It was a sore point. Following the Red Station debacle, it had become apparent that Clare Jardine had been receiving information from inside MI6, helping her to stay out of reach of the authorities. The friends responsible had so far remained hidden, but Harry was willing to bet that some still worked in the MI6 building.

'That's never going to happen,' Ballatyne said at last.

'Why? I'm hardly going to make their names public.'

'I'm sure you're not. But under the circumstances, having you galloping around London after members of Six isn't going to help matters – and I'd never get it sanctioned, anyway.'

Harry breathed easily. In spite of his words, Ballatyne hadn't made an outright refusal. He'd become used to the MI6 man's language, and he had a way of showing when he was amenable to persuasion. All it needed was the right kind of pressure.

'I'm not after the entire department. Just one person.'

Ballatyne looked wary. 'Christ, please don't tell me you actually have a name.'

'No. But it had to be a woman. Someone she worked with and trusted, although not necessarily in the same section.'

'Why a woman?'

'Because she doesn't trust men.'

57

Ballatyne stood up, a flicker of something on his face which might have been understanding. 'I have to go. I've got a round of meetings to stop this thing going global. I'll see what I can find out. In the meantime, let's just hope Jardine doesn't bump into any of Moscow's bogey-men.'

NINE

Clare pulled back her waistband and inspected her stomach in the bathroom mirror. With no electricity, she was relying on the pallid light coming through the small frosted window to see. It didn't help appearances much. Gingerly peeling back the edge of the bandage, she found the skin around the wound looking angry and swollen. It wouldn't look good on the beach, but she wasn't planning on going swimming any time soon. It wasn't itching as much as it had been, although she wasn't sure if that was a good or bad sign. Good if she was continuing to heal, bad if her body was shutting down around the wound because of infection.

Somehow, though, she felt it was improving. Her core fitness had a lot to do with it, and a resolve to survive, the latter something she had managed to keep a hold on even at her lowest ebb. All she had to do now was take care of the injury.

She put the dressing back in place and listened to the sounds of movement above her head. People were heading out to work, vans and trucks were coming and going, and the intensity of traffic was a faint buzz in the background. It was nine o'clock and another day was well under way.

She decided to wait. She had time and she needed to rest.

After leaving the squat in Pimlico for the first time, she'd scouted the area carefully, looking for somewhere else to stay. Keeping off the streets was essential until she could sort out what to do long-term. Mitzi had given her the addresses of two nearby squats, but she hadn't liked the feel of the atmosphere. Too many young guys for a start; mostly foreign and far from home, they had the arrogant air of males on the pull. She could do without the inevitable questions or the aggravation, let alone the danger to her wellbeing if things turned rough.

A walk in the area had soon netted her the two things she needed most: ready cash and a mobile phone. Her own mobile had been lost during the shooting. The money was in a Mercedes, several notes tossed carelessly inside the glove box, and the phone had been scored by a simple brush-past of a busy table in a café heaving with lunch-time trade. By the time the phone's owner realised it was gone, Clare was already halfway down the street, her jacket off and folded under her arm to change her profile.

She was now back in touch if she needed to be, and temporarily solvent. And she had a roof over her head.

The house was a narrow, three-storey building at the end of an alley a stone's throw from Victoria Station. The basement flat had its own entrance and wasn't overlooked, with no access points for tenants on the floors above. She'd spotted the wrought-iron gate purely by chance as she'd ducked into the alley to take a breather and check on the money she'd found in the Mercedes. It was the junk mail crammed into the letter box which had caught her attention, a sure-fire sign of an absent or lazy tenant. But she'd had to wait before being able to try the gate. The buildings on either side were dressed with scaffolding and protective sheeting, and builders' skips were piled high with rubble waiting clearance, reflecting the ongoing fashion for reworking the premises by attentive landlords and picky tenants.

On a return trip later that afternoon during a period of low activity, she had found the gate and the door to the basement flat simple to open, thanks to her earlier intensive training by an MI6 locksmith instructor. Inside, the place was dark and musty, the working surfaces and few bits of furniture layered in dust, indicating several months at least since the last occupation. There was a bed, a table in the small kitchenette and an armchair with sagging springs, but it was enough as a temporary base. She'd been in worse while on assignments abroad.

She'd slept the sleep of the dead.

She slumped in the armchair, a mug of coffee

cooling by her side, and stared at the phone's keypad, letting her mind relax. Calling a number regularly meant you relied as much on familiarity with the sequence of keys as you did on memory. Change the keypad layout and you could get thrown completely until the brain switched to the default of recalling the correct number. She had two numbers at the back of her mind: one she had used regularly, the other only recently. The first one was the one she wanted. But try as she might, it simply wouldn't click into place. It belonged to a colleague and friend in Six named Alice Alanya. Alice had been a constant in her life for a while, closer than friends, yet not partners. Thanks to her, after returning from Red Station in Georgia, Clare had stayed out of the reaches of MI5 and MI6, moving constantly and staying away from her previous haunts. It had been Alice who had kept her secretly fed with information on potential hazards, at great risk to herself and in spite of the huge error of judgement Clare had made earlier which had led to her posting to Georgia in the first place. That same loyalty had led her to remain a friend after Clare had dealt with Sir Anthony Bellingham, the deputy operations director who had tried to have her silenced to protect himself.

The thought jogged another, darker part of her memory, and she felt instinctively in her pocket for the round shape that had become something of a talisman. She took it out and looked at it.

It was a powder compact. Bright pink and plastic, it was gaudy, cheap and repulsive. But she could no more have left it behind in the hospital than have jumped out of the window. She opened the lid. Inside was the application pad and powder in a shade of orange she couldn't have worn if her life had depended on it. But that wasn't the point of it.

Rik Ferris had bought it for her, and it had taken her all of two minutes, even in a post-operative haze, to see the irony. The MI5 IT nerd with the irritating haircut and loud T-shirts had sent it after she had lost her own compact, the one with a concealed blade that had saved all their lives. It hadn't been a friendly gesture by Ferris, she knew that; but it had been one of appreciation.

She turned back to the mobile phone, hoping the distraction might have released the number. It was almost there, but the digits were floating just out of reach like fish in a pool.

She swore softly. The last person she wanted to call was the owner of the second number. Right now, though, she couldn't see any option. Alice she could trust implicitly. But she couldn't recall her home address, only that it was somewhere in north London, the details too scrambled to re-trieve. The only way to contact her would be face-to-face in the street, close to where she worked.

The MI6 building.

She dismissed that immediately. Stupid idea. If they were watching Alice, they'd have her on camera before she got close and the heavy squad would scoop them both up. Even a brush contact was risky and likely to compromise her friend.

She ran her fingers across the keypad, and found the digits coming clear and fluidly. *At last!* It started to ring at the other end. Then a man's voice answered, familiar and steady against a background rush of traffic.

'Harry Tate.'

She couldn't speak. Instead she cut the connection.

TEN

Harry stared at the small screen as he walked along Piccadilly towards Park Lane. The caller had hung up without speaking. He'd expected it to be Rik Ferris but the number on the screen was unfamiliar. Probably a misdial.

It reminded him that Rik was still looking for a way into HM Prison records, and if he became impatient, was likely to start cutting corners and delving into sites and files where he had no business. It was the reason he'd been kicked out of MI5 in the first place: in moments of boredom he'd gained access to files that the security services had wished to remain forgotten. No harm had been done, but, like Harry and Clare, his punishment had been a posting to Red Station and an intended ticket to a quiet oblivion.

He veered into the quieter sanctuary of Green Park and dialled Rik's number, checking his surroundings. A few tourists were milling about, unfurling maps and sipping drinks, and early walkers and runners were making their way along the paths and across the grass. But nobody was close by.

'Fong's Restaurant. We hep yew?'

'What are you doing?'

'Exactly what you asked,' Rik replied, and switched to a Yoda voice. 'No more it is, no less. Up against a hard place I am.'

'Cut it out,' Harry growled, 'or I'll confiscate your toys. You haven't strayed from the brief, have you?'

'No, I haven't. HMP only, just like you said. Honestly, between Five, Six and you, it's like working in a goldfish bowl.'

'Blame the digital revolution. It's for your own good, anyway. I've got another brief for you.' He gave him Tobinskiy's details. 'Run up everything you can on him, see if he had any friends in London.'

'Sure. Anyone in particular?'

'Yes. See if his world ever collided with Clare Jardine's.'

'Seriously?' Rik sounded surprised. 'Why would it? Anyway, if it had, it wouldn't be public knowledge, would it? Ergo, nothing on the web.'

'Maybe. It's just a thought. Check his name for any images, and look for her face.' It was a remote stretch, he knew. But stranger things had happened, such as a known face spotted in a crowd where no mention of them had been made in print. 'I'm on my way to your place. I'll tell you more when I get there.' He had a thought and added, 'You might also run Clare's name through

the mixer and see if you come up with anything
... friends, school ... social media contacts.'

'I did that once before, but no joy. I'll try
again, though, see if anything's leaked out. Are
you saying she's out in the wind by herself?'

'If Ballatyne's telling the truth, yes. She cut
and ran.'

'Jesus. That must hurt.' Rik spoke with feeling.
He'd been shot himself not long ago just a few
hundred yards from where Harry was standing,
and was well acquainted with the pain of a gunshot wound.

'Put the kettle on. I'll see you later.'

ELEVEN

'So, how do we find this damned woman, can
you tell me that?' Sergei Gorelkin didn't quite
pound the table, but it was clear to the three men
with him that he wanted to. Although smartly
dressed as always, in a neat grey suit and white
shirt, befitting his cover as a foreign businessman in London, to those who knew him Gorelkin
was ruffled. 'We have lost two days already. She
could be anywhere in the world!'

He and his companions were seated in the
corner of the Park Room in the Grosvenor House
Hotel in Park Lane. It was mid-morning and
reasonably quiet, but a suitable tip to the service
manager had ensured that nobody else would be

seated near them, guaranteeing privacy.

And they needed it. Having dealt with Roman Tobinskiy, a relatively simple matter for men with the right skills, they were now faced with a much more urgent one: the disappearance of a patient in a room near Tobinskiy's, who may have heard everything that had happened and could, if pushed, explode her news onto the world's stage. That, as Gorelkin had warned them more than once, simply could not happen.

Alongside Gorelkin were Lt Votrukhin, the team leader, and next to him, toying uneasily with a sugar bowl, Sgt Serkhov. Gorelkin's question, however, was addressed primarily to the fourth man at the table, who seemed unaffected by the senior Russian's rancid mood.

'We look in all the right places, Sergei.' George Henry Paulton looked cheerily back at him and tapped the table, commanding attention. 'You asked for my help in tracking someone down, and that's what I'm here for.' He shifted in his chair and gazed out of the window over the morning traffic in Park Lane, across to the green swathe of Hyde Park. He would have preferred being out there, feeling the springiness of the turf beneath his feet and breathing in the crisp morning air, rather than doing a grunt job of looking for some missing woman. But he had to be here with these three FSB thugs instead. It wasn't the best start to any day, but he'd had little choice when the phone call had come through. There were some people you didn't say no to. And Gorelkin, an unwelcome echo from his own past which right now he could not afford

66

to be made public, was one of them.

'Did you know, gentlemen,' he continued, 'that London has one of the highest concentrations of CCTV cameras anywhere in the civilised world?'

'What of it?' Gorelkin murmured. 'You British are paranoid. How does that help us with our problem?'

'Let me give you an example: I could tell Corporal Serkhov here to walk a mile from here in any direction and, given a couple of hours, I could track him every step of the way. I could tell you what he was wearing, what the traffic was like, if the sun was shining – even when he looked rather too closely at a pretty girl along the way.'

Sergeant Serkhov muttered something uncomplimentary under his breath at the implied demotion, but it wasn't entirely directed at Paulton. As a long-time FSB operative, he had no love of cameras.

'We have them in Moscow, too,' Votrukhin put in, sounding almost defensive. 'Are you saying you can use them to find this woman? That will take forever!'

'Not all of them, no. Just a few key locations to show us which direction she took, beginning with the area around the hospital. From there we track her progress, playing leapfrog.'

Serkhov looked puzzled, and Votrukhin explained what it meant.

'It's quicker than going through them all. Once we have one sighting, there's a new piece of body recognition software that takes care of the rest.' He smiled at their doubting expressions. 'It acts like a template, picking out any figure with similar characteristics, even in a football crowd.'

'You sound very sure of yourself,' said Gorelkin.

'I am. This is my turf, don't forget. I can use that to my advantage.'

Serkhov frowned. 'Turf? What is that?'

'He means it's his back garden,' Votrukhin muttered sourly. 'He knows it like he knows his home.'

'Quite right, Fyodor.' Paulton was indifferent to the lieutenant's tone. 'I have a feel for this city. I also know how frightened people think ... how they react when they're on the run. I know all the likely places they'd run to.' He tapped the table again. 'But we're getting ahead of ourselves. You still haven't told me the name of the person you're looking for.'

Gorelkin gestured at Votrukhin to go ahead, and the lieutenant said, 'The name on the hospital chart was Jardine. Clare Jardine.'

A few moments went by, and Paulton felt the air contract about his head as the name came whistling back out of the past. But he kept his face carefully blank as his mind raced over the possibilities. A giant coincidence? Or the playful hand of fate?

Jardine – if it was the same one – was just a name; he'd never had the dubious pleasure of meeting its owner. But clearly something these Russian clowns weren't aware of was that the woman they had mislaid, the same woman who had been in an adjacent room to where the troublesome Tobinskiy had breathed his final breath, could in all likelihood be a former MI6 operative who had killed her own boss with a concealed knife blade. Given half a chance, she would undoubtedly like to add his name to the list, too, if she ever laid eyes on him. The thought made his bowels twitch.

He also knew that Jardine had helped Harry Tate not so long ago on a job that had very nearly ended with Paulton's capture. He'd been lucky to escape that by the narrowest margin. Jardine, however, had been shot and very nearly killed by a Bosnian gunman working with Paulton. He hadn't given a thought afterwards about where she had gone to. Now, it seemed, he had a possible answer. How many Clare Jardines could there be, after all, being treated for gunshot wounds in specialist medical units?

He swore silently while pretending to run the name through his mental database. He could kid himself that if he'd known from the outset who he was being asked to trace, he would have refused to come. But deep down he knew that was a lie. In spite of staying below the radar, Gorelkin had been able to get in touch with him quite easily to make this demand. It would have been simple, had Paulton refused, for the FSB man to have passed on details of his whereabouts to MI5 and MI6, both of which had his name on search-and-detain lists.

In any case, he had to confirm first of all that it was the same woman. Even knowing something deep down wasn't enough; always check and double-check, a basic rule of intelligence work.

'Can you do this?' Gorelkin interrupted his thoughts. The Russian sounded excited. In his senior position in the Division for the Defence of the Constitution, he undoubtedly received a regular flood of information culled from all over the world about new technological advances, much of it aimed at security, surveillance, espionage and law enforcement. He would have heard of this latest digital development, might even have seen it working.

'I don't actually have access to it myself,' Paulton told him smoothly. 'But I have a contact in the Metropolitan Police who can arrange for a search to be made.' He rubbed his thumb and fingers together. 'It would take a small fee, of course, but I'm sure that's not a problem, is it?'

'How much?' Gorelkin's sour mood had evaporated, as if fanned away by the promise of positive action, and he was now almost jovial, like an indulgent parent being asked for pocket money by a child.

'It depends how badly – and how quickly – you want to find her.'

Gorelkin gave a cold smile. 'Very badly and right now. Good enough?'

Paulton nodded and took out a mobile phone. 'That's what I like to hear.' He excused himself and walked away, leaving the three Russians staring at each other.

'Can we trust this pompous little shit?' asked Votrukhin sourly. He was still smarting from being held responsible for not seeing a possible

70

threat from the Jardine woman. And now this Englishman with the all-knowing attitude was making the job look like a walk in the park across the way. 'Where does he get his expertise and contacts?'

Gorelkin looked at him. 'There was a time, Votrukhin, my friend, when that pompous little shit, as you call him, would have been tracking *you* right now through this city. He would have had a discreet mobile team around you the moment you stepped off the plane and would have known where you went, who you saw, when you scratched your arse and on which side. And you wouldn't have known they were there. And all that without this–' he waved a circular finger in the air – 'fancy camera technology. Paulton used to be an operations director for MI5. And he was very good at what he did.'

'So why is he helping us now?' asked Serkhov.

'He's a capitalist at heart; he joined the private sector. I believe it pays better and he gets to choose what he does.'

'So we're paying him?' Serkhov looked puzzled by the idea. He was more accustomed to telling people what to do; if they complied, which was nearly always, it was because he had the means and information that left them with little choice. Life was simple that way.

'In a manner of speaking.' Gorelkin considered the matter for a moment. 'Let me put it this way: Paulton owes me one or two favours. I helped keep him out of jail once he left his position in MI5, and he performed certain ... tasks for me in return. Tasks his former masters would almost

71

certainly not approve of. Paulton knows I like bargains to be kept, and his payment for helping us now is that he gets to live a little longer.' He glanced at Votrukhin as Paulton walked back into the room, slipping his mobile into his pocket. 'As to your question about whether we can trust him, not in a million years. He's a traitor born and bred. You should bear that in mind.'

Paulton sensed, as he returned to the table, that the Russians had been talking about him. It didn't bother him; he'd have been amazed if they hadn't. He was, after all, a former enemy, even though he was now helping them out in their dirty hour of need. Suspicions would be natural on both sides. But he was determined that this would be the last time Gorelkin crooked his finger at him like a master summoning a servant. He'd do this one job, but not merely because Gorelkin had demanded it. He had a much broader plan in mind; one which would see him triumph over adversity. He hadn't yet finalised the full details, but the framework was there.

Then a great many people would find the tables turned.

He'd made a call to his contact in the Met, just as he'd told the Russians. It added slightly to the risk of exposure, but his choices were limited if he wanted to make this visit as productive as possible. What Gorelkin and his goons didn't know was that he'd made a second call, this to a person high up the food chain, a person with the means and position in the intelligence community to assist his return to the UK – and not under a false flag and a silly beard, either.

That same person had also given him the information he was after: it was indeed former MI6 killer Clare Jardine who had been in King's College until the other night. Not that he was about to tell the Russians just yet. Better to keep some things back and retain a home advantage. But the information made his next course of action quite simple: find Jardine, turn her over to Gorelkin and his thugs, then set about selling them all as part of his retirement plan to come back home for good.

It made using his contact in the Met Police even more urgent. It might burn the man if anyone caught him with his hands on the CCTV search button, but that was too bad. He'd have to make it worth his while.

He was tired of running. Tired of looking over his shoulder. Tired of wondering if Harry Tate – no, *knowing* – was out there somewhere, waiting to take him down.

It was time to come in.

All he needed was a bargaining tool that they simply couldn't turn down.

'She's got nowhere to run,' he announced as he sat down. 'She's the product of a care home. She got caught in a gang shooting in Streatham, south London and King's College was the nearest unit.'

'But she understood Russian,' Gorelkin muttered. 'How is that possible for a girl from a care home?'

Paulton thought quickly. 'Simple. She was said

73

to be running with a couple of Ukrainians at the time she was shot.' The lie came easily. It was better than giving them anything they could fasten on and double-check, and was part of the trade-craft he'd learned many years ago: use elements of the truth for real colour, but sprinkled liberally with facts that were difficult or impossible to verify. The delay would give him time to engineer something himself. Part of the bargain for coming in. 'Even Ukrainians go in for pillow talk, don't they?'

'Ukrainians.' Gorelkin looked disappointed and Paulton knew why. In the Russian's world, family members offered a bargaining tool; a leverage point. But gang members weren't family and couldn't be coerced – even assuming they could be tracked down.

'Don't worry,' Paulton said smoothly, and indicated the two FSB operatives. 'I have my resources. Your men can start looking and I'll get things rolling. I should have some answers in a couple of hours. Perhaps I could have a mobile number to contact you?'

Gorelkin flicked a finger at Votrukhin to give Paulton his number. 'You can talk to him. He will pass messages to me.'

Paulton nodded. Gorelkin was being very careful, using his man as a cut-out. It was standard cell procedure. If anyone locked onto Votrukhin, it would end there.

TWELVE

'Nothing.' Rik handed Harry a coffee and nodded at the laptop screen, open on his living room table. The air in the room was stuffy and the machine's fan cooler was whirring busily, pointing to a long period of constant use. In the street outside, traffic noises signalled life in the Paddington area going on as usual.

'Nothing at all?'

'No mention of any prison transfers of females below the age of forty in the last five days. Unless they dropped her into the system without a tag, which I suppose could be possible, she's not in there. Knowing the way their bureaucratic minds work, they'd have had to provide her with a file, even if they'd given her a cover name. But the bio and physical details would have had to be similar, and I found nothing like a reasonable match.'

Harry agreed. Even given MI6's possible involvement, the civil service minds would have demanded some appropriate, if false, paperwork for a prisoner transfer, if only for health and safety reasons. And there was only so much fudging of details possible before somebody noticed and shouted out loud.

'What else?'

'About Tobinskiy, the usual stuff, mostly going back some years.' Rik pointed at a small stack of A4 sheets on a sideboard next to an inkjet printer. 'I printed off what was relevant for you, just in case. Since Litvinenko got iced, Tobinskiy's been keeping a low profile. He published some bits and pieces supporting calls for an investigation into the murder and Putin himself, but always through third parties. I trawled through photos as well, but they were all old, too. If the FSB taught him one thing, it was how to disappear. Until now, anyway.'

Harry flicked through the papers. Culled from newspapers, Wikipedia and similar sites, most of the material was the usual speculative biographical detail, larded with sinister hints about his former position in the FSB alongside Alexander Litvinenko.

He was surprised at the uncanny likeness between the two men. Perhaps there was some mileage in the suspicion voiced by Ballatyne that the wrong man had died. Not that it mattered now, anyway. Dead was dead.

'And no mentions of Clare?'

'Zilch. No photos, no tags on social media, no references anywhere. Unless Jardine was a long-term cover name, she stayed way off the net. It would help if we could check the name through Six. They'd know for sure.'

'I'm working on that. But don't hold your breath.' For some intelligence officers, using a long-term cover name or 'legend' instead of their own name, was to avoid the risk of their profession drawing attention to members of their family. Others used legends when working undercover for very long periods, allowing the false identity to take over completely. It was a risky strategy, however, as there was a danger of the line between the two becoming genuinely blurred and the officer losing sight of what was real.

He brought Rik up to date on his chat with Ballatyne. It didn't take long.

'The interesting thing is, Ballatyne's not a happy man,' he concluded. 'Something's going on back at the office and he's very jumpy.'

'Bit of internal political back-stabbing going on, probably. Lots of it about. Still, at least we've got a job. As long as he pays us, I don't mind. Where do we start?'

'We already have. Let's summarise what we know.' He sat down. It was their way of forcing clarity on a situation by brainstorming the possibilities. They usually had more to go on when tracing people, such as documents, tickets, background details, friends or work colleagues. But with Clare they had none. And unless Ballatyne came up with a name, even the work angle would be a non-starter.

'If Clare bugged out before she's ready, it's because she knew it wasn't safe to stay. Why would that be?'

'She heard something.'

'Right. Let's assume it was something Tobinskiy said in his delirium. If he was rambling, he could have been dredging up all manner of stuff. It could be something with serious implications for the Russians.' He stopped. Something that

77

hadn't occurred to him before needed answering. He took out his mobile and texted a simple question:

Does Clare spk Russian?

He pressed send and hoped Ballatyne got back to him soon.

'If Tobinskiy was knocked off,' Rik said, continuing the train of thought, 'she might have heard or seen who did it. That would have been enough to scare her off.'

Harry agreed. But he wasn't sure if that was the whole answer. Clare didn't scare. Unlike normal people, she was too messed up to know the meaning of fear. But she *was* ultra-careful. And boneheaded. It was what had kept her alive so far.

'So where would she go? No money, no easy contacts, what would she do?'

Rik shrugged. 'She'd do what she was trained to do: duck out of sight. But then ... I don't know. Christ, she's not exactly firing on all cylinders, is she?'

Before Harry could answer, his mobile gave a succession of beeps. He looked at the screen and saw there was an incoming message. It was a single word.

Yes

He tossed the mobile to Rik, so he could read the message. 'There's your answer. She heard and understood what Tobinskiy was shouting. Same if she heard anyone speaking to him.'

Rik nodded. 'Enough to drive her onto the street.' He returned the phone. 'If she's gone deep, she might never come up again. What then?'

'Then she's on her own. She'll have to rely on her wits – or someone she knows she can trust.'

Rik gave him a doubtful look. 'Someone like us, you mean? Could she be that desperate?'

'She might.' Harry stopped. He looked at the phone, remembering the call he'd received earlier on his way here. He'd assumed it was a misdial. But what if it wasn't? He went to the log screen to search his missed calls. There was just one. He read out the number and said, 'Can you trace the subscriber?' Professional instinct made him wary of calling it back until he knew who was on the other end.

'Sure. Then what?'

'Leg work. We know Clare left King's trauma unit during the night, but not the precise time or the direction she took. We might be able to narrow the time down using the nursing staff visits, but she was no longer critical, so I doubt she'd have been on a regular watch list.'

'Internal CCTV would nail it,' Rik suggested. 'If we can get a look at the drives.'

'That might not happen.' He explained what Ballatyne had told him. 'We'll have to go for private cameras. Can you trawl the neighbour-hood for business CCTVs, see if you can get something?'

'Sure. But wouldn't street cameras be quick-er?'

'They will, but Six will have already blocked them. Ballatyne might be able to get something, but I'd like to have our own line of evidence, just in case the footage disappears.'

Everything about the building housing the Major Trauma Centre looked normal to Harry. After arriving, he'd spent fifteen minutes on foot trawling the area surrounding the hospital for signs of extra security, but had seen nothing so far to indicate that the guard roster had been beefed up. Even so, he approached the complex via the glass-fronted Golden Jubilee building, banking on the bustle of visitors, patients and the collection of ambulances either side of the entrance to give him a degree of cover.

Before leaving for his search of the neighbourhood, Rik had run a quick check of the hospital website, checking facilities. The complex had its own security team with police backup, and considerable CCTV coverage inside and out, monitored by staff in a central control room. Any person entering and wandering the corridors for too long without any obvious aim would soon attract attention from one of the guards.

Harry waited for a family group of visitors to make their way up the steps, then joined them, holding the door open for an elderly lady and chatting easily to her about nothing of importance as they entered the foyer. It was enough to get him past a female security guard standing just inside the doors. She was short and sturdy, blank of face. Another ex-military person, he guessed. But not like the guards the other morning.

A second guard stood by the reception desk. Male, older, he was too busy joking with the receptionist to be scanning the crowd, and Harry peeled off from the old lady and walked away with the confident air of one who knew where he was going.

He found his way by trial and error to the trauma unit, and paused before approaching the security desk. There was no way of getting past this point without checking in; the set-up throughout the hospital was tight, but especially right here, and since the events of the other night, he expected efforts to have been tightened even more. Worse, if it was the same man he'd seen on duty last time, he was going to recognise him immediately. Even so, he was counting on the through-flow of patients and visitors not to be obstructed by undue procedure, and took a deep breath before stepping in front of the guard.

It was a new man, fresh-faced and friendly. He decided to go for broke, relying on a strong grain of truth.

'I'm here to interview one of the nurses,' he said, waving his MI5 card. 'About the ... uh, business the other night.'

The guard nodded, flattered by being assumed to be in on the events of two nights ago, a colleague by implication. He glanced at Harry's card, eyebrows lifting. 'Of course, sir. You know where to go?' He picked up a pen, ready to make a note in his log.

'Thanks.' Harry held up a hand. 'I'd rather you didn't do that, if that's all right. The fewer names the better with this.'

'Oh, right. Of course.' The guard looked impressed. Put down the pen.

Harry walked along the corridor to the nurses'

station, where a young woman he'd seen on his last visit was making notes on a clipboard. Her name badge read Casey. She had red hair and pale skin, like a girl from a Renaissance painting.

'Hello,' she said brightly. 'Can I help? Oh.' Her face registered recognition. 'You came to see Clare.' Then her expression changed. 'You know she isn't here, don't you?'

Harry nodded. 'Yes, I know. I heard you'd all been re-assigned.'

'Most, yes. Not me, though; I've been away, so they missed me.' She smiled. 'Lucky me, eh? Lots of excitement.'

Harry returned the smile and explained, 'I'm not here in an official capacity; I'm a colleague. I'm just worried about her.'

She looked round as the squeak of footsteps approached along the corridor, and her voice dropped. 'Actually, I've been wondering who to talk to. She needs help. You were the only person who ever came to see her. The others were just checking up, although they pretended to be work friends.' She frowned. 'I can't talk here, though.'

'Fine. Where?'

She glanced at her watch. 'I'm on a lunch break in twenty minutes. I'll see you outside in Bessemer Road up from the main entrance.' She looked past him and smiled brightly as a woman security guard walked by, then added softly with a wry smile, 'Sorry, but there's nowhere private in this place. I'm sure they've got the place bugged throughout.'

THIRTEEN

'Are you some kind of spook?' Casey lit a cigarette and gazed at Harry for a moment. 'You probably wouldn't tell me if you were, though, would you?'

'No,' Harry agreed, 'I probably wouldn't. But what makes you assume that?'

'I don't know, exactly.' She looked around as they walked side-by-side along the street, the bulk of the hospital building to their right. 'Something about you, I suppose. And the other men who came to see Clare.' She stopped. 'I've been doing this long enough to get a feel about people. Not just the patients, but visitors and ... others. Some have an aura, you know? My dad was in Special Branch. Some of his friends had this air about them, like they had secrets they couldn't talk about, that the rest of us weren't in on. Weird.'

'What did you want to tell me?'

She dropped her cigarette and turned to face him. 'OK, this is going to sound crazy, right. But the other night, when Clare left ... I had a feeling she was building up to something.' She turned and started walking again, then turned back immediately. 'When Melrose came in—'

'Melrose?'

'Yes, the Russian or Pole or whatever he was. He was admitted through the back door. I mean, literally, the back door. Like a delivery of new equipment. What the hell was that all about? I knew something strange was happening. Anyway, he was ranting and raving in his sleep – I mean, really shouting, like the worst kind of fever. But none of us could understand him, which didn't help. One of the auxiliaries is married to a guy from over that way and she thought he might have been Ukrainian. Then Clare told me he was asking for water.' She took out another cigarette and lit up. 'Sorry – filthy habit, I know, but if you worked in there, you'd ... Anyway, she told me he wanted a drink of water, so I assumed she understood the language. She denied it, and said she just knew what water was in Russian from school. *Varda* or something similar.'

She had understood a lot more than that, thought Harry. But he didn't tell Casey. 'Was that all?'

'Well, she didn't say anything else about him. But she seemed different after that. Like she'd had this kick of energy go through her ... like a light being switched on.'

'Is that unusual?'

'No, not really. Some get back into it quite quickly, others need something to jolt them. But Clare had been ... well, you know how she was: like a living corpse, poor thing. Anyway, suddenly she began to sit up and talk more, taking an interest, asking questions. She hadn't done that before. It was slow, of course, but getting there.'

'What sort of questions?'

She shrugged. 'Weird stuff, mostly. About the layout of the hospital, where the staff entrance was, was the place covered by CCTV, that sort of thing. I mean, I didn't think anything of it at the time, because I figured showing any interest in her surroundings was better than none. Before that, she'd just lain there, barely moving.'

Harry nodded. Clare hadn't said much the last time he'd seen her, beyond telling him where to go in two precise words. Even then, Casey had mentioned that she would only get well if she wanted to. At the time, it had not been an encouraging sign.

'Did she ever say where she might go – what her plans were after leaving hospital?'

'No, nothing like that. Some patients don't. They keep it inside until they're ready. Some don't ever let on where they come from, like they can't bear to talk about it in case they don't make it, I suppose. But if she was starting to think about going home, that was good, right? She wasn't near ready for it, though. I tried to tell her, but I don't think it got through.'

'What about Melrose? Did she say anything else about him?'

'No. She buttoned right up after that first bit about water. I assumed she felt sorry for him because he couldn't speak English. But thinking about it now, I wonder if something happened the evening she left.'

Harry stopped walking. 'Why would you think that?'

85

Casey tossed the cigarette into the gutter, as if she were unconvinced about the need for it. 'He'd been shouting again, although only Clare could hear him properly, being just across the corridor. I popped in to see her before going off duty, and she seemed confused.'

'How?'

'Well, she was pulling at the top sheet, folding and re-folding it, and asked me where her clothes were. She hadn't done that before, but we try to make patients feel safe – a sense of having their things close by – so I told her, in the wardrobe, where they'd always been. It wasn't a secret and I thought it might help calm her down. She couldn't have her blouse, though, which had been thrown away; it was covered in blood.'

Harry remembered all too well, but didn't say so. 'Go on.'

'I'd got her a spare T-shirt – we have an odds-and-ends cupboard for emergencies like that. I told her everything was in the wardrobe and she seemed to calm down a little after that. But that's not unusual; it doesn't take much to change their moods. I was going to recommend a sedative because I thought she was going stir-crazy, like some patients do – especially from the military. In the end, though, I didn't. I doubt she would have taken it, anyway.' She looked up at him. 'That was the last time I saw her. Or the new guard.'

Harry held his breath. 'A new guard?'

'Yes. Big bloke, not like ours. Looked like he could chew barbed wire. He arrived the same time as Melrose.' She shivered. 'He gave me the creeps. It was obvious he was there to look after Melrose, though. He never spoke to the other guards and used to sit inside Melrose's room most of time, except when he went on a break.'

Harry relaxed. If what Ballatyne had said was correct, he wasn't surprised that extra security had been placed on Tobinskiy's room. It made absolute sense to keep unwanted visitors away from their secret charge, if they didn't want news of his presence leaking out to the press. Like giving him a very British name while he was there; it was a simple precaution. Then Casey drove a truck through his reasoning.

'What I didn't understand was why he left early that particular evening.'

'Are you sure?'

'Yes. I'd been asked to stand in on another unit after my normal shift, and was just leaving when I saw him getting into a car down the road. When I went in the next morning, I found everything was in chaos. They said he'd left before his replacement came on, leaving a gap in security.'

FOURTEEN

Intelligence analyst Keith Maine strode north along Whitehall through the lunchtime crowd, enjoying the brush of cool air and the sounds of conversation going on around him. After the stuffiness of his office and the stack of reports he'd been checking all morning, it was good to escape and stretch his legs. His destination was a mile and a quarter from his shared office in Thames House, the home of MI5, near Lambeth Bridge, and he'd so far covered the ground at a pleasing clip, not bad going for someone approaching retirement.

Taller than most and smartly dressed in a grey suit, crisp, white shirt and burgundy tie, his quick, almost military gait automatically opened up a channel before him. He ignored the official buildings on either side: the Treasury, Foreign and Commonwealth, Ministry of Defence – all seen far too often to now make any impression – and made his way up the eastern side of Trafalgar Square, avoiding the souvenir stalls and their boiling clutch of tourists and sightseers, side-stepping a trio of elderly Japanese ladies arguing over a street map.

Veering off into St Martin's Lane, he eventually turned left into the shadowy confines of Cecil Court, a narrow pedestrian cut-through lined with bookstores and specialist collectors' shops. The light here was soothing, funnelled down between the high buildings on either side, and he paused to scan a trestle table layered with second-hand books. Familiar titles most of them, but none that attracted him. For Maine, looking was part of the pleasure of this place; his private retreat from the everyday tensions and scuttlebutt of the security services.

An amateur collector of first editions in his spare time, he was here today on a rare mission. A phone call from a friend had alerted him to the discovery of a very reasonably priced thriller that had just come onto the market. He'd immediately put in a bid and was now here to collect his purchase, an indulgence his single status allowed.

The shop he sought was at the far end, close to where the passage spilled out into the noise and rush of Charing Cross Road. Beyond it lay Leicester Square, the tourist trap and hunting ground for chuggers, the aggressively cheerful but pushy charity fund-raisers. He stepped inside the shop. Breathed the atmosphere with appreciation and a feeling of comfort. The walls were lined with solid bookshelves, the sheen of the polished wood reflecting their years, each one crammed with hardbacks. The floor consisted of roughened, bare oak boards, echoing with the hollow sound he loved and would have paid good money for at home, had he been able to afford it. But that, he reflected, had ever been the way. The cost of looking after his mother until her death twelve months ago had eaten up most of his civil service salary, leaving just enough for the occasional book purchase if the price was right. Everything else took a poor third place. He preferred not to think about the one time he'd allowed his indulgence to colour his judgement, and betrayal was such a harsh word. At the time, selling what he'd considered already outdated information had not seemed such a bad thing ... and as his conscience kept reminding him, it had been to an ally, so where was the harm?

He shook the unwelcome thoughts away as he crossed the shop floor. The bookseller was seated behind the counter at the far end, beneath a frosted window. He was scowling at a laptop and muttering under his breath. He wore a check shirt stretched across a broad chest, with a build unlike any bookshop owner Maine had ever met. There were no other customers, but Maine could hear the ripping sound of packaging tape being used down a flight of wooden stairs to his left.

The bookseller looked up and murmured a greeting with a hint of a smile. Reaching out a hand, he slid a hardback volume across the counter, wrapped in paper.

'I think you'll be pleased with this.'

Maine felt flattered by the recognition. But his excitement took precedence as his eyes settled on the book. It was a familiar feeling whenever something particularly special came his way. He picked it up, savouring the rustle of paper, the weight and texture, resisting the urge to sniff at the pages. Not unusually, he reflected that this precise moment, when taking hold of a book for the very first time, was better than sex.

The Man with the Golden Gun wasn't everybody's cup of tea, he knew that. But Fleming's work still carried a solid value and showed no signs of diminishing.

Minutes later, after the inspection and payment, and the obligatory exchange of small talk with the bookseller, who turned out to be the shop's owner, he walked out with his purchase carefully wrapped and clutched under his arm.

He paused to scan the table of seconds outside, reluctant to let the moment go. He wasn't remotely interested in the items on display, but felt a small obligation, after what he had just acquired, to give a fleeting nod to the mundane before moving on for a spot of lunch. Maybe today he would take some wine to celebrate this acquisition – a nice Merlot, perhaps.

Another customer was already browsing the titles. Neatly dressed, his tanned fingers were walking along the spines, flicking them aside one by one.

'I'm surprised at you, Keith,' murmured the man. 'You're looking positively smug.'

Maine faltered, tempted to walk away but surprised at meeting anyone here who knew him. An office colleague, perhaps, who'd ventured this way. He turned, feeling a momentary twitch in his gut. Echoes of the voice came back to him from a long time ago, uncomfortably familiar. Nobody from the office, he was certain. Yet the face, in profile, was not one he recognised. A slim beard, tanned, weathered skin, heavy glasses and dressed in a lightweight summer suit, the man could have been anyone, passing time just like himself. Not foreign but *from* somewhere overseas, somewhere hot. And yet there was something disturbing in the stance and the smile. He felt his gut lurch.

Surely to God...

Then the man had taken him firmly by the elbow and was leading him away, chuckling aloud for the benefit of any chance onlookers, a parody of the easy intimacy of an old friend meeting another after a lengthy gap. In reality, he was speaking between clenched teeth, a steely warning tone to his voice that left no room for argument.

'Now, don't make a scene, there's a good chap,' he muttered. 'Or I might have to hurt you. You do know who I am, don't you?'

'Yes.' Maine's head was spinning. He didn't know what to do. Felt a desperate urge to run, but knew that would be useless.

'Good. Then you'll know what I'm capable of. Shall we walk? Only I have an understandable aversion to staying in one place for too long. It's my one weakness.'

'What are you *doing* here?' Maine's voice was a strangled whisper as he felt himself propelled back along the passageway the way he'd come, powerful fingers digging into the soft flesh around his elbow, painfully massaging the nerves. This hadn't been part of his lunchtime mission. How the hell had this man found him?

'Don't pretend to be so surprised.' The newcomer steered him out into the flow of pedestrian traffic and across St Martin's Lane, stepping through a line of plastic garbage bags at the kerb, one of them spilling a scattering of packaging into the gutter. 'You knew I'd call on you one day. It's the way things work in this business, remember? Favours made, always repaid. You had your favour, now it's time to pay.'

Maine felt sick as he was led down a narrow alley alongside a gym. With no other pedestrians around, he felt horribly vulnerable. He stopped suddenly, ripping his arm free, fear giving him strength. But his legs wouldn't let him run.

'What do you want, Paulton? You must be crazy coming back here!' He cast around desperately, his earlier pleasure now gone, a man searching for a way out of a bad situation. Unfortunately, he saw neither police nor security men, although on reflection, he knew deep down that neither would have been of any help to him.

'Really? Why is that, Keith?' Paulton feigned surprise. 'Is it because I'm a black sheep in the intelligence community – a sordid little secret nobody wants to talk about?' He cocked his head on one side and showed his teeth. But it wasn't in a smile. 'Or is it because I scare you shitless and you can't face up to what you did and don't want to be found out?'

'No! I...' Maine choked on the words. 'What?' The single word was all he could manage, a sign of resignation. 'How did you know I would be here?'

'I didn't. But I know where you work, Keith.' Paulton's tone on the last few words was pseudo ghostly, the kind to frighten children. But this threat was very real.

'You followed me?'

'Of course. It's one of the things I've always been particularly good at, even if I do say so myself. But then, operate in some of the nasty places I've been to in my time, and you need to be good at something. You really should check your back more often, though, Keith.' He prodded Maine in the chest with a stiff finger, forcing him back against the wall of the building behind him. 'Now, I want you to help me find somebody.' Any feigned geniality had now gone, replaced by a harder tone.

A dulled look. 'Why should I?'

'Do you really expect me to explain that?'

'Is it someone important, is that it? I'm not going to help you kill anyone.'

'I'm not asking you to.' Paulton's voice was smooth, persuasive, but developing a harder edge. 'Not that it would make much difference if I were. I need some information, that's all; you have access to the files and I know you'll get it for me. Just one person, that's all I'm asking. Then I'll be gone for good and never bother you again. Scouts' honour.' He smiled. 'You'd like that, wouldn't you – me out of your life forever?'

'What will you do to this person?'

'Like I said, don't ask. That way, what you don't know can't come back and bite you on the arse.' He gave a huff of impatience and his voice dropped as a door opened along the alleyway and a bag of rubbish was dropped outside. 'Remember what I know about you, Keith. Five years ago you sold confidential weapons files to a French intelligence officer for hard cash.'

Maine flinched. 'I was tricked. I thought he was a journalist.' It was a claim he'd always made, but right now it sounded even more hollow than ever.

'Really? Was that what he told you? Boy, you were dumb. What was it he paid you – twenty-five grand? That must have bought you some nice little first editions.' He applied more pressure until Maine cried out in pain. 'Do you recall what happened to him, Keith?'

Pain etched Maine's face. 'No. I don't. Why should I?'

'He fell under a train in Norwood Junction. He

94

should have stood back from the edge like they always tell you.'

Maine looked horrified. 'I didn't know!'

'Nor should you. That was my job, cleaning up the mess left by people like you. But you didn't suffer, did you, Keith? Nobody found you out; there were no heavy knocks on your door at the dead of night. It stayed strictly between you and me, remember? Well, that was the favour; now it's time to return it.'

Maine was breathing heavily, his face ashen as the grim reality of what he'd done began to open up before him. The past few years since the Frenchman had disappeared had gradually absorbed the enormity of what he'd done. And the money had certainly helped. Now it was as if he'd been telescoped back to that time, with all the threat that had entailed. 'And if I don't?'

'Well, let's put it this way, Keith, I don't think your masters will like it, will they? They usually throw people in prison for what you did. It's called selling secrets, you know. Some might call it treason ... some of the old Eurosceptic die-hards, especially. They'd probably want to pull out your fingernails with pliers.'

Maine looked alarmed. 'You wouldn't!'

'Actually, I would. Just one phone call.' He snapped his fingers, making Maine jump.

'But you'd be implicating yourself. I'd tell them everything – about how you tricked me and forced me to help you escape after that Georgian fiasco with Bellingham.'

Paulton released his arm. It was a recognition that he was winning. Had already won. 'You really think that would help?' He waved a hand around them at the alleyway. 'What are they going to do – make my life more difficult than it is? They don't even know I'm in the country. I'd be gone before you finished dialling.' He smiled easily, eyes ice-cold. 'More to the point, you'd be dead before the week was out.'

Maine's face lost all colour as he recognised the truth in what Paulton was saying. He'd heard and knew enough about the man's history to know that he would stop at nothing to get a job done. His reason for leaving MI5 was proof enough of that. And silencing someone who crossed him would be no more difficult than choosing a new shirt.

He breathed deeply, rubbing his forearm, then said, 'Very well. What's his name?'

'She. A former intelligence officer, dismissed for misconduct, so no need to feel sorry for her. I want everything you have on her: addresses, family, photos, contacts, girlfriends.'

Maine looked puzzled. 'Girls?'

'Yes. Our Clare preferred the ladies. One of the reasons Six decided to dispense with her services. An outdated view of the world, but what can you expect of those dinosaurs?'

Maine shook his head. 'But MI6? I can't do that!'

Paulton's hand shot out and gripped Maine's arm once more. The pain was intense. 'Don't tell me you can't, Keith. Can't doesn't cut it. And don't try kidding me you failed, because I have a second source of information – and I *will* check.'

Maine tried to shake loose, but couldn't. Paulton's grip was too powerful. 'You're asking too much!' he protested, a whine edging his voice. 'They've put new systems in place ever since you ... since you left. Anyone trying to access certain files across the intel community triggers an alert. It's too tight.'

'Then you had better find a way round it, hadn't you? You know what the alternative is.' He took a pen from his pocket and yanked back the sleeve of Maine's jacket. 'Send everything you've got to this number.' He scribbled on the man's arm then let go, stepping back as a young woman carrying a bulging sports bag hurried by. 'Do as I ask and you can carry on with your masters in blissful ignorance until you collect your pension. Refuse and you can wait for them to come for you. It's as simple as that. Your choice.' He turned away.

'Wait.' Maine's voice was a whisper. He looked like a man facing death. 'Wait. I'll do it.'

Paulton turned his head, a sly smile of triumph on his face.

'By close of business today? Especially a photo.'

'What? No ... I can't.' Then he saw the look on Paulton's face. He nodded. 'Very well. What's the name?'

'Jardine. Clare Jardine.'

FIFTEEN

Harry was walking back to his car when his phone rang. It was Ballatyne.

'I've a possible sighting of Jardine. A female figure walking down Caldicot Road away from the hospital, timed at oh-two-thirty three. She was heading towards Coldharbour Lane, Harry. The imagery isn't great, taken from a CCTV camera at the far end of a car park, but it's all I could get so far.'

Harry felt a jolt of something approaching excitement. If it was Clare, it gave him a start point. Instead of having to cover the 360-degree field around the hospital, gradually widening the scope of the search and adding an impossible area of streets, road and buildings, they now had a single direction to focus on.

'What about inside?'

'So far, nothing. I've put in requests but I'm not holding my breath. The longer we wait, the less likely it is that we'll get anything. And waiting won't help her chances.'

'How did you find this one, then?'

'I couldn't get the hospital coverage, so I put one of my whizz-kids on checking out cameras outside the hospital perimeter. He got lucky.'

'You mean he broke some laws.' Harry had no

doubts that Ballatyne would do whatever it took to find what he wanted. Accessing NHS digital records was clearly not possible without a court order. But having his man hack into local authority or private contractor digital records was less of a problem.

'I don't know what you mean.' The voice was bland. 'Did you find anything?'

Harry relayed what Casey had told him. Ballatyne swore softly when he got to the bit about the guard leaving, but didn't volunteer an opinion. Undoubtedly he would begin an internal investigation, but finding out who the man was, or why he had left, might not be so simple.

'You'll have to take it from here,' Ballatyne said. 'I'll see if I can access street cameras in the area, but don't wait for me.'

'Are you giving me authority to break down a few doors?' He was certain Ballatyne had just given the silent nod to do whatever he could to track down Clare Jardine. That could only include using Rik's skills to the maximum effect.

'I never said that. I'll be in touch.' The phone went dead.

Harry rang Rik. The younger man answered, sounding bored and slightly out of breath. He was a hundred yards south of the hospital campus and had so far drawn a blank on any useful cameras.

'The ones in place are either busted or giving the wrong coverage.'

'Doesn't matter, we've got a lead,' Harry told him, and gave him directions to the junction of Caldicot Road and Coldharbour Lane. 'You take the east side and I'll take the west. We'll work our way north until we hit something.'

'Why north?'

'I think she'll make for the city centre. Anywhere else is too open. In her state, she'll stand out too much. She needs cover, somewhere to hide while she gets help and recuperates.'

'Fair enough. And if we don't find anything?'

'Then you get to let your fingers do the walking.'

'Yowzer,' Rik muttered quietly. 'At last.'

Votrukhin and Serkhov were just as keen to be doing something, but for different reasons. After making their excuses to Gorelkin, they had left the Grosvenor House Hotel and headed south and across the river, on their way back to King's College Hospital. Votrukhin had outlined his plan as they went, meeting no resistance from Serkhov, who favoured action rather than words.

'I'm not having that traitorous little Englishman looking down his nose at us,' he muttered darkly, as Serkhov pulled out into Park Lane. 'Did you see the look on his face? I wanted to lean across and punch that smile all over the room.'

Serkhov nodded sympathetically as he took the dark blue 3-series BMW skilfully across to the outside lane and squeezed between two taxis aiming for a space on Hyde Park Corner. Ignoring the looks from the other drivers, he accelerated hard and shot across towards Grosvenor Place. One of the training courses in the SPC was extreme offensive and defensive driving, at which he had excelled. 'You should have given me the nod,' he said tersely. 'I'd have followed him out and rammed that phone down his throat.'

Votrukhin gave an appreciative grunt. They were on the same page, Serkhov and him; neither man had enjoyed the lambasting that Gorelkin had given them for not dealing with the Jardine woman, but they could live with that. Operational errors happened in the best run organisations. What counted was putting them right in time and proving their worth for future missions. But having an outsider – a foreign outsider at that – present at the time and smiling at their discomfort was hard to take.

Votrukhin also had a bad feeling about Paulton. Even accepting the Englishman's previous job, which had required a talent for lies and deceit in spades, there was something in the man's face that had made him uneasy from the moment he'd met him. Gorelkin seemed unaware of it but Votrukhin had sensed it like an aura – especially when the ex-MI5 man had returned from making his telephone call.

'Why are you going this way?' he asked Serkhov. He knew the layout of London well and guessed that the sergeant was heading towards Vauxhall Bridge. It didn't really matter which one they used, but he was intrigued.

'Because,' Serkhov replied, 'when I joined the centre, I promised I'd spit on MI6 if I ever got close enough. Don't worry, I won't actually stop and gob on the building. Even I can handle symbolism.'

'You'd better not. They'll have our faces on film in seconds and their FRS systems will light up like St Basil's Cathedral.'

Facial recognition software was patchy at best, as both men knew, especially in moving vehicles with the play of light off windows. But neither wished to take the risk of being 'pinged' by a random lucky shot. The result would be embarrassing for all concerned, and career destroying at the very least for them.

Serkhov glanced across at his colleague. They had worked together several times, forming an effective team. But seniority in the SPC was a divider of men, and there was always a slight hesitation in both men when talking non-operational matters.

'What is it?' Votrukhin had noticed the look. Serkhov had something on his mind.

'I've never worked a black operation before. Have you?'

'No.' Votrukhin sighed. 'But it's what we do, isn't it? It's just a name. What's your problem?'

'This ... no contact stuff the colonel talked about–' he steered through a narrow gap and accelerated hard – 'it sounds extreme.'

Votrukhin didn't reply immediately. He'd been having similar thoughts. From what had started out as a tough but straightforward operation – if terminating a man could be called that – it had taken a slightly nasty turn. *Chyornyiy*. The word was so bland, in normal circumstances merely a colour. Yet here and now, it had taken on a completely different tone. Sinister. Now they were cut off from all outside contact, with only

Gorelkin and their wits to keep them out of trouble. And Votrukhin wasn't entirely sure why it had gone this way.

'It's extreme only if we get caught,' he concluded, and focussed on the job in hand. 'We'd better make sure we don't, right? Then we can go home.'

Forty minutes later, they pulled into a car park near the hospital and dutifully fed the meter. Only amateurs took chances; it was how they got caught. Then they set about scouting the area outside, trying to find a lead, any lead, that might point towards where the Jardine woman had gone. Inevitably, that proved fruitless, and merely increased the chance of them being noticed. Votrukhin finally led the way back to the hospital.

'Remember,' he said, as they approached the entrance to the Major Trauma Centre, 'this is quick and dirty. We get to the security control centre and shut it off, then get what we need and go.'

'Are you sure Gorelkin won't have us shot for this?'

'No, I'm not. But I'm certain he might have us sent to Afghanistan if we don't do something positive.'

'And if anyone gets in our way?'

'What do you think?'

'Fair enough.' Serkhov took out his gun. It was a 9mm Bernadelli P-018. He checked the magazine and slid it back into place, then put the gun away, every movement economical and practised.

Votrukhin produced a Spanish Astra 9mm and did the same. Both guns had entered the UK illegally, shipped in hold luggage with other weapons and ammunition, for which an American with dreams of easy riches was now awaiting trial in the US. If either weapon were lost, it would be traced to a gun shop in Concord, North Carolina. Not that either man was planning on that. As with all members of the elite SPC, Serkhov and Votrukhin were quite capable of dealing with problems quietly using their hands, or with whatever else might come within reach. But sight of the guns and the credible threat to use them would effectively ram home the message much faster than any shouting or physical threats.

Through the entrance, they already knew the way. Skirting the security guard by the desk, they followed the signs to the washrooms. But instead of going in, they veered off and followed the corridor, dropping down another set of stairs to a sub-basement level. Through a door marked STAFF ONLY into another, narrower corridor with dimmed overhead lighting and lined with unused furniture and electrical equipment awaiting clearance. Numbered doors were on either side, all closed. The atmosphere here was deadened and silent, other than the clank and hum of heating being pumped through the overhead venting.

Votrukhin was in the lead, fast and purposeful, checking for security cameras. He spotted one at the end of the corridor. Grabbing a broken chair he held it in front of him, obscuring his features. Serkhov did the same, hoisting an old overhead projector in front of his face. The air smelled of hot plastic and dust.

As they approached a door on their left marked 'Control Centre – No Admittance', Votrukhin reached for his gun and dropped the chair. He very carefully tried the door handle. Locked, as he'd expected. Standing to one side, he beckoned Serkhov to move up close. They had a couple of seconds at most if the guard monitoring the screens was awake.

'Open it and stay out here,' he said quietly. 'Anybody comes, stall them.'

Serkhov nodded, then swung his shoulders and heaved the projector at the door with almost casual ease.

The door smashed open under the onslaught, catching the single occupant by surprise and making him utter a squeal of fear. A cardboard mug dropped from nerveless fingers and bounced across the control desk, spilling hot liquid across the buttons. Shock and awe, thought Votrukhin happily. Works every time.

'Touch anything,' he told the guard in perfect English, 'hit an alarm or even speak, and you're a dead man.' For emphasis, he placed the tip of his gun to the security officer's forehead and held it there, finger curled around the trigger. And waited.

SIXTEEN

'You have backup discs for the cameras,' Votruk-hin told the guard softly after a few seconds. The short silence was enough to allow the fear factor to build just enough to make him compliant. Now to give him something to focus on. 'Two nights ago, from midnight to four. I want that footage.'

There were a dozen screens in two banks of six, showing various locations around the hospital. Every few seconds, the screens would jump to a new location: stairways, entrance, wards, canteens, delivery bay and so on. But it was the outside footage that interested Votrukhin. As far as he could see, though, all the exterior camera angles were close to the building, showing little or nothing of the surrounding streets.

The guard's mouth moved momentarily, but no sound came out. He was sweating visibly, and the smell of nervous body odour was heavy in the enclosed room. He needed a shave and a haircut. Votrukhin put his age at about forty. He was overweight and looked out of condition. He probably sat in this ghastly bunker most days, slowly dying of inactivity and eating his way towards going-home time.

'It's OK – I give you permission to speak. I

won't shoot you. Unless you decide to be a hero.'

The guard swallowed and croaked, 'I can't.'

Votrukhin's finger tightened around the trigger. 'Can't? That's a silly thing to say.'

'I can't – believe me! I don't know how to isolate specific time frames ... or any of that stuff. They haven't showed me. All I do is monitor the screens. They have an IT guy who deals with backup and storage.' He sniffed pathetically. 'I'm just here to watch, that's all.'

'Pity.' Votrukhin gave a sigh. 'You're not much use to me, are you?'

'Wait!' The other man held up a soft hand. 'I know where the drives are. They have separate ones in case of problems. They rotate them regularly.'

'Where?'

The guard pointed to a cabinet against the wall. Trunking fixed to the wall showed where power and feed leads ran into the cabinet. 'In there.' He turned to a separate monitor by his elbow, the sudden movement nearly earning a bullet from Votrukhin's gun. Tapping the keyboard, he scrolled down the screen. 'The one for the other night would have been ... hang on ... DS013. They change automatically. It's pre-programmed, so we just check the list.'

'Show me,' said Votrukhin. He cast his eye across the screens as the guard moved. No signs of alarm or panic anywhere so far. One of the screens jumped and revealed Serkhov, standing outside the door, looking like a nightclub bouncer. He was grinning at the camera. Idiot. 'Hurry.'

The guard complied, opening the cabinet door and pointing to an inner box housing four hard drives. They were each numbered from DS010 to DS013. 'That's the one.'

'Take it out.'

'Huh?' The guard looked puzzled.

'Take it out and give it to me.' Votrukhin emphasised the instruction with a prod of the gun barrel. 'Take out the drive, disconnect the wires. Or I shoot you.'

The guard did as he was told, grasping the hard drive and pulling it towards him. With shaking fingers, he disconnected the wires at the back and handed over the box.

'Excellent,' said Votrukhin. 'Now sit down.' He waited for the man to sit, then cast around. A canvas shoulder bag was hanging from a hook on the back of the door. He stepped across and dropped the drive into the bag, then threw the strap over his shoulder. 'You have been a great help.'

The guard pointed to the bag. 'Can I have my lunch box? It's in there.'

Votrukhin ignored him. He was looking around the room. There was nothing he could use to restrain the guard and stop him sounding the alarm, and they had already used up enough time. If the guard was worried about his lunch, it probably signalled a shift change coming up any time now. But they needed a few minutes to get out of the building and away. 'Where is the nearest outside door?' he asked.

'To your left.' The man's voice was dull, although whether out of fear or losing his lunch,

Votrukhin wasn't sure. 'Through the door in front of you and you'll be in a small lobby. Push the bar down and that opens onto the side of the building.'

'Is it alarmed?'

The guard hesitated just for a moment. Then he reached across to the control board and hit a switch. 'No.'

Votrukhin smiled. He almost got caught, there. So the man had some guts after all. Or maybe he'd genuinely forgotten. He reached in the bag and felt a bottle and a plastic box. He took out the box and tossed it in the air. 'Here.'

As the guard reached up to catch it, Votrukhin lifted the gun and shot him. The noise was loud in the room, but he doubted it would be heard outside.

'You eat too much,' he said, as the guard flopped to the floor. He stepped out into the corridor and pulled the door to behind him.

Serkhov looked at him. 'Did he get to be a hero?'

'Not really. I think it was a chemistry thing. Come on.'

SEVENTEEN

Rik Ferris struck gold not long after beginning his trawl for CCTVs along Coldharbour Lane. Close to where it intersected with Denmark Hill, he came to a short stretch of shops. Above a beauty salon, he spotted the blue glass eye of a camera beneath a protective dome. He checked the point where the bracket was fitted to the wall. He could see a power lead but no data cable. It was a wireless unit. His laptop carried a useful software programme called Eye Drop; it gave him the ability to plug in to wireless CCTV feeds and copy any recorded footage. But why stand out here and do it if he didn't have to?

He entered the shop, where the air was hot and perfumed. It was little more than a reception area and trade counter, with glass racks of beauty products around the walls. A curtained doorway led through to a larger room at the back, from where he could hear laughter and the hum of a hair dryer.

He asked to see the manager, and the girl behind the counter disappeared through into the back, to be replaced moments later by a slim, striking woman in her fifties. She was wearing a white overall and peeling off rubber gloves.

'Can I help you? I'm Maria Carvalho, the

owner.'

'Nice to meet you, Mrs Carvalho.' Rik smiled winningly and handed her his ID card. He explained that he was helping in the search for a young female patient who had discharged herself from the hospital. 'She hasn't completely re-covered,' he said. 'We think she may be in shock, and confused by what happened. She was seen heading in this direction, and your camera might have picked her up.'

The woman looked him up and down with a momentary suspicion, then seemed to relent. 'We fitted the camera after some break-ins,' she explained, in a soft accent. 'Our insurers insist-ed, and it seems to have worked well so far.' She shrugged philosophically. 'Or maybe we've just been lucky.'

'How long do you keep recordings for?'

'For no more than two weeks. It's movement activated, so we don't fill up the drive with pointless rubbish. At least, that's what the man who sold it suggested.'

Rik nodded. He was familiar enough with the technology. The less footage he had to trawl through, the better. 'Could I see it? It would cover just a couple of hours of recording, that's all.'

She gestured towards the curtained doorway. 'Of course. Come. I'll show you where we keep the machine.'

Rik followed her through the main room, which was a combination beauty treatment and hair salon, nodding at a clutch of assistants and their customers. Mrs Carvalho led him to a small office and gestured to a shelf with a hard drive and monitor. The monitor's screen was dark, but a green operating light was blinking on the hard drive.

'Help yourself,' she offered. 'I've got a colouring job to finish, so please excuse me.'

Rik watched her leave, then got to work, calling up the programme menu and selecting a time frame which focussed on the night Clare left the hospital.

There were many brief snatches of movement, mostly of cars stopping at the kerb then moving off, and several pedestrians walking by. Conducted in silence, it had the eerie feel of a cheap horror film, with snatches of movement and the play of car headlights forming shadows across the pavement. The footage was grainy and stuttering, and whoever had sold Mrs Carvalho the system hadn't gone for high-end technology. But it was clear enough to make out some detail of faces and clothing.

He'd been at it for nearly forty minutes when a figure went by just beneath the camera. He almost missed it, but for the glint of light off the metal stick in the figure's hand. He hit rewound then played the scene again. A buzz of excitement went through him. It wasn't a stick; there was an odd shaped attachment at the top.

A metal crutch.

He breathed easily and replayed the footage over and over, watching the figure ghost by, seemingly hugging the building and bent over. Female or slim male? Female. There was something about the build. From what he recalled

112

about her, Clare wasn't exactly sylph-like, but neither was she a weightlifter.

Then the area around the figure flared with light as a car pulled up at the kerb nearby, and the face became clear.

It was Clare.

Rik took out his mobile and called Harry.

'Got a sighting.' He gave the address of the beauty salon. 'And I think the manager fancies me. Her name's Carvalho. You'd better hurry – I'm frightened.'

'Keep your legs crossed,' replied Harry. 'Two minutes.'

Rik ducked his head through into the main salon and beckoned to Mrs Carvalho. She followed him and he showed her the footage, pointing out the glitter of the crutch.

'A colleague's on his way to verify it, but I think this is her.'

'Poor dear,' the owner replied softly, a frown of concern etching her forehead. 'Why is she walking like that?'

'She had a stomach operation. It's not fully healed yet and she shouldn't be on her feet.' He tapped the hard drive. 'Can I isolate this section and email it to my computer? I'll need to distribute this to others helping in the search.'

'Of course, yes.' She watched while he did it then said, 'I hope you find her. This is not a good place for a young woman alone late at night.'

Voices approached and Harry walked in. He nodded at the woman and said, 'Thanks for your cooperation, Mrs Carvalho. It's good of you.'

'Miss,' she corrected him, and patted her hair,

113

eyelashes fluttering. 'Always happy to help.'

Harry peered at the screen. 'It's her.'

They made their escape, leaving the owner excitedly regaling her customers with the story.

'She was heading north,' said Rik. 'But I'm not sure that helps us much.'

Harry took out a street map and stabbed it with his finger. 'There's a four-way junction up ahead with side streets. It's going to be messy finding out which way she went from there. But it's all we've got.'

It took them a further two hours of false starts, broken cameras, reluctant owners and poor footage around the large junction to find other premises with a private CCTV that offered a decent, useable clue. This one was above a bingo hall in Camberwell Road, showing Clare's figure heading due north towards the area known as Elephant & Castle. She was bent over and seemed to be leaning on the crutch more than she had been earlier.

'She must be hurting,' Rik commented. 'Could you do that? I couldn't.' His voice carried a hint of admiration.

'No,' said Harry. 'Nor me. Come on.' He thanked the bingo hall manageress for her help and led the way back onto the street.

'Where to?'

'She's going for the river,' said Harry. He made a note in his notebook. He'd been plotting the position of street cameras as they went, building the progress line ready to hand over to Ballatyne. The MI6 man might not be able to do much with

114

it very quickly, but being able to give him precise positions where Clare had passed by would narrow down the search time considerably.

It made him wonder what Clare had in mind, and whether she was absolutely clear about her intentions. The closer she got to the centre of London, if that's where she was heading, the greater became the density and coverage of street cameras. And that exposed her to enormous risks of discovery by the MI6 trackers as well as the Russians. On the other hand, tracking a single figure through the streets, camera by camera, was not that simple, unless someone had access to real-time footage and knew exactly where to look. If the followers on either side got that much, then they would have Clare in their sights, unless he and Rik could get to her first.

He consulted a street map. The Elephant & Castle would be a nightmare for the two of them to check out. There were several roads leading off from the main gyratory system, and a maze of smaller streets Clare could have ducked into to stay out of the open. Covering them all would be impossible without an army of helpers or direct access to the street cameras from a central position.

He followed the map with his finger, leap-frogging ahead. Clare probably knew this area as well as he did. If so, she'd have probably headed for somewhere familiar, somewhere she could join the army of night people gathering in the area and lose herself among them. That meant only one logical destination: Waterloo Station.

He texted Ballatyne.

115

EIGHTEEN

'Where are you right now?' It was Ballatyne, in answer to Harry's text. He sounded rushed.

'Near Waterloo. We've had a sighting of Clare.'

'Never mind that. This is not an instruction for you to get involved, but an update. There's been a shooting at King's College hospital. The security control centre was raided by two armed men. They forced their way in and made the operator hand over a hard drive with CCTV footage of the night Tobinskiy was killed. Then they shot him.'

'Dead?'

'No. He's alive but hurting.'

'Any indications who they were?'

'The guard was able to talk just before he went into the operating theatre. He said the man doing all the talking sounded English at first, but an accent came through a couple of times. There was another man who stayed outside the control room. He looked East European and was built like a wrestler. There's footage of him and the shooter leaving the building together through a side door. Then nothing. The police are working on cameras in the area, but my guess is these jokers will merge into the background.'

'Russians?'

'Undoubtedly. Looks like the FSB team decided to get hold of the footage. Comes across as panic measures to me, probably to cover their tracks from their visit the other night.'

'Why would they bother?' Harry countered. 'There's the footage from today's entry. They're clearly not worried about leaving evidence. Not that it proves who they were.'

A long pause. 'Good point. In that case they must be counting on tracking down Clare before we do and getting out of the country. Thanks to the obstruction by the hospital authorities, they now have a lead on us. As soon as they scan that hard drive and put out pictures to their resident network on the streets, Jardine's hours are numbered.'

'Wasn't there a backup drive?'

'That *was* the backup. And the hospital's still dragging its heels in releasing the original footage.' His breathing echoed down the line. 'I give them about four hours before the executives are hit with a massive court order which will freeze their balls.'

'Good luck with that.' Harry gave this new development some thought, then said, 'It would help if we could cut this short.'

'How do you mean?'

'Following her trail is taking too long; she could be anywhere. She'll probably be looking for help by now, and there's a limit on who she'd approach. Do you have that name for me? There must have been at least one person she was friendly with. Nobody works in a complete vacuum.'

'Damn. You never give up, do you? OK. I got one. Her name's Alice Alanya. She's a Russian language specialist, thirty-four and single, lives in Harrow, north London. She was friendly with Jardine, but as far as I can make out, no more than that. They shared briefings on a couple of Jardine's assignments, and Alanya gave her some refresher sessions to keep her language up to date. As far as I can make out without disturbing the water, she was about as close to Jardine as anybody.'

'Disturbing the water?'

'I'm having a problem with the deputy head of the Russian desk. It means going through back-channels to avoid her.' Internal politics. He didn't elaborate further. 'I'll email you a photo in a minute.'

'Is Alanya clean?'

'You mean with her surname? There's no reason to think she isn't. Her great grandfather was a Russian émigré, but any allegiance to the old country ran out a long way back. She's just another member of Six, that's all.'

'Where do I find her?'

'She's a creature of habit. She leaves the building about six thirty unless there's a buzz on, and gets home via Harrow-on-the-Hill.' He read out an address. 'Go easy on her. I don't want this spreading fire and panic throughout the service. Use my name if you have to but keep it low-level.'

Harrow-on-the-Hill tube station was no more or less prepossessing than any other station Harry had used, although it had the disadvantage of possessing two entrances on opposing sides of the line. The northern exit and ticket hall gave access to the main shops and town centre off College Road; the southern exit gave out onto a back road opposite a small recreational park. Alice Alanya's home address, a small block of private flats on a residential street to the east, was reachable from either direction.

Harry watched as the flow of passengers walked by from the northbound line. He was checking faces while trying to look bored, occasionally checking his watch like a man on a date. Rik was across the way, doing the same in case Harry missed the target. They had decided to wait at the tube station for her, rather than following her from SIS headquarters, on the grounds that the less time they shared the same space, the less likely Alanya was to pick up on their presence. Even non-field operatives were trained to be alert at all times, in case of being under surveillance from foreign agencies, but according to Ballatyne, Alanya had been involved in special operations because of her language expertise, so she would be even more aware of the need for caution.

Harry checked the print-out of the photo Ballatyne had emailed him. Alice Alanya was slim, about five feet eight inches, with long dark hair, pale skin and a nice smile. He hadn't been able to think of a better word; she was pretty without being beautiful, but would attract attention from most men without trying.

Which made him wonder why she was single.

Ballatyne had been unable to help on that score, as closer questioning of her colleagues would have aroused suspicions and chatter in the office – something he wanted to avoid.

Another trainload decamped and walked by. Equal numbers of men and women, mostly office workers but a few in more casual gear or work clothes. The flow dropped to a trickle, then ones and twos in no particular hurry, some using mobiles. A minute passed by and Harry looked across at Rik, who shrugged and got ready to wait some more.

In the sudden quiet, they heard footsteps. A young woman, walking at normal speed, head up, alert. Shoulder bag, smart suit, white blouse. Officer worker. She was heading for the northern exit.

Alice Alanya.

Harry already had his phone clamped to his ear. He started talking, saying he was on his way and he'd be there in five minutes, an imaginary but entirely plausible conversation heard a hundred times a day. It was a signal to Rik to start walking away, front-running the target to keep his face hidden, but assuming the normal route home unless told otherwise by Harry.

Alanya stopped just a hundred yards from the station and entered a store advertising East-European food. Harry called Rik to tread water and wait for her to emerge, while he carried on walking. He was playing safe in case she had ducked into the store for more than just groceries; she might have done it to check her back. He passed Rik without speaking, and turned the corner and waited behind a builder's van parked at the kerb.

Moments later his phone rang. It was Rik.

'She's coming out, heading your way. Carrying a plastic bag. I'm following.'

Harry watched as Alanya came into view and crossed the road. She appeared unconcerned, walking at the same speed, another worker on her way home, now with the makings of dinner.

He gave her a hundred yards, with Rik following, then crossed to the other side and joined in.

Five minutes later, she entered the block of flats they had scouted out earlier. A single front entrance beneath a canopy, three floors, a smart building, well maintained. Harry joined Rik fifty yards past the block.

There were no signs of other watchers.

'You going in first or me?' Rik asked.

'I'll do it. I look more like Internal Security. You look more like a cat burglar.' He was looking at Rik's clothes for the day, which, unlike his jacket and slacks, were jeans, a nondescript T-shirt and scuffed trainers. His normally spiky hair had been tamed by an application of gel to prevent him standing out.

Rik grinned. 'Cheers. That's the kindest thing you've said all day. I'll hold the fort out here.'

Harry nodded, then walked back to the block of flats and through the entrance.

Alice Alanya was waiting just inside. She looked calm.

She was holding a can of Mace in her hand.

NINETEEN

'Why are you following me?' She was holding the Mace ready, knuckles white. One blast and he'd be on his knees clutching his face, eyes streaming. One well-placed kick if she'd been trained right and he'd be out for the count.

She was good.

Harry already had his MI5 card in his hand. He held it up as her fingers tightened around the can. 'Official business. If you use the Mace, my colleague will come in and jump all over you.'

It wasn't true, but might make her think twice.

She blinked, eyes flicking towards the entrance. 'You mean the scruffy young guy in glasses and trainers? He looks lightweight.' Up close, she looked fit and capable. The nice bit had sunk beneath the surface.

'That's the one. He'll love you for noticing. Can we go inside ... or somewhere more public?'

'Who do you think I am?' She was nervous now, more so than when she'd thought he was just a prowler. Investigators from the Security Service landing on your doorstep usually had that effect, especially when you're in the same business.

'You're Alice Alanya, age 34, Russian language specialist for Legoland,' he recited, using the

MI6 nickname for the quirky building at Vauxhall Cross. 'I could go on but I'd have to shoot everyone in the building in case they heard.'

She blinked but said nothing. Then she lowered the can. 'Your mate stays outside, you can come in.'

She led the way up to the top-floor landing and opened one of two doors, switching on the light.

The flat was neat, sparsely furnished, and comfortable. Lots of shelves around the walls, filled mostly with books. Russian and eastern history, travel books, dictionaries, reference works. Other shelves held paperbacks, a mixture of novels and non-fiction; a few crime and thrillers, and one or two literary works. A small TV on a low shelf in one corner, towards the rear, and an exercise bike in another corner with a bottle of water in a holder and an MP3 player and headphones looped over the handlebars. A swivel to the right would give a view out of the front window, but it looked as if the bike had never moved. She liked to focus.

No sign of sharing the space, though. No photographs or discarded clothing, no shoes left lying by the door. One person's space; private and unencumbered.

'I live alone,' she said. She'd been watching his reaction. She dropped her keys on a side table and took her bags through to a small kitchen. 'Do you want coffee or tea?'

'Coffee, please,' said Harry. 'Strong as you like.' Sharing preferences was a subtle way of breaking down barriers. But Alanya was MI6; she'd know all about that.

He looked through the front window. No sign of Rik, but he wouldn't be hanging around. Strangers standing about in this kind of road would attract attention. Especially scruffs in jeans and trainers.

After the roar of a kettle came stirring sounds, then Alice returned. She handed him a mug of coffee, dark as sludge. Her own looked like green tea or camomile. She sat down neatly on a two-seater settee and sipped her drink, gesturing for him to take the armchair opposite. The can of Mace was close by her side.

'What's this about?' she asked. 'Have I been pinged?' An in-house term for an alert sounded about an officer's behaviour.

'No. Nothing like that. I'm sorry we approached you like this, but we need your help.'

'Really? You couldn't go through channels?'

'It's not that kind of help.'

She blinked, analysing the statement. Harry let her think about it; he wanted her slightly off-balance, unsure of what this was about. Reactions were easier to assess that way, especially with someone as aware as Alice Alanya.

'So you don't want my superiors involved. That means it could compromise me.' She stared at him. 'Boy, that's going to take some persuading.'

'Clare Jardine.' He let the words lie without embellishment or explanation. That could come in a second or two. He was interested in reading her face. It didn't take long. She frowned slightly, the mug halfway to her lips, then lowered again.

'Clare? I don't understand.'

She was either exceptionally good or completely and genuinely surprised, Harry couldn't tell which. Her voice had carried just the right tone of someone having a name from their past thrown at them out of the blue, but a practised liar would manage that easily enough.

'Have you heard from her in the last six months?'

'No. Is she all right?'

'You were friends, though, right?'

'Yes. More like good colleagues, but we got on. Is there a problem with that?' She waved a hand in mild exasperation. 'Look, I went through this before – we all did.'

'All?'

'Everyone who worked with her. If you're really Five you'll know.'

'I'm just checking, that's all.'

'Fine. Then you'll also know she left SIS under a cloud.' She looked away for a second. 'It's no secret what she did. If you must know I never blamed her, not like some of the others.'

'Blamed her for what?'

She paused, then shrugged. 'Bellingham. What she did to him. That view is on record, if you need to check, so don't go getting heavy on me. She was set up to be killed, along with the others.'

'You sure that wasn't rumour?'

Her eyes flashed. 'Are you kidding me? There is rumour and rumour. The corridors were buzzing with it. You can't keep something like that going if there isn't an element of truth.' She took

125

a deep breath. 'Anyway, after that, she got shot and I haven't heard from her since.'

Harry sat back. So far she'd been right on the button. Credible and angry in just the right proportions. Except for one thing: she hadn't mentioned being in contact with Clare after Red Station. The easiest lies were by omission.

'You heard about the shooting?'

'We all did. It's not often a field officer gets shot, past or serving. It rattled a lot of cages. But you probably wouldn't know about that, would you?'

She was angry and resentful, Harry noted, lashing out with concern for a friend. He could ignore the fact that she might have – probably *had* – helped Clare out with information after Red Station. But she seemed genuinely unaware of any contact since.

'Because I'm with Five, you mean?'

She didn't meet his gaze. 'Forget it. If you're not tapping my shoulder about my behaviour, why are you concerned about Clare?'

Harry decided to go with the truth. He'd been hedging enough and it wasn't getting anywhere. 'First off,' he said, 'I'm no longer with Five. But I am working with Ballatyne's approval. He's the one person you can ring if you need verification.'

'I might do that.' It was a sign that she recognised the name.

'I was one of the "others" you mentioned, along with Clare. The place was code-named Red Station in Georgia and Clare and I came out together, along with the scruff outside, whose

126

name is Rik Ferris. He's also former MI5. We were all let go out of official embarrassment. When Clare got shot it was by a Bosnian called Milan Zubac, working for a group of deserters called the Protectory. She managed to disable Zubac with a compact knife and was lucky to get to hospital in time. She spent the last few weeks in King's College, at the Major Trauma Unit.'

'You seem to know a lot about it. How come?'

'I was with her at the time.'

TWENTY

Candida Deane, Deputy Director of the Russian Desk in SIS, stepped into the Donovan Bar in Brown's Hotel in London's Mayfair, and scanned the tables.

George Paulton waited as her gaze passed over him, paused, then came back. He raised a hand, at the same time checking his watch. Right on time.

Beyond her the doorway was empty. No obvious heavies lurking – a point he'd insisted on, although he knew they wouldn't be far away. Deane wouldn't have been able to dump her personal protection altogether without questions being raised by internal security. But the one person she wouldn't like to be seen meeting in public was a former Operations Director of MI5 who was now on a watch-and-detain list at all ports, accused of offences against ... he still wasn't entirely certain what the legalities were of what he'd done, but no doubt government lawyers had done all the necessary paperwork.

He stood up as she approached, and saw her frown as she took in his appearance. It reminded him that although they had met before, it had been a while ago and on different levels. And she had never seen him in this guise before.

'Thank you for coming, Miss Deane,' he said politely, and sat down again. 'I thought you might appreciate the ambiance here.'

She glanced around, in spite of herself. The walls were lined with Terence Donovan photographs, while behind the bar, with its high stools, was a startling stained glass window depicting St George of dragon-slaying fame. He wasn't particularly bothered whether she liked it or not, but if he had made a serious error of judgement in coming back to London and arranging to meet her, he at least wanted to have a pleasant memory to take away with him.

They ordered; she took a vodka and tonic, no ice, while he asked for a second Donovan Martini, their signature drink. He figured he could afford the slight fuzziness it would bring and he had a lot of catching up to do.

'I'm not a traitor,' she said calmly, as soon as they were alone. 'And I won't do anything that makes me into one. Get used to it.'

Paulton lifted an eyebrow. 'Ouch. So defensive.' He picked up his drink and raised it in an ironic gesture towards her. *'Salut.'*

'Just so we're clear on that point, that's all.'

128

'Oh, I'm clear on it, don't worry. It's why I contacted you in the first place. I'm already out in the cold as it is; why tie my future to someone who might just get found out for some other offence further down the line?'

Deane said nothing.

'Thing is,' he continued, 'I know how ambitious you are. You'll use me, the service and anyone else you come across to get what you want.' She looked ready to protest, but he waved a conciliatory hand. 'Not that I blame you; a top job in Six is worth having. And we all do what we think is right to get to the top of our respective dog piles, don't we?'

She stiffened. 'Well, you stuffed that up for yourself, didn't you?'

'Now, now. Don't play nasty. We're supposed to be friends.'

Her eyes flashed. 'Friends? We'll never be friends as long as we live, George, so don't give me that crap.' Her south London accent became more noticeable as emotion took over. 'You contacted me for one thing and one thing only: you want to come in out of the cold without being marched straight into Wandsworth at the start of a long sentence in solitary. You said you'd bring me something worthwhile to help you do that. Well, I'm waiting.' She took a slurp of her drink, her face flushed.

Straight for the throat, thought Paulton. Like an attack dog. It was a reminder not to push her too far. In her position she would know people she could call on if she wanted someone taken care of quietly.

129

'And I keep my promises,' he assured her smoothly. 'For example, I know of at least five agents-in-place in the UK, still active, still gathering intel, still reporting back to Moscow, Langley and Beijing. At least one of them is turnable.' He smiled. 'That's what you're really after, isn't it? Someone you can add to your credit list of achievements.'

He saw by her expression that he had struck a nerve. Look at any SIS officer, and you would see what you'd expect to see – a spy in plain clothing. But peel back the skin, the carefully crafted outer layer, of the ambitious ones, and you'd find a bureaucrat with an eye to the main chance – the gold chalice of spy-running: having their own double-agent on tap. And one with a potential line right into Moscow Central was still the purest gold of all.

'I'll need more than that.'

'Of course you will. And I have something better. A lot better.'

'Paulton, if you're stringing me—'

'I'm not. And before you tell me what nasty, despicable things you can have done to me, remember that I know things you and some of your friends in high places would rather I didn't know.' He shrugged. 'Some of it is, shall we say, less than current. Old hat. Passé, even. But still embarrassing to those in power. However, let's not fall out over that. No, I have what dear old Gordon Brown used to refer to rather boringly as "a package of measures". Only my package comes with a lot more meaning.'

Deane waited, eyes dull.

'Clare Jardine.'

Deane frowned. 'What about her? We had her, then she ran. I told you.' She pulled a face. 'I can't say I'm surprised. But there are people above me who agreed to leave her be, as you know. She's untouchable.'

'But you didn't agree, did you?' Paulton resisted the temptation to grin, knowing her secret. This wasn't the moment for triumphalism. 'You want her to pay for what she did to Bellingham. Quite right, too. I sympathise. And she will pay, I can assure you.' He uttered the words, feeling the weight of the mobile phone in his pocket, which held the data Maine had sent him. It had been very last minute, and not as helpful as he'd hoped. But the intelligence analyst had done his best.

What Paulton now knew was that there was little chance of tracing Jardine in the normal way. She appeared to have gone off the grid after returning from Red Station and killing Sir Anthony Bellingham, and had no home address, no family and no close friends. But he had a good facial photo of her, which should help Gorelkin's gorillas in their search.

A pulse was beating in Deane's throat. Paulton recognised the signs of anger beating beneath the surface. Deane had worked under Bellingham in MI6. She had been one of his protégées, one of a posse of SIS recruits loyal to him and hanging on to his coat-tails. Ironically, had Bellingham survived, Deane's advance in the service would not have been quite so rapid. But sudden gaps in any organisation created opportunity for the ambitious. He doubted Deane had ever considered it, but with his death, there had been a vacuum and she had moved on up ahead of her colleagues. The fact that he considered her totally unsuited to the job was beside the point. Played right, she could still be useful to him.

'Do you know where she is?'

'I have an idea, yes. But that's not the only part of the package.'

'Really? Who else have you got – Lord Lucan?' Deane didn't bother hiding her scepticism. 'Not interested.'

'Not even close. I know who put an end to poor old Roman Vladimirovich Tobinskiy in King's College.'

Deane's eyes showed a spark of interest, quickly supressed. 'How can you know that?'

He grinned. *What she meant was, even she doesn't know that.* 'I know how they found Tobinskiy, I know about the guard leaving his post the night he was killed ... and I even know the name of the man who came over especially from Moscow's Special Purpose Centre to run the kill team who carried out the assignment.'

The thought processes as Deane ran through the permutations were almost painful to watch. Paulton let them run without interrupting. He knew what was happening. Boxes were being ticked, targets lined up, scores being calculated for the final personal triumph.

Finally, she said, 'Are you saying Jardine wasn't involved?'

It was a minor point, but one he knew she

would consider. Vengeance is a hard goal to let go.

'She knew nothing about it.' As her face fell, registering disappointment, he added smoothly, 'But in the final analysis, who will be able to tell? She was right there when it happened, she knows the Russians, she was already a bad apple in the barrel.' He shrugged meaningfully. 'You can do with that what you will. I presume you have people looking for her?'

She gave a hint of a nod, but no more. She would have to be careful committing resources to look for a person of no official interest purely for her own ends; but he had no doubts that she already had a team working on it. Outsiders, probably, a bunch of contractors from one of the many shadowy private security companies with offices in Mayfair.

He watched while she worked out the prizes this could bring her: the team responsible for the murder of a Russian dissident in a London hospital, including their senior Moscow chief; the woman who had murdered her boss, Bellingham. A shot at the top job.

Game, set and match.

TWENTY-ONE

Alice Alanya stared at Harry. 'I didn't realise. How did it happen?'

Harry didn't want to go through the shooting again; he'd done that enough already. But he owed Clare some recognition with her friend. 'She was helping Rik and me track down Zubac. We found him but he got the jump on us and shot Clare. He was going to finish her off, then me, when she used a knife on him. She saved my life.'

'That's why you want to help her.'

He nodded. 'And she helped someone else. I owe her for that, too.'

'I don't know what I can tell you,' she said after a moment's thought. 'I haven't heard from her, if that's what you're asking. Not since ... well, ages.' She stopped speaking.

'But you used to, before she was shot.'

She shook her head, but it didn't amount to a denial. He decided not to push it.

'You've heard of Roman Tobinskiy?'

'Of course. What about him?'

He told her about Tobinskiy's death in King's College Hospital. She looked shocked, even stunned; with her position in MI6, working on the Russian side, she would be well aware of the gravity it would bring to international relations if the death was proven to be suspicious.

'Clare was recovering in an adjacent room,' he added. 'She may have heard something that made her run. If she did, then the killers will be after her.'

'Killers?'

'Two men raided the security control centre at the hospital earlier today and took the CCTV hard drive. It would have held footage of the night Tobinskiy died and of Clare leaving the hospital minutes later.'

Alice touched a hand to her mouth, eyes wide. The implications were clear and she knew what it meant for Clare. 'My God. How awful.'

'Yes. I'm surprised you haven't been told.' He was more surprised that she hadn't been hauled in and questioned by internal security. Maybe, with stunning lack of efficiency, they were working through Clare's past list of contacts in reverse alphabetical order.

'I didn't know – honest. How bad was she hurt?'

'She was out of the woods and recovering well, but not enough to have a couple of killers on her trail.' Or a vindictive bunch of MI6 heavies, he wanted to add, but didn't. That might colour her judgement. 'Last seen, she was heading towards Waterloo Station and central London. Best guess is she'll go to ground and find someone she can trust. But she has no ready access to money or ID, unless she had a stash somewhere.'

'You mean with a friend. Like me.' She gave him a flat look. 'You think I'm hiding her?' She swept a hand out. 'Do you want to search the place? Go through my things, check my phone log and laptop to see if we've been having cosy chats? Go ahead.'

Harry shook his head, about to deny it, but was interrupted by his mobile ringing. He excused himself and took it out.

It was Rik. 'Don't want to cause panic, boss, but two blokes in a blue Focus just did a couple of slow drive-bys, eyeballing the flats. Might be coincidence but I don't think so. I got their number.'

'Did they see you?'

'No.'

'Meet us round the back. We're heading out.' He shut off the phone and looked at Alice. 'I'm sorry to do this to you, but we have to leave. Now.'

'Why?' She blinked like a startled doe. But she stood up and reached for her bag, her security training taking over.

'Two men in a car showing an interest. They could be from Six, but it would be best not to risk it. They're probably looking for Clare. Do you have somewhere you could go until you hit work tomorrow? Ballatyne will fill you in then.'

'I have an aunt in Uxbridge.'

'Good. Show me the back way out and we'll see you safely to a taxi.'

Alice turned left out of her flat and led Harry through a narrow door leading onto some back stairs, concrete and unfinished. The air was cool and musty. At the bottom, she turned right at a glass-panelled security door leading out to a small enclosed area with parking spaces and garages.

Rik was standing with his back to the door, watching the entrance off a feeder road from the street. If the men were the Russians, they would come in the back way through the feeder road. They hadn't got much time.

Harry opened the door and Rik nodded before heading off at a brisk walk.

Alice stared at Rik's right hand, held close down by his side. 'He's armed.'

'I know. I keep telling him about it but he's addicted.'

'You're carded, then?'

'Yes. Is there a footpath away from here?'

She nodded. 'Turn right and through a stile at the end. We can double back towards the station. My God, what kind of work do you two do?'

'Most of it's boring and repetitive. But every now and then we get to shoot people. Come on.' He hustled her along, and she gave directions, showing the entrance to a narrow alleyway between rear gardens. Bordered by trees and wooden slat fencing, it was concealed from the road, and Harry called a halt long enough to send a text to Ballatyne.

Did you put watchers on Alanya?

No. Why?

He got the car registration number from Rik and texted back to Ballatyne: *Two men in blue Focus* followed by the number.

Four minutes later, as they left the path and entered another residential street, a reply came through.

Not mine. Suggest avoiding action. Talk later.

Harry put the phone away. Ballatyne was going operational. The time to talk would come once they had got clear and lost the watchers. For now they had to focus on staying out of sight.

Alice led them back towards the station by a roundabout route, with Rik and Harry alert and ready to duck into cover if the car with the two men should return. As they entered Station Road from the north, Harry spotted a passing cab and dialled the number on the roof panel. The despatcher told him two minutes and asked for the passenger's name.

Harry led Alice to the doorway of a closed store to wait, while Rik wandered along the pavement to keep watch.

'Go to your aunt's and don't contact anybody,' he told her. 'In the morning, go to the office as usual, but keep with the crowd. When you're out, stay on the move and go straight to see Ballatyne. He'll brief you.'

Her eyes looked huge with worry, but she remained calm. 'OK. What are you going to do?'

'Try to find Clare before anybody else does.'

She nodded and shivered, her first real sign of nerves. Then she said quickly, 'Do you know why she was posted to that place in Georgia – why they sent her there?'

'The basics, yes. Why?'

'It wasn't just a mad fling in the middle of an operation, you know. It was serious – on both sides.'

'Are you sure?' According to Mace, the station chief in Georgia, Clare had become the victim of a reverse sting. It had cost her her job and nearly her life.

'Yes. She told me all about it. I know, she shouldn't have, but she had to talk to somebody. She was gutted when they found out. She'd managed to control it at first, hoping she could find a way of breaking off the assignment as unworkable. But they realised what had happened and pulled her out of the field. She was marked as unreliable. I suppose they had no choice. You know the rest.'

A cab approached and pulled into the kerb. Rik checked the passenger name and gave Harry a nod.

As Alice ducked into the car, she turned and gave them both a wan smile. Seconds later, she was gone.

'She's clear,' said Rik, coming to join him. He blew out a puff of air. 'Now what?'

Harry was thinking about what Alice had said, wondering if he wasn't grasping at straws. *It wasn't just a mad fling in the middle of an operation. It was serious.*

But the words were bouncing around in front of him, loaded with meaning. Bloody hell. It was obvious. If Clare couldn't go to friends, there was possibly only one person she could go to.

He texted Ballatyne. *Need talk.*

Rik had been watching him. He gave a start. 'Hey – I forgot, I got the details of that subscriber you asked for; the misdial.' He took out his own phone and scrolled to the notepad function. 'His name's Fortiani; he's a trader of some kind in an office near Victoria.' He handed over the phone and Harry read the details. 'You playing the markets now?'

Harry shook his head and dialled the number.

It rang out and went to voicemail. A man's voice. 'This is Ray Fortiani. I'm unavailable right now. My apologies. Please leave a number and I'll call you back. Thank you.'

Harry stared at the screen. Fortiani, whoever he was, sounded educated and confident. A businessman. Not the sort to misdial, but if he did, he would apologise and not leave someone hanging.

He checked Rik's notepad and saw another number, this one a landline. Home or office. He dialled the number.

'Fortiani.' It was the same voice.

Harry apologised for calling so late and asked Fortiani if he had recently lost a mobile phone.

'What? Yes, I have, actually.' He sounded excited. 'Have you found it?'

'Not exactly.' Harry explained about the call he'd received. 'Have you reported it lost yet?'

Fortiani sounded sheepish. 'No. To be honest, I don't know for sure if I left it in the office or if it was stolen. I didn't want to have it cancelled in case it was handed in by the cleaners at work. There's a ton of material on there that I'd like back, though.'

Harry asked where else it might have gone missing if not at the office.

'Well, the only place I can think of is a place in Pimlico: The Grove. It's a wine bar I go to a lot with a group from work, and it's the last place I remember using it. I mean, if that's where it happened, it was done so smoothly I couldn't actually recall having it with me. You know how it is when you're with a bunch of friends and colleagues? The place is always packed and half the time you can't hear yourself speak. But I can't imagine any of the usual clientele stealing phones; it just doesn't gel.'

Harry didn't have such reservations about other people's honesty being guaranteed by the places they frequented, but he didn't bother enlightening Fortiani. 'When was that?'

'I was there the evening before last until late, and again yesterday afternoon. I have a work mobile, too, so I've been working with that. I guess I should report it, for the insurance.'

'Can I ask you not to do that yet? If I can, I'll get it back for you. But it's important that we don't alert whoever has it that we know.'

Fortiani sounded puzzled. He said, 'Are you police?'

Harry cut the call. It saved having to explain the unexplainable.

Then he looked around and spotted an Indian restaurant along the street. It reminded him that they hadn't eaten properly.

'You hungry?'

Rik nodded. 'Could eat a horse. What's going on with the phone?'

'It wasn't Fortiani who called, trying to sell some bonds.' He explained about the trader's phone lifted from a café table in Pimlico.

Rik's eyebrows lifted. 'You think it was Clare? That's a reach.'

'I can't think of anyone else. She's resourceful enough.'

'True. Maybe she'll call back.'

'Maybe. In the meantime, it tells us where she is. Or was.'

They were well into their meal by the time Ballatyne called back. He didn't sound happy.

'My wife's going to kill me for this. We're supposed to be at dinner.'

'I didn't know you had a wife,' said Harry, and gave him a brief report, avoiding names. He finished by asking, 'Clare's target – the one she got canned for.'

A cautious pause, then, 'What about her?'

Her. So the target had definitely been a woman. His response was too instinctive to be a mistake. But Ballatyne was too experienced not to have read the files. He'd have brushed up on all their histories as a matter of course, the moment this business began.

'Do you have a name and a location?'

Another silence, this one lasting several seconds. Finally Ballatyne said, 'You must be bloody joking.' The phone went dead.

Harry put his phone down with a wry smile. Ballatyne's obtuse way of not saying no.

Rik looked up from his chicken korma, one eyebrow raised. 'I bet he didn't like that. You're not serious, though, are you? She wouldn't go there, surely?'

'Why not?' Harry repeated what Alice had told him before getting into the taxi. 'What would you do if you were that desperate?'

'I don't know. Find a friend – any friend, I guess.' He frowned. 'But her target was a Russian, wasn't she? If they find out she's gone there, she'll never see daylight again.'

'Maybe she knows that and figures she has nothing to lose.'

TWENTY-TWO

Clare awoke suddenly, her heart pounding. A loud noise had ripped into her subconscious, like the crash of a door bursting open. She sat up, panic overtaking her, and was on her feet without thinking. *Somebody trying to get in!* Then she bent over as pain creased across her middle, an unsubtle reminder that she wasn't in any fit state for gymnastics.

She breathed in and out, allowing her heart rate to settle. The room was silent and chill, smelling of damp. A gloomy space but not dark. The sickly glow of a street light filtered in across the floor. She'd been dozing in a battered old armchair. She recalled the building work further down the street earlier; tips being filled with rubble, workmen shouting, a cement mixer chugging constantly. Like a small war going on. Then silence when they packed up for the day. And sleep.

She'd been woken by a delayed playback, that was all. The mind playing tricks. She forced herself to relax further and assessed her surroundings. She was alone, the garden door locked and jammed shut against outsiders. The connecting door to the rest of the building had been nailed up by whatever previous tenant had isolated him or herself down here in the basement. There was nobody in the room and she felt angry at herself for losing her grip. This wasn't her, not this jittery, disconnected heap of jelly who jumped at every slight sound.

She straightened up by stages, like unfolding an old newspaper, stopping at each ragged tug of pain, until she was more or less upright. It took a while. Then she breathed in and out, the taste in her mouth sour and bitter.

Jesus, was this what it was like to be *old*? If so she wanted none of it. She checked herself over, a slow examination of her physical extremities first. Legs stiff, arms ditto, stomach burning but not as bad it had been. Sleep had helped. She peeled back the bandage under her waistband. Hissed at the redness of the skin around the gunshot wound, but it was better than it had been. Maybe the effort of getting here had helped, forcing her body to flush with healing power, to fight off infection.

But where was here?

Her inner senses took over, remembering the hospital. Images came to her slowly, an unravelling film reel of her rush from the building and through the shadow-filled streets, overhead lights harsh and painful to the eyes, her feet sore from not having worn shoes for a while. She'd met a German girl – Mitzi? – then gone to a squat, followed by the outdoors again and more walking. Until she found this place.

Pimlico. She remembered now. Near Victoria Station, busy streets, residential and businesses cheek by jowl. Lots of people.

Safety, of sorts.

Other images forced their way in from further back. The hospital smell, night-time, the sound of the men in her room; before that the man across the corridor, Tobinskiy, shouting in Russian, angry and at times incoherent, but according to the nurse, never fully conscious. Educated, though, she would have known that by his use of words, even if she had never heard of him before. Raging at the state, the persecution and murder of his friend, they were trying to kill him, he'd gabbled; sending assassins just like they did with Alexander. Why could nobody see it? Why would nobody believe him? The torrent of words had at times been unintelligible.

He would be next, he'd moaned once. Then they would believe.

She'd wondered for a while who Alexander was, her mind still foggy. She had known, once, she was certain. It lurked on the edges of her mind, a vague whisper of sound, from a briefing or the news ... maybe something she'd read. But it wouldn't come. Then suddenly it did, in a rush like a floodgate opened: Alexander Litvinenko, former FSB officer, asylum seeker in Britain, journalist and hater of Vladimir Putin. Polonium 210. Radiation poisoning. Photos of Litvinenko in hospital, hunched and dying. Grey going on white.

Now dead.

She eased herself carefully down in the armchair. The elbow crutch was nearby but she ignored it. Sighed with relief when the pain subsided. Felt the mobile phone jammed down between the cushion and the arm.

She picked it up, switched it on. Waited while the icons flickered into life. Checked the amount of power left. Three bars. Not bad but not great. The time on the small screen said 23.15.

There were several missed calls and eight voicemail messages. Jesus, she'd stolen the phone belonging to a talk freak. She ignored them all. Didn't want to waste power by deleting or checking them.

Tomorrow, she'd call ... who? Still couldn't recall Alice's number. Pointless asking directory enquiries or 192; MI6 didn't encourage easy access for any of their personnel.

Harry Tate? She saw his number in her head, floating past with perverse immediacy, tantalising. Why was that?

She switched off the phone, put her head back. She was hungry, her stomach tight with the need for food and fluids. She should hit the street and find an all-nighter, get something inside her. Maybe in a while. When she felt better.

Seconds later she was fast asleep.

TWENTY-THREE

'We need to step things up.' Sergei Gorelkin was annoyed, but holding his mood in check. Getting pissy with Votrukhin and Serkhov would serve no immediate purpose other than to make him feel better. He could save that for later. Right now they had to find the Jardine woman and silence her before she got to the press with anything she knew.

He had called them in early to the office in Mayfair. He dispensed with the sweep for bugs; he didn't have time. Neither did he allow them any breakfast, a distraction from the main topic. He had, however, arranged strong coffee, to ensure they were wide awake and listening.

'How?' Votrukhin queried. 'We don't have enough feet on the ground, we can't use the embassy and we're not allowed near any of the residents.' These last were deep cover agents unknown to the embassy, but supported at arm's length in their legends and daily activities. Deeper still and even more remote were the gold standard of spies, the sleepers, although, as some wags in Moscow had been heard to claim, since the fall of communism not even Moscow knew who *they* were anymore.

'We hit the streets.' Gorelkin reached down

147

and picked up a cardboard box from the floor. It was twice the size of a shoe box. He tore off the lid and tipped the box up, spilling out some of the contents, which skidded across the table in a fan.

They were a mix of two shots. Half were photos taken inside a plain corridor, the flare of overhead lights reflecting off a shiny tiled floor. The subject was a woman walking beneath the camera. The format was clearly from CCTV footage, the best few frames frozen for all time. The others were file shots, face-on and serious, like passport shots, but larger and better quality, provided by Paulton, although he hadn't disclosed where he had got them.

Clare Jardine.

Votrukhin and Serkhov picked up samples and scanned them quickly, committing the images to memory. They hadn't seen the CCTV stills before, but had handed over the hard drive for Gorelkin to process the moment they got back from the hospital. The images weren't perfect, but good enough. They showed a young woman in her thirties, possibly older, gaunt in the face and pallid, walking with one hand clasped across her middle, the other holding a metal crutch. She wore dark trousers and a jacket over a white top, and if she was aware of the camera above her head, seemed unconcerned.

'She's on the street,' Gorelkin told them, 'most likely in central London. As the Englishman told us, she has no family and nowhere to go. She'll have joined the rabble. So that's where we look for her, using the people she mixes with.' He

148

tapped one of the photos. 'And that crutch is going to make her stand out.'

Votrukhin fanned his face with one of the photos and nodded. 'I get it. Use the rabble to find her. But which ones?'

'All of them. But concentrate on illegals from the east; them we can talk to.' Illegals had more to lose, and far more to gain by earning any kind of reward. And those from the east had a much stronger network of their own kind to use and mobilise. In addition, if Votrukhin and Serkhov had to lean on anyone, the last thing an illegal would do was complain to the police for fear of compromising their position.

'What about the Englishman?' Votrukhin asked. 'Did he come good?'

'Yes, he did.' Gorelkin opened out a map of London. It had a series of coloured dots on it. The furthest south was a short distance from King's College. There were six more, all in a line leading towards central London, all black. The last black dot was at Waterloo Station.

'These black dots represent firm sightings of Jardine,' Gorelkin explained. 'They end at Waterloo Station, but there's an imperfect shot of a figure across the river near Charing Cross Station which could be her.'

'The blue ones,' said Serkhov, 'are they possibles only?'

'Yes. Either the image was poor or it was too far to tell for certain. There would have been others bearing a similarity to Jardine, of course, but the blue ones are in line with where she might have gone, so we don't discount those.'

He placed one hand on the paper, forming a curve with his thumb and forefinger. The curve embraced the area of Battersea in the south right up to Waterloo Station and the Embankment in the north, including where the river bent eastwards towards the area of Southwark and London Bridge. 'Start here by the river and work your way across to the north and west. She is in that area somewhere. Maybe north of the river by now, maybe not. Use those you can trust to spread the photos.'

'What does Paulton think?' Votrukhin ventured a question. 'He's the expert. Does he have an opinion he'd like to share with us?'

'Only that Victoria is probably a good area for anyone to hide. Lots of tourists, lots of movement, cheap hotels and faces nobody remembers.'

'It's still a hell of an area.' Votrukhin picked up the map and folded it, nodding at Serkhov to bring the box of photos. He might not like what they had to do, but refusing Gorelkin's orders was not an option.

Gorelkin smiled and checked his watch. 'You're correct, lieutenant; it's a big area. It's now eight o'clock. Do it right and you should have this part of London covered by nightfall.' He stood up, straightening his jacket. 'Find her, deal with her ... and you might just be forgiven for letting her go in the first place.'

Harry and Rik had had the same idea, although they were working with a better head and shoulders shot of Clare, from JPEGs supplied by

Ballatyne. They were at least three years old but clearer than any CCTV shot. They also had the advantage of being less likely to arouse suspicion among those they approached that she had been filmed by a security camera, and was therefore on the run from the authorities.

Harry had abandoned any idea of checking the neighbourhood where Clare had once lived, on the simple grounds that she wasn't the nostalgic sort and wouldn't bother returning there.

They reached Victoria Station and began to ask around, having decided to split up and work their way south towards the river. It was dog work, requiring them to go into the darkest corners they could find, but necessary if they wanted to reach the most obvious people – the ones Clare might have met in the past few days. They approached street hostels, rough sleeper communities, figures huddled in sleeping bags and beneath layers of cardboard; they checked doorways and empty premises, squats and renovation sites, spoke to traffic wardens and sweepers, rail workers and café owners. The response became numbingly similar, mostly in the negative. But equally depressing were the possible sightings too vague or too long ago to follow up easily, from individuals trying to help, yet offering a tantalising hint that Clare was out there somewhere.

By midday, they had exhausted their supply of photos, and were forced to take Rik's memory stick into a printer to get more produced.

'She might have moved further out,' Rik suggested, as they sat and drank coffee, waiting for the photos. 'Or north of here. There are plenty of squats beyond Park Lane, fancy big places waiting to be renovated.'

Harry knew he was right. But they couldn't afford to spread the search too thin. They were already overstretched as it was. Clare could be anywhere in the city, he knew that; but it was simply his instinct that placed her somewhere within reach.

He took out his mobile and composed a text. This one wasn't for Ballatyne.

We can help you. Ring me. He paused, wondering what he could use as an identifier. To Clare, on the run and hurting, this text could easily be a trap to lure her out of hiding. Then he had it. He added, *Pink Compact. So not your colour.* He dialled the number of Fortiani's mobile and pressed Send.

TWENTY-FOUR

'Have you seen this woman?' Serkhov shoved the photo under the nose of a man sitting in the doorway of a day hostel a hundred yards south of Victoria Station. The doors were locked and the alcove reeked of urine. Serkhov tried not to throw up at the rank body odour coming off him.

'Say what, pal?' The eyes were slate grey and unfocussed, his greasy skin a network of veins and ingrained dirt. The neck of a bottle stuck out from his coat pocket.

Serkhov swore silently and gave up. He'd seen drunks like this too many times to be surprised. Back in Moscow they were a feature of the landscape, high on illicit vodka or *samogon*, and the cheap *chacha* as it was known in Georgia, all liable to be dangerously toxic. He placed the heel of his hand on the man's forehead and slammed his head back against the door. He wished instantly that he could wash his hands and turned away in disgust.

Across the street, Votrukhin watched and shook his head. He placed a mint on his tongue, allowing the sharp flavour to spread around his mouth. Given time, he'd have used more subtle methods and picked their targets more carefully, chatting first to gain their confidence, maybe even buying them a drink or two. But time was something he didn't have, and subtlety an art Serkhov had never possessed.

They had already handed out dozens of photos in the area, and secured the dubious promises of several illegals to hand out more and spread the word about the missing woman to the north and east. For the most part, that meant waiting to see what came back. But in the meantime, doing something was better than nothing, and might keep Gorelkin off their backs.

He turned and walked along the street, Serkhov following a parallel path on the other side. A street sweeper in a bright orange tabard was scooping up some litter. He stopped alongside him, holding out the still of Jardine taken from the CCTV footage.

'Excuse me,' he said. 'Have you seen this girl? She's thought to be in the area. She discharged herself from hospital and could be in danger.'

The man squinted at the photo for a second, then shook his head. 'No, pal, I haven't seen her. Like I told the other bloke, there's a thousand look just like her walk past here every day. Sorry.'

Votrukhin thanked him and was about to walk away when he stopped. 'The other man? Big with a shaved head?' If it matched, it would be Serkhov, but he hadn't been working this area until now – and then only across the street.

'No. Young guy, spiky hair. Looked like a charity worker but he wasn't.'

'Why do you say that?'

'Dunno. Something about him. A bit sure of himself, if you know what I mean. I reckon he had copper written all over him. Have you told the cops about her?'

'Ah, of course. That would be it.' Votrukhin thanked him and moved away, his antennae twitching. He caught Serkhov's eye and signalled him to wait, then walked across the street to join him.

'We have company,' he announced, scanning the area carefully. 'A young man with spiky hair, could be police, also showing a photo of Jardine and asking if anyone has seen her.'

Serkhov pushed his lip out. 'Could it have been one of our drones?' A name for the more trusted illegals they had recruited to broaden the search across London.

'No. There's no way any of them would be

154

mistaken for police – not by a local, anyway.'

'So who are they?'

'Security services, I think. MI5, MI6 ... even sub-contractors. She disappeared the same night as Tobinskiy died, so it makes sense that they will be looking for her to ask why.' He felt bad for not dealing with the woman as Serkhov had suggested, when they'd had a chance. Unless they recouped the situation and got to Jardine first, this was going to come back and bite him, he was certain. Team leaders shouldn't make these kind of mistakes. 'This is getting too crowded for comfort.'

Serkhov scowled. 'Do we carry on? If it's Security, they might spot us before we see them.'

'We have no choice.' He fixed Serkhov with a hard stare. Now was not the time for doubts. 'There might be more of them working the area as a team. Keep your eyes open for anyone flashing photos.'

'And if they see us first?'

'*Chyornyiy* rules, remember? Deal with it.'

TWENTY-FIVE

To Harry, in spite of Fortiani's beliefs to the contrary, The Grove wine bar looked exactly the sort of place to pick up a spare mobile phone. It was a high-end bistro and restaurant on two floors, standing on a prominent corner spot a few minutes from Victoria Station. One look inside and he'd already spotted several phones prominently displayed where anyone trained in brush-past techniques would scoop them up in an instant. With so much laughter and talk, busy waiters juggling trays of food and drinks, clients coming and going, often from one table to another in pursuit of gossip and connections, it was like an ants' nest of furious activity.

Just the kind of place Clare would have targeted.

He stood on the corner outside, trying to get a feel for the area. The buildings here were up-scale and neat, the streets open. Not the best place for a fugitive to hide in. While The Grove would have been ideal for a fishing trip, to pick up a mobile phone, Clare would have been looking for somewhere more compact to duck into, with plenty of interconnected run-throughs and preferably without cameras. Victoria was attractive, with thousands of business travellers and tourists to use as cover, but anybody pursuing her would make that the first place to look. And a young woman with a stick would stand out.

He consulted his map and felt his spirits sink. Pick anywhere with a pin. It would take a team weeks to go through the lot.

Rik joined him, shaking his head. 'Not even any possibles.'

'Me neither.'

'We're not the only ones looking for her, though.'

Harry looked at him. 'I know. I've had a couple of comments. What did you hear?'

156

'Four people mentioned guys flashing photos around – photos of a young woman. One said the photo looked like a still from a security camera. No reliable descriptions, but they all said they had foreign accents. A couple I spoke to reckoned they were Czechs or Poles, like illegals.'

'Or Russians.'

'Exactly. But the descriptions were of young guys, probably no more than twenty, and not well dressed. The line they were selling said the same thing: the woman had discharged herself from hospital.'

Harry nodded. Any other story would not have elicited the same sympathy or desire to help. But the men doing the asking sounded unusually young. Reliable FSB operators working overseas were usually older, having proved their trustworthiness and picked up a bagful of experience and scars along the way. Twenty was too young.

'They've been clever,' he concluded. 'They're using the street traffic. Doing what we're doing but on a bigger scale, and using illegals or overstayers to spread the word. Put out enough photos and someone somewhere will hit pay dirt and get the reward.'

His phone rang and he grabbed it eagerly, hoping it would be Clare.

It was Ballatyne.

'I've spoken to Alanya and checked the operations log. The two men in the Focus were a security surveillance team sent to check her out.'

'Why?'

'For the simple reason that she was buddies with Jardine. This business has got everyone in a

157

spin. Deane's got internal security turning the place inside out for anybody who so much as looked squinty-eyed at Jardine. Alanya happened to be top of the shit list.'

'Is she all right?'

'She is now. She thinks you're midway between Superman and a saint, by the way. Personally I think she's deluded, but there you go.'

'It's a strain, I know. Who's Deane?'

'You know I can't tell you that.'

Harry had a sudden thought. Clare worked the Russian section and Alice Alanya was a Russian language specialist. 'He's Head of the Russian desk, isn't he?'

'I told you—'

'I know – you can't tell me otherwise you'd have to send round one of your hotshots to shoot me. I get that. But who else would have an interest in this Tobinskiy business? Does this Deane know there's a Russian wet team out there?'

Ballatyne breathed heavily down the phone. It was enough to tell Harry that he was correct. 'She, actually,' he said finally. 'And if she does know she's not saying. Her name's Candida Deane. She's deputy head while her boss is off sick. It's an open secret that she's hoping he stays that way.'

'So she's ambitious.'

'With good reason; from the Russian desk to the upper reaches of the totem pole is an easy stretch. It carries more responsibility, it takes more budget and it has a lot of history. Bets are that she'll make it, and she won't care who she burns on the way, me included. I never told you any of that, of course.'

'She sounds like a toughie.'

'Like a junk yard dog. She's not to be messed with, Harry. She's one of the new breed; all MBAs and focus meetings and barbed wire knickers. But she's no shrinking violet. She likes to collect trophies and she's built a team around her who think the same way.'

'Warning noted. What about that other thing I asked you for? The target.'

A longer silence while Ballatyne played with his conscience, then: 'Jardine's target was a woman – a Russian. Her name was Katya Balenkova, and she was a captain in the Federal Protective Service, or FSO.'

'Is that what I think it is?'

'Probably. Give me five and I'll call you back.'

TWENTY-SIX

Lieutenant Katya Balenkova strode through the arrivals hall at Vienna Schwechat International Airport, scanning faces among the groups of meeters and greeters. Most looked local, with a few business types standing around exchanging pleasantries or deep in conversation on mobile phones. While she couldn't imagine any of them possibly presenting a threat to the three government financial specialists from Moscow coming along behind her, it was her job to ensure that their passage was unhindered and safe.

She dismissed each person quickly, automatically checking body outlines for the bulge of concealed weapons, and eyes for a look too intense and focussed for this place. When she was certain the way was clear, she turned and gave a signal to Bronyev, her FSO colleague. He nodded and herded the three bankers towards the main concourse and exit, where a limousine would be waiting outside.

She felt almost naked without her service weapon, which they were not permitted to carry on flights for obvious reasons. But it wouldn't be for long; as soon as they reached the city, she and Bronyev would be issued with side-arms from the embassy's armoury. It would not be a fact made known to the Austrian authorities who, like most countries, would take a dim view of the carrying of guns on their sovereign soil. But the Russian government's view was that bodyguards without weapons were like bulldogs without teeth.

She stepped back to avoid the senior of the three men, a particularly loathsome bureaucrat named Dobrev, who had been eyeing her openly ever since they had met the previous day. Overweight and pasty, with gelled hair and a heavy gut like excess baggage, he had made no secret of his intentions on this trip, suggesting that a drink at the earliest opportunity once they reached the convention hotel in Vienna would be an excellent way to show his appreciation for her security services. He had ignored Bronyev's disapproving stare, resting his pudgy hand on Katya's arm just a shade too long, snuffling pig-like with pleasure and pressing himself against her.

She had resisted the desire to knee him in the balls, and instead feigned a quick move to check out a nearby cab driver loitering for a fare. Having already been demoted from captain to her present rank of lieutenant after getting caught in a foreign espionage sting – although she had been cleared of any deliberate intent by an enquiry panel – dropping a fat banker to the floor with a Grozny handshake would only make things worse. And she had no wish to see what the job felt like at an even lower rank. Probably shepherding local dignitaries in some God-awful backwater in the Urals, just to make them feel valued and important, a small but vital cog in the machine that was the new Russia.

The official driver from the embassy was waiting by his car, a black Mercedes, as arranged. Katya watched from the side as Bronyev ushered the three men out of the main entrance and across the pavement, under the eye of two policemen who knew an official car when they saw one, even though it carried no pennant on its nose to smooth the way. It was all done with much petty fussing by the bankers, keen to have onlookers notice them and wonder at their importance, even if nobody quite knew what they represented.

So different, she thought, to the charges she had once worked with and guarded so assiduously. Diplomats, ministers and military men of

the highest ranks, they knew the game and played it correctly. Grandstanding in public was for
special days, parades and national celebrations;
every other day out in the open, wherever they
were, demanded rigorous adherence to protecion
rules. That meant no wandering off, continuous
movement unless told to stop by their guards,
and no ostentation likely to attract the attention
of political extremist or terrorists.

And at all times, following the advice of their
minders.

It was mostly bullshit now, she realised that. In
the main, the men – always men – wore civilian
clothes, unless on parade or at a function, and
were as faceless as the next man, albeit far better
dressed. But wearing a fancy imported suit
merely made them envied or resented, rarely if
ever a target.

Even so, their lofty positions and crucial jobs
had made them valued assets and therefore to be
protected at all times and by the best in the
business. And Katya Balenkova had been one of
the finest to graduate from the FSO academy and
training centre.

But that had all ended when the British had
decided she was a worthy target of a sting – a
honey trap, as it had turned out. A visit to London had resulted in a chance encounter with a
young woman. The encounter had moved to
drinks, to friendship, to meetings ... and eventually, in Brussels, where the other woman had
been visiting on business at the same time as
Katya herself had been working, something
more.

Later, in Frankfurt, the ground had fallen away beneath her feet when the other woman, Clare, had disappeared, hustled away from outside the hotel where they were staying by two men in suits, obviously guards of another kind.

It was when Katya herself had been called in for discussions on her return to Moscow that she had discovered who and what Clare Jardine was.

An MI6 operative.

Now she found herself bored and resentful. Unexcited by the lowly, tedious routine of safeguarding self-important drones like Dobrev, whose biggest threat, apart from her knee, was the copious amounts of drink he consumed; angry at her fall down the career ladder. And emotions like these, in this job, were dangerous. They led to lack of attention and a lowering of one's guard.

'You coming?' Bronyev was standing by the rear of the car, a faint frown on his face.

She nodded and joined him, climbing in the front passenger seat as her position required, and buckling in for the journey.

Bronyev sat in the back, close to the kerb. Younger than Katya and allegedly fresh out of the academy on his first posting, he was cautious and wary. And ambitious, too. But pleasant enough to work with. And he had more conversation than most male FSO members, whose main topics were limited to Spartak or Dynamo Moscow football teams.

She wondered not for the first time if Bronyev had been slotted into the team to keep an eye on her. Unlike many newcomers to the guards, who were usually full of themselves, he was likeable and considerate, and had confessed to wanting to progress in the FSO ranks by getting some solid experience behind him. But right from the start she had noticed signs about him that gave her cause for concern; there were times when his movements were just too practised, like an operative who had gone through the motions too many times before to be a simple newbie. Inexperienced guards betrayed their lack of skill in small ways: moving in a stop-start motion, as if unsure about who was in control of the speed of progress from car to building; standing in the wrong position and becoming a hindrance to their more experienced colleagues' line of sight; failing to scope the area in a 360 fashion and allowing large gaps to appear in the screen around their charges.

Bronyev, however, made none of these mistakes, and that worried her. She had also caught him watching her, as he had been just now. It wasn't in a sexual way, which she would have understood; hell, she might have her preferences which left men out of the equation altogether, but he wasn't to know that. No, she felt he was watching her for other reasons.

She breathed deeply and watched the neat and ordered countryside slip by outside, trying to relax. Three days here, unless there was a change of programme, and she'd be on her way back home. If he had been put in to check on her, she had better not give him anything to report back on.

TWENTY-SEVEN

It was nearer fifteen minutes before Ballatyne rang again. His voice sounded oddly dead, free of any natural echo, and Harry guessed the MI6 man was in a sanitized chamber with a secure outside line where not even God would hear a word he said.

'Sorry about that. More information coming in all the time, some of it you need to hear. First things first, though. I hope I never live to regret this, but I happen to think you might be right about Jardine's original target. But understand this: this conversation is so far off the record, it's inaudible except to dogs in Outer Mongolia.'

'I get it.'

'Balenkova's job is the equivalent of our own Diplomatic Protection Squad, only her unit's got much bigger muscles. Their mandate is vast, with some estimates giving them over twenty thousand members, all military trained. Some are formed into regiments, the best being special forces or Spetsnaz equivalents, with others working in outwardly civilian roles. They cover the president and other government officials as well as important installations such as IT centres, public utilities, nuclear sites and weapons storage and production units. They also travel

165

abroad when needed, and there are reckoned to be anywhere between ten to twenty assigned to any major city with a Russian presence. But they're not just armed guards with attitude; they're state security by nature and breeding, going back decades.'

'KGB?'

'Yes, but also known variously as the Ninth Directorate and the GUO – I forget what that means.'

Harry wasn't surprised. The Russians had any number of secretive agencies, most interconnected and linked through the KGB and its fore-runners, now through the FSB and its governing body. His work with the security services had not brought him into close contact with individual members, but it had often been said that every single member of Russia's vast security network was connected by one string or another, like a giant spider's web. Pull one and the tug was felt right down the line.

'I must have been out of the room when they lectured us on that one,' he said. A thought occurred to him. 'If their role is protection, what made Balenkova a target for an approach?'

'Christ, you're going to get me shot, you know that?' Ballatyne gave it a few seconds, then said, 'Balenkova first got lit up when she was working personal protection with a team of about twenty men and women, assigned to shadow a small but important group of military personnel. These were all high-ranking officers with responsibilities for communications, weapons and strategy, including nuclear installations. Balenkova and

166

her colleagues were the elite of the FSO, proficient in languages and top-level protection. They went everywhere with their charges, including overseas. The psych evaluators we employ to tell us clever stuff about our friends and enemies reckon they would hear and see things we can only dream about. Each one of them probably carries more secrets buried in their brains than any other members of the security apparatus.'

It explained a lot. Who wouldn't want to try draining one of these super-guardians of information, especially the intimate details of what the top military personnel had been chatting about over dinner and drinks when their barriers were down? Even gossip and scuttlebutt was useful if applied correctly. It was a spy's daydream.

'So Clare was assigned to get close to Balenkova and milk her.'

'Yes. Balenkova's name popped up again when she accompanied a couple of generals from the Northern Command to London for talks. She was seen as a possible target.'

'Why?'

Ballatyne hesitated. 'It's not what you think. Balenkova was friendly, outgoing and there to smooth the way for talks while protecting her charges. She speaks excellent English and knows how to mix it with people. But she was heard to make some remarks off the record that our psychological profilers judged to show a degree of disenchantment with the regime in Moscow. It was too good a chance to miss, so Jardine was told to make an approach, get friendly and build a rapport. It began in London and travelled across to Brussels as the Russians moved around. There was another meeting three months later, in Paris this time, when the Russians were talking to the French, and a final one in Frankfurt. That's when Jardine got her chain yanked. She'd gone too far and got noticed. She'd got involved.'

'Did her handlers know in advance?'

'What – that Balenkova was gay? Apparently not. They didn't know Jardine was, either. One of those things. Equal opportunities and inclusivity and all that, we're not supposed to ask anymore.'

'So where do I find this Balenkova?'

'You're really hot on this one, aren't you? What makes you think she even cares about Jardine, let alone that she'll help you? Word is, she got busted down the ranks as a security measure after Jardine got close.'

'I don't know. But Clare might try to contact her. If she does it might give us a lead on where she is.'

'Balenkova might simply turn her whereabouts over to the wet team, have you considered that?'

'In that case, we've nothing to lose by asking. You know she'll get nothing out of me.'

'Let's hope not. Trouble is, I don't know where she is. If I had a hotline into the FSO database, I'd tell you. But I don't.'

A dead end. Or was it? Ballatyne had a habit of storing information and acting on it later.

'Another bit of news,' Ballatyne continued, 'is that Tobinskiy died choking on his own vomit.'

'Seriously?'

'That's the public version. Truth is, there are small signs that question the facts; minute signs of bruising on the lips, which could have come from a hand placed over his mouth; and marks on his shoulders suggesting he might have been restrained, although the medical staff logged two occasions when he had to be held down for fear of hurting himself, so that's not proven. He was nauseous, anyway, and vomiting had been recorded, but I'm told it's easy to induce in a patient suffering gunshot wounds and running a fever. It'll keep the conspiracy theorists busy for years.'

Harry digested the information, the scene running in his mind. For a man in a weakened physical condition and suffering a bullet wound and pumped full of drugs, it would have been a simple job physically to hold him still and complete the task. Quite what it would have called for mentally was another thing altogether. Killing was hard enough; killing a man in his hospital bed required a detachment and cold-bloodedness that he hoped he never acquired.

'Do you have any leads so far?'

'We got a name of the man who might be running this job. His name's Sergei Gorelkin. He's one of the FSB's senior figures responsible for special operations overseas. He went off the radar in Moscow a few years ago, and it's thought he went into another department or got demoted. Then he popped up again recently as right as rain. He was seen boarding a flight to Frankfurt several days ago. Two other suspected

169

FSB operatives were identified passing through Paris Charles de Gaulle by a French intelligence officer on his way back to their embassy in Moscow. He recognised one of them from a penetration operation eight months previously by colleagues in the DGSE. All three were travelling under cover names. It's only a guess but I'd bet my pension they were converging on London.'

'Did your lady friend on the Russian desk tell you all this?'

'The Russian desk claims to know nothing about it. I think they're playing silly buggers and hoping to bag the prize. I got all this through back channels of my own.'

Harry grinned. 'You're more devious than I thought.'

'I have my moments. But if you think I'm devious, Gorelkin's got a reputation like a box of weasels. He's old-school KGB and as hard as nails. If he's over here, it means the Tobinskiy job was given top priority. Gorelkin has a chain of command like everybody else, but it's known that he takes his orders from the presidential office.'

'Would their embassy know he's here?'

'I doubt it. Whatever Gorelkin's doing, the last thing Moscow wants is a politically motivated assassination leading right back to their front door.'

Harry digested the information, then said, 'What about the other two men?' He and Rik must have come very close to running into them earlier, and he didn't like the idea of two FSB heavies walking up behind him with orders to kill.

'The French say they're specialists. You know what that means.'

'Killers.'

'Correct. I don't have names and only the vaguest descriptions, but I'll mail those over to you as soon as I have something firm. Why – are you getting nervous?'

Harry told him about the other people hunting Clare Jardine. 'They'll spread the net further and faster than we can. Can't we get the Met involved?'

'Sorry. No can do. They're under pressure elsewhere, and this is messy enough as it is. There's already chatter on the wires about a patient disappearing from the hospital. If we get the plods looking for her, it'll hit the news before tea time that there's a manhunt going on. God only knows what the media would make of that.'

'Clare's in danger. You don't think we owe her our full protection?' Harry tried to keep his tone level. Getting angry at Ballatyne was pointless and would merely make him dig in his heels. And deep down he knew the MI6 man was right.

'Of course we do. But you're it, I'm afraid. Five is too busy with other things, and it's pointless drumming up support with inexperienced officers who wouldn't know their arse from their knee joint. Jardine knows the score; she'll keep her head down. If she's still got the instincts we drummed into her, she'll call in and ask for help. Smaller is safer, as you know.'

Harry cut the call and found he'd been holding

his breath. He was facing an unpalatable truth: as far as the establishment was concerned, Clare Jardine was on her own.

Unless he and Rik could find her before the bogeymen did.

TWENTY-EIGHT

Clare had made a mistake. She had slipped out of the basement flat just before midday, no longer able to stand the enclosed space. All the while she could hear sounds of movement in the rest of the building, and the construction noise further along the street, she was growing more and more convinced that discovery was not far away. In the end she had had to leave, taking the crutch and the mobile in case she couldn't make it back again. A lesson learned from her former life: never leave behind anything incriminating, never take anything you don't need to carry.

She had hugged the buildings, moving vaguely away from the direction of Victoria, where she felt sure that SIS watchers for one would be conducting surveillance for her. Where the Russians would be was beyond her; they did not work to the same set of rules as other intelligence agencies, and that was the greatest danger. They could pop up anywhere.

She had walked for twenty minutes, moving slowly in a zigzag pattern, aware that if she continued for long enough, she would end up completing a circle. It was the way that those being pursued often ended up, walking in what they were certain was a straight line, but which eventually drew them back to their start point.

To get her bearings, she had stopped, trying to picture the layout of the streets in the area. The last thing she needed was to walk out into the open, where a woman with a crutch would stand out.

Then a man had turned a corner on the other side of the street, where three streets converged on a small paved triangle containing a cluster of trees and raised flower beds, and a small toilet block. The man was young and thin, with the gaunt, hard looks and fair hair of an east European. Possibly a waiter or kitchen worker – there were plenty of restaurants in the area employing both. He was dressed in jeans, trainers and a bomber jacket, all bearing the creases of long use and not recent purchases.

She moved into the doorway of an upscale carpet shop, with Persian rugs and no prices, and watched the man as he strolled along the pavement. He was acting casual, but scanning the pedestrians around him just a little too intently. Then he'd stopped a postman and showed him a piece of card, asking a question. The postman took the card and held it at an angle as if to catch the light. He shook his head and handed it back.

Clare felt her stomach go tight.

A photo. *The man had showed him a photo.*

She debated moving away from him. But that would mean walking along a quiet stretch of pavement with little traffic. She would be exposed, her crutch clearly visible. Maybe she should ditch it. It was acting like a beacon to those who knew she had it; and she was certain that her pursuers would by now have a CCTV still of her. It was what she would have done, and all those in the same business. Get a picture and show it around.

But getting rid of the crutch was a non-starter; she needed its comfort and support in a literal sense, as her muscles were still not able to do the job they had been trained to do. Instead, moving as quickly as she dared, she walked towards him, one eye on the man, the other on a small parade of stores eighty yards away, with a cluster of scaffolding rising to the roof tops.

She began to draw level with the man, watching from the corner of her eye as he stopped and put a phone to his ear. He had his back to her, looking at the ground and kicking idly at a small stone or something, distracted. Her nerves were screaming at her to run, to hobble, to do anything to move faster, to get away. *All he had to do was look up and turn his head, and he'd see her!*

Then she was past the first scaffold poles and beneath a familiar green awning, and ducking through the doorway into the welcome warmth and smells of coffee and amid the noise and comfort of people.

She ordered an Americano from the barista, spilling a few coins onto the counter one-handed, keeping her back to the door and window. Then she took her drink and slid into a corner seat, juggling the crutch awkwardly past two mothers

174

and their toddlers, expensively casual and bliss-
fully unaware as they discussed schools and
husbands, and how hectic their schedules were.

Noisy and shouty but great cover. Clare relaxed. Took out the mobile, opened the back and
slid the battery back into place, a cautious move
against the phone being triangulated and traced.

One could never be too careful.

The phone vibrated in her hand, and beeped
loudly, making her jump. An incoming message.

The two mothers scowled in disapproval as if
their me-time had been spoiled, and one of the
children watched Clare, waiting to see what she
would do.

She ignored them, aware that she was attracting attention but unable to avoid it.

*We can help you. Ring me. Pink Compact. So
not your colour.*

Harry Tate. It had to be. Or Rik bloody Ferris.
The reference to the compact was the decider;
the identifier to stop her running for the hills.
Clever.

She switched the phone off and stuffed it back
in her pocket. She needed time to think. To get
her mind in order. Peace and quiet hadn't helped
her, in that basement, so maybe this noisy en-
vironment, with the threat of discovery not far
away, would work instead, getting her brain cells
firing on all cylinders.

She took out the pink compact and turned it
over, the plastic smooth and comfortable to hold.
Amid all the craziness that had happened recently, this was the one normal thing she had in her
possession. She stood up and went to the wash-

room, leaving the crutch against the chair. She was shaking with nerves, and her stomach was sending shivers through her whole body. She's pushed herself too hard and was now paying the consequences. She washed her face and rinsed her mouth with water, then washed her hands. She needed a shower or a bath; she felt gritty and sweaty, and her clothes were beginning to smell. She'd managed to rinse her underclothes, but that was all. She dabbed on some of the powder from the compact, but gave up when it stuck to the moisture in her skin.

She returned to her table. The women and children were gathering themselves together, like a small tribe moving on to pastures new, scooping up their clutter. She sat and watched them leave by stages, edging towards the door, and sipped her coffee, going over her options.

She ran her fingers across the mobile in her pocket. She'd almost had the number for Alice earlier. It had hung there, taunting her, the digits swimming around like fish in a tank, one second in place, the next confused. Then gone.

The same had happened with another number. But that one was a definite no-no. She had ignored it, knowing it would come to nothing. But then the numbers had come back clearly, and one by one, fallen into line like balls in the National Lottery. And perversely, when what she really wanted was Alice's number, there they had stayed, tight and ordered in her mind's eye, waiting to be dialled.

Why couldn't the number she *wanted* do that, instead of this ... forbidden one? It had been so tempting to try the keys. Katya Balenkova. The familiar image of the slim face and short blonde hair hovered before her, causing an ache she thought she had long suppressed.

An echo of the ache that had led to her downfall.

But calling Katya would trigger alarm bells in more than one place, of the kind that would end in disaster for both of them. After she had been pulled off the assignment by her controller at Vauxhall Cross, she'd had no news of the FSO officer's fate and had heard nothing since. For all she knew, Katya might be dead.

She leaned forward to check the street, her view now clearer with the mothers and children gone. The young man had disappeared. She'd been lucky; just a few seconds more out in the open and he would have seen her.

She sat back with a sigh and watched in a detached way as a blue BMW drew up at the kerb and two men got out. They ignored the reserved parking sign for deliveries, and a workman in a yellow tabard and hard hat protesting about needing the space.

The men crossed the pavement and stepped inside. The first was tall and dark, military in bearing. A leader. The second was stockier, heavy across the shoulders. A follower. She labelled them instinctively, businessman and driver. She felt tiredness wash over her. This was taking more out of her than she'd thought possible. She needed to get back to the empty flat; to get her head down and sleep.

The two men ignored her and went to the

177

counter, ordering tea and coffee.

She must have dozed off momentarily, because suddenly they were sitting down, the tall one by her side, the other across from her.

Blocking her in.

The taller man shifted in his seat, bringing him slightly closer.

With him came the familiar smell of peppermint, giving her a jolt of recognition more acute and identifying than a face.

'Miss Jardine,' he said softly, looking into his mug of tea with distaste. He placed it to one side and added, 'You've embarrassed us, my colleague and me. Led us quite a dance. Is that how the saying goes?'

Her instinct was to ask him who he was, what the hell he was talking about, to dissemble and act the outraged lone woman accosted by two predatory men. But she knew that wouldn't work.

He was speaking Russian.

TWENTY-NINE

Clare stared at him. The shock of hearing him use her name lasted a brief moment before she managed to clamp down on any reaction. Of course he'd know it; he'd have got it from the hospital. The moment they'd found her gone, after dealing with Tobinskiy, they'd have gone into overdrive, deciding what, if any, were the implications of her disappearance, and what to do about it. How they had found out she spoke and understood Russian was incidental. They'd probably drawn that conclusion from her sudden departure. It would have been enough to have had them calling in expertise, checking records, chasing down CCTV records and trawling the streets.

Now they'd found her.

If she hadn't been so stunned, she'd have been impressed.

'What do you want?' She remained calm, studying both men, analysing what kind of opposition they presented. She wasn't going to outrun them or fight them off, not in her condition; they looked too fit, too determined. Professionals. FSB or their contractors at the very least, to have been sent here after Tobinskiy. That meant they wouldn't be easily stopped. But she had to find a way out somehow without involving anyone else.

She felt the mobile in her pocket. Eased it out to lie by her leg, where they couldn't see it. Pressed the re-dial key.

'We would like you to come with us,' the tall one answered. 'No fuss, no trouble.' He flicked a finger sideways to indicate the other customers. 'We don't want to ... alarm these good people, do we?'

For alarm, read hurt, she thought. *They were actually going to take her out of here.*

She didn't need to look around to know exactly who was in the café. Her training had kicked in and she already knew. There were two baristas behind the counter, with five customers in the place; two at the counter, three at tables. All women. All innocents. If these were the same two men from the hospital, they were unlikely to be here on legal papers and would not react well to confrontation, or to her refusal to go quietly.

It would be a bloodbath.

She could hear the phone ringing out. Just a tiny sound. Or it might have been her imagination. Surely they would hear it, too? They couldn't be that deaf.

Come on, Tate. For Christ's sake pick up!

But they appeared to be unaware. Or maybe they didn't care.

The ringing stopped. She couldn't hear a voice responding, but she imagined it. A beat or two, the cadence of an incoming call with no voice, followed by another query: *Hello?*

'What are you going to do, shoot them?' she said. She held her chin down, trying to project her voice down at the phone without the nearest customers hearing her. The last thing she needed was panic.

'If we have to, we can do that,' the shorter one replied. He leaned forward over the table, unwittingly putting his face nearer to the phone. 'We could shoot them all, before you could make a sound.' He grinned coldly, enjoying the moment.

She swallowed at his nearness. *All he had to do was look down and he'd see the phone by her leg, the screen clearly lit up.*

'You wouldn't dare.'

'Of course we would.' He picked up the powder compact where she'd placed it on the table and studied it, turning it over as if studying a particularly interesting relic. 'Perhaps I will take this as a souvenir of our visit. I have a girlfriend who likes this trash. What do you say?'

Clare tried to snatch it back, but he was too quick. He sat back and continued toying with the compact, then put it in his pocket, a sly smile on his face.

The tall one said, 'I hope you realise that it would be quite simple for us to just shoot you here and walk out. Do you really want us to harm them – just because of you? We are new here, the authorities don't have our faces on their data-bases and we will never come back. So who cares? Simple.'

'How did you find me?' In spite of the threats, Clare was puzzled by the speed with which they had tracked her down. From a standing start, they had moved with amazing speed, in a city where finding a single person should have many taken days.

In response, he dropped a couple of photos on the table. One was obviously a still from the hospital CCTV; she recognised the bland NHS décor even with the grainy finish. The other looked vaguely familiar, but she couldn't think why. It had a string of numbers printed across the bottom and could have come from anywhere. It had been taken face-on, a bland head and shoul-ders shot like a passport, only bigger. She tried desperately to recall where it could have been taken, but her mind was a blank.

She swallowed the rise of fear and despair that

rose in her throat. Something about this photo meant something; but she couldn't think why. And that helplessness made her more frightened than anything else. All she knew was, they had found her so quickly, that all her efforts had been laughable. But there was a core deep inside her that refused to give in. She breathed deeply, watching the tall Russian's face. He seemed unaware of how much the photo had affected her. Or maybe he assumed she was just acknowledging that she was caught.

'Where did these come from?' she asked.

'We have our sources.'

'Sources?' It was a vain hope that he might tell her something, but she had to try.

'You think we're amateurs, Miss Jardine? You think I'm going to tell you who got them for us?' He shook his head slowly, but looked very pleased with himself. 'Dream on, I think the saying goes in English.'

Clare hoped Harry Tate was listening and scrabbled for a way of conveying to him where they were. It might take too long to respond, but she couldn't think of another way of doing it.

'This is Starbucks in Pimlico Road, London,' she muttered, changing tack and putting on a tone of outrage, 'not Grozny. You do know the Iranians have a consulate building just along the street, don't you?' It was a lie, but she was counting on these two not knowing that. Active units like this would be focussed on finding their target, staying below the local radar, completing their assignment – and getting out fast. What they *would* know, however, was that Iran was nobody's friend at the moment and the likelihood was that its buildings would have watchers in place and armed police in close proximity, in case of protests and trouble.

Their eyes didn't waver a jot. They were too good for that. But she sensed something passing between them, like an electrical signal.

'You're lying.' The short one spoke. But he didn't sound certain.

'Please yourself. Why don't you try something, see how far you get before there are more cops with guns here than you can count? Try explaining that to your bosses in Troparevskiy Park.'

The tall one didn't even blink. But his colleague's mouth dropped open just a fraction. It was enough to tell her she'd made a mistake, and she cursed herself. Fuck. That had slipped out unbidden. What she had said told them that she was no ordinary person who'd just happened to be in a hospital ward next to one of their own dissident countryman; ordinary people don't know about the Troparevskiy site, the very secret training base south of Moscow for the FSB's Special Purpose Centre.

The tall man was studying her like a sample on a lab tray. He asked softly, 'Who are you, Miss Jardine? Or maybe I should ask, *what* are you? You speak almost fluent Russian and you know things most Russians don't know.' He seemed to notice her crutch for the first time, and leaned over and picked it up. He weighed it in his hand and gave a dismissive shrug, then took off the rubber ferule and studied the flattened end. And smiled.

'Nobody. I'm nobody.' But she knew it was a futile argument. She'd as good as told them in a few careless words.

Just then a blur of colour moved into view out in the street, catching her eye. The workman in the yellow tabard had stopped a police car and was pointing at the Russians' car. Behind it, a skip lorry was waiting to move into the kerb.

Sensing this was her only chance, Clare reached across and flipped over the tall man's tea, spilling it across the table at his colleague.

'*Suka!*' the shorter man yelled, and jumped up as the hot liquid poured into his lap.

It was enough of a gap. Clare stood up and forced her way past him, gritting her teeth against the pain, aware of the tall man reaching out for her, but missing.

THIRTY

Harry heard the words coming out of the phone and stared at Rik, who stopped pacing up and down at the sound of the familiar voice. He'd automatically switched it to loudspeaker mode the moment he'd answered. They could hardly believe what they'd heard.

'*This is Starbucks in Pimlico Road, London, not Grozny...*'

'She's in trouble,' said Harry. 'Where the hell is—?'

184

'It's right here!' Rik pointed at the street sign above their heads on the restaurant's wall. 'We're in Pimlico Road right now.' He spun on his heel and looked along the street, then grabbed a waiter coming out of The Grove. 'Where's the Starbucks?'

'Pardon?' The man looked affronted.

'The Starbucks in Pimlico Road. How far down?'

The man shrugged off Rik's hand. 'I don't know – maybe two hundred yards down that way.' He gestured with his chin. 'On the left, with all the scaffolding.'

But he'd already lost his audience as Harry and Rik took off along the street.

Harry saw the police car in the road while they were still a hundred yards away, and heard the sharp crack of gunshots. Two men appeared from inside a doorway, and raced across the pavement towards a car at the kerb. Men in workmen's tabards and hard hats stood around in shock, and a figure in uniform lay crumpled in the road alongside the police patrol car.

There was no sign of Clare.

Rik raced ahead, hauling out his gun and shouting at the workmen to get out of the way. They did so, diving back into the shelter of the buildings, a discarded hard hat bouncing and rolling into the gutter behind them. Someone screamed and a car horn sounded as the car the men had jumped into screeched away from the kerb, clipping another vehicle on the way and scattering broken yellow glass as it went.

Rik ran out into the centre of the street and

stopped, bringing his gun to bear on the departing car. He aimed, then stopped. It was already eighty yards away and accelerating. Too far for accuracy and a scattering of innocent pedestrians had already formed a random and unwitting human shield around it. One stray shot and he'd have a disaster on his conscience.

Harry slowed to a jog and scanned the people in the area. If Clare was around, she'd either been shot and was still here or she'd already disappeared.

Sirens sounded in the distance and people gathered around the fallen policeman, who was struggling to sit up. A woman in a Starbucks T-shirt stood on the pavement, her face drained of colour and her mouth open in shock.

Harry looked inside the café. It was empty, one of the small tables and a couple of chairs up-ended, mugs and plates lying broken on the floor.

'What happened?' he asked the employee. He had to repeat the question before she answered.

'I don't know,' she mumbled hurriedly, her accent Spanish or Italian. 'Is crazy. One second, two men are sitting with a woman. Next she is rushing out and one of the men is shouting.' She gestured at her front. 'His clothes is wet and he is shouting but I don't know his words. Foreign, I think, not English. Then the men walk outside after her and *paff, paff* – they start shooting and a policeman he is falling and...' She rubbed at her face as tears poured down her cheeks. 'Why would they do this?'

'Where did the woman go?' Harry asked. The

sirens were now very close and he guessed he had only seconds before armed response units arrived and the area was cordoned off.

She looked puzzled. 'What?'

'The woman – the one with the men. Where did she go?'

'I ... I didn't see.'

'Did she leave the building? Did they take her with them?'

'Yes. I ... I don't know – maybe. No, wait. She walk out first and disappear. The men are chasing her but she is already gone, I not see where.'

Harry whistled to catch Rik's attention, and thrust his hand in his jacket as a signal to put his gun away. If the first responders were armed, they would come out of their car zeroing in on anyone with a gun.

'She can't have gone far,' he said, when Rik joined him. 'But we can't get caught up in this. Let's go.' He walked away across the street. The area here opened out into a small paved triangle with trees and flowerbeds where three streets intersected, and he was heading for the widest area, the most difficult to close off. It was also where he figured Clare would have made for, planning on putting as much distance and confusing scenery between her and the men as she could. Staying on the same street and in direct line of sight of a man with a gun would have been a death sentence.

They crossed the paved area, past a line of bikes chained to a rack; a squat public convenience block with two women frozen to the spot outside the door; then more bikes and some seats. Everything was neat and ordered, tidy and upscale; a bit like a model toy-town, Harry thought. Take out the gunfire and it would have been ideal.

They stopped on the far side, checking the two other streets. Gawpers were converging in numbers to see what all the fuss was about, but nobody was walking away. No woman with a crutch.

'She can't have moved that quick,' said Rik. 'Not in her condition.'

Harry agreed. She must have gone under cover somewhere. It's what she would have been trained to do, to get off the radar and keep her head down until it was safe to move on. Having two gunmen on her tail would have been encouragement enough to make it quick.

He spun on his heel, and was staring up at a camera fixed to the top corner of a building when two squad cars pulled up and disgorged armed officers. They each immediately grabbed a likely looking witness and began to question them, isolating witnesses from new arrivals. Others began to seal off the area and direct traffic away.

Harry ignored them. Time was running out. If he and Rik got dragged inside the cordon, they would be too caught up answering questions about why they were carrying weapons to go looking for Clare. If she got pulled in, she'd be exposed and vulnerable. They had to get her away from here.

But first they had to find her. There were alleyways and a few side entrances to the shops that she could have ducked into, but checking those out would take too long and be noticed. He studied the onlookers, most of them with their backs turned, staring at the action going on outside the Starbucks, and the people helping the wounded policeman. One of the two women outside the public convenience block had joined the crowd, but the other was still where Harry had first seen her, shifting from foot to foot.

The policeman. He'd been shot by one of the Russians. And where he had fallen was in direct line with where Harry and Rik were standing. And in line with the convenience block.

'Come on.' Harry walked across to the woman who was staring impatiently at the locked toilet door.

'Problem?' he queried.

The woman looked at him, suspecting a flanking move to get inside first. 'She's been in there ages,' she muttered, nodding at the door. 'She might be disabled and all that, but really ... you know?' She gave a toss of her head and tutted at woman's inhumanity to woman.

'Disabled?'

'Yes. On a crutch. You know, those metal things. Not that she was moving slow. It was just after all that banging and shouting.' She jerked a thumb over her shoulder, evidently unconcerned by the fact that a shooting had happened only yards away from where she was standing.

Harry said, 'Excuse me – I think I know who she is.' He turned so that he was shielding the door from the police across the road and put his head down. 'Clare? It's Harry. I got your message. We need to leave. Now.'

'Hey – what are you doing?' The woman tapped him on the shoulder. 'What's going on?'

'We're looking for a young woman who walked out of a secure unit,' Rik told her. He tapped his head. 'She's ... confused, you know?' He waited until she nodded, then said, 'We're here to take her back, so she doesn't come to any harm.'

Then the door clicked open and Clare Jardine stepped outside.

THIRTY-ONE

Harry and Rik virtually lifted Clare off her feet and steered her away from the police activity. Surprisingly, she didn't put up any protest. In fact, both men kept looking at her; this was not the Clare Jardine they both knew. Gone was the spiky attitude, the energy and the 'leave me alone or suffer the consequences' aura she habitually wore around her like a force field. Instead she looked drained, her face greasy and pale and her shoulders slumped in a display of defeat.

Once they had a couple of street corners between them and the police, Harry slowed and gestured at a low stretch of wall outside an apartment block. Clare was breathing heavily and he was worried that she was going to collapse if they pushed her too far.

She slumped down on the wall and looked at

both men. 'Is this where I say thank you, you big brave boys, and go all gushy and grateful?'

'Christ, that's more like it,' Rik muttered. 'I thought they'd overdone the meds and made you into a human being.'

'Spin on it, Ferris,' she murmured, but there was a glint of something resembling humour in her eye. Then she added, 'OK, thanks.'

Harry sat beside her. 'Who were the shooters and what did they want?'

'Russians. One of their direct actions units, probably. They were the same two who came to the hospital and killed Tobinskiy. I suppose he was killed? I haven't heard any news.'

'Choked on his own vomit. That's the official line, anyway. But there are signs he was smothered. It won't be made public until they get full autopsy results and make up their minds how to play it. How do you know they were the same men?'

'One of them likes peppermints. They also threatened to shoot everyone in the café if I didn't behave. Like it was an everyday thing. And they weren't joking. Is that good enough for you?'

'How did they find you?'

'I don't know. I think they had spotters out looking for me. There was this young guy on the phone near the Starbucks. He pretended not to see me, but he wasn't a pro. He disappeared and minutes later, those two arrived and started with the threats.'

'What did they say?'

'They wanted me to go with them. They didn't

191

explain why, but I think if I'd put up a fight, they'd have slotted me on the spot. Then a cop car stopped outside because their car was blocking a reserved space for builders. That's when I decided to leg it.' She took a deep breath and shivered. 'That's when the shooting started. Was anyone hurt?'

'A cop,' said Rik. 'But he looked OK. The Russians got away.'

Clare nodded and looked at Harry. 'Have you still got friends in dark places?'

'You mean Six? Yes, why?'

'I got their registration.' She recited the number and make of car. 'It's probably been dumped already but someone might see who left it.'

Harry texted Ballatyne with the details. He didn't hold out much hope of it carrying a trace, but it was worth a try this early on in the day.

Ballatyne called him five minutes later. 'You've got Jardine there with you?' He sounded surprised. 'I suppose it would be asking too much for her to pop in for a chat.'

'Why don't you ask her.'

Harry passed the phone to Clare, who listened for a second, then said, 'Dream on, Ballatyne. I'll deal with Tate and Ferris, but that's it.' She passed the phone back and pulled her jacket around her.

'She's a little charmer, isn't she?' Ballatyne commented. 'Still, can't blame her, I suppose. Leave this with me and I'll put out a city-wide search.'

'You do that.' Harry thought about the street camera and its scope of coverage. 'You might have someone check out a camera across the junction from the café, above a kitchen shop. If it's working, it should give you a clear shot of everyone arriving and leaving the Starbucks where Clare was approached. They were the same two from the hospital.'

'What are you going to do?' Ballatyne clearly meant with Clare.

'For the moment, keep our heads down.'

'Where?'

'You don't need to know.'

'That sounds ominous.'

'Don't blame me. You're the ones with the leaky windows.'

Ballatyne gave a grudging murmur. 'Fair comment.' He paused, then said, 'I want you to come in for a meeting. We need to get some action decided and I need your input.'

Harry thought about arguing against it; he hadn't been near Vauxhall Cross or Thames House since leaving the Security Service, and didn't want to do so now. But it might give him some advantage if he knew what the official security agencies' line was. Sitting in on a meeting wouldn't be so bad.

But Ballatyne took his silence for assent and pre-empted him. 'There's a security office door opening onto Great Scotland Yard, next to the Civil Service Club. Ask the guard inside to direct you to room 101.'

Harry nearly laughed. 'You're kidding.'

'I wish I were. Life imitating art, I'm afraid. It's a genuine meeting room where embarrassing or annoying issues get shelved for good. You should feel quite at home there. One hour. Please don't be late.'

He hung up without saying goodbye.

'Where are you taking me?'

They were in Harry's car heading north. Clare was bundled in the back seat, hunched over and clutching her stomach. She looked deathly pale and Rik was keeping an eye on her from the front passenger seat. They had hit the area around Sloane Square barely five minutes from the scene of the shooting, leaving behind a growing atmosphere of activity and blue lights, with a police helicopter already coming in over the rooftops and hovering overhead.

'Hospital would be a good place to start,' said Harry, steering them up towards Knightsbridge. 'You need checking over.'

'Forget it. I've had enough of hospitals. Give me some painkillers and I'll be fine.'

'Your call.' Harry knew enough not to waste time arguing. 'We'll go to Rik's place. It's not far and you can rest up there until we decide what to do.'

'Why bother? Let me out anywhere – I told you, I'll be fine.' She sat up and peered through the window to get her bearings, eyeing the up-market stores and the expensive cars jostling for space at the kerb. 'Jesus, not here, though. Too many cops and security guards.'

'Too many cameras, too,' said Harry. 'It's how they got onto you in the first place.'

She scowled and leaned forward between the seats, working on the implications of that. 'I was wondering how it happened. I must be getting slow. But how could they do it without help?'

'That's what we'd like to know,' said Rik. 'They moved bloody quick, considering. Maybe they've been here before and know the ground.'

'They haven't.' She winced and grabbed for the seat as they squeezed through the lights and headed towards Hyde Park Corner. 'The tall one, the one in charge, he said they were new here and they'd never be back. He meant he could shoot me and walk away. It's how their direct action teams work; in and out and move on. God knows, they've got enough personnel to rotate them a hundred times over if they need to.'

'You seem to know a lot about them,' Rik commented.

'I had to, once; it was part of the job. The FSB were the enemy. Still are.'

Harry said, 'Did they give any clues about why they're here or who they report to?'

She shook her head. 'No. They were in the hospital to deal with Tobinskiy, then came after me. They must have realised I'd bugged out of King's because I'd heard too much. If I could speak Russian, I was a threat. So I had to be eliminated.' She gave a wry smile. 'They don't change, do they? They have a problem, they take it out.' She spoke matter-of-factly, as if discussing the disposal of trash.

'So why didn't they just shoot you inside? Better still, wait for you on the street and deal with you there?'

'Beats me. I think they were having fun, showing how clever they were.' She paused. 'The tall

195

one said I'd embarrassed them and led them a dance. I don't know what he meant by it, but I can guess.'

Harry didn't say anything for a few moments, focussing on the traffic. Then he said, 'So can I. Getting away from the hospital the way you did put them on the spot. They weren't supposed to leave any witnesses. They might have wanted to take you back alive to regain the lost ground with whoever's controlling them.'

'That makes me sound like a bloody trophy,' Clare muttered. But she didn't argue the point and lay down with a soft groan, her head on the seat.

'One thing's for sure,' said Rik bluntly. 'They weren't going to hang on to you for long.' There was no answer and he glanced at Harry. 'What are you going to be doing?' he asked softly.

'I've got a meeting to go to.' Harry didn't enlarge on it. It was better not to give Clare another reason to cut and run. In her condition she wouldn't last five minutes out there. 'Can you watch her? Don't let her go out.'

Rik nodded with a wry smile. 'Will do. She's still a grumpy cow, but I owe her that.'

THIRTY-TWO

While Harry drove them north towards Paddington, the two FSB men were on a similar course, but further east, eager to get clear of the inevitable police cordon being thrown up around Pimlico.

'Who is that bloody woman?' Votrukhin was finding it hard to contain his anger at losing Jardine so easily, and slammed a fist against the passenger door panel. The same questions he'd asked Jardine had been going through his mind in an endless rote, demanding answers. 'How the hell does she know about Troparevskiy?'

'The Internet,' Serkhov ventured. 'Every school kid with a PC can find out where we are these days. When we get back we should get the Sixth-Oh-Sixth Rocket Regiment to use some of their specials to shoot down the Google Earth satellites. They're nothing but trouble.'

Votrukhin ignored him. He was too busy trying not to think about their next meeting with Gorelkin. The colonel would be uncontrollable at this second failure, and would probably have them on the next plane back to Moscow in disgrace. The likelihood of them surviving as members of the Special Purpose Centre were about as high as an armed Chechen terrorist in the middle of Red

Square with a smoking bomb in his hand being invited in for vodka and *zakuski*.

Serkhov said nothing. It had been he who had opened fire, shooting the cop who had leapt out of his car to stop them, in spite of Votrukhin's orders. He focussed instead on driving and keeping his eyes open for police cars or road blocks. Neither of them was sure how the British authorities might react to the shooting, but it was likely to involve a concerted raid on cameras on the ground and in the air. They had already seen how easy it was to track an individual on foot across the city; following a car, even among a flow of similar vehicles, would not be a problem. The added advantage of number recognition programmes would pin them down very quickly.

'We have to get rid of this car,' Votrukhin said, regaining his calm. It would not help their case, losing it, but cars were disposable assets and this one, like others they could use, was untraceable. 'Did you check any places we can use?'

Serkhov nodded. As the driver, it was his responsibility to find a way of disposing of the car should they run into trouble, like now. 'There's a place near Shepherd's Bush. They can make a car disappear in an hour.' He made a chopping motion with his hand. 'Tiny pieces, then melted down. No traces, no fingerprints, nothing.'

'Good. Go there now.'

Ten minutes later they were cruising along Park Lane when Serkhov swore. Two police cars had appeared in the distance behind them, lights flashing to help them carve through the traffic.

More blue lights were flashing up ahead and there was already a build-up of cars and buses blocking the road around Marble Arch.

'What the hell?' Votrukhin twisted in his seat to watch the two following cars with a feeling of alarm. 'They can't have traced us yet. It's impossible.'

'So why are they sitting on our tails then, and blocking the road ahead? They must have the description of this car.'

Votrukhin thought about it for a couple of seconds before logic took over. He sat back and faced the front. 'Yes. But they're throwing up an outer cordon, that's all. They can't yet know who we are or where we are for sure. But if we get caught inside it, we're stuck.'

'What do we do? We can't dump this right here – they'd see us.'

'I know.' Votrukhin glanced quickly around, feeling a lot less calm than he sounded. They were just coming up level with the Grosvenor House building, where they had had their meeting with Gorelkin and the English traitor, Paulton. There were streets on that side, where they could lose themselves long enough to dispose of the car and walk away. But that was on the other side of Park Lane, with an expanse of grass, flowerbeds and trees in the central reservation behind a V-shaped metal barrier that looked too strong to burst through. On this side there were no streets, just the railed-off expanse of Hyde Park, which offered no escape whatsoever.

'There!' He pointed ahead to a ramp going into an underground car park. Any CCTV system would have the car instantly, but by the time the authorities got round to studying it, he and Serkhov would be long gone. They wouldn't dare risk coming back to the car, but that was too bad.

Serkhov responded calmly, signalling and cutting neatly into the inside lane. They were already dropping out of sight as the two police cars swished by.

'Keep your face averted from the cameras,' Votrukhin warned Serkhov. 'This isn't over yet.' He pointed at a corner space, jammed between a Jaguar and a 7-Series BMW. 'In here. Leave the keys in the ignition. With luck it will be gone within the hour.'

'What about Gorelkin? He'll go nuts if we dump it.'

'Gorelkin can go screw himself. We're the ones in danger here, not him. Now do it.'

Serkhov did as he was ordered and parked the car. Moments later they were walking away from the car, heads down and with their faces partially covered by their mobiles, two businessmen hurrying to a meeting.

But their departure wasn't entirely unseen. In the shadows, behind a primped-up van with fat tyres and tinted windows, two men stopped trying to open the doors and watched them go, drawn to the interior light of the BMW and the partially-open passenger door.

THIRTY-THREE

Richard Ballatyne was waiting to greet Harry on the second floor landing of a building in Great Scotland Yard. The security guard nodded and left them to it, and Ballatyne walked away trailing a crooked finger.

'Sorry about the rush,' he said quietly. 'But this was an opportunity to get several important heads together on record without going through a full-blown meeting with everyone and their brother from the Sec of State down. We've got two gofers on a watching brief from the wider cabinet office and one from COBRA; a sit-in for the Joint Intelligence Committee; Commander John Crampton from CO19 ... and Candida Deane of the Russian Desk.' The pause there was, Harry sensed, deliberate. A warning.

'Nobody from Five?' His old employers. He was surprised. Anything involving the activities of foreign agents in the country should have had MI5 representatives here in droves, jostling for the prize.

'No. For reasons I'll tell you about later, they've agreed to let us run with this. But they are still involved.'

'Great,' Harry murmured. 'And Deane? Should I be worried?'

Ballatyne threw a brief smile over his shoulder as he turned a corner in the corridor and walked towards a heavy oak door at the far end. Unlike the others, it bore no number or name plate. 'Not really – not inside this place, anyway. She'll be muzzled by the presence of the others, although she might still try to bite. And she's no friend of Clare Jardine's. You'd do well to remember that.'

'Any specific reason?' Clare had worked the Russian department. It wouldn't be too surprising if there was history involved.

'Deane was a protégée of Sir Anthony Bellingham.'

Christ. That was more than reason enough.

Ballatyne opened the door and ushered Harry through, stepping past a tall man with a flat-top haircut and broad shoulders standing just inside. Clearly a minder. The room was functional and spare, with a long table bordered by chairs and a sideboard holding a stack of notepads and, oddly, a Bible. The walls were panelled with oak and hung with pictures that had probably been there since the place was built. It smelled to Harry of paperwork, ink and dry, dusty talk, and possessed all the soul and atmosphere of a coal bunker. Just right, he thought, for disposing of embarrassing issues. It reminded him of another room not far from here, where his own career in MI5 had been consigned to a skip by a committee of faceless suits, before being posted on what had very nearly been a one-way trip to Georgia.

He nodded at the faces around the table as

Ballatyne made introductions, instantly forgetting the names of the civil servant attendees. He received a cordial enough smile from Commander Crampton, which told him that the Met's firearms unit officer didn't know who or what he was, and a cool look of assessment from Candida Deane, a blonde with a cool, businesslike stare behind large glasses, who undoubtedly did. Crampton looked like a rugby player who had played just a little too close to the ball.

Deane looked even tougher.

'This is a little off the cards,' Ballatyne began, once they were all settled, 'because the situation is a little unusual. You all know the basics, but just so that we're all up to speed, I'll outline it in extremely simple terms, to save time.'

'Just a moment.' Candida Deane was looking at Ballatyne but flicked an imperious finger towards Harry. 'Does Tate have clearance for this meeting? I don't recall his details being submitted for approval.'

Ballatyne appeared to have been expecting the interruption. He merely smiled and said, 'Mr Tate is a former MI5 officer and has my full confidence. He has completed various assignments for us both here and overseas, and worked with the UN in highly confidential circumstances. He is also carded which, as some of you might not know, means he has been security vetted to carry a firearm. That places him higher on the secure list than many people who habitually sit in this room. May I?'

Deane nodded grudgingly and made a pointed note on a pad in front of her. But not before shooting Harry a final glance of assessment.

'Earlier this afternoon,' Ballatyne continued, 'two gunmen shot and wounded an unarmed police officer on Pimlico Road, SW1. The officer was answering a call by a member of the public standing on the pavement. The two men had left their car in a reserved bay and entered a Starbucks café in search of a former MI6 operative named Clare Jardine. Miss Jardine left the café pursued by the men. They fired shots at her, which is when the officer was hit, but I understand she managed to escape unharmed.'

'Who were the gunmen?' one of the suits from the Cabinet Office queried, pencil poised to make a note. 'And why would they be after a former officer? Is this a revenge thing?'

'I was coming to that. They are thought to be Russian FSB operatives, most likely from their Special Purpose Centre, and responsible for the death of Roman Tobinskiy in King's College Hospital's Major Trauma Unit three nights ago. As you might know, Tobinskiy was a close friend and associate of Alexander Litvinenko, and shared his disenchantment with the Russian government. He had also made public those views, like Litvinenko. However, the reason for their attack on Miss Jardine was because she was a patient in the same corridor as Tobinskiy and witnessed the men's presence in the unit.'

'*Was* a patient?' Deane lifted an eyebrow as if this was news. All heads swivelled her way, then back.

Ballatyne didn't miss a beat. 'Yes. She speaks Russian and had heard Tobinskiy rambling while sedated. It told her enough to know that he considered himself at severe risk – a fact already reinforced by his own shooting in Brighton several days before, which was why he was in the unit in the first place ... as you know.' He waited a brief second for the meaning to sink home to the others, then continued, 'The attacker then was thought to be East European, most likely also FSB or at least a contractor. The moment Jardine heard the two men speaking, she guessed what they were going to do and that they wouldn't want any witnesses. There was nothing she could do to stop them, so she left the hospital before they could return.'

'What did they do to Tobinskiy?' asked a woman from the Joint Intelligence Committee. 'I mean, I suppose they weren't there for his health, were they?'

'No. They weren't. They held him down in his bed and suffocated him.'

THIRTY-FOUR

There was a stunned silence as they digested the blunt words. The woman from the JIC looked almost embarrassed, as if she had attended the event in person and wished she hadn't.

Harry glanced around the assembled faces. Only Deane and Crampton seemed less than shocked, and he guessed they had already heard the grisly details.

'The purpose of this meeting,' Ballatyne continued, 'is to bring everybody up to speed so that we're aware of the ramifications. Tobinskiy was probably killed on orders from Moscow – like Litvinenko. Exactly who stands to gain by it is anybody's guess. It could be old scores being settled, or a prelude to something else involving friends of the government jostling for position.'

'That wouldn't be unusual,' the woman from the JIC murmured. 'They're like a nest of hornets, anyway.'

'Yes. Either way, we have to handle this with care. More accusations against the Russians of wrongdoings without proof will not help international relations. I'm aware of the need for continued trade talks and negotiations regarding events in the Middle East, and that we must try to avoid fouling the atmosphere. But that is more long-term. What I want to highlight is that our problem is much more short-term and immediate.'

'Really?' Deane looked up. 'Involving the Jardine woman? Where is she, by the way? Do we know?'

'Just a second.' The representative of COBRA – the Cabinet Office Briefing Room committee, which dealt with regional and national emergencies – spoke up. 'I'm unclear as to why this Jardine woman was in this hospital in the first place. Isn't it a specialised unit? And am I correct in my understanding that she was let go from MI6 following serious disciplinary measures – and accused of a violent attack against another officer?' He spoiled his supposedly independent stance by glancing at Candida Deane with a faint smirk.

Ballatyne's face was blank, but Harry knew him well enough to guess that the word 'bitch', aimed at Deane, might have floated across his mind. The COBRA representative had clearly been got at.

'She was there,' Ballatyne said quietly, 'because she had been shot and nearly killed while assisting Mr Tate here, in mopping up a gang involved in trading secrets to foreign powers. She saved his life and that of a colleague, and undoubtedly saved many others by bringing down this gang, known as the Protectory. I don't think it was asking too much for her to be given the best possible treatment in return. Do you?'

The man said nothing, but flushed under the gaze of the others.

'What about her now,' said Deane, filling the gap quickly. 'Where is she?'

'She's safe. She's still recovering from her wounds and this hasn't helped.'

'But you can tell us where she is, surely. Unless you think this room is bugged?'

A chuckle went around the table, but Ballatyne stopped it in its tracks.

'That's on a need-to-know basis.' The words were flat and left no room for discussion.

'So what now?' Commander Crampton, the CO9 officer, queried.

'For now, we keep looking for the two gunmen. I'm grateful for your unit's cooperation, commander, and we'll conduct an exchange briefing later. What we do if we catch them is not for me to decide, however.'

The meeting broke up shortly afterwards, leaving Deane at the table. The minder remained by the door, giving Harry a clear indication of who he worked for.

'I object strenuously to having an outside contractor involved in this,' she said, once the door had closed behind the last of the suits. 'I take it Tate is a contractor?'

'Your objection is noted,' Ballatyne replied, shuffling some papers into a folder and standing up, pointedly refusing to answer her question. He waited while she digested that, then got to her feet and moved to the door.

'I'll be making a full report of this, Richard,' she warned as a parting shot. She threw a last look at Harry. 'This isn't over, believe me.'

Once Deane had gone, scooping up her minder on the way, Ballatyne sat down again and looked across at Harry. 'You're very quiet.'

'I'm still trying to figure out why you brought me here. I obviously couldn't contribute, being an outsider.'

Ballatyne waved a hand. 'I wouldn't feel too bruised about what Deane said. She was just sounding off. Anyway, she uses contractors all the time; the bloody asset files attached to the Russian desk are bursting with former military and security spooks. It's cheaper and reduces costs. You'd be amazed how much extra National Insurance payments can add to the budget every year.'

Harry wasn't convinced. He'd been ushered

here for a reason, like a prize dog at Crufts. 'I was on show, wasn't I?'

'Not at all. Why would I do that?' Ballatyne looked innocent.

'I haven't figured that out yet. To make a point, perhaps.'

Then he had it.

'What?' Ballatyne caught something in his face, thoughts betrayed.

Harry thought about formulating his next words with care, but decided it was too late for that. The shit was already sliding off the shovel. If professional sensibilities got bruised along the way, it was too bad. Anyway, he suspected Ballatyne already knew.

'That was the point you were making: they were too organised and you wanted to make it obvious you knew.'

'Who – the Russians?'

'Yes. They had a plan to deal with Tobinskiy, which was one thing. But then they realised Clare had disappeared from the hospital. That shouldn't have bothered them; by now they should have been long gone, back to Moscow or Minsk or wherever.'

'So?' Ballatyne's expression was bland, waiting.

'They didn't; they stuck around. Worse, they went after her, using people on the street as a collective search team. They probably used CCTV footage, too, the same as we did.'

'That's quite a suggestion. Are you saying they hacked into the systems?'

'Why not? If they were desperate enough to go

back to the hospital and take the CCTV, the hard drive *and* shoot a security guard in the process, breaking the Computer Misuse Act wouldn't trouble them one bit, would it?'

'True. But it's standard procedure, even for the FSB. They worked the evidence, the same as any cop would do.'

'But this isn't their back yard, is it? They came in to do one job. It's the way they work: fly in a team, do what they have to and fly out again. No local contact, no mess, and most of all, no records. But this lot are different. They're not residents, yet they knew how to work the terrain, knew the most likely area Clare might head for to hide in a crowd: Victoria. Why not Piccadilly or Trafalgar Square or a dozen other places?'

Ballatyne shrugged. 'I think you're reading more into this than is wise.' But his eyes were glittering as if he were enjoying the idea being unravelled.

'They weren't messing around, either,' Harry continued. 'They came ready to shoot. They were desperate.'

A lengthy silence from Ballatyne, then: 'Meaning?'

'I'm saying they had help. That's what you were punting in the air ... to see who reacted.'

'They probably did have help. There are plenty of long-term embassy people who could have lobbed ideas and local knowledge at them.'

Harry shook his head. 'That wouldn't happen. You said they came in on false papers.'

'Yes.'

'That means they wouldn't be able to go

210

anywhere near the embassy. In fact they'd be under strict instructions to stay well away. And a job like this, especially after the Litvinenko scandal, they'd be like untouchables.'

'Call me slow,' Ballatyne muttered, 'but there's something you're not saying. What is it?'

'I don't know.' Harry shrugged. He had no proof for what he was thinking, merely a gut feel about the way things had worked out. But hiding it wouldn't solve the problem. 'How many people knew Clare was in that hospital unit? I mean, really – how many?'

'A few. A handful, no more. There was no need to spread the news, especially with her background. Why?'

'A handful. But how many of that handful knew she was someone the Russian hit team wouldn't – no, couldn't – ignore ... someone who had to be traced and silenced?'

The silence was longer this time. Ballatyne shifted in his seat as he digested what he was hearing. Harry didn't think the MI6 man was being deliberately dumb; he was far too astute for that. But he might have been struggling to accept the fact that the Russians had somebody supplying them with information.

'You're suggesting the Russians had inside help ... where? The hospital? If so, they wouldn't have needed to bust inside and steal the hard drive. And for the street camera footage: the Met? City of London Police? The London boroughs? The list is a long one.'

'The Met control rooms would be the quickest.'

Ballatyne gave a dry smile. 'Did your mate Ferris tell you that? He'll get you into trouble, that boy.'

'It makes sense. How else could they have tracked her so quickly? They must have used the same key cameras as your people. Find a start point – outside the hospital in this case – to identify her on screen, then leapfrog camera displays to build up her direction of travel. Lose her on one and you simply go back to the last one to see where she might have changed direction. There are operators who do it all day, every day. They play the cameras like a video game. I know because I've used them.'

'You make it sound easy.'

'It is if you've got a target with a distinctive walk and using a crutch. Clare might as well have been carrying a placard with her name on it.' Harry stood up. He'd done all he could. If Ballatyne chose to ignore him, there was nothing else he could do. 'You know I'm right. They've had orders to find her and silence her because they know what will happen if she talks. Why else go to all that bother and shoot up Pimlico for a nobody?'

'As you say, they were desperate.'

Ballatyne was playing dumb again, happy to let him do the running. But without more con-crete proof, it was obvious he wouldn't act on mere speculation.

Harry left him there and walked out. He need-ed to get proof that there was a bad apple in the woodpile.

He needed to speak to Clare again.

THIRTY-FIVE

'What's this – a level one interrogation?' Clare looked sour and angry, but she didn't look as if she had the strength to put up a real fight. Harry had suggested they sit down and go through everything the Russians had said to her in the café, in case there was something they could use to pin them down.

'You know what it is,' he said patiently. Rik watched them from across the room, saying nothing. 'You've done this before. Look on it as a debrief.'

She sighed but said nothing, so he continued. 'If we don't stop them, they'll keep going until they find you. You're a witness; you saw and heard them in the hospital just before Tobinskiy died, and now you've seen and met them face to face. You know them. That makes you a liability. You know how they treat liabilities.' He let that sink in before saying, 'Try and remember everything they said, no matter how insignificant, from the time they walked in and sat down.'

Slowly, fighting against tiredness, she did as he asked, recounting everything that had happened, from the moment she spotted the young man on the mobile phone across the street, to the second the car stopped outside and the men appeared. It came haltingly and with several backtracks to scoop up details, most of it of no great importance. But Harry kept pushing her to go over things again, in the hope that her professional brain was still active and would click on and begin to rifle through the images and words he needed.

After the first run-through, which lasted thirty minutes, he got Rik to arrange some food. This wasn't going to be a quick job, and they needed to keep up their energy levels, especially for Clare. But once they had eaten, he got her right back on track.

Her initial tiredness now gone, Clare didn't react well. 'Look, Tate, what are you hoping for?' she burst out. 'That they gave me their names and unit numbers? Their email back in Moscow so we can exchange greetings? It doesn't work like that. They were a black ops team. I've seen their type before and know the way they work. They threatened to shoot me; they didn't tell me how they'd found me, only showed me the photos they'd used. That was the tall one – he was the one in charge.'

'Photos. From CCTV cameras? They'd have got those from the hospital hard drive.'

'Yes. I suppose so.' Then her face froze and she sat up. Thoughts of the photo had triggered other thoughts ... and one specific memory.

'What?'

'Christ, I've been stupid,' she whispered. Her face flushed and she turned away. 'He showed me a photo, but it wasn't from any CCTV. And I've just remembered where I've seen it before –

or one like it.'

'Go on.'

'It was a black and white, full facial, blown up to postcard size. It had a number series across the bottom.' She looked up at Harry. 'It was my file photo from Six. I recognised the style.'

Harry sat back. This was worse than he'd thought. How the hell could a team from Moscow get a personnel photo from inside MI6? There was only one way.

'I asked him where the photos had come from,' Clare continued. 'But he just looked smug and said he wasn't going to tell me.'

'What did he say – the exact words?'

She frowned, struggling to recall. Then it came to her. 'He said something like, "You think I'm going to tell you who got them for us?" Like it was his own big secret and he was enjoying himself. Then he told me to dream on.'

'Was this in English or Russian?'

'Russian.'

Harry looked across at Rik, who shook his head in wonderment. They were both analysing the words. 'You think I'm going to tell you who got them for us.' The meaning was clear: the Russians didn't have a direct insider after all. But they had the next best thing: somebody with access to MI6 who could get them information through other means. Quite what level of access that was remained to be seen.

Harry's phone rang. It was Ballatyne.

'We caught a lucky break. The BMW from outside the café in Pimlico was spotted heading along the Edgware Road in north London less than an hour after the shooting.'

'So you got them?'

'We got the driver and his mate ... but they weren't Russian hit men. Just two local neds who happened to be scoping the underground car park in Park Lane for easy pickings. They saw two men in suits park the car and walk away, leaving the keys in the ignition and the doors open.'

'They wanted it gone.'

'Absolutely. And the thieves obliged. They didn't get far, though. An armed unit recognised the car's description and they were in the bag.'

'Did they give a description of the Russians?'

'Yes. One tall and slim, one short and chunky – like a wrestler, they said.'

It was them, Harry was certain. But why dump the car under Park Lane? If they had wanted to make it disappear for good, they could have dropped it anywhere south of the river and made their way back north by tube. The chances of it being gone for certain before they had reached the next corner would have been dramatically higher there than near Hyde Park. The Park Lane area was awash with cameras, and only chance had brought two witless thieves along at the right time. And now the police had the car and would be scouring it for forensic details. It made the chances of an arrest considerably higher, although he wasn't ready to lay bets on it just yet.

'They must have a bolt-hole nearby,' he concluded aloud. 'They probably panicked and left it on impulse. Are there any addresses on the list of Russian properties in that area?'

'We're combing through it right now and doing visual checks as we go, to see if we can spot anyone. We're having to be careful; there's a chance we could frighten them off if we go in heavy handed.'

'They won't go far.'

'What makes you think that?'

'They'll want Clare even more now. She's seen their faces, she heard their voices ... and now they know who she is – or was. And she knows who they are.'

'What do you mean?'

'She says they're probably black ops personnel.'

'*Chyornyiy*,' said Clare. 'Tell him. He'll know what it means.'

'She said they're *chyornyiy*.'

A silence. 'How does she know that?' But, Harry noticed, Ballatyne didn't argue.

He related what Clare had told them. When he got to their speculation about someone with access to MI6, Ballatyne began muttering darkly in the background.

'Leave it with me,' the MI6 man said finally. 'I'll get back to you.'

Less than a mile away, in a rented office they would never use again, Gorelkin was also swearing, but for different reasons.

'So what is she – SIS? Security Services? No. You're mistaken. How can that be possible?' He slammed a hand on the desk in front of him, making the two men with him jump. Votrukhin and Serkhov had witnessed one of Gorelkin's

217

occasional bursts of temper, and neither wished to come under its spell again. But right now they had nothing to offer in their defence.

'We don't know for sure,' Votrukhin ventured a slight correction. 'But how else could she know about Troparevskiy?' He ignored Serkhov's raised hand. 'It's probably no longer a big secret, I know, but she spoke as one who knew what she was talking about.' He snapped his thumb and forefinger. 'It came out like that.'

Gorelkin nodded and stared around blindly at the functional office walls, trying to find some solace in the situation. It didn't work. He knew what the lieutenant meant, and it wasn't good news. Those in the business would know about Troparevskiy. They wouldn't have to think about it – it would come automatically. But would they give themselves away quite so easily? Maybe, if they'd been shot in the gut like the woman. He was about to speak again when the door opened and Paulton was ushered in.

'Mr Paulton,' Gorelkin murmured, indicating a chair on the other side of the table. It sat squarely between Serkhov and Votrukhin, and he'd planned it that way. He still hadn't worked out whether Paulton was playing them or not. If he was, he would live to regret it. 'Now then,' he said quietly, and leaned forward, not allowing time for the Englishman to settle, 'would you care to tell us precisely what you know about Clare Jardine?'

Paulton looked relaxed, but something moved in his face. Gorelkin didn't miss it.

'I'm not sure what you mean,' Paulton replied

cautiously. 'I had only the information I was given—' He stopped speaking when Serkhov reached out a hand and grasped his shoulder. He winced as pressure was applied, and went pale.

'Let us start again,' Gorelkin murmured. 'My colleagues have already wasted enough time chasing shadows. Now we hear that this woman you said came from a care home and was running with Ukrainian gangsters is actually a British Intelligence operative. Would that explain why she also speaks Russian, do you think?'

Paulton tried to shrug off Serkhov's hand without result until Gorelkin gave the signal to let him go.

'I stand by what I was told,' the Englishman insisted. 'There was obviously an attempt to cover up her real identity while she was undergoing treatment. It's a public facility and it would be normal for members of MI6 or MI5 to be given cover names.' He smiled weakly. 'The press keep a constant eye out for special forces personnel passing through the hospital; the security or intelligence services would rate even higher in news value.'

Gorelkin thought it through. It sounded reasonable enough. He was aware of how voracious the British media was for exclusives, no matter how far that intruded into national security matters. In Russia there was no such laxity permitted. Any journalist who poked too far into the establishment found himself on a short journey to a maximum security cell until they forgot what they had been searching for.

But he still didn't trust Paulton further than he could spit. 'Very well. I want you to find out *now* about this woman. Everything you can tell us.'

'Of course.' Paulton stood up, straightening his jacket where Serkhov's hand had scrunched up the material. He looked flushed now, as if realising just how close he had come to disaster. 'I'll get onto it immediately.'

'How soon?' Gorelkin asked.

'Give me half an hour.'

'Make it twenty minutes. Or I make a phone call.' The threat was uttered without drama. But he meant it.

Paulton nodded, and Gorelkin and his men watched him go. And waited.

Paulton returned eighteen minutes later. He sat down and folded his hands together, every inch the repentant, even embarrassed, man.

'You were correct,' he announced. 'Clare Jardine is a former MI6 operative.'

'Former?' Gorelkin picked up on the word.

'Yes. She was fired by them for gross misconduct but continued to work in the security field. She was wounded while working with a former MI5 man named Tate, which is why she was being treated in King's College.' He stared around at the three of them. 'But she has no credit whatsoever with SIS or MI5, and is now off the grid with Tate. She's what some gamers call RTK.'

'What does that mean?' asked Serkhov.

'It means,' Gorelkin murmured, 'Ready To Kill. You can go and get her.' He was looking at

Paulton while he spoke. 'Isn't that right?'

Paulton nodded. 'Quite correct.' He slid a piece of paper across the desk. It held three names and addresses.

'What's this?'

'The first is Jardine's last known address, although I doubt she'll have gone back there. The second is Tate's, in Islington. The third is another former MI5 man named Ferris. He's an IT drone who works closely with Tate.'

Gorelkin flicked the piece of paper towards Votrukhin. 'Excellent,' the FSB chief said quietly. 'Now we are getting somewhere.' He glanced at his two men. 'Go. See to it.'

They stood up. Votrukhin looked worried.

'What are your orders?' he asked.

'Take them out, of course.' Gorelkin was looking once more at Paulton. 'Take them all out. Then we can all go home.'

THIRTY-SIX

'I think I know where the Jardine woman is.' Candida Deane shuddered as if the telling was being forced out of her, and watched the leaves above their heads shifting in the early morning breeze across St James's Park. It was just after seven and they were alone save for a brace of joggers shuffling round the lake and the distant hum of early rush-hour traffic in the background.

'Really? Is that why you called this meeting?' George Paulton sniffed at the air, one eye on the perimeter roads of Horse Guards and Birdcage Walk. Not that he could do much about it if Deane had summoned a snatch squad to take him in. He was too old for running and wasn't about to fling himself in the duck-shit filled water in a desperate attempt to kill himself rather than face the ignominy of prison. But he didn't think she had finished with him – at least, not yet. She had too much invested in using him for her own ends, as no doubt calling this meeting would prove.

'Isn't that enough to start with?'

'So why don't you pick her up? I thought you wanted the kudos.'

'No,' she corrected him patiently. 'As I understood it, you saw it as part of a package to sell me in exchange for my help to rehabilitate you.' She eyed him from behind her large glasses, her cool stare unblinking and steady. It reminded him that this woman was ambitious, experienced and nobody's fool. The thought made him uncomfortable.

'So it's a benefit trade-off, is it?'

'If you want to call it that.'

'But what could I do with her? Jardine has no value to me. She's just a washed-up MI6 killer with a dubious history.'

Her face showed interest. 'That's something I've been meaning to ask. Bellingham sent her to Red Station, didn't he? Some misdeed or other.'

'To join other miscreants, yes.' Paulton knew what was coming; he'd been waiting for it. It showed he was back in the bargaining business on the upper side.

'Why? What did she do that was so bad? It must have been serious, for him to see it as an alternative to dismissal ... or prison.'

'You mean you don't know?'

'No.' Her face clamped shut with a spark of irritation. 'Those files are sealed and I can't gain access at my level.'

'That's a shame.' He cleared his throat. 'Let's place that one on the table as well, shall we? A little *amuse bouche* – a taster for the main event. You get me what I want, and I'll tell you everything I know about Clare Jardine's plunge from grace.' He smiled, pleased at the imagery.

'Will it be worth hearing?'

'Oh, I think so. Believe me, once you hear, you'll want her far more than I ever could.'

Deane made a sharp noise. 'Come off it, Paulton. You and I both know I'm not the only one. What about your friends.' She lowered her voice as a couple of student types in baggy shorts and beanie hats sloped by. *'They* want her and they're expecting you to deliver. Tell me I'm wrong, *droog.'*

Paulton felt a cold shiver down his back. He didn't need to ask who she meant by 'they'.

She had used the Russian word for friend.

He revised his opinion of her. Bellingham had been more astute at spotting her potential than he'd given him credit for. This woman really was dangerous.

'Sorry. You've lost me.'

'Bollocks. You know who I mean. Must be

nice in Kensington Palace Gardens at this time of year.'

The location of the Russian Embassy in west London.

It was like a door slamming in his face. If she genuinely suspected him of working for the Russians, there was no way that she would ever sanction his return to the UK. The best he would get was a fast ticket to a maximum security cell; the worst was a bullet behind the ear.

Unless.

'They're not my friends, I promise you,' he said calmly. 'In fact, they'd see me dead in a moment if they saw any immediate benefit to it.' He paused as an elderly man shuffled slowly past, wheezing heavily. Dressed bizarrely in tight jogging bottoms, huge trainers and a long vest, he wore a set of huge, battered headphones and a Manchester United scarf, and looked close to expiring.

'Christ,' Paulton muttered, watching him, 'the things you see when you haven't got a gun.' He waited for the ancient to move away before changing the conversation. 'What would you give to see Jardine go down, Candida? She killed your boss, didn't she? Your mentor, Sir Anthony Bellingham.'

Deane's eyes flickered, betraying her feelings, and she said, 'I could pick her up today if I wanted to. Right now, in fact. What can you offer?'

'Actually, that's not quite true, is it? You have nothing to hold her on.' He allowed another jogger to go by, then added, 'Given a public hearing, Jardine would make sure Bellingham's past misdeeds with Red Station came out. Mine, too, I grant you, but that's a risk I'm prepared to take.'

'How noble of you.'

'But your present masters wouldn't allow it. Too much stink attached. It's one dirty little secret they would rather forget about. On the other hand, the longer she's out there, the more she gets under your skin.' He saw that strike home, and felt calm again. Deane wanted Jardine, all right; like a drunk wants another drink. But prison wasn't enough. She wanted her dead. And if he read her correctly, she was expecting him to arrange it. 'Very well. I'll see what I can do. But there's got to be a quid pro quo.'

'I haven't forgotten.'

'Good. So where is she?'

'A man named Tate has her hidden away. He's former MI5.'

'I know who Tate is. I should do – he used to work for me.' He took a deep breath. Somehow he'd known it might come down to this. But how had Deane found out? 'You know this for a fact?'

'I was introduced to him yesterday. Ballatyne was parading him at a meeting like a pet ridgeback.'

'Ballatyne? Do I know him?' He'd been out of the loop too long. People had moved on or moved up, the civil service version of musical chairs. The game had changed.

'He worked with a man named Marshall in Operations. Marshall died and Ballatyne moved

225

into his chair.' Her tone of voice betrayed her innermost thoughts on that one. 'Ballatyne's clever, though. And committed. I'm having to watch my back with him.'

'It comes with the trade.' His voice was bored. 'You were talking about Tate.'

'Apparently he helped Jardine escape from the two gunmen who shot the hell out of Pimlico and wounded a policeman.' She leaned forward. 'Find Tate and you'll find Jardine.'

'And when I do?'

'Don't be coy, George. You know what I mean. I know you've arranged things like it before.' The use of his first name gave no hint of intimacy; the subject under discussion was too chilling for that. 'Whatever you do to her, it had better be permanent. Remember, I want all of them: Jardine, the Russian gunmen and their boss ... *and* the name of the insider.'

'Insider? I don't follow.'

'Oh, I think you do. You see, I've just been informed that somebody has been ferreting through our files, plucking out details. Now, I have no proof, of course, but I'm willing to bet your testicles that he or she is working for you.'

Paulton said nothing. It was bound to happen sooner or later. Maine wasn't a field man, and not clever enough to have avoided leaving any traces of his searches. It was a pity, but he was going to have to ruin Maine's collecting habit for good. He'd have to let him fall, a casualty of battle. Just as long as he did it without dropping himself in a cold, lonely cell.

'We haven't found out who the ferret is yet,'

Deane continued. 'But we will. You could save me some time, though. Give me everything you know and we'll talk rehabilitation. But don't take too long. We're getting close.'

She produced a small square of white card. It held a line of neat handwriting. 'Tate's address. I ran a check on him, just in case you'd forgotten how.'

He took the card, although he didn't need it. Let her think she was one up on him.

As she turned and walked away, he was left wishing he'd got a sniper stationed on a nearby rooftop. If he had, he'd have given the signal to pull the trigger and put the bitch out of his misery.

As she disappeared beneath the trees, he took out his mobile and dialled a mobile number. This couldn't wait any longer. His future was resting on a knife-edge. It was time to play a massive hunch, to see if he was right. He didn't know Jardine from a hole in the ground; but he had an intuitive feel for the way somebody in her position might think. And right now she was probably looking for any friends she could find. Tate and Ferris were colleagues of circumstance, he was certain. But that wasn't enough for someone under the kind of massive stress Jardine would be under. She would want someone much closer.

If he played this right, he would get the information he needed and get rid of a monumental risk at the same time. Two birds, one carefully lobbed stone.

'Yes?' It was Keith Maine.

'I need to see you. Urgently,' Paulton said, and

told him where, and what else he wanted. The last thing he wanted from this man.

'Jesus – I can't do that!' The analyst's voice was pitched low. He was probably in his office somewhere, on early shift, and terrified of anyone hearing.

'You can and will.' Paulton didn't give him a chance to panic and cut the call. 'Ten thousand if you come up with what I want. It's a known name; it will be on the current WAR list.' Watch and Report, the rolling surveillance log with open access to Five and Six, to avoid agency clashes on suspects and persons of interest. He knew the way both agencies worked, knew that there was every chance that the information he wanted would be there. If his hunch was correct, it might give him a clue to Jardine's intentions. And wherever she went, so would Tate and Ferris.

Maine didn't argue. Instead his voice became slightly louder, more open. 'Very well. But I want to see it before I buy. There are so many fakes about – and I insist on it being in top condition.' Paulton knew the signs: a work colleague was close by and he was pretending to be taking a call from a collector. But there was a sub-text. What he was really saying was that he didn't trust Paulton to send the money, and wanted cash in hand.

Paulton named a spot on a public street not far from Thames House, south of the river. Close enough to his work for Maine to feel safe, far enough away to retain a measure of secrecy about who he was meeting.

The promise of money helped, as he knew it would.

Next he dialled another number. Votrukhin answered with a terse hello.

'The Jardine girl is with Tate,' Paulton advised him. 'Have you moved on them yet?'

'No. Why?'

'You should do so, soonest. Where Tate goes, Ferris is close by.' He paused, trying to determine whether any of this could rebound on him. If the Russians collared Jardine and the two men, all to the good. He would get the credit from Deane for Jardine's demise, and he wouldn't need the information Maine was getting for him. But he preferred to have insurance in place, just in case. To hell with it. 'They will be armed and ready, of course.'

Votrukhin grunted. 'So? You think we will not?'

THIRTY-SEVEN

There was a grey light and a threat of rain outside the windows of Rik's Paddington flat. Harry got up from the sofa where he'd been sleeping and checked his gun, which had been close by on the floor. He stretched, then showered while Rik went out for coffee and to check the surrounding streets for unusual activity.

Clare had slept in the spare room. Her batteries

229

had eventually run down last night, exhausted by her efforts and the stress she'd suffered over the past few days. He'd let her sleep; they all needed rest and he was convinced nothing else could be accomplished before morning.

But he and Rik had slept in stages, taking turns to watch the streets and check the building regularly for sounds of movement.

'We need to talk about something,' he said, when they were all having breakfast. His remark was directed at Clare.

'Christ, give it a break,' Clare muttered, tearing off a piece of croissant. 'Let me get this down first.' But she didn't sound as touchy as she had the night before, he noticed. He put it down to wear and tear. The longer this went on, the more she would have to rely on them acting as a team.

'What is it?' asked Rik, spooning down a yoghurt. 'We going nuclear or what?' His gun, a Ruger SR9, like Harry's, lay close to hand.

'In a way.' Harry looked hard at Clare. 'How do we stop this black ops team?'

'What? Why ask me?' She stared at him. 'I'm out of the game, remember?'

'You think?' Rik countered. 'What are you doing here, then?'

She didn't respond, but gave him a sour look.

'You know them better than we do,' Harry told her. 'You know how they work, you said. So, how do we stop them coming after us?'

'Short of killing them, you mean? Getting a direct cease and desist order from Moscow?' She thought it over. 'Finding them won't be simple. They're trained, like our guys, to operate alone or in teams of two or three, depending on circumstances. They have no profile, they stay off the embassy circuit and use papers which take long enough to check to allow them to get away if compromised. They'll be incommunicado, answerable only to their field controller, whoever he is.'

'Gorelkin. Ballatyne says a man named Gorelkin was spotted coming this way on false papers. He's high up in the FSB's Special Purpose Centre.'

Clare blew out her cheeks. 'Jesus, that's all we need. I've heard of him but I thought he'd retired. He's one of their grey wolves from the old days. A hardliner.' She frowned. 'Hang on. He did retire, I'm certain of it. He fell out with his new bosses when the FSB took over from the old KGB. He didn't like the new touchy-feely approach and thought they'd lost their edge.'

'Ballatyne said he disappeared for a while, then came back recently.'

She raised her eyebrows. 'It happens. But only in special circumstances.'

'Like what?'

'Well, think about it: if someone's needed for something deniable, he'd be ideal. He's retired and has no provable link to official operations.'

'That's a bit lame, isn't it?' Rik said. 'Like anyone would believe it. Once FSB, always FSB, I thought.'

She gave a hint of a shrug. 'You asked. I told you. They're deniable or...'

'Or what?'

'Or they're here without sanction. Completely

off the books.'

'Is that likely?'

'If the right man gave the order, yes.' Her tone of voice told them who she thought that right man was. There was only one.

The Russian president.

'They did Litvinenko,' said Rik. 'So why not Tobinskiy?'

'But this time,' Harry pointed out, 'they know the world is watching.' He thought it over. Tobinskiy had been murdered, according to early suspicions, although there was no guarantee that the UK authorities would come out and say so. The scandal would be immense unless they could provide solid proof to the world's court of opinion. If not, there would be a diplomatic and trade backlash from Moscow. Without it, they would have to sit on their hands, powerless to make a solid case.

But Clare Jardine was the proof; she was the only witness who could put the Russians at the scene of Tobinskiy's death. And their clumsy attempt to kill her in Pimlico would only add fuel to the suspicions.

Unless they could silence her for good.

He turned back to Clare, trying to find a way of convincing her to help. He had run several ideas through his mind, but nothing seemed to fit. Because ever since last night, he'd been thinking of only one way to find the two Russians and stop them coming after them. 'There must be a way to stop them. If we don't, they'll keep coming. And if they've got inside access to security and intelligence personnel files, they'll know your details ... and they'll soon know ours.'

Her eyes were unfathomable, and he wondered if she wasn't suffering some kind of sensory overload. He would have been in similar circumstances. But somehow he had to reach her.

'You're in danger,' he said. 'The only way to stop this is to catch the hit team or to blow it wide open. Or threaten to, anyway. Then you have to disappear. For good.'

'How?' Her voice sounded distant, tired. Lost.

'We get in touch with the one person who might be able to help you.'

'Who?'

'Katya Balenkova.'

There was no reaction. In fact Clare showed no signs of having heard him. The silence in the flat was total.

'Clare?' Rik spoke up, one eye on Harry.

Harry's phone rang. He ignored it. Now wasn't the time to break the spell. They had to get her to respond.

'Are you saying Katya wouldn't help? Or couldn't?' he said carefully. 'Think about it. She's in the Federal Protective Service. She might be able to get word to someone who could stop these bozos.' He didn't want to mention that there had once been a relationship of sorts between the two women; that in times of dire need you used what you could, real or tentative. Neither did he want to find out that they had parted in hate and he was wasting his time.

The phone was still ringing. Then it stopped, leaving a note hanging in the air.

233

Almost immediately, Rik's landline began ringing. And his mobile.

Harry's radar twitched. Something was wrong.

He reached across and hit the audio button on the landline base. It was Ballatyne. He sounded terse, his voice bursting hollowly in the room.

'Harry, you have to get out of there. Two men paid an early morning visit to Jardine's old address. The owners were away, but the place was trashed as if they were searching for something. A neighbour called it in and the address showed a red light. If they've got her old address, we'd best count on them having yours and Ferris's, too. There's a squad on the way to your place and another on the way to Paddington to intercept, but you'd better not wait. Call me when you can. Now go.'

The phone went dead.

THIRTY-EIGHT

'Out,' said Harry. 'Grab and go.' He snatched up his gun and checked the load. Rik was already doing the same and reaching for his car keys and a panic bag. Clare was slower in moving, but it was obvious her training was kicking in. Neither of them bothered asking why; they knew.

'Down the fire stairs,' said Rik softly, closing the flat door behind them. He set off along the corridor to a plain maroon door in the corner. He eased it open, allowing the air to move without any movement or sound. He peered through the gap into the stairwell.

Empty.

With Harry helping Clare and watching their backs, they descended the stairs, listening to sounds coming from the other flats and from the outside. More than anything they were listening for the sound of footsteps.

They reached the ground floor and Rik pointed to a door at the side of the building. It had a fire bar and a glass panel, and a view across a path to a gate in a brick wall. Through the gap they could see pedestrians and cars and an adjacent street.

Rik nodded towards the gap. 'Go. I'll get my car and meet you in the street.' Then he stepped towards the fire door and pushed it open, checking that all was clear before signalling the others to follow. The moment they were out in the open, he moved away and was gone, striding across a small car park with his mobile pressed to his face and his gun held inside his jacket.

His Audi was parked in the far corner. He reached it and opened the door, climbed in and started the engine. Placed the gun on the passenger seat, covered with an old newspaper.

As he went to drive forward, two men appeared at the entrance to the car park. One was tall and slim, the other was heavyset, like a wrestler. The tall man continued walking towards the front entrance; his colleague turned and entered the car park. He had one hand inside his jacket.

Rik watched, hardly daring to move. He was

parked in shadow here, and unless the other man looked directly at him, he should avoid detection. Even so, he reached for his gun and slipped the safety in readiness.

The wrestler approached the main rear door, through which most residents came and went, and which was too often left open. Like now. He reached out with his free hand and pulled the door open, hesitated, then stepped inside and disappeared from view.

Rik let out his breath and put his gun back on the seat, safety on. Go or stay?

This could all end now, if he played it right. Up behind the wrestler, take him out and wait for his colleague to come down the stairs. No more need for Clare to run, no need to wait for the knock on the door. Except that things didn't always go the way you planned. The tall man might go for broke and take a hostage, or shoot his way out. Others could get hurt. And what if the squad Ballatyne had sent turned up right in the middle of it? They were unlikely to ask for ID before opening fire on a man with a weapon in his hand.

He left the gun where it was and started the engine, drove out of the car park and into the street, turning right to complete the square and bring him back down the street where Harry and Clare were waiting.

Harry, meanwhile, had moved through the gap in the wall and found himself on a quiet one-way street. Cars were parked on one side only, with a line of wheelie bins huddled across the other side, awaiting collection. He beckoned Clare to come out, and she emerged, holding her stomach but moving freely.

Everything was quiet.

A car started up behind the wall. Harry recognised the throaty hum of Rik's Audi. It idled for a few moments, then moved away and was gone.

Harry looked back at the block of flats. There was a chance if they stayed right here that anyone looking out of a rear window at the top might see them. He grabbed Clare's arm.

'Come on,' he said, and led her up the street towards the top where Rik would have to enter. By the time they got there, Rik was waiting.

Two minutes later they were out of the street.

Harry texted Ballatyne. *Away & clear. We need to meet now. Richx*

'What the hell are we doing here?' Clare stared around her with a look of disbelief at the décor of Richoux in Piccadilly. She was huddled in a corner seat, arms crossed tightly over her middle. 'I thought we were going to see Ballatyne.'

After a fast drive from Paddington, with Rik taking a series of diversions in case they had been followed, they had ended up in the restaurant and grabbed a rear table well away from other customers.

'We are,' said Harry. 'But he's shy about introducing us to his colleagues. He thinks we might put our feet on the table. Anyway, the coffee here is better.'

'And we don't have to give up our weapons,' Rik murmured.

At that moment, Ballatyne walked in and approached their table, leaving his minder by the door, watching the street.

'If I didn't know you better, I'd think you fancied me,' the MI6 man said to Harry. He sat down, signalling for the waiter to bring coffee, and placed a bulky brown envelope on the table by his side. 'Signing off a text with "Richx" is a bit risky, isn't it? You never know who might be hacking into your phone these days.' He nodded at Rik and received a vague hand wave in return, and gave a wan smile to Clare. She didn't respond.

He raised an eyebrow and said, 'So what happened?'

'We were leaving,' Harry replied, 'and Rik spotted two men answering the description you gave us. We got out just ahead of them. Thanks for the tip.'

Ballatyne's eyebrows went up. 'Close call. I checked with the squad we sent round, but they didn't see anyone. They were held up in traffic.' He shrugged. It happened. 'What can I do to help?' He was speaking to Harry but looking at Clare.

'Katya Balenkova. How do we get hold of her?'

Ballatyne looked surprised. 'Boy, you don't ask much, do you? Why do you want to contact her?'

'If we don't stop these guys,' Rik replied, 'they'll stop us. If we do stop them, they'll send someone else – someone we don't know.'

'And you think Balenkova might help you? Dream on – she's a Federal Protective Service officer, which makes her all but FSB in name only. Why would she put herself at risk?'

'She might consider it's worth it.' Harry gave a fractional tilt of his head towards Clare.

'What – you think because of their little fling Balenkova will turn on her old bosses?' If he thought the comment undiplomatic, he didn't show it.

'Litvinenko did. Tobinskiy did.' It was the first time Clare had spoken, and surprised them all. Her voice sounded cracked and dry, as if she had got out of the habit. She was staring at Ballatyne, eyes dulled by tiredness but a firm line to her mouth.

Ballatyne didn't respond at first. Then he said, 'You're ready to go along with this insanity?'

'Not really. I think Tate's nuts, but what choice do I have? Anyway, Ferris is right: if the two men who approached me don't finish this, they'll send somebody else; maybe not straight away, maybe not even this year. They'll let the dust settle, then one day they'll send in another team. It's the way they do things, you know that.'

Ballatyne looked grim. 'Fair enough. I suppose I can't stop you trying.' He checked his watch. 'About now, Balenkova's babysitting three Russian government financial heavyweights at an international banking symposium in Vienna. They're in the city for three days, glad-handing and talking roubles, euros and dollars.'

'I don't believe you.' Clare spoke forcefully, but with a tinge of uncertainty.

'Why – you think escorting bankers is beneath her? That they don't merit equal protection to military chiefs and politicians?'

'Damn right. She's one of their best people. She was heading for the top spot, guarding Putin himself.'

'Was.'

'Huh?'

'After you were busted and had to be pulled out, we heard she was suspended for a year or more, under suspicion. Then she was put on a roster looking after bureaucrats and low-level functionaries travelling in and out of Chechnya. Sounds like a punishment squad to me.'

'She would have hated that.' Clare sounded saddened by the revelation.

'Probably. She must have had a hard time convincing her bosses that she hadn't got anything out of you ... or that you hadn't managed to turn her. Whatever her specialist FSO skills, she'll have a good head on her shoulders. She will have heard things in private spoken by her charges, got to know who has doubts, who has a taste for money, women, boys or drugs or any other weakness that can be exploited.' He tilted his head. 'It's attractive stuff for the shrinks who like to know about these things – on both sides.'

'You've been monitoring her?'

'Of course.'

'Why? It was a busted operation, for God's sake!' She sounded angry, with twin spots of red growing on her cheeks. She slumped back in her seat, as if distancing herself from them all. 'What was the point?'

'Get over it.' Ballatyne's voice was flat, unapologetic. 'You know targets are never forgotten that easily.'

Harry and Rik sat very still. Ballatyne clearly knew more about Clare's aborted operation than he had let on, right down to the fine details. It was a reminder that he had been in the game for a long time, working his way up in the ranks at Vauxhall Cross. He would have been involved in numerous operations, either on the periphery or right in the centre. If he hadn't, he'd have made it his business to acquaint himself with the file.

'We were doing exactly what Balenkova's bosses were doing,' he continued, eyes fixed on Clare. 'We had to play safe, so we kept a watching brief. How did we know *you* hadn't got turned instead? We didn't. The only way we could be sure was if Balenkova got busted down the ranks or suspended. Which she did.'

'So what now?' said Harry, after a few moments of silence. 'We need to contact her.'

'Tonight they're attending an opening gala dinner. Tomorrow the Russian delegates are dining with the Russian Ambassador at the embassy in Reisnerstrasse. Balenkova and her FSO colleague, if they follow previous habits, will cut loose and do their own thing, leaving the embassy security team to play tag. Separately, I might add. The colleague likes to go and do his own thing when he's not working, so he shouldn't be a problem.'

Harry stared at him. 'You knew what we were thinking of doing.'

'Not really. But it's what I would have done in your boots.' He smiled at Clare. 'Sorry, but if you hadn't spoken up, I'd have vetoed the idea. You know her better than anyone; just be sure

241

you're not walking yourselves into a cold, dark cell.'

Clare shifted in her seat. 'Does that mean you won't help us if we get into trouble?'

'Officially, I can't. But I'm having Balenkova and her party watched, in case of any deviation from their plans. I can also give you a safe house to go to on the outskirts of the city, with an escort, after you make contact. The rest, though, is up to you.' He stood up, reaching for the envelope. He took out a slim white folder and dropped it on the table. 'Flight details and passes for each of you on a military flight out of Northolt this afternoon. Don't be late.' He held the brown envelope out to Clare. 'Where you're going, you'll need your passport. It's in there with the rest of your personal stuff from the hospital. Don't say I never help you.'

He walked away, back rigid, and paid at the counter before leaving the restaurant.

THIRTY-NINE

'I think I'm in love,' Rik murmured. 'What's got into him all of a sudden? He's usually on our case all the time.'

'He's helping, but it's off the books.' Harry turned to Clare. 'You know what this means: you're coming with us. Are you up to the trip?'

Clare tipped out the contents of the envelope

242

and scooped up her wallet, passport, coins and other personal belongings she'd had on her the day of the shooting. 'Fuck off, Tate.'

'I think you said that already.'

'Why would Katya talk to me, after what he said?' She tipped her head towards Ballatyne's departing back. 'I caused her nothing but grief and lost her God knows how much credibility in her job. She probably hates my guts.'

Harry didn't have a definite answer to that. But they had to try.

'You haven't been in contact with her since?'

She shook her head. 'Like when? I've been too busy being busted, then sent to that shithole in Georgia and helping save your arses. It's not like I was sitting on my hands doing nothing.'

It was a glimmer of humour. Not much, and tinged with a core of anger. But it was an improvement on anything they had seen so far. 'Anyway,' she continued, 'I didn't think she'd want to hear from me.'

'You might be right. But if you meant anything to her, she wouldn't want to see you taken out by a couple of FSB hotshots, would she? The simple fact is, she won't give Rik and me the time of day, no matter how we dress it up. But I'm betting she'll give you a hearing, at the very least. That's all we need.'

'What do you hope to achieve?'

'She might have an answer to this problem. She might not, but it's worth a try. And it gets you out of the country for a while and away from those two shooters.'

Several moments went by, during which Rik

signalled for more coffees. The waitress brought them and left them alone.

'I don't know how to contact her,' Clare said at last, stirring a generous portion of sugar into her coffee. 'I knew her mobile number once, but I still can't remember it.' She made a winding motion with a finger to the side of her head. 'It's all mixed up. Funny how I remembered your number, though.'

'And mine?' said Rik.

'I never had yours. Anyway, why would I bother?' She gave him a hard stare.

He blushed, although they all knew it wasn't out of any romantic notion. 'I put it in the compact ... on a slip of paper under the powder.' He looked mortified. 'You mean you didn't even look? I'm hurt.'

A hint of a smile touched her mouth and hovered for a fleeting second before disappearing. 'No. I didn't look. Now that bloody Russian thug's got it. He said he was going to give it to his girlfriend. Bastard.'

'Hey, it was only cheap.' Rik waved it away. 'If you liked it that much I'll get you another one.'

Now it was her turn to blush, but accompanied by a feigned look of disgust. 'Are you kidding? It was vile.' She dropped her spoon into her cup. 'But I want it back. Can we go now? I need some new clothes. I feel like a bag lady.'

They were about to board their flight for Vienna at Northolt when Harry's mobile rang. It was Ballatyne, his voice like a flat tyre. He was in the secure room again.

Harry dropped back and signalled for the other two to carry on.

'Tell me Ferris hasn't been letting his fingers walk where he shouldn't.' Ballatyne threw himself straight into the conversation without preamble. He sounded peeved and ready for a fight.

Harry was cautious. Ballatyne must know that Rik would have been accessing files somewhere; he'd even given them the nod to do so. 'Where specifically?'

'Specifically? Six, of course. The bowels of Vauxhall Cross. Forbidden bloody territory on pain of castration.'

A quick tug of relief. 'In that case, no. Why?'

'Because somebody's been trying to access our HR records – the section housing personnel details of former operatives no longer active.'

'You mean Clare Jardine?' It had to be; hers was the only name in play at the moment.

'Yes.'

'It wasn't Rik. You have my word on that.'

'Good. Glad to hear it.'

'What brought this on?' At the exit door to the tarmac, a member of the ground crew was signalling to Harry and a couple of other latecomers that it was time to roll. Harry avoided his eye. This was too important and he doubted he would get a signal once on board the flight, which would be basic and noisy.

Ballatyne muttered something beneath his breath. 'Ever since Bellingham and Paulton ... and some other security-related issues, new systems have been put in place across Five, Six, GCHQ and other selected agencies. Anybody trawling for information outside their remit, or attempting to use insider channels to do the same from one agency to another without the proper codes and passwords, which are changed frequently, sets off an alarm. It happens every now and then when somebody new tries to access a file without the current passes. Mostly it's an officer or analyst searching the databases to cross-ferment files and gets careless.'

'And this wasn't?'

'Not this time. He was blocked automatically first time round by the system lock-outs. Then he got creative and got into the guts of her file.'

'And you don't know who it was?'

'Not yet. He or she was clever enough to use an access log-in code belonging to an officer on sick leave.'

'That's pretty crude.' It indicated somebody without the specialist knowledge to by-pass the systems ... or someone brazen enough to care little about using a fellow-officer's code.

'Maybe. Or they might have been doing a quick and dirty one-time trawl and didn't care for subtlety. There was a time it would have worked, but not now.'

'How long will it take you to track them down?' Harry didn't know what the current levels of visual security were at MI6. They probably had CCTV on every floor, in strategic flow areas such as stairwells and general corridors, and Restricted Access points where security was at its most severe. What it might not cover were staff or officers using individual workstations.

'If it was somebody within the building, it will

be a process of elimination: who was present on that floor, who wasn't where they should have been, who had visitor access, who had a bad annual assessment last time round.'

'And if it's somebody outside?'

'Actually, that might be easier. If it's an outsider with access through a common server, they'll leave a trail that can't be erased. And there are only so many points of origin they could have used.'

A whistle came from the departure door, and Harry said, 'I've got to go. The flight's leaving.'

'OK. I'll call later with any news.'

FORTY

Votrukhin and Serkhov were beginning to get rattled. None of this was going the way they wanted. The girl had escaped – twice. And now they had failed to get the two men helping her. Worse, they had only just missed them, the knowledge of how close they had come to regaining some credit with Gorelkin taunting them like a dying laugh. Serkhov had picked the lock to Ferris's flat within seconds, and it was immediately apparent by the condensation from the shower and the remains of breakfast that the flat had been vacated in a rush not long before.

'They had a warning,' he muttered sourly as they hurried along the street. For the present they were without a car until a replacement was sourced, and having to rely on public transport and taxis to get around. Yet another reason to be anxious; every second they spent on buses, in taxis and on the Underground, quite apart from using the streets on foot, risked them being spotted and recorded. By now their descriptions would have been issued city-wide, and only luck would continue to keep them out of the hands of the British security authorities.

'Who else would have known, though?' Serkhov shouldered through a group of immigrant workers waiting for a work bus, oblivious to their protests. 'Nobody but us knew we were going there.'

'The Englishman. He knew.'

'Sure. But why would he risk playing games with us? Gorelkin has him by the nuts.' He mimed crushing something with a powerful fist. 'One phone call and he goes to prison for treason, or whatever it is they charge them with here.' He spotted a café and nodded at the steamy window. 'Wait. I need some tea. Even the vile mixture they serve here is more than we'll get from the colonel. And I don't think I can face his temper on an empty belly.' He swerved across the street, reaching for some money.

Votrukhin was forced to follow. The last thing he wanted was an argument with the sergeant; right now they needed to be acting as one and focussing on what to do next, not squabbling over food and drink.

They sat inside and sipped strong tea and ate a sandwich each, surrounded by a mixed clientele of building workers and student types. Accustomed to short, sharp breaks and no guarantees when the next one would come along, they knew the value of keeping their physical energy levels high. Eating also kept their mental faculties alert, especially when in the field as they were now and having to rely on split-second decisions to cope with an ever-changing situation.

Votrukhin stared out at the passing traffic. His expression was grim. For the first time in a long while he was feeling uncertain of himself. And Serkhov's touch of insubordination wasn't helping. In fact he should have slapped him down for it, but he hadn't the heart.

'Are you thinking what I'm thinking?' Serkhov had tuned into him, the way close colleagues do in operational situations. He took a large bite of his sandwich and fished out a segment of gristle, flicking it onto his plate.

'I've no idea. Tell me what you're thinking apart from filling your belly and I'll let you know.'

Serkhov swallowed some tea. 'This assignment's going to hell in a bucket, is my opinion. And we're stuck like a couple of tarts right in the middle of it.' He hesitated as if suddenly remembering that he was merely a sergeant talking out of turn to an officer, then ploughed on hastily. 'I know we have to work to orders and in isolation so we can't spill our guts if we get caught, but what happened to briefings, backup and some help? In any case, I'm not sure the colonel's being entirely open with us.'

'How do you mean?'

Serkhov shrugged. 'The way he's not allowing us any contact with the embassy or anyone else.'

'So what? It's standard operational rules. We've worked like this plenty of times before.'

'Yes, but we've always had fall-back positions available. Lose a car and we know immediately from pre-briefs where to go for another one. Here we are in the busiest city in the western world, with more Russians outside Moscow than most places on earth, and we can't even do that straight away. And we're now using one-time-only meeting places, like that dump of an office we were in last time.'

'So you're getting choosy about where we meet, now? Have you forgotten those places we used in Beirut? Or Athens? They were toilets compared with this.'

'You know what I mean. It's like we're right off the grid all of a sudden and having to survive on our wits, with no chance of backup. But where's Gorelkin while we're running our arses off around London?'

'He'll be somewhere near, waiting for us to report. It has to be that way, you know it.' Votrukhin sounded uncertain, even to himself, and felt instantly guilty. Team leaders weren't supposed to show doubt to those beneath them, no matter how desperate things were. The problem was, he was under exclusive orders from Gorelkin, a senior officer, and those orders included a no-contact rule with anyone outside of their three-man cell. It also precluded any practical displays of initiative, such as getting the hell out of here on the first flight while they still could.

'And there's the Englishman,' Serkhov muttered. 'What the hell is that all about? He's ex-MI5 and therefore a sworn enemy. If he betrayed his country and his service, he certainly won't think twice about dropping us in the shit if it suits him. Has he been cleared through central command to work with us?'

'I've no idea. Why – would you like me to call them up and check?'

'I bet he hasn't. The thing is, how do we even know for sure he's not still employed by MI5, huh?'

Votrukhin shifted in his seat, a worm of doubt in his mind. He'd been having the same thoughts ever since meeting Paulton. It wouldn't be the first time a team had been sold a fake pony. 'Don't even think that, you idiot. Gorelkin's not an amateur at this game; he'll have checked him out very carefully. Anyway, I think they know each other from way back. Haven't you sensed the atmosphere between them? They've worked together before, I'm certain.'

'Big deal. Once turned, a man can be turned again in my opinion. Paulton now knows our faces, full descriptions – even our mobile phone numbers. Don't tell me you haven't thought about it.'

Votrukhin said nothing. He was supposed to be above such rebellious considerations. And as an officer in the Special Purpose Centre, he should by rights be reporting Serkhov for his words and having him shipped home on the next flight out to face an unpleasant investigation and a period of retraining. Yet much of what the sergeant had said was correct. Something in the way Gorelkin had been acting was like a man waging his own private war, not trusting his men to know any of the background details. All they knew was that after dealing with Tobinskiy, the situation had been going steadily to hell, as Serkhov had phrased it so acidly, in a bucket. And now they were in pursuit of not only a former female member of MI6, but two former members of the Security Services, MI5, who were guarding her.

'So what are you suggesting?' Votrukhin said finally. 'That we tell Gorelkin that we're withholding our labour? That we don't want to play anymore? He'd have our balls on a stick inside the hour.'

Serkhov looked depressed. 'I don't know, do I? I'm just saying. It doesn't feel right.' He pushed his mug and plate away and stared out into the street through the condensation on the window. 'Give me a gun and a bunch of terrorists and I'd be happy. Not this game of round-the-houses.'

FORTY-ONE

George Paulton watched from the cab of a battered builders' van as the tall figure of Keith Maine appeared at the junction of Lambeth Road and Kennington Road. The analyst was dressed in his usual suit and carrying what looked like a plastic

Tupperware box. The pavement behind him was clear, with no obvious signs of pursuit or surveillance. Indications of either would have meant Maine was already being watched, or had panicked and sold Paulton out to the heavy treaders of MI5.

Paulton put the Ford Transit in gear and drove slowly along the street as if looking for an address. Half the skill in appearing normal was to do normal things. Nobody noticed the mundane and everyday activities, the background clutter of people going about their lives and jobs. And builders' vans were ten-a-penny, not worth a second look, especially when aged and scuffed to anonymity. Not unless the builder he had liberated this van from happened to have made the trip all the way from across the river in Blackfriars in search of his beloved vehicle and saw him.

He timed his arrival just as Maine was beginning to betray signs of nerves. The analyst was looking around and evidently already feeling out of his comfort zone, his face creased with concern.

Maine did a double-take as the van stopped and he saw Paulton beckoning from the driver's seat. For a second he didn't recognise who was under the baseball cap and wearing a set of paint-spattered overalls, then he gave a weak smile and climbed in. The smile faded as Paulton set off south and took the first left down a side street.

'Where are we going?' he demanded. 'I've got the information. Have you got the cash?'

'Calm down,' Paulton replied, taking a right

turn, then another left. 'We need to get off the main street, that's all.' He grinned, showing his teeth. 'We don't want everybody and his brother seeing our little transaction, do we?'

'No. I suppose not.' Maine sat back, careful not to brush against anything dirty, and held onto the door handle.

Paulton pulled into the kerb behind an old VW Golf, and cut the engine. They were situated between two tall buildings here, with no windows immediately overlooking them, a point Paulton had carefully scouted out earlier. There were no street cameras just here either, and he felt as secure as he could be.

He reached down by the seat and produced a heavy brown envelope. He opened it to show packs of cut paper, and peeled them back to show the edges of twenties and fifties. 'Sorry I couldn't get small denominations,' he said, 'but I figured the smaller the package the better you would like it.'

Maine's eyes opened wide at the proximity of so much cash. He smiled nervously and opened the lid of the Tupperware box. Inside was a pack of sandwiches and a banana. He lifted the sandwiches and took out a memory stick with a plastic lid. He unsnapped the lid. 'It's all on there. I copied the file for you. There's not much on it ... just a bunch of surveillance logs and the subject's movements over the past six months, and some historical annotations and comments.'

'What sort of comments?'

'Who the subject is, her background, how she first came to be a person of interest.'

254

Paulton smiled like a tiger. 'How interesting. That should save me a lot of chit-chat.' He didn't bother to explain what that meant.

'It runs up to five p.m. yesterday. There's a small delay for overseas traffic from our watchers, so we don't know if she has moved since then.'

'Excellent, Keith. Excellent. That wasn't so difficult, was it? We'll make a field man out of you yet.' He took the memory stick before Maine could stop him and handed over the brown envelope. He was counting on Maine being too scared of being outed to his bosses and losing his pension, to have double-crossed him. 'How did you manage it, by the way?' He wasn't really interested in the detail, but allowing Maine to preen was a useful way of deflecting his attention.

Maine almost smirked as he slid his fingers inside the envelope and ran them over the notes. 'Easy enough, as it happened. There's a common surveillance log on targets open to all agencies so we don't trip over each other. Any one agency wishing to move on an individual or organisation merely checks the log to make sure there's no on-going operation against them, and signs off the details as going "live". Everyone else steps back until given the all-clear.'

'The wonders of organisation. Are you certain you left no trail?'

'Of course. I'm not an amateur, you know.'

Paulton smiled. 'Of course. Aren't you going to count it?' He glanced in the wing mirrors on either side, and felt his blood beginning to race.

The street was clear. No pedestrians or vehicle traffic, nobody watching. It was now or never.

Maine bent his head to check the money, the pull too much to resist. As he did so, Paulton reached down again and picked up a steel meat skewer from the floor. The curved end was wrapped with a pad of rag and gaffer tape which he'd arranged earlier, to protect his hand.

'Wait a minute.' Maine had noticed something wrong. 'This isn't right—'

His protest was cut off sharply as Paulton brought his right hand round and up in a vicious jab, aiming at a point just above the analyst's belly. With his full shoulder weight behind it, he drove the point of the skewer into Maine's body, punching through his suit, then his skin, and into his heart.

Maine grunted and turned his head to look at him, his jaw dropping open in shock. His eyes went wide for an instant in accusation, and he mumbled something unintelligible, and tried to shake his head. It wouldn't work. A bubble of spit appeared at the corner of his mouth, and popped.

Paulton checked his pulse. Nothing. He glanced in the mirrors. Still clear. And no shouts of alarm. He sat back, breathing heavily, and flexed his right hand. In spite of the padding, his palm was going to be bruised to buggery. A pack of ice should sort that out, along with a stiff drink. He figured he owed himself that, at least. Then he needed to check the contents of the memory stick, to see what Maine had come up with.

He reached across and gave the skewer a sharp

tug. It took a sharp twist before it slid free of the body with a faint pop, the cloth of Maine's suit cleaning the metal of most of the blood as it came away.

He smiled and patted the dead man's jacket back into place. Some things were just so simple. All it took was the brass neck to plan it and carry it through. And neck was something he'd never lacked.

He wrapped the skewer in a rag and put that in his pocket for disposal the moment he saw a rubbish bin, then picked up the brown envelope and tucked it inside his jacket.

As he climbed out of the van, he gave Maine's shoulder a tug and allowed the body to slump sideways across the seats, so that it was below the level of the windows.

Locking the van carefully, he walked along the pavement to the VW Golf, another borrowed vehicle he'd acquired near Victoria Station. Seconds later, he climbed in and drove away.

FORTY-TWO

Vienna. The old spies' playground between the wars.

Harry wondered where all the old spies were now. Blown away, probably, by the winds of change that swept off many of the old-style espionage methods of backstreet meetings, dead-letter drops and shadowy confrontations on railway platforms and in smoky bars, to be replaced by electronic eavesdropping, satellite surveillance and computer hacking.

Clare had been silent all the way from the airport, as if nearing proximity to Katya Balenkova was making her shrink in on herself. She had been staring moodily through the window when Rik had spotted the city's famous Ferris wheel. Clare had immediately asked the taxi to stop along Ausstellungstrasse, a main boulevard running east-west and within sight of the iconic landmark.

The three of them climbed out and stood on the wide pavement, breathing in the fresh air as the taxi took off in search of another fare. They were close to the hotel Harry had booked from the information desk at the airport, and carrying overnight bags only, and Clare had insisted that she was capable of walking.

'I fancy a go on that,' said Rik, staring at the wheel, with its clunky-looking but quaint cabins, like small railway coaches, inching their way round into the cool air.

'Surprise, surprise,' Clare muttered. But she followed his gaze, lifting her head and standing up straighter than she had in a while.

'No time, children,' said Harry. 'We have grown-up stuff to do. According to Ballatyne, Balenkova and her party are not here for long. We have to make contact with her this afternoon, try to set up a meeting.'

'What if she freaks out and calls the heavy mob?'

Clare made a sound of disgust. 'Christ, Ferris, where have you been? She *is* the heavy mob. She doesn't need help. She's the best there is.' Her tone was one of open admiration for the woman.

Harry nodded. 'She's right. But if Balenkova does react badly, then better we know sooner rather than leave it too late and lose her.'

'So what's the plan?' Rik still had his eyes on the wheel.

'They're staying at the Imperial Hotel, near the embassy. But so are some bigger Russian wheels along with their security teams.'

'Ouch.'

'Quite. Any approach there would be too risky.' He looked at Clare. 'Especially for Katya.'

She nodded. 'So where, then?'

'Somewhere open, where she can see you coming. That way she gets to choose whether to stay or go.' He forestalled her speaking by adding, 'This is all about her. We need her help, but she has to know who she's doing it for. Rik and I would stand no chance of a direct approach. She'll think it's entrapment.'

'Cheers.' Clare looked glum. 'So I'm the gay stalking horse, am I?'

'More like a tethered goat, but that's just my opinion.' Rik smiled as he said it. 'Nobody's getting at you – you know it's the only way to play it. We're just there to see fair play, right, Aitch?' He glanced at Harry.

'Correct. And if you call me that again, I'll put you on the wheel and lock you in for the night.' He lifted his chin towards the area of park where

259

the wheel was revolving at a majestically steady pace. 'My guess is, they'll come here sooner or later, because everybody does. But to be certain we need to lock onto her and her group and see where they go.' He glanced at Rik. 'You'd best do that. You know what she looks like?'

Rik patted a small, slim leather case. It held his iPad. 'Sure do. Ballatyne's man here just email-ed it over. I just hope she hasn't had her hair styled since it was taken, though.'

'I haven't seen that.' Clare scowled at him as if she felt left out.

Rik shrugged and took out the iPad. He switched it on and called up a full-screen photo. It showed a slim woman with short, fair hair and a confident stance. She was frowning slightly, and standing on a city pavement next to a man in a suit. A car number plate at the edge of the scene showed it to be somewhere in Moscow. The man in the suit had the bearing and stolid lumpiness of a bureaucrat, and appeared to be waiting for permission to move. Balenkova was looking off to one side, her jawline determined. She had a curly wire tucked down into her collar and was carrying a small comms device in one hand. She looked every bit the steady bodyguard, in spite of her slim build.

'She hasn't changed much,' Clare remarked. 'A bit thinner, maybe.' She turned away from Rik and the photo, anxious to be on the move. 'Can we do this sooner rather than later?'

Harry looked at Rik. 'Suits me. Did Balla-tyne's man say where they are now?'

'Yes.' He consulted the iPad messenger.

'They've just arrived back at the hotel. They've probably got some free time before the dinner at the embassy.'

'Right. You get over to the Imperial and make contact with him, then let us know where they go. We'll drop your bag at the hotel and catch up with you.'

Rik handed over his overnight bag and turned as a cab crawled by, the driver eyeing them as potential fares. Seconds later he was gone.

'You love all this stuff, don't you?' Clare said, pulling her coat around her. 'The intrigue, the chase.'

'It's part of the job.'

'Really? What about catching Paulton? Isn't that part of the job, too?'

'What's Paulton got to do with this?'

'Nothing. But he hasn't rated a mention yet. Have you forgotten what he did, with Bellingham?'

'Of course not.' Paulton and what he'd done was never far from his thoughts, but life had to go on. He had a feeling Clare didn't share that view. 'His time will come.'

Clare leaned closer to him, her face intense. 'Damn right, Tate. Because if you don't get him, I will.'

Back in London, Paulton was staring at his laptop, checking the details of the MI6 surveillance log on Katya Balenkova, former captain in the FSO, now a humble lieutenant. He didn't waste time reading the commentary about her suspension and punishment following her secret assig-

261

nations with Jardine; he knew most of it anyway, and was much more interested in the here and now.

He scrolled down the list of sightings and reports, most of it undecipherable to an outsider, but offering a ready picture to a man with his experience. She was being watched along with several other persons of interest, her progress tracked with surprising ease by the watchers employed by Five. But then, she wasn't using covert means and was operating quite openly in an otherwise mundane job, escorting a variety of government appointees on their daily business and being a good girl until she could be rehabilitated back to her former position.

Vienna. The latest surveillance log entries had her entering Austria with three financial bureaucrats attending a conference in the city. Three charges with Balenkova and one other to keep them out of trouble. Good luck with that, he thought. Once free of the watchful eye of Moscow, three bureaucrats could kick up a ton of grief for a security team trying to keep them under control.

He glossed over the rest. It didn't tell him much other than where she was right now. It certainly didn't explain to him what her frame of mind was, which would have been a lot more interesting. Just beneath the final words of this entry was a blue hypertext link. He frowned. What had Maine been playing at – copying anything that came to hand? He clicked on it.

The screen flickered and opened up a cross-connection of KAs – Known Associates. It was a standard format on files for persons of interest; you might know their names and addresses, but more often than not, their associates gave you a far greater grounding in what their specific interests were. The greater the KA file list, the clearer was the subject's probable intentions.

He chuckled knowingly. Clare Jardine was at the top of a very short list. She was a KA, all right; about as KA as you could get without being married. But so what?

Then his heart skipped a beat.

An entry had been made further down showing a further link, this time to a file being run by a Richard Ballatyne of MI6, requesting an all-eyes lookout for Clare Jardine, a former officer currently on the loose in central London with two former members of Five. Their names were Tate and Ferris. The look-out was tagged LAR – Locate and Report. In other words, no direct action until otherwise ordered.

Beneath that, like the good little bureaucrat that he was, Maine had cut and pasted a reference code from a travel docket raised by Ballatyne.

Three return tickets to Vienna. Tate. Ferris. Jardine.

Bingo. Or game set and match of his own.

He reached for his mobile and dialled a number. Rule 1 of intelligence gathering: check and double-check the source of your information. Rule 2: never trust a source completely, even then.

The phone was answered immediately. He identified himself and said, 'Now why would

263

Tate, Ferris and Jardine possibly go to Vienna, do you think? For coffee and cake? A bit of Strauss?' The sarcasm was deliberately heavy, because he sensed he was being ignored.

'I don't know. I only just heard myself.' Candida Deane sounded testy. There was a long pause, then she said, 'How come you know?'

'I have my means. I'm intrigued by any departure from the norm. What on earth would attract them to Vienna – have you thought about that? Tate and Ferris are hardly the cultural type, and Jardine's a nasty little killer.'

'Maybe it's as good a place as any to hide, knowing who's after them.'

Paulton considered that seriously only for a moment. Vienna as a hiding place was ridiculous. Too full of government officials of every kind, therefore security people as well, it was too conservative a city for fugitives to stay for any length of time without standing out. Even experienced people like Tate and Jardine would be pushing it to go there with the intention of finding a secure hole longer than a couple of days.

'No. That doesn't fit,' he said. 'Vienna is a specific destination; they would have gone there for a reason.'

'And you think I would know?'

'Well, not you perhaps, Candida, dear.' His voice was purring with a vicious undercurrent he was finding hard to retrain. 'But somebody in that nest of vipers you call a workplace does. Try finding out who.'

'You know something.' The accusation was immediate.

'Suspicions, actually. But there's nothing I can do about it. Much better if you do, don't you think? Gain some more kudos.'

'Why the hell should I? I don't need this.' The south London tones came thick and harsh on the edge of anger. 'This is getting pointless, George. I'm thinking I should cut you adrift and let you fend for yourself.'

'I wouldn't do that. You'll regret it, I promise.'

'Are you threatening me?'

'Hardly. But then I don't have to. If Tate and Ferris get Jardine clear, the FSB team will pack up and go home because there's no point in them staying. If they do that, you'll have nothing to take to your bosses: no Jardine, no hit team – and if you cut me loose, there's no way I'll ever tell you who the inside man is.'

He heard her gasp at the promise he was offering. At the same time, he knew she wouldn't let him go that easily. She needed whatever he could offer and, most of all, she needed him. He had no illusions about her real plans; she wanted him wrapped, parcelled and stamped for the senior men and women in MI5 to call their own. He was, after all, a rogue intelligence officer. And rogues had to be brought down.

He decided to let Deane stew in her own juice for a while. She might be getting difficult, but he knew she would have already begun a search among the files to see what he knew.

He cut the connection and dialled another number. Time to switch the game a little. Perhaps this was something Gorelkin would have to handle. Tough luck on Deane, losing one of her hoped-for trophies, but that was the way the game played out. And he knew just what to say to make the man from Moscow take immediate action: an MI6 officer and two former MI5 officers, known subcontractors for the government, were on their way to Vienna to make contact with an officer of the Federal Protective Service. That should certainly light a *Katyusha* rocket under his arse. And with a bit of luck it would bring down the ceiling on Katya Balenkova's career for good. He didn't know the woman, didn't care if she lived or died. But anything she suffered would put a serious kink in Jardine's life, and that alone would be well worth celebrating.

Gorelkin's familiar, gravelly voice answered.

'Sergei, my friend,' Paulton said smoothly. 'How would you like to bag Jardine, two British intelligence offices and one of your own turned double-agent into the bargain?'

FORTY-THREE

Harry had just dropped his bag in his room when his mobile rang. He expected it to be Rik telling him that Balenkova and her charges were on the move. It was Ballatyne, sounding energised.

'Right, we've discovered the rat in the woodpile. His name's Keith Maine. He's not inside Six; he's a senior intelligence analyst with Five.

He used a loophole in a joint server to gain access to Jardine's file in Six. We think it's the same person who tried a while back, on a fishing trip.'

'Wouldn't it have been easier to find someone inside the building to do that? Why go through Five?'

'Actually, it wasn't so shabby. Maine used to be with GCHQ in Cheltenham, working closely with Five. When Thames House began recruiting their own analysts with specialist experience, he requested a transfer. Said he wanted more of a hands-on challenge. They grabbed him with both hands. As for finding someone in the building, believe it or not you can't just trawl through the faces and pick someone at random, you know. Staff get a bit suspicious at that kind of carry on.' He sounded almost jaunty, Harry decided, at finding that the rat was at Thames House, not Vauxhall Cross.

'What's his history?' Harry instinctive thought was whether the transfer had been instigated by an outside influence, to get a man inside MI5. It had been tried before more than once.

'On the outside, he's clean. Single – pretty much a carer for his mother until she died last year – no overt political leanings, belongs to two books groups, a small collector of first editions and other rare books. Colleagues think he's a good guy, but boring. Good at his job, but coming up for retirement.'

Harry nearly laughed. That profile alone would fit nearly any person discovered to have dipped their fingers in the secrets drawer over the past fifty years. But it also fitted a vast number of totally innocent and hard-working members of the intelligence community.

'The original grey man.'

'Not to somebody, he wasn't,' Ballatyne murmured. 'I doubt he was doing this out of conviction. I think he was got at.'

Harry knew what that meant. Money or a weak point, not political gain. 'What's happening now?'

'The internal security heavy mob is running his entire history through the meat grinder as we speak. They're going to town on his background, friends, where he's been, the bookshops he visited – everything and anything. You know how it works.'

Harry knew very well. The effect of that kind of close security vetting on everybody around Maine wouldn't be pleasant. The net result would be that he would shortly discover just how many loyal friends he had left in the world. The likelihood was, very few.

'If he had the nous to use a back door into Six, how did he get found out?'

'The usual thing: he got careless. He dropped a receipt from a bookshop near another officer's terminal – an officer who's been in Afghanistan for three weeks. Thames House knew what we were doing, so they did a deep system sweep which led to Maine's desk. They found a twelve-digit code on the underneath of a notepad. It matched entry codes to personnel records in Six. They've got him lined up for a heavy chat.'

Harry frowned. There was something in Balla-

268

tyne's voice that wasn't right. 'You mean they haven't done it already?'

'They can't find him. He didn't report in after lunch today and his mobile's switched off. He logged out of Thames House for lunch, and was seen walking south across Lambeth Bridge. Last thing anyone saw of him.'

They were too late. 'Is that normal?'

'No. His colleagues say he keeps regular patterns, rarely if ever varying. He's a creature of habits. Heading south across the river wasn't one of them. That's where the internal hunters are focussing their search.' He cleared his throat. 'But that's not all.'

'Go on.'

'He delved into an open access surveillance log on Katya Balenkova. All agencies can check it, given the correct codes. Maine had been doing some analysis on surveillance report patterns, so he had authority to go in there.'

Harry didn't want to ask, but had to. 'Why is that a problem?'

'Well, very few people knew of the link between Clare Jardine and Katya Balenkova. The techs can't tell me how much he read yet, but whoever was running him had clearly made the connection between the two women, and knew just where to point him for maximum effect.'

'I thought that file would be closed.'

'It is – or was. But I think I have the answer to that. When they did an initial audit of Maine's activities, they pulled up traces of another search he'd made. This one was closer to home, in Thames House. It was a read-only file, but it looks like that's all he needed. He was reading up on an old friend of yours. I think Maine was looking for a smoking gun to protect himself.'

Harry knew instinctively what Ballatyne was going to say. There was one other person he could think of who knew all about Clare Jardine and Katya Balenkova

George Paulton.

In an annexe to the Russian Embassy on Reisnerstrasse, a single phone call was all it took to have a team of specialists ready and briefed to go out on the streets in force, armed with photographs of Clare Jardine and Katya Balenkova. They knew who and what Balenkova was, but none had ever met her. The tone of the phone call from a source in London left no doubts about how important this was.

'Trace and report,' Captain Yuri Symenko, the resident commanding officer of the FSB security detachment told his men, after handing out the photos and briefing notes. 'Do not apprehend either of these women until I give the order. There are British spies involved and I want to scoop up all of them, you hear?' He smiled in spite of the gravity of the situation. He had been here almost two years now, and had never witnessed anything this exciting before. British spies, for heaven's sake! He'd never even seen one, let alone arrested one. If all went well, this could lead to a posting to somewhere far more interesting, like Paris or even New York.

'But Balenkova's FSO,' whispered one of his deputies, staring at the briefing notes as if they carried the seal of the Kremlin. 'Are you sure about this information, sir?'

'The instructions come from an impeccable source, lieutenant,' Symenko said loftily, waving away the officer's concerns. Even so, he experienced a tiny moment of doubt. Arresting a member of the Federal Protective Service was unheard of, and would be like charging a member of the inner cabinet in Moscow with treason, such was their reputation. They were above reproach, vetted and trained to the highest level, especially Balenkova, of whom he'd heard. Yet he had also heard of Colonel Gorelkin and knew enough of his background to realise that arguing with him would be to bring his own career to an abrupt and painful end. It was sufficient to reinforce his decision. 'When I give the order, separate Balenkova from her FSO colleague, Bronyev. Neutralise him if necessary but don't harm him. He is not part of this. But above all, do it quietly. We do not want an international incident on our hands.'

FORTY-FOUR

The area known as Riesenradplatz, with the giant wheel at its centrepiece, and the amusement arcades and rides that had attached themselves to it like noisy, brash pilot fish, was bright with colour and movement as the afternoon slipped

271

into evening. Tourists anxious to get an exclusive photograph of the wheel made famous in the film *The Third Man* were shuffling around the site like paparazzi, looking for a memorable viewpoint against the fading light without including the gaudy neon of a MacDonald's franchise or a haunted castle.

Harry felt a momentary doubt at the movement of the crowd. It would be too easy to miss Balenkova and her group here, and too easy for the Russian to see Clare first and bolt at the possibility of another approach by MI6.

He checked on Clare's position, and saw that she had settled on a spot under the cover of a tree near a group of Japanese students, hunched and low-profile, a dark, anonymous figure in the crowd. Harry had also merged into the background, attaching himself to a group of Americans on a whistle-stop tour of Europe, allowing their shift and flow to absorb his presence.

'They're out of the hotel and heading for the wheel.' Rik's phone message had come after a lengthy wait, just as Harry was trying to think of another way of allowing Clare to contact Katya Balenkova. They had promptly left the small hotel where they were staying and walked to Riesenradplatz to wait for their quarry to arrive.

The American group began to drift away to the south, making noises about finding somewhere cheap to eat, before the restaurants got too busy. It left Harry feeling exposed, and he looked for another group. But none was static enough to provide sufficient cover, so he kept on the move, his mobile in his hand, glancing occasionally at his watch, playing the late-date scenario, but never moving out of sight of Clare's position.

As he walked past a stall selling ice creams and soft drinks, his phone rang.

'Harry Tate?' The voice was male, with a vaguely American accent.

'Speaking.'

'A man in Vauxhall said you might need supplies. My name is Richoux.' The last was a code word identifier, taking the name from the last place the two men had met in London. Ballatyne had been busy making arrangements.

'Good timing,' said Harry, and told the caller where he was.

'Stay where you are. I'm a few minutes away on foot. I know what you look like, don't worry. I'll approach from the north, across that round-about in the centre. We're old friends and you forgot your briefcase when you visited me. My wife's name is Inge.'

Harry thanked him and cut the connection. Only spies made a big thing about walking up to somebody in a public place. In the normal world, it happened all the time and nobody questioned it. He continued walking, making a slow tour of the area and keeping Clare in his line of sight. While doing so, he called Rik.

'Where are you?'

'Five minutes away. One of the suits stopped the cab and went into a chocolate shop with the male guard. What's the German for I think my wife's cheating on me with four other men?'

'Why?'

'My driver's getting arsey about following

their cab.'

'Tell him *"meine Frau betrügt"*. He'll think you're a total wet, but he'll enjoy the chase.'

He stopped in the shade of an overhead canopy and waited. He was facing the roundabout 'Richoux' had mentioned, where he had seen cars come and go. There were various approach roads but they all fed into this one place. A noticeboard with a map of the area showed the attractions on offer. A number of business cards had been inserted behind the rim, including taxi and limousine services. He plucked one out and stuck it in his pocket.

'Harry!' A man in a sports coat and flat cap appeared by his side. He was carrying a black briefcase and made a show of relief at seeing him. Red-faced and chubby, he held the briefcase aloft and made a brief pantomime about how nice it had been to see his old friend, but that Harry had left his briefcase behind and Inge had sent him out on pain of death to get it back to him.

'Tell her she's an angel,' said Harry, playing along. 'Next time I'm in town, I'll take her out for dinner. Not you, though – you've had your share.'

The two men laughed and 'Richoux' glanced at his watch before throwing his arms around Harry, claiming for the benefit of anyone close by that he was late for dinner and had to dash.

Harry watched him go before checking inside the briefcase. It held two soft cloth bags, of the kind up-market shoes were sold in. He could tell by the weight and look that they each contained a handgun and a spare magazine. The briefcase also contained a Yale key attached to a piece of card by a length of string. The card carried an address in the suburbs.

The safe house.

His phone rang again.

'Just arriving,' said Rik. 'They're in a cream Mercedes.' He read out the number.

Harry turned and saw a cream-coloured cab stop near the wheel and disgorge a group of passengers. Four men and a single woman. Three of the men were soft looking, obviously bureaucrats; the fourth looked alert and fit, moving with athletic ease. A bodyguard.

The woman was Katya Balenkova.

Harry glanced across at Clare. She had spotted the group, too, but hadn't moved, which was good. He doubted Katya would see her clearly enough to identify her, which was also good. Any sudden move or a direct approach would be enough to warn Katya's colleague that something out of the ordinary was unfolding, and he would have to make a move to neutralise the situation. Just as he'd been trained.

The three bureaucrats looked up at the wheel, gesticulating and laughing, clearly intending to take a ride. One of them hustled off, beckoning for the male bodyguard to go with him, no doubt to pay for their tickets. The other two men trailed in their wake, with Katya bringing up the rear and scanning the area like a true professional.

Harry stayed where he was, aware that if she turned now just as he began to move, she might spot him. He rang Clare's mobile.

She answered with a dull voice. 'I see her.'

'Wait for the three suits to get on board,' he told her. 'If the male guard goes with them, make your approach. But not too fast.'

'I've done this before, you know.' She cut the connection. He turned his head and watched as she moved out from under the tree and walked towards the wheel.

Katya had stopped a short distance back from the last people in the queue. She was well clear of the men but watching as they shuffled towards where the cabins arrived at the embarkation platform, laughing and jostling like children on a day out.

Harry felt a sudden jolt.

There was no sign of the male guard.

He moved position slightly. The guard might be the truly paranoid type; the type who might have gone on ahead to check there wasn't a bomb under the seat set to blow his charges sky-high. Or he might have doubled back to watch their backs.

Clare turned her head and looked back at Harry. She was just thirty yards behind Katya, standing among a small knot of passengers who had just exited the wheel and were clustered together looking for direction. For once she looked uncertain, no longer confrontational, almost lonely. He felt for her, and tried to imagine how he would feel in such circumstances, meeting up with a person he had once been close to; someone he had caused to lose position and prestige, and who might turn and react badly.

Then Clare was moving, striding forward with

purpose. She stopped alongside Katya, not so close as to invade her space, but within earshot. Then she was talking; he could tell by the way she held her head, facing slightly away, chin down.

Balenkova took a moment to react, no doubt having had to break her concentration. She turned her head, then snapped it back into position at once, her whole body stiffening.

Contact.

Harry's phone rang.

He ignored it. Too much going on here right now. It stopped once to go to voicemail, then started ringing again immediately. He accepted the call.

Ballatyne.

'Don't hang up – I don't care what you're doing. Just listen.' The MI6 man's voice was tense. 'Keith Maine's body was discovered thirty minutes ago in a Ford Transit off Kennington Road. He'd been stabbed once with some kind of long spike. On the floor of the van was a lunch box and the cap from a memory stick, but no sign of the stick itself. It looks like he got it out of the building in the lunch box. There was clearly a handover, but the other party didn't keep their side of the bargain. I checked back with the techs. Maine accessed a travel file in Six and picked up the ticket reference to your name, and copied details of your trip to Vienna. Safe to say that whoever he was working for now has the stick and whatever data it contains. He knows where Balenkova is ... and where you are.'

Harry swore silently. He'd been here before. If

the information had been passed to the two Russians, it wouldn't take them long to get a team in Vienna to track them down based on Katya's movements. All they had to do was follow the group's itinerary.

He cut the connection with Ballatyne without a word. He had to warn Rik to keep his eyes open. But the most vulnerable was Clare – especially right now when she was face to face with Katya herself.

FORTY-FIVE

A whistle sounded, piercing the music and noise from the amusement stalls and other rides. Harry looked round.

Rik was standing near where the cab had dropped Balenkova's party. He was making a subtle chopping motion with one hand across his throat, fingers out straight. He must have tried to ring Harry but couldn't get through because of Ballatyne's call.

The signal was clear.

Abort.

Behind him, Harry saw why. Four men were getting out of a black Mercedes SUV. Dark suits but definitely not business types. Too alert to be casual visitors. One of them flicked a hand to usher away the other three, their orders to disperse. Then he looked off to one side, where a footpath led through to a green space and an adjoining approach road, and gave a subtle nod.

Harry turned his head to follow the look.

Two more men had appeared between the trees. They were scouting the area, trying to be casual but looking more like attack dogs on the hunt.

Harry turned and walked towards Clare and Katya. Playing out the same scenario as Richoux had done, he lifted his arms in welcome and called her name.

She turned and stared at him in puzzlement, but he gave her no time to object. Placing his arm across her shoulders, he bent as if to kiss her cheek, but instead muttered, 'Move it. We're blown.' Then he led her away, smiling down at her and catching a brief glimpse of Katya's face, her mouth open in surprise.

As they left the area, one of the men from the car approached on the trot, calling Katya's name.

'Wait!' Clare hissed, struggling against his arm. 'We can't leave her!'

Harry increased his grip on her shoulders, making her gasp. 'There are at least six of them – probably more. What do you want me to do, shoot them all?'

'No, but—'

'What did you tell her?'

'That we had to meet, to talk. She didn't say much. I think she was in shock.'

Harry looked up and saw Rik standing by the entrance to a café. He turned and disappeared inside. They followed him and found a table at the back. It wasn't a big place but crowded enough to provide cover for a while. If the men from the car were combing the area, they would look for anyone leaving the site and heading across the open spaces or roads nearby. Staying right under their noses was not the wisest move, but might be enough to fool them.

'I'll stay outside,' said Rik. 'They didn't see me.' He disappeared through the door.

'Talk me through it,' said Harry, after ordering drinks and making sure the briefcase was safely out of the way.

Clare still looked angry, but was beginning to calm down as she saw the sense in Harry's sudden intervention. If the men had suspected Clare was making an approach, they would have scooped them both up immediately, dealing with any legal fall-out later. Or maybe they had orders not to worry.

'I thought she didn't recognise me at first,' said Clare. 'Then she said my name. That was all. I told her I was being hunted ... that some men were trying to kill me after Tobinskiy was murdered.'

'How did she react?'

'She looked stunned. I said I was a witness and that Tobinskiy's killers were now after me, and I thought they were under orders from Sergei Gorelkin, who's in London. She looked at me as if I was nuts.'

'And?'

'Nothing. She just said "That can't be". Then you rocked up.'

Harry wasn't sure what to do. Either Katya had believed Clare or she hadn't. Time would tell. A lot would depend on what the men who had come looking for her would say and do – and what their orders were. If they had been briefed against Balenkova, they would probably take her in for questioning. If so, that would be the last they would see of her.

'I told her where we were staying,' said Clare, her voice sombre. 'In the hopes that she was able to contact us later. Sorry.'

'Doesn't matter,' said Harry. 'We'll move somewhere else.' He would leave the hotel a contact number in case, isolating themselves from any possible move against them. Something was puzzling him. 'She said "That can't be". What do you think she meant?'

'Like I told you earlier, I didn't think Gorelkin was still around. If he is, he's been brought out of retirement for a special assignment. Katya must have thought the same thing.'

'She'd know him, then?'

'God, yes. Everyone in the FSB knows about him – he's a legend.'

'What do you think she'll do?'

'Gut feel?'

'Yes.'

'I think she'll call.' She dropped her eyes. 'I hope she will, anyway.'

Harry said nothing. It was the most vulnerable he'd ever seen Clare. And no wonder. She had been through the ringer recently, and had put up with more than most people ever have to suffer. Now she was hoping that the one person who had ever meant anything to her, someone whose career she had brought to a stuttering halt, would

281

give her a fair hearing rather than simply turn her over to her bosses.

Rik appeared in the doorway. He walked across the floor and took a seat.

'They've gone. There was a bit of a row with Katya, but she used her mobile and was looking up at the wheel. I think she was talking to her mate on board with the three stooges. Then they all left.' He looked at Clare apologetically. 'Katya went with them.'

Back in London, in a service office near Marble Arch hired for the day, Sergei Gorelkin was being brought up to date with events. He listened to the call on his mobile, then shut it down and stared across the table at Votrukhin and Serkhov.

'So. Balenkova is now being interviewed by the head of the Vienna team. It seems they were remarkably efficient in finding her.' His expression dared the two men to object to his barbed comment, and he continued, 'However, she was on official duty with a colleague and their three charges when they found her, and there was no sign of the Jardine woman or the two men who are helping her. Balenkova did not know what they were talking about.'

'What will they do?'

'Nothing. As the information we were given and passed onto them comes from an admittedly unreliable source, the team leader says he will not act on that alone.'

'Idiot,' Serkhov muttered darkly. 'If what you told us is true, and Balenkova got cosy with Jardine a couple of years ago, how do we know

Balenkova's trustworthy? She could be playing a waiting game.'

'Really? A waiting game?' Gorelkin's eyebrows went up in amusement. 'Now that is an expression I never thought I'd hear you utter, Sergeant Serkhov. You suddenly have the utmost confidence in what Paulton tells us, do you? I thought you didn't trust him.' He switched his gaze to Lieutenant Votrukhin. 'Neither of you did.'

'No further than I can piss, like you,' Votrukhin replied mildly, being careful not to suggest that Gorelkin had been taken in by the Englishman. 'He's already lied to us once, about Jardine being tied in with a Ukrainian gang. Who's to say he didn't plant bogus information on that memory stick just to keep us fooled for his own ends?'

'He probably did,' Gorelkin agreed mildly. 'Or at the very least, told us what he thought we wanted to know.' He paused and looked up at the ceiling, taking a long, deep breath. 'Either way, I think Mr Paulton is, shall we say, edging past his use-by date.'

'What do you mean?' Votrukhin's face said he knew what the term meant, but his tone was requesting direct orders, not vague suggestions.

'For the moment, I mean nothing. We stay on the move, we have nothing more to do with Paulton until we know more.' He nodded at the lieutenant's mobile phone sitting on the table by his elbow. 'Dispose of those – he has your numbers. We go silent and we wait to see what else happens in Vienna. If the Jardine woman comes back, it means her approach to Balenkova for

283

help – if that's what it was – has failed. Then we will deal with her as we should have done in the first place.'

FORTY-SIX

The area around the hotel where Harry and the other two were staying was secluded and quiet. Any night life was a few blocks away, where the more conservative residents of Vienna could be spared the garish sights and sounds of the tourist trade that passed through their fair city, washing it with the kind of raucous music that owed nothing to Strauss, Mozart or their illustrious colleagues.

Harry had chosen the early shift, and was now standing in a darkened doorway, watching the front of the hotel they had now vacated, waiting for a sign of late night visitors. He had guessed that if Balenkova chose to make a move, with or without her colleagues, she would do so when there were fewer pedestrians about and when the likelihood of running into traffic would be slight. But she wouldn't want to leave it too late; movements in these quiet streets would stand out, especially if she had a unit of armed FSO personnel as backup.

A taxi turned into the street and stopped a hundred yards away. A couple climbed out and the man stood on unsteady legs and paid the driver. A burst of laughter followed and the female half of the couple, a large lady in a long dress, tottered off along the pavement, shimmying to an inner tune and leaving her companion to stumble along in her wake.

A dog wandered by, sniffing at doorways, and jumped back in surprise when it saw Harry. It continued on its journey, leaving him to the night.

Twenty minutes later, he heard footsteps approaching, and peered out from his cover. A lone figure was coming down the street. He waited for the walker to pass beneath a street lamp. Slim, not too tall, in trousers and a half-length coat. He couldn't see clearly yet but something about the movement was definitely female.

Another street lamp washed its light over the figure. A woman with fair hair.

Katya Balenkova.

She turned in at the hotel, and with a glance along the street behind her, disappeared.

Harry felt the weight of the gun in his pocket. A Walther P88 9mm, its twin was now with Rik in the other hotel. He hadn't been convinced of the need for weapons, but seeing the display of force sent to intercept Clare, he wasn't prepared to take chances.

Three minutes passed. No traffic and no other pedestrians. He could hear the hum of vehicles in the distance, and the tinny sound of a nearby radio or television, but that was all.

He gave it another two minutes. They had left a phone number with the receptionist, saying that they had been called away on urgent business out of the city, but would retain their room for the following night. If Balenkova was playing them, it would be sufficient to make any watchers think they could catch up with them the following evening.

His phone buzzed. It was Clare.

'She called. She's agreed to meet.'

'Where?'

'Here, at the hotel – but I didn't tell her where it is. I told her what you suggested and she said fine.'

'That's very trusting of her.'

'No, it's not. If she doesn't like you, she'll kill you. She's very capable.'

'Thanks for the warning. Is Rik outside?'

'He's on the roof, keeping watch.'

'Right. Five minutes.' He cut the connection and waited. If Balenkova had help nearby, now was the time she would call it in. It gave Harry a chance to spot any watchers, while remaining unconnected with Balenkova save for a short period before they entered the other hotel. As a precaution, he took out the gun and placed it on a ledge in the doorway. If he did get scooped up here and now, there would be no going back if found in possession of a weapon.

A door scrape echoed along the street, and when he looked out, he saw Balenkova step into the open and look left. Then she turned and began to walk towards him. He picked up the gun and walked away, making sure she saw him.

Two minutes later, he waited in a recess be-tween two buildings for her to come along. When she did, he stepped out, hands empty and clear of his body so that she could see he meant her no harm.

She stopped a few feet away from him. She looked perfectly balanced and relaxed, but had one hand in her coat pocket, which looked a little dragged down on that side.

'Mr Tate?' Her voice was accented but clear. Confident but wary.

He nodded. 'I'd like to check you for devices, if you don't mind.'

She cocked her head to one side. 'And if I do mind? I still don't know who you are, only your name.'

'Which Clare told you.'

'But I don't know you. Why should I trust you?'

'You're here, aren't you? She wants to see you. She's in danger.'

'Yes, she said that. What makes you think I can help?'

'I don't know if you can. But she believes it – wants to, anyway.' He pressed on before she could talk further, aware that she could be playing for time, in which case they needed to be away from here and off the street now. 'Follow me and I'll take you to her.'

She didn't respond for a moment. Then she took her hand out of her coat pocket. It was empty. She lifted her hands clear of her body, holding the coat open.

'What are you proposing to do – a body search? The last man who tried that is still walking with difficulty.' Her tone was light, but he guessed she wasn't fooling.

'Nothing like that. I just wanted to see if you were willing to go along with it, that's all. Is the gun loaded?'

'Of course. Is yours?'

Harry nearly laughed. He hadn't heard such cheesy lines since watching a very bad spy film a few years ago. But it broke the tension between them. He turned and led the way along the street and round a corner. The hotel was across the street.

Inside, they by-passed the reception area without being seen and took the lift to the fourth floor. Up close, he saw that Katya had nice eyes but a pock-marked area of skin along one side of her jaw. She smelled of soap and was wearing jeans and a plain sports jacket with flat-heeled boots.

She watched him assess her and did the same back, lifting a dismissive eyebrow before concentrating on the mirror on one wall.

Outside the room where Clare was waiting, he was about to knock when Katya held up a hand.

'Please. Can I speak to her alone for a few minutes? I promise I won't harm her. She owes me that.'

Harry nodded and stepped back.

FORTY-SEVEN

'We all clear?' Harry stepped onto the roof, where Rik was keeping an eye on the streets below. The air was fresh and slightly damp with the promise of rain, free of the traffic fumes further down. They were on a maintenance veranda running all the way round the building, with a clear view of the approaches to the hotel. Unless Katya had been coached since the meeting in Riesenradplatz and was under orders and playing a devious game to reel them in, they should be safe for now.

'So far.' Rik shivered. 'How was she?'

'Prickly, suspicious. What you'd expect.'

'You left them alone?'

'They need to talk.'

'Bit risky, though, isn't it? They could be punching seven bells out of each other.'

'It might ease the tension a bit if they do. I'll give them three minutes to decide.'

'What do we do if she agrees to help? She's not exactly in a position to call off the dogs, is she?'

'No.' Harry still wasn't entirely sure what he'd hoped to achieve from this. Getting Clare out of harm's way was one thing, and they'd almost achieved that until he'd heard Ballatyne's news about the details lifted from secret files on the memory stick. The Russians had moved even faster than he'd expected, drumming up a search team to track down Katya. But luck had been on their side. Just.

He hoped it would continue.

His phone rang.

Clare said, 'We're good. You can come down. She promises not to shoot you.'

Harry left Rik on guard and walked down to the room, using the rear emergency stairs, which were deserted and little-used, although impressively carpeted. He rapped on the door and stood back so that whoever answered the door could get a good look at him.

It was Katya. She had one hand out of sight behind the frame.

'You can put that away,' Harry said. 'If I was going to slot you, I'd have done it in the street.' He marched past her into the room. Clare was sitting on one side of the bed. She looked oddly bright-eyed and alert, in spite of the rough day, and was sipping from a miniature of brandy from the minibar.

'Celebration?' he asked, and felt embarrassed. 'Sorry. I didn't mean that the way it came out. What's the situation?'

'Katya's agreed to help us,' Clare announced. 'She thinks her future's shot, anyway, so why not?'

'Really? That was quick.' Harry studied Clare for signs that the miniature wasn't her first. In her weakened condition intoxication would be much faster than normal, and he didn't want her impaired any more than she already was. He also wanted to avoid false promises and expectations on both sides. If Katya had already made a decision which would affect her entire future, it had to be the right one.

'Really.' Katya advanced into the room and stood in front of him. Her gun hand was hanging down by her side. She looked more formidable up close, and Harry could see why she was so good at her job; attitude radiated from every pore, but without brashness. In basic terms, she gave off the right vibes to inspire confidence in her charges and a sense of power in anyone who faced her.

'Help us how?'

'I can help you find Sergei Gorelkin. Find him and you will find the men trying to kill Clare.'

'OK.'

'But first you must promise me full protection and entry to the UK without months in one of your asylum centres or a debriefing cell.' She looked him in the eye, her stare unwavering and cool. 'Otherwise I walk out of here and you never see me again.'

Harry hesitated. For someone negotiating their future, she was amazingly self-possessed. But the simple truth was, there was no way he could guarantee any of what she was asking. However, he knew a man who might. 'I'll see what I can do. That's all I can say.'

'Bullshit,' Clare intervened. 'You'll have to do better than that, Tate. Katya's giving up everything for this. The least the UK government can do is allow her residency and new papers.' Her lip curled. 'The MOD does it all the time for

291

Iraqi and Afghan interpreters, and I know Six has done it before for blown assets. She's going to help you find the killers of Tobinskiy. Surely that counts for something.'

'I agree with you. But I'm not on the official payroll. I promise I'll speak to Ballatyne.' He looked at Katya. 'The first priority, though, is to get you out of here.'

She nodded and put a hand out to prevent Clare from arguing further. 'Very well. That is enough for now. This man ... Gorelkin. He's a special; one of the old guard. He retired years ago. Some said he was not a fan of modernity, others said he was simply tired of the game.'

'Game?'

'He started out in the GRU – military intelligence – and was very active during the Cold War in Germany and the West. He also organised counter-terror units during our Afghan War and was highly decorated during that time. He transferred to the KGB and worked under Vladimir Kryuchkov until Kryuchkov's forced retirement in '91. Gorelkin continued but some say the fight had gone out of him, that he was not happy with the new ways of the FSB or of the new government.'

'Of Putin?'

'Especially of Putin. But not even a man of Gorelkin's status could voice those opinions for long without attracting trouble. Eventually he dropped out of sight. There were rumours that he was doing special work for the government, but they were like many rumours, impossible to prove. It was part of the mythology of men like him. Then, I think two years ago, it was said he had died of cancer.' She glanced at Clare. 'I tell you this only so that you know who you are dealing with. If Sergei Gorelkin is, as you say, controlling the team in London, then he was asked to come in and do so at the very highest level.'

'Why? The FSB can't be short of good leaders.'

'They are not. But a man who retired, disillusioned, then died? Who would think it? I can barely believe it myself.'

'Why not?' Harry countered. 'It makes him very deniable. Was he involved with the death of Litvinenko?'

Katya paused before answering, and blinked, as if adjusting her thinking. Then she said, 'I don't know. Nobody does. That is a subject not talked about anywhere in the FSB. There is a saying among the ranks, "You can think your thoughts but do it quietly".'

'And Lugovoi?' Harry said it before Clare did – or in case she could not. Andrei Lugovoi, a former member of the FSO, like Katya, but now a member of the Russian parliament, was the prime suspect in Alexander Litvinenko's murder in London, and Litvinenko's widow was pushing hard for an investigation. 'Is he also a non-subject?'

She looked straight at him. 'I never knew him and I don't know if he did it or not. We are trained to save lives, not take them.' Her face moved momentarily in some kind of inner conflict, but she said nothing else.

'My point,' Harry said gently, 'is that if Gorel-kin played any part in the tracking down and killing of Tobinskiy, he could have done it before. It would have made him a natural choice.'

She nodded fractionally. 'Yes, I agree. It would.'

'So where do we go from here?' said Clare. She looked nervous, as if the talk was irritating her, and was tapping the empty miniature on her knee in a furious drum-beat. 'We can't stay here forever, can we?'

'No.' Katya looked at her with sympathy, then at Harry. 'After seeing you at the wheel, I was ordered back to the FSB office in the embassy. I was questioned about my motives for going to the wheel and asked if I had arranged to meet somebody. I denied it, of course; I didn't even know Clare was here in Vienna. But they kept asking me, over and over. They checked my mobile phone, they searched my luggage, they questioned my colleague and the three banking experts we were guarding. It was only then, and the bankers all agreed that it had been entirely their idea to visit the wheel, and that I had not even mentioned it, that they seemed to believe me.'

'But?'

'They did not, of course. Mud sticks, isn't that what you say? Especially as I suspect somebody had told them about my record.' She looked angry for a moment, then continued: 'It is not often that anyone is given a second chance in the FSB – or anywhere else in our security system. One infraction and that is the end of your career.

I know there were some who believed I was guilty all along, and this would have been enough to confirm it in their minds.'

'Would Gorelkin have known?'

'Possibly, but not likely. It was all too recent for him. But he is a very experienced man; he would have made it his business to find out.' She hesitated. 'Especially, as I say, if the poison had been administered in the first place.'

The memory stick, Harry thought. Or did they have some other source of information?

'How did you get away now?'

'They let me go. They had no reason to hold me or send me back. I'm due to return to Moscow tomorrow afternoon, in any case.'

Harry walked over to the window and looked out. It was dark now, with a glitter of lights over the zigzag-pattern rooftops. He wondered what was going on out there. Were they having Katya followed? He had taken great care in bringing her here and watching out for tails, but shaking off a good surveillance team was not an exact science. Not that he could do much about that.

He turned back. 'And you're sure you don't want to go back? It's a big step.'

She shook her head. 'I'm sure.'

'What about Gorelkin's men in London?' he asked. 'Is there any way of stopping them?'

Katya frowned. 'Legally, I'm sure there is. If they have been recruited to kill a foreign national outside of the direct rules of conflict, then possibly they are acting against the constitution. Since 2010 there has been a new set of rules governing the use of force by all military and security personnel.'

'Does that include the FSB?'

She gave a thin smile. 'I cannot answer that.'

'How about a non-legal answer?'

'If they are acting under the direction of a person who is not part of a government agency, then they are classified as criminals. The only way to stop them would be by direct force.'

The words, voiced without drama or heat, seemed to lower the temperature in the room instantly.

'Then that's what we have to do.' Harry was reaching for his phone to call a cab, when it buzzed.

It was Rik.

'Bogeys are on us,' he said quietly. 'Two cars, one at each end of the street, plus two on foot. Looks like a war party, and they know exactly where we are.'

FORTY-EIGHT

'They've found us.' Harry relayed the information to the two women. He drew his gun. This really wasn't the place for a fire-fight, but he wasn't about to let any of them be taken without some kind of resistance. If these new arrivals were acting on orders from Gorelkin, then they were looking to silence Clare and anybody with her. Finding Katya would be a bonus and her future would be equally short-lived.

'That's impossible,' said Katya. She had gone pale, but looked quite calm. 'How could they know?'

'No idea – unless you were followed or have a tracker on you.'

'No.' She shook her head. 'I was not followed, I promise you. Absolutely not.'

'Then it's a tracking device. But let's get out of here first.' He went to the door and opened it a fraction. The corridor was empty. He didn't waste time checking the front window onto the street, but led the way along the corridor to the back stairs. Clare was in the middle with Katya bringing up the rear, gun still drawn.

Unlike most hotels, this one believed in making the fire stairs as comfortable as possible, with a decent carpet to deaden the sound of footsteps and lighting to make the descent easy. Harry went one floor ahead to check the way, cracking the floor doors a little each time to listen, in case the Russians had had time to insert anyone ahead of the main force arrival. But the building was quiet save for the hum of air conditioning and the occasional sound of music or voices.

They had just arrived at the ground floor where a lobby gave access to the kitchens and office, when a door to the front reception area opened and Rik appeared.

'They stopped outside for a powwow,' he told Harry quietly. 'But they haven't split up yet. I think they're waiting for orders. The two on foot are right by the front entrance. They're all in casual gear.'

Harry was still puzzled by how quickly the followers had got here. He was certain the hotel wouldn't have had any reason to tell the authorities. And if they had, the new arrivals would have been police, not men in street clothes. But there had to have been something.

He looked at Katya and said quietly, 'We can't stop here, but you need to start dumping anything that could have been fitted with a radio tag. Otherwise there's no point in us running; they'll catch us wherever we go.'

She nodded and pulled out a wallet and her mobile phone. 'I have never given my wallet to anyone. But this,' she hefted the phone. 'They took it away while I was being questioned. I think they were checking my calls and contacts.' She put her gun away and ripped off the back of the phone, and took out the battery. *'Dura!'* she swore softly. 'I'm an idiot.'

'Show me,' said Rik. He took the phone and slid out the battery. Behind it was a paper-thin disc, with a tab placed to share the phone's power supply. He took it out and handed back the phone. 'They didn't trust you much, did they? Leave this with me. I'll lose it. Come on.' He turned and went through a rear door fitted with an emergency handle, although this was down. The door was propped open by a block of wood, no doubt where the staff took their breaks.

They emerged onto a small yard piled with beer crates, aluminium casks and a stack of delivery cartons, all lit by a single overhead light. It was impressively tidy. Double gates led out onto a service alleyway running parallel to the front street. It was shut fast. Harry pointed to a door set in a high wall bordering the side of the yard. 'Where does that go?'

Rik stepped across and slid a bolt. The door opened to reveal a narrow passageway running between the buildings on either side, no doubt a left-over from when the area was criss-crossed with narrow channels to allow pedestrians easy access without venturing onto the streets.

'They'll know we went out that way,' said Clare.

'Not if it stays bolted,' said Rik. He held it open while they filed through, then closed it behind them and slid the bolt. Using one of the beer casks to stand on, he put his hands on the top of the wall and kicked the cask away before clambering up. The cask rolled away and came to rest across the yard, near the rear gates. Dropping down the other side, he trotted after the others, flicking the tracking bug away into the dark.

'Go!' Captain Yuri Symenko gave the order to his men and switched off his radio. The rest was now up to him. A chance to prove himself worthy of better things.

The team piled out of the car and crossed the pavement to join their two colleagues at the front entrance to the hotel. Four of them moved inside while two others trotted along the street to an intersection to check the rear of the building. Symenko followed at a more relaxed pace, enjoying the feel of power at the flick of a finger.

Inside the hotel, a man was sitting behind the reception desk, reading a book on French architecture.

'BVT.' After two years, Symenko's German was fluent enough to pass muster. He flashed an ID card stating that he represented the Federal Agency for State Protection and Counter-Terrorism. 'You have suspects in this hotel we wish to interview.' He produced photos of Clare Jardine and Katya Balenkova and slapped them on the counter in front of the clerk, who seemed bemused by the show of strength rather than intimidated.

'The dark haired one, yes,' he said, pointing at the picture of Jardine. 'But I've never seen the blonde one. What have they done?' He stared around at the men with Symenko, all dressed in jeans and jackets, none of them bothering to hide the automatic weapons they were carrying. They seemed to fill the space with their presence and were all staring at him in silence.

'Never mind that. Which room?'

The man told them, and stood watching as two men headed for the lift and the others took the stairs. 'Don't break anything,' he called after them, then shrugged and went back to his book. They hadn't even asked for a key. He made a note to get the cleaning ladies in early tomorrow; no doubt they'd be needed.

Upstairs, the team gathered along the corridor leading to the English woman's room and waited for Symenko to give the order to go. When he nodded, one of the men leaned across, knocked on the door and waited. No answer.

'Force it.' Symenko moved back to allow the men to kick the door in, which they did with a crash.

The room was empty. They checked every drawer and the bathroom, but there was nothing of interest.

Symenko was about to call in the results when his radio crackled.

'They went out the back.' It was one of the men outside. 'I can see them moving along an alley-way.'

'Follow them and keep them in sight. And keep this channel open.' He ordered his men out and back to the vehicles.

Symenko was smiling in eager anticipation. This was no longer a simple trace and report; it was now turning into a hot pursuit.

FORTY-NINE

'What's the plan?' asked Rik, as Harry led them across an intersection towards a darkened area in the distance. 'We're not going down in the sewers, are we? I saw that film. It gave me the creeps.'

'Relax,' Harry murmured. 'If we do I'll send one of the girls down first to shoo away the nasty spiders.'

They were passing between a seemingly end-less collection of four-and-five storey apartment blocks set back on streets that were too wide for comfort. All the Russians would have to do was hit the right street and they would be caught out in the open.

'Where are we going?' asked Katya. She seemed calm enough, but there was an air of tension about her that spoke volumes about the kind of men pursuing them.

'There's a safe house we can use,' Harry replied. 'If we can get to it. But we can't do that with them following us.' He had tried calling Richoux, but there was no response. The man's local knowledge would have been invaluable, but they were going to have to fall back on their own resources. So far they had seen no sign of a taxi, and hanging around for one to turn up was not an option. If the Russians called up reinforcements and flooded the area, it would be only a matter of time before they were seen.

Up ahead the glow from the street lights between the apartment blocks appeared to fade, showing an area of relative darkness. Harry had mentioned it to be a park near the Praterstern, a large gyratory system connecting a number of roads like spokes of a wheel. If they got to that safely, they could go under cover in the park until they managed to pick up a taxi and head south to the district of Favoriten, where the safe house was located.

'Fair enough.' Rik turned to check on Clare, who was being helped along by Katya. She had refused his help earlier, and he'd figured she was better off doing it herself if she chose.

He was about to turn back when he noticed a

flicker of movement a hundred yards away. A figure was jogging along the street, flitting in and out of the shadows. He'd seen some movement before, but had dismissed it as normal. Now he wasn't so sure.

'I'm going to drop back,' he told Harry. 'I think we've got a tail. I'll catch up at the park.'

Harry turned and looked behind them. The pursuer had vanished. 'You sure you can handle it?'

'No worries.'

'OK. Don't take all night; his buddies won't be far behind.'

Rik stepped of the street and into a small belt of trees and bushes bordering an apartment block. The trees conveniently blanked out any view of the windows above and behind him, leaving him in almost complete darkness. He allowed his breathing to settle and listened to the night, trying to block out the hum of traffic and focus instead on noises closer at hand.

He heard the man before he saw him. Whoever he was, he had a clumpy tread and was breathing heavily with a faint wheezing sound, like a worn-out prize-fighter who had encountered too many punches. Rik waited until the last second, then peered out as the man passed beneath a street light. He was short and stocky, dressed in jeans and a nylon jacket. He had close-cropped hair and a developing paunch, but walked with the resolute gait of a man accustomed to long route marches.

The glint of a weapon showed in a hip holster to one side.

As the man drew level with his hiding place, Rik stepped out and hit him across the throat with his gun.

Whatever his physical state, the man had good instincts. He moved to one side the moment he sensed trouble, lifting his forearm to block the attack and uttering a sharp expletive. But he was a fraction of a second too slow. His arm took most of the blow, but the gun barrel glanced off the solid mass of muscle and bone and thudded into his throat. He grunted and made a choking sound and pitched over backwards.

Rik bent and dragged the man into the bushes, picking up the gun which had slipped from its holster. He flipped the body over and took out the man's shoelaces, then tied his little fingers and thumbs together, palms outwards to prevent him from breaking them, and used the man's belt to secure his ankles. It wouldn't last long, but would give them breathing space to get away unseen.

He stopped, hearing footsteps approaching along the street. Another one? He waited, then heard a snuffling sound, and came face to face with a red setter ducking its head beneath the foliage. It stared at him, tongue hanging out, then whined. He wasn't sure who was most surprised, but was thankful when the dog retreated at a sharp command from a woman walking by just a few feet away.

He allowed her to move away before going back to searching the unconscious man's pockets. He felt a bulky object in the jacket. It was a shortwave radio. He made sure he didn't touch the controls and put it in his pocket to dispose of later. Then he set off after the others.

'Preshkin's not answering.' One of Captain Symenko's lieutenants, a recent addition to the team, had been monitoring the lead man's progress along the back streets. He had been getting a regular commentary by radio about the direction in which the fugitives were moving, but that had ceased, accompanied by some interference and background static. 'Hello, Preshkin. Come in,' he barked, as if to prove it.

'Leave it.' Symenko could read the signs well enough; Preshkin had pushed too far ahead and got jumped. He swore, drawing surprised looks from the men in his car. But he had good reason: they were now running blind with only a vague idea where the fugitives might be. But what if they had a car nearby? Then all his fantasies about catching foreign spies – and one clearly traitorous former FSO officer – would be so much dust.

He turned and looked into the back of the Mercedes, at a man sitting scrunched between two of his men. All was not yet lost. He had an ace up his sleeve.

'Well, Bronyev,' he muttered, 'it looks like you may have an opportunity of redeeming your failure to have spotted the treachery in your colleague, Balenkova.'

'What do you mean?' Bronyev was angry, but powerless to do anything. As an FSO officer, he had a high degree of leeway over other departments. But Symenko outranked him and his own position had been further weakened, as had been pointed out already back at the embassy, by his claim that he had no inkling of Katya Balenkova's plan to defect. He had tried arguing that it was not so far a proven defection, but that had carried no weight. If anything, it had made his situation worse.

'You worked with Balenkova. She knows you. Trusts you.' Symenko showed his teeth in a nasty grin. 'Of course, if I hadn't been told different just a short while ago, I'd even believe you were shtupping her on the side. But that's not likely, is it – eh? You know why?'

Bronyev made no answer, his face blank.

'She doesn't like men, does she?' Symenko continued. 'I bet you didn't know that, did you?'

'No.' Bronyev shook his head at a hard elbow in the ribs from the men on his left.

'No. I thought not. It seems your former colleague has a bit of history in that direction. I'm amazed she was allowed to continue serving. Still, we'll soon have her back. Then she'll find out what being a minority really means.' He tossed a mobile phone into Bronyev's lap. It was Bronyev's own. 'Call her. Tell her to come in. We'll talk ... give her a chance to explain herself. No doubt she was overcome by foreign agents and has had no opportunity to break free. That kind of shit. I'll leave it to you – you know what to say.'

'She won't talk to me. Why should she?'

Another elbow in the ribs from the man on his left made him grunt. In spite of his position, Bronyev turned his head and stared at him. The man was big and solid, with a broken nose. A professional FSB bruiser. 'You do that again and I promise you your nose will be even less attractive than it is now. I'm an officer of the FSO who has done nothing wrong, so accord me some respect.'

The man looked back at him and sniggered, his breath sour with the smell of onions. Then he followed it up with another dig of his elbow.

Symenko opened his mouth to tell his man to back off; he knew just what members of the FSO were capable of, especially at close quarters. He'd seen plenty of their kind in his time, passing through this city with powerful and important men. And Bronyev was right – he had done nothing wrong.

He was too late.

Without a flicker of warning, Bronyev rammed his own elbow upwards at an angle, using his torso to gain full torque and pushing his bunched fist with his free hand for maximum effect. The result was catastrophic for his attacker; his nose, already badly abused, took the full force of Bronyev's blow, which snapped his head backwards into the roof of the car. A rush of blood sprayed down the front of the man's jacket, but he was beyond caring, and lolled loosely in his seat like a stringless puppet.

Bronyev didn't stop there. Sensing the man on his right beginning to move, he thrust his hand down between the man's legs and grasped a handful of his testicles, and squeezed.

The man froze, eyes going wide.

'Enough,' said Bronyev softly, eyes on Symenko. The captain looked stunned by the speed of his reactions. 'This is unnecessary and you know it, captain. I have it within my right to report you and your men for brutality against a fellow officer.'

Symenko nodded. 'Yes. Of course. I was about to stop him.' He glared at the man on Bronyev's right, who stopped wincing long enough to signal that he was not moving.

'Good.' Bronyev released the man and picked up the phone. He hit a speed dial number and waited while it rang out.

FIFTY

'It's Bronyev, my colleague.' Katya had switched on her mobile as they approached the end of the street. Seconds later it had buzzed. She had taken it out and was staring at the screen. 'They're using him to try to get to me.'

Harry looked past her and Clare, and saw Rik jogging along the street towards them. He was moving easily and had clearly suffered no damage.

They were standing beneath some trees on the edge of a small park not far from Riesenradplatz and the giant wheel. Between them lay the dual carriageway that was Ausstellungsstrasse, running east-west and connecting to the Praterstern gyratory. It was wide and too well lit, and still busy with traffic – an enormous gulf if the Russians had men staking out the most obvious points to watch.

'Can you trust him?' Harry asked.

'I don't know. I think so, but...' She shrugged. 'He will be under pressure to help them. I've put him in a terrible position.'

'Forget it. It's done. He can't do anything for you now.' He was aware that it sounded harsh, but he knew what the situation would have been like had their positions been reversed. The man commanding the pursuers was responding with whatever he had to hand in order to reel them in; and that included leaning on Katya's former colleague.

A few minutes ago he had called the number of the taxi company on the card from the amusement arcade. Then he had tried Richoux one more time. Still nothing. The lack of response wasn't good news; local assets like Richoux were chosen for their knowledge, contacts and reliability, in case an operative needed help on the ground. That help ranged from the provision of equipment, like guns and a safe place to stay, to simple background information on a place or a person which only a local resident could pick up. If an asset was indisposed for any reason, there was always a backup message to explain it. Going off-line in the way Richoux had done meant that he had been intercepted and blown.

End of game.

'Can they lock in on your mobile?' He was aware that some phones had anti-tracking devices. He'd never seen the point, since software development invariably put the ungodly just one shade behind the good. But using a mobile that was open to triangulation or tracking the signal would be a sure way of being caught very quickly. And Katya's colleagues would almost certainly have a search going on right now for her signal.

'No. The risk is too great for FSO protection officers. All our phones are fitted with blocking software.' She looked at him with a faint smile. 'Don't you have it in your department?'

'I don't have a department. Life's much simpler that way.'

As Rik joined them, a light coloured Mercedes cruised to the kerb and stopped. It was a taxi. The driver looked across at them with a questioning lift of the head. Stopping for an unknown pick-up on the edge of a park was a risky business in any city, even Vienna. But taxi drivers have to make a living, too.

Clare stepped into the light, her arm through Katya's. The driver nodded and beckoned them aboard, listened to the destination Harry gave him, and set off for the Praterstern and the south.

The area known as Favoriten was a mixed residential and commercial zone, the cultures of its residents leaning heavily in favour of Turks, Croatians and Serbians, all workers who had populated the area over many decades. The safe house had been chosen, Harry guessed, for this very reason. In an area where incomers were frequent and varied, and their backgrounds often too obviously tragic to question, nobody would pay much attention to a few more moving among them. Hopefully, it would only be for one night, before moving out again the following day.

He got the driver to drop them off not far from the exit from the A23, which ran north-south through the district, near a collection of large apartment blocks. They waited for the Mercedes to disappear before turning and following Harry along the street to one block of five set among parkland.

'We should check it out first,' cautioned Rik, as they surveyed the building from the shadows beneath a belt of trees. It was neat, bland and four storeys high, with bedding and washing blowing out from verandas along its length. Nearly every window showed a light, testament to the working day being over and a sign of normality. But entering this place without care was asking for trouble, especially with Richoux having gone silent.

Harry agreed. 'I'll go with Katya. You stay here with Clare.'

He and Katya set off, walking close and slowly, like a couple returning home, their bags and the briefcase close enough to resemble shopping to throw anyone off-guard. Once off the street they followed a neat pathway to the main entrance, and inside, used the stairs. Both had their hands on their guns, aware that if trouble was waiting for them, they would have split seconds to react and fight their way out.

The apartment that was their safe house was on the first floor. They walked past it once, studying the lock for signs of a forced entry. It looked good, and after reaching the end of the corridor, they turned and went back.

Harry knocked while Katya stood to one side. No answer.

He inserted the key and pushed the door. It stuck for a second, then opened, releasing a gust of warm, stale air. Harry stepped inside, dropping his bag and moving swiftly forward along a short hallway into an open living room. Katya slid past him and checked out a bedroom, kitchen and bathroom.

'Clear,' she said, and returned to join him.

Harry dialled Rik's number and gave the all-clear to come in.

'We need food,' said Katya. 'I saw a store along the next street where we were dropped off.'

Harry nodded. It made sense. Going out in a group to eat would attract attention. They were clearly not Turkish, and their clothes in a well-lit restaurant would mark them out immediately as foreigners, and therefore a subject of interest. 'Good idea. Cold meats, preferably, and bread. Coffee, too.' He held up his mobile. 'I need to make a couple of calls.'

Katya nodded and went out.

As soon as Rik and Clare arrived, Harry dialled Ballatyne's number. It rang without answer. He tried again in case he'd misdialled. Still no response.

'Problem?' Rik was standing by the kitchen door, watching him. Clare had gone into the bathroom.

'Could be, but I don't know what. Ballatyne

isn't picking up.'

Rik delved into his bag and opened his iPad, waiting for a connection. Seconds later, he was tapping away one-handed on the screen's virtual keyboard.

'What are you doing?' Harry queried.

'Just checking something. Won't be a minute.'

Harry left him to it and took a walk round the apartment. He wondered how many people had used this place before. It was minimally furnished, with two single beds, chairs, table, small sofa and cupboards. No carpet but a simple tiled floor. It reminded him of British army accommodation around the world: basic, unfussy, plain and cheerless. There was probably a specialist department somewhere in Whitehall, with an order book full of details about such furniture very similar to this.

He turned off the room lights before approaching the windows, and checked the view of the parkland and street outside as carefully as he could. There was too much shadow and darkness to be certain of anything, however. He considered that ironic seeing as how he had been relying on that very thing to survey the apartment building before coming in.

Rik appeared in the doorway to the bedroom, waving his iPad. 'Six have had a system shutdown. They issued an inter-agency security statement two hours ago saying all non-essential comms channels have been suspended for security checks. It includes a short-term interruption to most call networks.'

'What does that mean?'

313

'Sounds like they've been hacked. But it could be they're tracking down the insider. It would explain why Ballatyne's been out of touch.'

'How did you get this?' He knew Rik wouldn't have had time to get into any of the security agency systems, and nor would Six have gone public with the situation. The one thing you don't do is alert your enemies to the fact that you've suffered a system meltdown.

Rik smiled. 'Friend of a friend. Don't worry, I didn't hack into Six.'

Harry said he was going downstairs to check the outside more closely, and left the apartment, scanning the corridor carefully before stepping out. He passed the doors to other apartments, where for many, life was going on as usual; an argument in one, music from another, a child crying, a football match commentary.

He left the building and walked along one of the paths, passing two Muslim women with a baby buggy and shopping bags, their heads covered in hijabs. Once they had gone, he stepped off the path and melted into the trees. Then he stood and breathed in the atmosphere, using his senses to tune in to the night.

Cars passed along the street nearby, and there was a steady roar from the A23 dual carriageway which they had joined to bring them down from the city centre. But there was nothing that suggested there was anybody here who shouldn't be – except maybe himself and the others.

He wondered what Katya was doing.

FIFTY-ONE

Katya was standing outside a small Turkish-run general store, studying the street. She was clutching a plastic bag of groceries in one hand, while the other was inside her jacket, resting on the butt of her gun.

The weapon, a slim-line PSM 6.35mm pistol, issued on arrival by the embassy's security armourer, was designed to sit snugly beneath the jackets of personnel of both genders. It felt uncomfortably small compared with her usual service weapon, a heavier Viking MP-446 9mm. She had used the PSM before, but never in a hot action, and never out on the street. Right now, it left her feeling vulnerable and exposed. If anyone decided to launch an attack on her out here, she would have felt better prepared with a heavier weapon carrying more punch.

She walked away from the store towards a darker area at the end of the building, and took out her mobile. What she was about to do was crazy, and she knew Tate, the Englishman, would advise her against it. But she had no choice. If she could find out who was ranged against them, and what they knew, it gave her a better chance of getting out of this city with her life, or locked up in a cell awaiting a trial back in Moscow. In aligning herself with Clare and her colleagues, she had already gone too far to turn back now.

The truth was, she didn't want to go back. Whatever her life had been was over. From here on in, the future would be whatever she could make of it, with Clare, hopefully.

But to do that, she had to live. They all did.

She sent a text message to Bronyev consisting of a single dot. Her number would not show up on his mobile, but he would know it was her. They had once discussed a colleague using it to get a friend to call her back when needing back-up or an escape from a clingy or boring compan-ion – a dating SOS. If anyone with Bronyev should see the dot, it would look like an incom-plete or blank call from an unknown number.

She waited for him to call back, sinking into the shadows of a doorway and watching the street. There was no way they could trace the call, but she didn't know how clean of telltale signals Clare and her two friends were. If either one of them used their mobile and the local FSB unit somehow got a trace on it, they would be here within twenty minutes.

Her phone buzzed. A dot and a question mark.

It was Bronyev. He was asking where she was. She smiled. More than that, he hadn't given her away. If he had, he'd have called her, tried to keep her talking and find out where she was. And every moment she spent on the line would reduce their chances of remaining free. The downside was that in using this brief communi-cation, he was also telling her that his freedom was severely restricted.

At least he was still in one piece and not confined to a locked room in the embassy basement.

She wondered what to do. Ironically, neither of them could communicate freely now. She because whoever was with Bronyev would be waiting for just that event; Bronyev because he would be being watched.

She had to get back to the apartment building. Tate and the others would be getting anxious about how long she had been gone now. She was about to put the mobile back in her pocket when it buzzed again. She checked the screen.

'888'

She frowned, then went cold. Bronyev had once told her that his mother had studied numerology, and had talked about it often with her son, explaining the importance of numbers in spiritual matters. All numbers meant something, he had explained to Katya, and had gone through a list from 0 to 9 and their repeat sequences. She'd forgotten most of the list because it meant nothing to her. But 888 had stuck because it had once been her mother's apartment number in the concrete housing block where she had lived and died several years ago. Too lacking in imagination to name the blocks after anyone interesting, such as heroes of the former Soviet Union, the then Cold War authorities had settled instead on the dull conformity of numbers.

Apartment 88 in Block 8. 888.

In spirituality, the three numbers 888 meant a phase in one's life was about to end – a warning so that one could be prepared. She recalled telling Bronyev at the time that he was being over-imaginative. Numbers were to be added and subtracted, not feared. Anyway, she hadn't wanted to think about her mother dying alone in that place while she had forged a career in the FSO.

Bronyev hadn't argued, but had smiled indulgently, something which had made her think he was more spiritual than their superiors might approve of. For a man whose job was to potentially kill in order to protect the lives of others, it could be seen as a sign of weakness.

She swallowed and wondered if she wasn't now imagining things.

888. The numbers glowed in the poor light.

Then she heard the car engine.

In this part of the city she was pretty certain that 4X4 Mercedes of the type she had seen used by the FSB simply did not exist. The vehicles were highly tuned as a matter of course, with reinforced glass and panels, and she could pick out one of their engines quite easily in a quiet location such as this. The only cars she had seen here so far had been standard road models, small and mostly in poor condition and badly maintained.

But not this one.

It appeared at the end of the street, slowed and stopped, one indicator winking. A gleaming black M-Class vehicle with tinted windows and heavy duty tyres. She knew there would be at least four men inside, all armed.

She stepped back into deeper shadow, her stomach going cold. Somehow they had found her. Worrying about how was a problem for later, if ever. Right now she had to warn the others. Warn Clare.

She began to dial the number, panic for a moment making her forget whose phone she was ringing – Clare's or Tate's?

Her own phone started ringing, and she jumped.

At that moment a man stepped out of the Mercedes down the street. She shrank back against the wall, shielding the light from her mobile behind her, and scrabbled at the keyboard to shut it off.

She managed to hit the 'off' key and the ringing ceased. But it was too late. The man by the Mercedes had swung round and was looking towards her. She recognised the stance: that of a hunter sniffing the wind. Then he turned and muttered something to the others in the car.

The doors opened and three more men stepped out. One had a gun in his hand, the street lighting glinting off the barrel. The others would be similarly armed.

They weren't here to take her back, then.

She dropped the bag of groceries and started running.

FIFTY-TWO

Harry stared down at his mobile. He'd rung Katya to find out where she was. It had been ringing out, then stopped in mid-ring. It could only mean one thing: she was in trouble.

He started moving across the parkland towards the streets where Katya had seen the store. She must have seen something. Or somebody. But why kill the phone without answering? It could only mean she wasn't in a position to pick up. He used the trees for cover, jogging through an area heavy with bushes into a clearing with a bench and a picnic table. A single light threw a pale glow over a play pit full of sand and a makeshift see-saw. A child's football lay punctured to one side, and a coil of rope, abandoned until another child found a use for them.

A small car clattered by on the other side of the next line of trees, beyond some bushes, its muffler stuttering and throaty. He slowed and drew his gun. He was close to the road and guessed the store must be nearby.

A man's voice called out in the dark, unintelligible. Another answered, then came the sound of footsteps receding. They were light, fast. Running.

A woman.

As Harry ducked through the trees he caught the hum of a car engine coming closer. It sounded powerful, high-performance, unlike the rust-bucket he'd heard moments before. Then came the crunch of tyres on gravel. Whatever it was, it was heavy.

The man shouted again. This time Harry understood the word.

'*Skoree*!' Hurry.

Russian.

Damn. *How the hell had they found this place?* But the answer was obvious: Richoux. He was the only person who knew where the safe house was located. He must have talked. Pushing the thought away, he focussed on the sound of running feet. It had to be Katya they were after. If so, he had to intervene somehow, to give her a chance to get away.

As he brushed aside a hanging clump of foliage, he saw a black Mercedes 4X4 standing in the street in front of him, the engine ticking over. The front passenger door was hanging open, and he could see the driver holding a radio or phone to his mouth. There was a burst of conversation and static. There were no passengers, though. They must have decamped to go after Katya.

Then a man stepped out from behind the 4X4 and scanned the parkland. He was strongly built and dressed in jeans and a nylon jacket. He had a gun down by his side in one hand, a radio in the other. He was coordinating the search.

His head swivelled away, eyes brushing across where Harry was standing, checking the scenery

321

for movement, his job to watch for interference and direct his colleagues. There was no reaction for a split second, and Harry thought the man had missed him.

Then his head snapped round again.

The gun came up and the man went into a crouch, instincts and training driving him.

Harry responded in the same fashion. He dropped away to his right knee and moved sideways all in one movement, allowing his body to roll. He felt grass beneath him, smelled the musky aroma of dead foliage; heard a shot and felt the air shift as the bullet snapped past his head. Then he was coming up again, this time with his gun held in front of him, the butt cupped in his left hand, a move he had practised many times before. The barrel centred on the Russian, and stopped. The man stared in disbelief at having missed, his mouth open as he tried to bring his gun across to centre on the target.

Harry absorbed the scene automatically, running the details through his head. The man was standing against the 4X4; a solid body mass; nowhere for the bullet to go afterwards; no pedestrians in danger. No options but to shoot.

He squeezed the trigger twice.

The Walther sounded horribly loud, the gunshots echoing all around him and battering the air. He wondered how good the local cops were at responding to late-night gunfire. Not great, he hoped; they needed time to get clear and away.

The Russian was slammed back against the 4X4, dropping his weapon. For a second he hung there, scrabbling with his feet to stay upright.

Then the massive shock invaded his system, overpowering his muscles and co-ordination, and he slid sideways and hit the ground.

Harry turned and ran. He wouldn't get a better chance. Staying on the grass, he used the trees to give himself cover from the street and the driver of the 4X4, who was shouting for backup. Dodging through the bushes, he kept the street within sight, wondering how far away Katya was now. She was young and fit, and would cover the ground quickly. But the men following, if the 4X4 had been full, would split up, reducing her chances of escape in an area that was wide open with few hiding places on the streets, unless she was lucky enough to find an open door.

He hit an open space and saw a junction in the street ahead, and fifty yards further on, a bulky figure trotting along, hugging an apartment block. The man was carrying a gun.

Harry whistled. The man didn't hear him at first, so he whistled again, and ran for the trees on the far side of the open space. It put him in a shooting gallery, and the man didn't waste time in responding. He turned and fired twice, then again. But the shots didn't come near, the man's aim spoiled by his body twisting.

Harry hit the trees and carried on through. The gunman would no doubt expect him to stay still, using the cover to wait for pursuit and pick off anyone who followed. But that wasn't the game plan. He angled towards the street and burst out of the trees, and saw the gunman crouched in the angle of the building, waiting to take a shot. But he was looking slightly off, his gun following his

323

line of sight.

Harry fired once, aiming low. He didn't expect to hit the man, but to scare him. It worked. The man shouted and jumped as the wall beside him erupted into fragments with the force of the bullet, then turned and scurried back in the direction he'd come from.

Katya was running along a wide street, her footsteps echoing off the nearest building, her breathing coming louder as her energy levels diminished. Somehow her instincts had deserted her, and she had made a wrong turn. Now she was in a wide space, almost a boulevard between two large apartment blocks with no obvious cover. If she didn't get off this street soon, they would catch her. Or simply use her as target practice and shoot her down.

She saw an opening in the building on her right. It looked like an access way for maintenance vehicles to get into the heart of the building, where rubbish was dumped down chutes for collection. But when she turned into it, she saw it was a tunnel running through the building to the other side. Maybe there was a doorway down there, somewhere she could hide until they gave up and moved on.

She ran into the gloom. There were only a couple of dim lights on the wall to show the way, and she slowed her pace to avoid obstacles. At the end of the tunnel she could see a boulevard just like the one she had left. It wasn't much better than where she had come from, but it was a chance; perhaps the only one she had.

Then, with just twenty yards to go, a man stepped around the corner and into the light.

It was Bronyev.

FIFTY-THREE

Katya gave a cry of despair. This wasn't supposed to end this way! All that training, all the set-piece exercises at the academy, the live firing, all the scenarios they had gone through over and over again to speed up reactions to events like this.

She skidded to a halt, bringing up her gun, her breath catching harshly in her throat as she tried to swallow against the dryness. She felt exhausted, as much by fear as by the running, a counter to the adrenalin rush earlier when she had first seen the men arrive.

She stared at Bronyev, wondering what he was doing here. Deep down, though, she knew there could be only one reason: he knew her better than anyone else, and had been ordered to bring her back. She desperately didn't want to shoot a close colleague, a man who had trained in exactly the same way as her and with the same beliefs; but right now she was faced with no choice. If he tried to stop her, she would have to shoot. There was too much to lose otherwise.

'Wait!' Bronyev was holding his hands out from his sides, his voice low and urgent. 'I'm not here to stop you, Katya.' He looked, in spite of the situation, relaxed and in control, yet wary. And she realised that he hadn't got his gun out.

'Why not?' she asked, gulping air. The gun felt slippery with sweat in her hand, its slim shape like a toy. 'It's your job. You have to do it.'

'Yours, too. Or had you forgotten?' He was breathing visibly too, although whether from the chase or nerves, she couldn't tell.

'Was,' she replied, and sagged against the nearest wall. 'The job changed, you know? Things changed.' That made her sound idiotic. She couldn't explain and didn't have time. He probably wouldn't understand, anyway. He was infinitely more of a product of the system than she was.

'Like the English woman?'

Katya felt herself go cold. *He knew?*

'What do you mean?' An automatic form of denial. It was all she could think of to say.

'Come off it, Katya. Sorry – I suppose I should call you lieutenant. But I'm not a fool. I heard the rumours about your...' He paused and waved a vague hand.

'Indiscretion? It's all right, you can say it.' She risked a glance over her shoulder. If the other men showed up now, she was dead.

'Yes, that. And that's all they are for the most part – rumours. Not to me, though. I have a sister who's gay, you see, so I know. But I couldn't care less. There are some up the ladder who think you'll get it out of your system one day and ... well, get your focus back. Daft, I know.' He shrugged and looked embarrassed at the absurdity of it.

Katya nearly laughed. God in heaven, what a bunch of dinosaurs! Could they really be that stupid? Did they think she was possessed of a *fever*? Didn't they know this was the twenty-first century? That there were actually gays in modern Russia, just like the rest of the world?

'It's not entirely their fault,' said Bronyev sympathetically. 'They actually want to believe we're all perfect citizens, fitting the world they have created for us.'

'There's no such thing,' Katya snapped. 'Any fool knows that. Don't they ever look around them?'

'Outside the FSO, probably not. You're right. But they *want* us to be perfect, that's my point. Makes them look good.'

'Christ, what are you, Bronyev – a closet sociologist? That's worse than being gay!'

He smiled. 'Just trying to make my way, that's all. And to help you.'

'So why this chat? Are you telling me you're sympathetic?'

'Why not? Like I said, my sister's gay – and she'd never forgive me if I told her I'd stood in your way or tried to bring you in.' He cleared his throat, and Katya thought he looked a little sad. 'I love my sister, you see. I look out for her. I know how tough it is for her every day, everywhere she goes. We live in a very unforgiving place, you know that?' He looked around, checking the space behind him. 'Thing is, saying that makes me less than perfect, too, in their eyes. Join the club, huh?'

She stared at him, wondering if he wasn't simply trying to string her along, to get her to drop her guard. But he merely looked back, waiting. Then she knew he was speaking the truth. And wondered how she'd never realised before. No wonder he had never come onto her, never tried to share down-time with her on assignments when their charges were tucked up safely in their hotels or embassies, or handed over to the care of another team. Not once had he made an improper remark or stepped over the line the way so many other men did, their intentions thinly coated in coarse humour. Somehow she had got used to that, being part of the barrack room system, knowing from early on that to respond in a negative fashion every time would mark her out for ever more ugly treatment as word got around that she could be easily wound up.

'All because of your sister?'

'Yes. Our parents freaked out when she told them. It was ugly for a while. But they've been wonderful ever since.' He shrugged. 'Not that they can talk about it much. It's fine by me, but tough for them, I suppose.'

She felt as if she were in a dream. First thinking Bronyev was a threat, then finding out he wasn't. Now realising he'd known all along. And said nothing.

'So what do we do now?'

'*We* do nothing. You get out of here. I, of course, like a diligent FSO officer, will scour the city for my deviant colleague who I wish wasn't leaving because ... well, because.' He sighed and waved a hand. 'Of course, I won't find her, and they'll send another team out to look for you. I'll get a roasting for not watching you more carefully and realising what a threat you were, but in the end what can they do?' He looked sad once more. 'You realise you'll never be able to come back, don't you?'

'I know.' It was something that hadn't been voiced before; something she hadn't even thought about. The simple enormity of hearing it now hit her like a sledgehammer. But she knew instantly that it was the right thing – the only thing – to do. Anyway, unlike Bronyev, she had no family. 'Thank you for the warning, by the way.'

He grinned. 'Hey – no biggie, as the Americans would say. See, I knew the numbers would come in useful some day.'

'But not for this.'

'No, not for this. Just you be careful and don't get brought back in chains. I'd hate to have to stand up in court and speak out against you.' He nodded at the street behind her. 'I'm going to walk past you and out the other side. You go the other way.'

'All right. Are you sure?'

'Of course. I'll look back when I get to the end.' He swallowed. 'Don't be here when I do.'

She smiled and felt a flood of emotion, and wanted to throw her arms around him. But she knew that would be fatal. He was telling her to go. Before he changed his mind.

'Will you be OK?'

'Me? Hell, yes, I expect so. Once the fuss is

over I'll probably get promoted.' He hesitated, then said, 'I never told you who my father is.'

'No. Does it make a difference?'

'His name is Dmitry Alexandrovich Bronyev, General Lieutenant of the Land Army Eastern Command. Only a handful of people know that. And that's how I'd like to keep it. Now you know, so don't let me down. He'd be really pissed if this got out.'

She felt as if her head was in a spin. She'd never made the connection of the names before; in any case, scions of top army officers weren't supposed to become bodyguards, willing to throw themselves in front of their charges at the first hint of danger. No wonder Bronyev was better than a normal recruit; with a father like his, he'd have been absorbing and absorbed in the military life ever since he was old enough to open his eyes.

'I won't tell anyone.'

There was nothing more to say. She watched as he approached her, and as he walked by, lifted a hand in a brief salute.

Then he was gone, and she walked quickly away in the opposite direction, her footsteps echoing his.

FIFTY-FOUR

Harry jogged back into cover and waited for Katya to appear, squatting to get a view of the ground below the level of the hanging foliage. He was looking for movement where there shouldn't be any. It was pointless going any further in search of her; she could have gone in any direction and he would have to trust her to get back to the apartment somehow. All he could do was watch for the men to return this way.

Once he was certain of being alone, he rang Rik.

'Jesus, was that you?' the younger man said. 'It sounded like a war zone out there. You could have called me to help.'

'No point. It would have given them another target. But they're now one down and smarting, so they'll be back.'

'How do you think they found us?'

'Richoux, is my bet. Them turning up here is no coincidence.'

'Unless Katya's carrying another tag.'

'If so, they'd have found us earlier. But if she shows up, check her out.'

'Will do. What do we do now?'

'Stay put but be ready to move. There was only one car, but I doubt that will last.'

'Got it. I suppose you didn't manage to find Starbucks while you were out, did you? I could kill for an Americano.'

'You and me both.' Harry switched off and took another look around. Very quiet. And not even a police response to the shooting. That could work in their favour if they had to move; being seen out on the streets following a shooting was a sure-fire way of being picked up.

Then he saw her.

Katya was moving through the trees, stopping at intervals to scout ahead. She was heading for the apartment building. She didn't look hurt, so he guessed she must have outrun her pursuers. He followed, angling away so that he could watch her back, until he reached the open space and the pathway leading to the building entrance.

He followed her in, then waited just inside, eyes on his back trail. No movement, but it didn't mean they weren't out there, watching.

He rang Rik to warn him that he was on his way, then scooted up the stairs and tapped on the door. He found Katya inside, hugging Clare unselfconsciously. They turned as he walked in.

'There was shooting,' Katya said. She sounded surprised. 'What happened?'

He told them in brief detail. Katya said nothing on learning that one of the FSB men had gone down, and agreed to allow Rik to check her clothing when Harry explained about how fast the pursuers had got there.

'I don't think it's you,' he told her. 'But we need to leave here now, and I don't want them following us to the airport.'

'Is that wise?' Katya asked. 'They will be there already, in case we try to fly out.'

'Do they have enough men?'

'Yes.' She looked sombre. 'For this they will have called in more. In any case, it is too late now to get a flight.'

She was right. With everything that had been happening, he'd lost track of time. They had to find another way.

They left the apartment and found another way down which took them through the basement and up the other side in case the Russians were waiting. Rik went ahead to scout the area leading to the main streets and pick up a taxi.

On the way, Harry's phone rang.

It was Ballatyne.

'What happened to you? Is everyone all right?'

'Fine so far,' said Harry. 'But you need a new local asset in Vienna.'

'I heard about Richoux.' Ballatyne sounded tired. 'Sorry, I've been a bit tied up here. We had a total shutdown and I've been fire-fighting most of the day. Richoux left his apartment late this afternoon and nobody's seen him since. His girlfriend said he emptied his bank account and told her he wouldn't be back. He didn't say why.'

'He's got new friends, that's why.'

'It figures. We've already rolled up the network over there. They'll be replaced as soon as we can get new faces in place.'

'They know about the safe house, so we're getting out of here now. I'll tell you the rest later. But we can't use the airport at Schwechat; they'll have it sealed up tight.'

'Hang on.' There was a muffled silence, then he came back moments later. 'Right. You need to get to Wiener Neustadt Ost. It's a civilian airfield forty kilometres south of Vienna. I'll have to use up some favours but I'll have a military flight waiting tomorrow morning.'

'Good. Tell them we'll have one extra.'

'Balenkova?'

'Yes. She needs full entry and protection. She won't be going home again.'

'You know the powers that be will want a quid pro quo from her?'

'Good luck with that.'

'Thanks. Call me when you get in,' he added curtly. 'We need a debrief.'

In London, in the Mayfair office where they had held their first meeting, Sergei Gorelkin was raging. News that Jardine was still at large had been compounded by hearing that Katya Balenkova had defected and the FSB team sent after her was a man down.

'Federal Protective Service officers do *not* defect, Symenko!' he shouted down the phone, slamming a fist down on the table. 'The FSB does not *lose* personnel!' He gripped the handset hard enough to crush it, eyes glinting like pieces of ice. 'This is unacceptable! If you do not find these women and the men helping them, I will have you replaced, do you hear me?'

Across the table from him, Lieutenant Votrukhin and Sergeant Serkhov stayed very still. To comment now, even to move at the wrong moment, would be to invite disaster. They felt a measure of sympathy for the man Symenko, on the other end of the phone, but only insofar as his being the focus of Gorelkin's anger meant they, for the time being, were not. They knew, however, that it would not last for long. If Jardine and Balenkova managed to get back to London, their peaceful world would shatter in an instant.

'Fucking idiots!' Gorelkin slammed the phone down, bouncing it clear across the table so that Serkhov had to retrieve it. 'You two had better upgrade your efforts, I can tell you. That incompetent donkey Symenko won't be able to stop them leaving Vienna, which means they will be back here by tomorrow at the latest.'

'Might they decide to go somewhere else instead?' said Votrukhin hopefully, who was wishing he could get on a plane to Moscow right now. Anything was better than staying with this sinking ship. He was now in full agreement with Serkhov; that Gorelkin was following some kind of secret agenda, and they were trapped like flies in his web until he let them go. Worse, he couldn't help but feel that Gorelkin had finally lost control of the situation, and he and Serkhov were in danger of being dragged down with him. But getting out was not a luxury they could afford.

'No. They will come back here. You must redouble your efforts to find Jardine.' He rubbed at the side of his jaw. It was the first sign of nerves that the two men had seen in him, renewing their concern about what this operation had turned into. 'This cannot be allowed to go any further,' he muttered. 'We must end this now.'

'And if we don't?' said Votrukhin. 'We don't even know where they are. And every day we stay in London is a day closer to our being identified.'

'Don't!' Gorelkin snapped. 'I will not have defeatist talk! This is vital work, much more so than either of you two clods can imagine. Now get out there and do your jobs!'

Votrukhin stood up, an angry retort on his lips. But Serkhov grabbed his arm and stopped him.

The two men walked out without a word, leaving Gorelkin staring at something very far away.

FIFTY-FIVE

'What do you want, Ballatyne? I'm busy.' Candida Deane barely looked up as Ballatyne stepped into her office, focussing instead on a file she was reading. The soft lighting, essential for all the inner offices of SIS Headquarters like this one, made her features seem less harsh than normal, as if she had been airbrushed.

'Just a chat.' Ballatyne wasn't fooled by the businesslike tone; she was puzzled by his appearance. He pushed the door closed behind him, something that he knew would put her nerves further on edge. Other than the required briefings and meetings which brought all department and desk heads together, he and Deane rarely had reason to speak alone. Even with everything surrounding the Russian hit team and their attempt on Clare Jardine, their encounters had rarely been without other heads involved, and therefore somewhat impersonal.

He sat down without being asked, and crossed his legs, flicking away some imaginary dust. He glanced around the office, which was not yet hers until her superior gave his final notice, and saw signs of her already settling in; a few books, a set of tiny hand-painted Matryoshka dolls, some photographs of foreign places.

'About what?' She put down the file and sat back.

'Your meeting with George Paulton, for one.'

She stared at him, her face showing no emotion, then said, 'I have no idea what you're talking about. Why would I meet with him?'

'That's what I would like to know.' He reached into his jacket pocket and produced a single photo. 'But before you go all girly and deny it, take a look at this.' He dropped the photo on the desk in front of her.

It showed Deane standing in St James's Park. Alongside her was George Paulton.

'It's a fake.'

'Of course it is.' Ballatyne allowed a full measure of sarcasm to coat his voice, and put his hands together. 'As was, I suppose, the old man who jogged by at one point. He was dressed in jogging gear and wearing enormous headphones. He looked as if he was about to die. In fact Paulton was quite rude about him; said something about not having a gun – I have the full transcript which I can give you, but I can see by your expression that you don't need it.'

Her eyes were like ice and her voice just as frosty. 'What do you want?'

'Please let me finish. The old chap's name is Emil Panowski. He was one of the best Cold War field operatives we ever had, did you know that? You should look him up in the archives. He used to cross the Berlin Wall back and forth like a rat up a drainpipe. He still does the occasional job for us where we need an invisible presence. He's getting on for eighty, you know.' He sniffed. 'He had a full sound recording on you the moment Paulton showed up. Very interesting it was, too.'

'I don't believe you.' Deane had gone quite pale, he noted, but she was still defiant.

'Really?' He took a small digital recorder out of his top pocket. 'Perhaps this will convince you.' He pressed play and Deane's voice echoed into the room in a sequence of brief utterances.

'I think I know where the Jardine woman is.'

'Tell me I'm wrong, droog.'

'Find Tate, you'll find Jardine.'

'And when I do?' It was Paulton's voice this time, before switching back to Deane.

'Don't be coy, George. You know what I mean.'

And finally.

'Whatever you do to her, it had better be permanent.'

Ballatyne switched off the recorder. 'I got my boys to do a bit of simple editing, I admit, but I think you'll agree, it's a game changer. This little selection alone puts you in a meeting with a wanted traitor and enemy of this country; it shows you had knowledge of events and facts that you have chosen not to share with an on-going investigation; and you actively sought the murder of a former MI6 officer – all as a means of gaining promotion. Or did I get the wrong end of the stick?'

Deane's voice, when she spoke, was shaky. 'So why haven't you used it? You want Paulton and the Russians for yourself, is that it? Grab all the glory for yourself?'

'I couldn't care less about Paulton. He's finished, anyway, as I'm sure he must know by now. If Gorelkin doesn't get him, Harry Tate will.'

'But?'

'But he has his uses until then and that's what I'm focussing on. I want to know where he is.'

'How would I know that?'

'Because you're not stupid, that's why. You had one of your tails on him from the moment you first met. You've had him followed and pinned down ever since. Paulton's good, but he's been out of the game too long, unlike your young shadows.' He stood up. 'I'll do you a trade. Give me Paulton and I'll sit on this recording. And you do nothing – and I mean *nothing* – to warn him or to make a move against me.'

She made an ugly noise. 'Like I should trust you.'

'I agree it's a bit one-sided, but that's the offer. Take it or leave it.'

He walked to the door without waiting for her answer, and let himself out.

FIFTY-SIX

'What is this place?' Katya Balenkova looked
with suspicion at the oak panels and heavy
pictures on the wall, made drab by a yellowish
light coming in from the outside. It was the room
in Great Scotland Yard where Harry had attended
the meeting with Ballatyne and the various
security-related committees. She sat down
gingerly between Harry and Rik. Clare was on
her way to a private clinic arranged by Ballatyne,
to undergo some tests. She had, in any case,
refused to attend anywhere official after arriving
back from Vienna, on the simple grounds that
she didn't trust Ballatyne or any of his sort not to
lock her up and throw away the key.

'We call it Room one-oh-one,' said Ballatyne, settling in his seat at the head of the long
table.

Katya gave him a flinty smile. 'Of course.
Where nasty things happen. How appropriate.'

'You've read Orwell?'

'Of course. It was how we learned about life in
the west.'

Ballatyne realised that she was laughing at
him. 'How droll. Don't worry, the only nasty
thing likely to happen here is if you drink the tea.
They use it down in Portsmouth to de-scale the

hulls of clapped-out destroyers.' He tapped the table, attracting the attention of Harry and Rik, John Crampton of the Met Police CO19 team, a young male official with a notepad and a lean and tanned individual seated at the far end, dressed in a plain suit straining at the shoulders. 'Shall we get on?'

'Who's the strong silent type?' Rik was the first to speak, jerking a thumb towards the man at the end.

'He's an observer,' said Ballatyne. 'Hopefully we won't need his services, so introductions aren't necessary. Our singular purpose for holding this meeting is to find a way of locating and stopping the two FSB operatives who killed Tobinskiy and tried to eliminate Miss Jardine. Beyond that, we do not go.' He glanced at Katya. 'Miss Balenkova, I understand your position; you don't wish to operate against your countrymen, although it seems to me that you're already doing that by being here. However, your presence here is a courtesy. You are not expected to take part in any direct action.'

'I understand.'

Ballatyne shuffled two pieces of paper and continued. 'We now have identifiable footage of the two men we believe assassinated Roman Tobinskiy in King's College. The same two men subsequently raided the hospital's security control centre and shot the guard after taking the hard drive to the cameras. They were then filmed both inside and coming away from Starbucks in Pimlico, and shooting an unarmed policeman in the street outside.' He glanced at Katya. 'They weren't here to play games.'

'How are the wounded men?' asked Harry.

'Recovering, although unlikely to ever work again. The shooter and his mate were seen dumping their car afterwards in the Park Lane underground car park. It all tallies rather nicely with footage of them entering the country six days previously, proof for cynics that the cameras do have a genuine function.' He smiled drily. 'I had my men canvass the area around Park Lane, and they turned up a doorman on the Grosvenor House Hotel who remembered them.'

'Lucky break,' said Crampton. 'Or were they careless?'

'Luck, apparently. But we all need it from time to time. This particular man used to run security in the casinos in Monaco. His skill was remembering the faces of professional card sharks and so-called lucky players. These two weren't players, but he remembered them the moment he saw the photos. All we had to do was match his memory to the security cameras inside.' He looked very pleased with himself for a moment, then said, 'We came up with a surprise package. Our two shooters, whose names we don't know, were there, having a cosy chat with one Sergei Gorelkin. And who else should walk in but a man known to us all, but most especially to Harry, here. George Paulton.'

Harry found he'd been holding his breath. He'd had a feeling Ballatyne had uncovered something important, but hadn't known what it was. Now he knew.

'Where is he now?'

342

'Right now, no idea. You don't sound surprised.'

'I'm not. This business has his thumb-prints all over it. Gorelkin's men must have been tipped off about who and what Clare was, and her connection to Katya and Six. Paulton would have known about both. You said Maine pulled his details off the files, possibly to find some dirt as a safeguard if Paulton cheated him.'

'Correct. Sadly we can't confirm that now Maine's dead. But it's almost certain that Paulton silenced him. I ran a check on Paulton's operational log. It seems he and Gorelkin popped up simultaneously in Stockholm, Berlin and Madrid, among other places, several years ago. Paulton was running at least two officially sanctioned fishing operations against him, although the debriefs show nothing of significance was achieved. With hindsight, I think we can treat that with a certain amount of disbelief. I reckon he and Gorelkin came to an arrangement over the years, and may have even worked together since Paulton went rogue. He's been out in the wilds, and unless he won the Spanish lottery, he'll have needed funds.'

'You think Gorelkin brought him in to help kill Tobinskiy?' Crampton asked.

'I doubt it; that was already an on-going operation. But he might have brought him in to gain access to MI6 and MI5 files, to find Jardine. That's where Keith Maine comes in. He had the means and the knowledge, and Paulton would have known him well enough to exert pressure.' He sat back. 'Now I've established who did

343

what, we need to find Gorelkin and his men before they latch onto Jardine again.' He looked directly at Katya. 'You told Harry that they might be operating illegally – or, at least, without proper sanction from the government.'

'Yes.'

'And that makes them criminals.'

'Correct.'

'It would save a lot of mess,' he said slowly, 'if we could get them pulled out by their own people. What are the chances?'

She thought it over, eyes on his. 'You want me to contact someone about these three men?'

'It would help if you could.'

'But why would they believe me? In their eyes I'm now a criminal and a traitor. I could be acting on your instructions ... which I would be, of course.'

'Plant the seed; that's all I ask. You must know somebody you can call. If it means finding a private phone number, I'm sure we can help.' He smiled knowingly.

She sat back, eyes clouding over, and thought about it for a full minute. 'Maybe there is one person.'

'Dare I ask who?'

'His name is Bronyev. He was my colleague in Vienna. We were friends, too. He is a good man.' She looked a little sad at the memory.

Ballatyne was sceptical. 'A bodyguard with the FSO? Does he have any clout?'

'Not him, no. But his father does. He is an army general. Is that clout enough, Mr Ballatyne?'

344

'Good enough for me.' Ballatyne nodded sideways at the young male official. 'Go with Julian, here, and he'll show you to a secure communications room. Take your time. Just tell them about Gorelkin and the others. If what you told Harry is correct, and they were acting illegally, somebody will take notice.' He reached into his breast pocket and produced a memory stick. 'This has still photographs of the men involved, taken in various locations. They're good enough that even their own mothers will recognise them. Julian will help.'

They waited for twenty minutes, during which time Ballatyne arranged for coffee and biscuits, and the man at the far end of the table got up and disappeared to the bathroom. The atmosphere was heavy and utterly quiet, with almost no sound of movement in the corridor outside and just a hint of traffic noise from the street.

'You spoke to Clare,' said Rik.

Ballatyne nodded. 'We had a brief chat. She seems to be bearing up remarkably well, but I thought she should have someone take a look at her, just in case. She must be feeling better; she asked for a laptop.'

Rik looked surprised. 'Really? I could have lent her mine.'

'No need. I arranged for one to be delivered to her at the clinic. It was the least I could do after all she's been through. I asked if she wanted any help, but I gather she's quite the IT buff on the quiet.'

Harry said, 'What did she want it for?'

'She wants to sort out her future, she said. *Their* future, actually; hers and Miss Balenkova's. I believe they're looking for somewhere to go away, far from the madding crowd of spies, lies and security officers. Not that I blame them.'

'And you just gave her a laptop.'

'On loan, actually. But why not?' Ballatyne looked innocent. 'She's hardly likely to run off with it, I shouldn't think.'

Harry said nothing. He was prevented from asking further questions by Katya returning with her escort. She looked pale but composed.

She sat down without meeting Ballatyne's gaze and said, 'It's done.'

The MI6 man glanced at Julian, who nodded in confirmation.

'Good.' Ballatyne clapped his hands. 'I think we're finished here. Thank you, Miss Balenkova. I appreciate that wasn't easy for you. Mr Ferris, can you watch Miss Balenkova's back? I need to talk to Harry.'

Rik nodded. 'Sure. I've got nothing else on at present.'

FIFTY-SEVEN

'What was that all about?' Harry and Ballatyne had stopped along the gravel path of Victoria Embankment Gardens, skirting small groups of tourists and office workers on their lunch break. Ballatyne had led him at a brisk walk from the building and down towards the river, forging ahead on the busy pavement in a manner that avoided conversation. 'Why the play-acting with Crampton and the Special Forces liaison?'

'You know him?'

'No, I recognise the type.'

'I was covering my back. You know how these things work.' Ballatyne turned and looked towards the river, chewing his lip. 'This job is as much about politics these days as it is about gathering intelligence. Departments have their own priorities and agendas, and as much blood is spilled in the corridors as out in the field. I just have to make sure none of it is mine, which is why those others were at the meeting. I needed them to hear the basics.' He gave a thin smile. 'Crampton and the nameless one will spread the word about Paulton; I'll do the rest from another direction.'

'So why am I here?'

'We need to stop this in case Miss Balenkova's

347

message doesn't get through. I wasn't entirely open and honest in that meeting. We've actually got more information about the two shooters than I let on. First of all, though, there's Paulton.'

'There always is. Do you know why he was here?'

'In a nutshell, he wants to come in from the cold.'

'You're kidding.'

'I wish I were. Maybe life out in the wild isn't all it's cracked up to be when you've got a price on your head. It seems his plan was to bargain his way back by bringing something of value to the table. And for that he needed a sponsor ... someone who would give him the time of day without having him shot on sight. Somebody who would appreciate something to trade – if it had added value.'

'How do you know this?'

'A birdie told me.'

Harry had been thinking a lot about who else would have benefited by Clare's death apart from the Russians, who wouldn't have wanted their part in Tobinskiy's murder revealed. But exactly who that was meant someone else had to be pulling some strings. As an old instructor had been fond of saying, when you've considered and rejected all possible options, all you're left with is the blindingly obvious. But naming names wasn't his job.

'Who?'

But Ballatyne was enjoying himself too much to let it all out at once. 'Well, let's remember that Clare Jardine figures closely in all of this. First of all, who would have a grudge against her? The list is not very long, strangely enough. Second, who has the ambition, balls and position to risk talking with Paulton as a means of getting to Jardine? Who would also give anything to get the Tobinskiy hit team – and their controller? And who would bring Paulton back into the fold – and potentially turn on him as a personal coup?'

Harry knew who Ballatyne was talking about. The only person he had referred to who might fit. Candida Deane. What he didn't know was why the MI6 man was going after one of his own colleagues in such an open fashion.

'I take it this person would have known about the Russians being here in the first place?'

'Too right. They read reports and summaries just like I do, and that one would have been hot enough to snap her knicker elastic. They knew where Tobinskiy was, they probably had a good idea what this team were here for – although, to be honest, tying the two together might have taken a while, because they'd have assumed that finding Tobinskiy wouldn't have been easy.'

'So how did they find him?'

'Laughably easy: I think the shooter in Brighton who first plugged Tobinskiy had a backup man in place. Once the shooting was over, the gunman disappeared, and all his colleague had to do was keep an eye on the hospital and wait for Tobinskiy to croak. When he didn't, he simply followed the ambulance to London. A second team was called in to finish the job. It's how I would have done it, anyway.'

'Is that why the guard on the ward disappeared? Was he part of it?'

'No, he was perfectly innocent, if incompetent. A mix-up over rotas. He saw another guard entering the building and thought he was his replacement, and took off without handing over. It left a ten-minute gap which the Russians exploited. But they'd have probably planned on taking out any guards, anyway.'

'So Deane wasn't using Tobinskiy as bait?'

'Probably not, much as it pains me to say. She's as nasty as a tank of piranha fish but she has her limits. She was playing Paulton along and hoping to implicate Jardine in the killing *and* get the hit team all nicely wrapped up. I can't prove it because she's not saying much, but I suspect she was planning on turning Paulton in as a bonus.' He sniffed. 'I told you, she's ambitious. Proving any of it might be a problem, but she's finished in that job, anyway.'

'Unless you can find Paulton.'

Ballatyne shrugged, his eyes hooded. 'You and I both know that's not going to happen.'

'So what's this other information you have?'

Ballatyne took a slip of paper from his pocket and passed it to Harry. He was surprised to see that it held an address in Knightsbridge, west London.

'What's this?'

'We tracked the shooters to this location. The tech boys in the Met got a lucky strike with an FRS camera along Knightsbridge. The building's not on the list of Russian holdings, which makes me think this whole operation was very deep and black. It's the second-floor flat of a short-term rental property. They were there last night and I've got a man on watch to make sure they don't slide out unnoticed.'

'Couldn't you get Crampton's men to go in?'

'Too risky. There are two foreign embassy buildings in the same street, both unfriendly, one openly harbouring a fugitive facing terrorist charges in the States and cocking their noses at us. If the boys in blue show up in force anywhere within two hundred yards, they'll scream from the rooftops.'

'What about Special Forces?'

'The MOD won't risk sending in anything less than a full team. Can you imagine the noise?' He shuddered. 'We'd never hear the last of it from the Harrods board, either.'

Harry breathed out. He knew what was coming.

'So what's the plan?'

'You and Boy Wonder could do it.' Ballatyne straightened his jacket. 'It would send a message to Gorelkin's controllers, telling them they can't do this on our territory without consequences.'

Harry wanted to tell Ballatyne to go jump in the river; that he didn't do hit jobs, no matter what the reason. But he knew deep down that it wouldn't wash. If the two Russians were in there, it wouldn't be a hit, it would be a fight.

There was a lot more he wanted to ask, especially about Clare. For example, why was Ballatyne suddenly so keen on her welfare, when before this he had been indifferent to downright cold. But now wasn't the time.

Ballatyne turned to go. 'Don't leave it too long, or they'll be gone until they can pop up and take another crack at Jardine. And I hate to be melodramatic, Harry, but they do know where you live.'

FIFTY-EIGHT

From the scrum of journalists and onlookers jostling about on the pavement, it was clear where the suspected terrorist was seeking sanctuary. The street was just behind the world-famous façade of Harrods in Knightsbridge, and the kerbs were lined with luxury model cars of every make, many with chauffeurs in attendance.

Harry and Rik walked past the red-brick house where they had been told the two Russians were staying, and joined the crowd eyeing the embassy building, where an official was reading a statement for the press. It was clearly not the first such statement of defiance in a running war of words, and even the press personnel looked slightly bored with the rhetoric and fist-waving. But it gave Harry and Rik an opportunity to take a look at the target building without being too obvious.

The proximity of the press and onlookers, quite apart from the flow of pedestrians, gave Harry cause for concern. If things went badly wrong and the two Russians took the offensive, there could be carnage. And that was to be avoided at all costs.

'Come on, we're going to have to do this ourselves.' He walked further along the street and turned down the first intersection. He had already scanned the area for Ballatyne's watcher, but whoever he was was keeping well out of sight. No doubt he was holed up somewhere comfortable, waiting for instructions.

They circled the block holding the target building, and eventually ended up in a narrow street at the rear. The structures were extensive, and broken up into a rabbit warren of offices and residential spaces. Harry had already seen that some had access through from front to back, but these were mostly by secured passageways and doors. Unfortunately, not all the rear passageways were identified, and there was no way of telling which ones had access to the front.

'No option,' Harry said. 'Front way in.'

They returned to the front entrance and stopped by a flight of stone steps leading to a basement flat, carefully avoiding looking up at the first-floor apartment windows. A chauffeur was polishing the already gleaming bodywork of a large blue BMW nearby, but paid them no attention.

'I used to live in a place like this in Earl's Court,' said Rik. 'Full of backpackers and layabouts. It was connected to the rest of the building by narrow back stairs, from when they had servants' quarters. We might strike lucky.'

Harry nodded. They hadn't got any alternative. They descended the steps and knocked on the door. A woman opened up and peered out at them, large dark eyes in a coffee-coloured face above an overall and an apron.

'Yes?'

'Police,' said Harry, flashing his MI5 card. 'I wonder if you could help us?'

'Police?' The woman looked frightened. 'What I do? Why you come here?'

'It's OK.' Rik leaned past Harry and smiled broadly at the woman. 'It's not you we're after, love.' He jerked a thumb over his shoulder, towards the press pack across the street. 'We need to get a view of that crowd, to make sure there's no trouble.'

She frowned, mollified but puzzled. 'But from here? Is too low.'

'You're dead right. But if we could get further up ... say, on the second or third floor, we'd have a great view. Are there stairs going up?'

She shook her head. 'Yes, but they are locked. Only manager has keys.'

'Great.' Rik gave another winning smile. 'And where is the manager?'

'Belize.'

'That's a bit far. Do you live here?'

'No, I cleaner and make sure everything is working.'

'Brilliant.' Rik delved in his pocket and took out some notes. He held them up. 'I'm a magician with locks. You take this and go put the kettle on, and we'll be through and gone before the water's boiled. And I'll lock the door behind us so you don't get into trouble.'

The woman stared at the money for a long

time, eyes flicking to both men and back. 'Is this what British policemen do?'

'In very extreme circumstances, yes.'

'OK.' She reached out and took the notes, and stood back to let them in, closing the door and leading them through a set of offices to a narrow door in one corner at the rear of the building. 'This go up to ground floor,' she explained in a hushed voice. 'Turn right and stairs go up to other floors.'

She turned and disappeared, evidently not keen on staying to watch her part in their moment of larceny.

'I didn't know you were a magician with locks,' said Harry.

'There's quite a lot you don't know about me.' Rik grinned and produced a short length of plastic. Inserting it between the door and jamb, he wiggled it about, at the same time leaning hard against the door, which gave a little under the pressure. The plastic moved and sank into the gap, and suddenly there was a click and the door was open.

Harry checked the cleaning lady wasn't looking, then drew his gun and followed Rik through, closing the door behind him.

They were at the bottom of a flight of stairs piled with cardboard boxes and stacks of floor tiles. At the top was another door with the Yale lock and handle on this side.

The door opened onto a polished tiled hallway. To their right another flight of stairs led upwards, and beyond that, the hallway ran down to the front of the building.

The stairs to the upper floors were wide, carpeted down the centre, with a wood and metal banister polished with years of use.

'Straight up?' whispered Rik. He drew his gun and slipped off the safety.

'Might as well. Knock and wait.' In Harry's experience, pretending to be a water official or a delivery man only worked if you had sight of the people you were calling on and their suspicions were low to zero. Anyone armed and in hiding on the other side of the door would take any such pretence to be just that, and were likely to start shooting instead.

Rik reached the door first and knocked a light rat-tat, then stood to one side and waited, with Harry on the other side.

No answer. He knocked again. A door slammed down the hallway, to the rear of the building, followed by the sound of footsteps. Another door banged.

Harry stepped out from the wall and looked down the hallway.

'It's them – they had a back way out.' He began running, while Rik took a step back and kicked the door open and disappeared inside.

Harry reached a door at the end of the hall, down a short flight of steps. It was part of an extension to the main building, with a side window giving a narrow view to the rear, and he guessed it gave out onto the street he and Rik had seen at the back. He tried the door. Solid and unmoving, opening towards him. It would take an axe to get through it.

He ran back to the apartment and found Rik

standing in a living room littered with discarded pizza boxes and beer cans. A huge plasma television was on with the sound muted, showing a children's programme.

'If it was them,' said Rik, 'they travelled light.'

Harry bent to one side of an armchair. He picked up a small can of Birchwood Casey gun oil lying on its side, dripping its contents onto the parquet flooring. Near it, just under the edge of the chair, something shiny caught his eye.

It was a single round of 9mm ammunition.

FIFTY-NINE

Harry put down the can and called Ballatyne. The MI6 man answered immediately. 'Where's your watcher? The targets are on the move out the back. We're blocked and need some eyeball backup.'

'No problem.' Ballatyne sounded unnaturally calm. 'We've got a live map of the area on-screen. Make your way to the front. Bruce will be waiting for you. His controller will guide you from there. Out.'

Harry turned and ran through the building and down the stairs, with Rik hard on his heels. Going out of the front door, he remembered to put away his gun in time before coming under the curious gaze of the press pack.

The blue BMW was still there, the engine

ticking over quietly. The chauffeur lifted a hand. 'Tate and Ferris? Jump in and buckle up. The name's Bruce.'

'I'm Harry, he's Rik.'

The BMW tore away from the kerb, narrowly missing a photographer being artistic outside the besieged embassy. As he came to the end of the road, Bruce hit a button on a central console, and a stream of radio chatter came out over the powerful hum of the engine.

'Targets on foot ... could be heading for a multi-storey right behind. No, wait. Targets approaching dark saloon ... an Astra, in Pavilion Road. Getting in and heading south, south, along Pavilion. Stay on that heading.'

Harry was amazed. 'You've got a helicopter up there?'

'Good timing, huh? Your boss thought they might come out like rats from a burning barn. They cruised into position five minutes ago.' He calmly steered the BMW through the narrow streets and locked onto the course provided by the controller's commentary.

'They're going south,' said Rik.

Bruce nodded. 'Chelsea Bridge, I reckon.' He squeezed through a gap between a builder's lorry and a taxi, shifting skilfully through the gears and playing the brakes and accelerator for maximum effect. All the time he sat back as though in an armchair at home.

'How do you know it's them?' Harry asked.

'Your two subjects were in all night and they were using the Astra yesterday. It's a hire car but we haven't got the name yet.'

'It'll be false, anyway,' said Rik.

'Makes sense. They popped out earlier for breakfast. We didn't have the resources for a full box surveillance, so I stayed on them all the time. Easy enough job, though.'

'Just you?' said Harry. He knew well that mounting a full, round-the-clock surveillance was very heavy on manpower and resources, but Ballatyne had said nothing about the level of commitment given to this operation.

'Just me. There were no stops, no drops and no contacts. Can't tell what they were doing once they were inside, of course. The tall one's in charge and shorty's the driver.' He paused to listen as the controller gave an update feed on the Astra's location. 'This driver's good, whoever he is. Very good. I don't think he knows we're on him yet, but if he gets a sniff of us, we might have a chase on our hands. He must know the ground pretty well.'

'He doesn't,' said Harry. 'As far as we know it's their first time here.'

'Really?' Bruce was even more impressed. 'Good thing we've got eyes in the sky, then.'

Harry wondered at his calm demeanour, and sensed he was happier chatting, even when concentrating. 'Do you do this a lot?'

'As much as I can.' He grinned. 'I used to drive interceptors with Essex Police, in Subaru Imprezas. Then I got a transfer to this lot. This is a lot more fun.'

'Let's hope it stays that way,' Harry told him. 'You know these two are armed, don't you?'

'So I noticed. Bad boys.'

'Bad enough. How did you notice?'

'The way they walked, the way they sat, holding one hand against their jackets. Classic signs when someone's carrying.'

A burst of chatter interrupted to tell them that the speeding Astra had crossed the river and was heading towards the south-east. Moments later, it was crossing the A3, still heading in the same direction and using back streets which were less busy. Local police patrols were being warned to stay well clear and give the men in the Astra no reason to start shooting.

'Where's he going?' Bruce mused aloud. 'There's Heathrow, Gatwick or the Channel – that's all there is down this way, unless he's got another hidey-hole.'

'Blue One, the target's picking up speed.' The controller's voice was cool, economical. 'Estimates are he's heading for Herne Hill, Dulwich and Catford areas, then further south.'

'Why would he pick up speed?' asked Rik. 'He can't see us.'

'He doesn't have to,' said Bruce. 'He knows we're here.' He accelerated again, whipping past a bus and two cars, slipping past a traffic island on the wrong side before slotting back onto the right side of the road. 'The good ones have an instinct. If they've done this before, they pick up the signs somehow. Same as us when we see a suspect car; it doesn't look right. Can't tell you why, it just does. Nine times out of ten, we're right. He might not even be trying to outrun us – he could be fixing to get some space between us so he can dump the car and walk away.'

Suddenly the controller uttered a mild curse. *'Signal's going ... we're losing pictures. Trying to recover ... Blue One, picture's gone ... last seen target was slowing down, slowing down hard. Be ready to decamp.'*

'Why no picture?' Bruce cried. 'And why now?'

They were fast approaching a crossroads, with minimum traffic in sight. Then, just beyond it, they saw the Astra. It had almost stopped, and seemed to be idling in the centre of the road. They were now close enough to see two figures inside. Suddenly it sat back on its suspension and pulled away hard, blue smoke issuing from the exhaust.

'He's off,' said Bruce. 'Over to you. What do you want me to do?'

Harry considered the consequences. The longer this chase continued, the more likely it was that the Russians would either panic and start shooting, or they would get away. Without the overhead camera coverage, there were too many side roads the Astra could duck into, losing their pursuers in an instant.

'Go for it,' Harry said. He and Rik took out their weapons and did a quick check, then sat and waited for Bruce to find a suitable place to stop the Astra. This was his expertise and they were just along for the ride.

'Hold onto your panties, girls,' Bruce murmured, and tramped hard on the accelerator, sending the BMW streaking towards the traffic lights, which were green and clear. The row of houses and shops became a blur, and figures on the pavements seemed frozen in mid-step.

'Look out right!' Rik yelled a warning just as a dark shape loomed up on that side, filling the windows.

A large 4X4 had deliberately jumped the lights.

Before Bruce could react, there was a sickening blow against the rear wing, ripping the BMW off-course and sending it into a neck-wrenching spin. The tyres shrieked in protest and a shower of glass fell around the interior of the car as the windows gave way under the force of the collision.

Harry managed to stuff his gun inside his jacket and hold on, grabbing hold of the door handle and the seat belt to stay upright, while feeling the sharp torque of the whiplash effect as the car spun and rocked on its suspension, with Brice fighting the wheel to keep it upright.

Then the world stopped moving just as suddenly as it had started, and they were left in total silence as the engine stuttered and died.

'He's gone!' Bruce shouted furiously, twisting in his seat for a sighting of the vehicle that had hit them. He spat out a mouthful of blood. 'Damn, I bit my tongue. *Bastards*!'

Harry unhooked his seat belt and climbed out, followed by Rik, nursing his elbow from the collision. Bruce was right, there was no sign of the other car, and the Astra had also disappeared.

'It was a set-up,' Bruce muttered sourly, joining them on the side of the road and stretching his neck with a wince of pain. 'They had another car waiting to run interference.' He looked at Harry. 'Who the hell are those people?'

'Foreigners,' Harry told him. 'They all drive like that.'

'Blue One ... come in. Blue One ... you OK?'

SIXTY

'What a shit hole.' Serkhov shivered and pulled his jacket collar up around his chin. He and Votrukhin were standing outside an abandoned cottage with a corrugated iron roof, set against a grey, sludgy expanse of the Thames where it spilled out into the sea.

After being forced to flee the apartment in Knightsbridge, they had taken a prearranged route through south London, using small hotels for one night each while awaiting further instructions, aware that this mission was now almost certainly over.

Votrukhin in particular had been shocked at coming so close to being caught by the two security men, and had angrily asked Gorelkin how they could have been traced to that address. Gorelkin had expressed no specific opinion, suggesting in a roundabout fashion that he and Serkhov must have been careless. It had been enough to leave the atmosphere between them soured and distrustful.

The next time Gorelkin called, it was with orders to make their way north to a point on the coast of Essex, just across the Thames.

'What about the hire car?' asked Serkhov.

'The car doesn't matter,' Gorelkin insisted. 'You won't be returning it, anyway.'

Their destination was near Canvey Island, on the Thames Estuary. The car's satnav guided them along a winding lane lined with houses and fields. Then the houses stopped, leaving nothing but scrubby fields and what looked like mud flats. It looked bleak and unwelcoming, driving both men into an even more sombre mood than before.

'Wait right at the end, on the point,' Gorelkin had told them earlier. 'A deep water channel runs close to the shore. A trawler will pick you up and take you to Ostende, where you'll be picked up.'

'Why can't we fly out?' Serkhov had queried. He was past caring what Gorelkin thought of his questions and just wanted to get the hell out of this godforsaken country any way he could.

'All airfields are being monitored, that's why,' Gorelkin had replied tersely. 'You go anywhere near one and you'll be picked up. Nobody is watching trawlers leaving the coast.'

It made sense and Serkhov had shrugged it off. As long as the trawler didn't sink, he could put up with a few hours at sea. Anything was better than sitting around waiting for the British security services to pick them up.

'We'd better wait inside,' Votrukhin murmured, and walked over to the cottage and kicked open the door. The interior was a ruin, the brick walls bare of plaster, the floor a concrete slab riddled with cracks and littered with old bricks and planks, the roof a mass of holes. But it would do until they could leave.

'What about the car?'

'Leave it. People come down here to walk dogs and watch birds. By the time the boat comes it will be almost dark.' Votrukhin piled two stacks of bricks and placed a plank across, forming a rough bench. He sat down gingerly, then pulled out a packet of mints. He took two and offered the packet to Serkhov, but the sergeant shook his head and sat beside him.

'I still don't get how Gorelkin arranged for us to dodge those security people,' Serkhov murmured. 'They nearly had us, then suddenly, gone.'

'Don't question it,' Votrukhin replied. 'We followed instructions, it got us out of a jam. End of subject.' Even he, however, had been left wondering how their boss had managed it. From having no support whatsoever, they now had someone watching their backs and intercepting a close pursuit. All it had taken was a phone call instructing them to slow right down at a particular set of traffic lights along their route, then take off the moment they saw the other car coming.

All he knew was that it was the best piece of stage-management Gorelkin had ever managed.

They sat in silence after that, neither having much to say. After working together so long, more often than not in dangerous situations, the two men had developed the art of silent companionship, speaking only when necessary.

Through the thin walls came the sound of boats passing in the channel; small work vessels, engines clattering, the occasional fast launch crashing over the water, and heavier vessels seemingly taking an age to go by and making the ancient building shudder with their noise.

After thirty minutes, with the light fading outside, Votrukhin's phone rang. He answered it and listened, then shut it off.

'The boat's on its way in. We wait inside for a signal.'

Serkhov sucked on his teeth and spat across the room. He'd been getting more and more restless, and didn't think much of the arrangements. Nothing to eat or drink, in danger of some local idiot dog walker seeing them here and reporting them to the police, and neither of them knowing what was going to happen afterwards.

'Seems a dull way to leave the country,' he commented. 'There was a moment when I thought we might go out like that film ... *Butch Cassidy and the Sundance Kid*, shooting our way out through a bunch of English cops.'

Votrukhin said, 'You think too much.'

'No. I'm being realistic. Your trouble is, you believe all the crap they sold you about duty for the country and service, and how being an officer lifts you up the ladder. Me, I stopped listening to that years ago. We're still at the same shit level we were at ten years back, and it doesn't look like getting better, after what Gorelkin put us through.'

'So why are you here, then? You want to die a hero's death, is that it?'

'Well, it might be better than wasting away in a foreign prison. Or finding that we're going to carry the can for Gorelkin's cock-up and end up

366

in a recycled *gulag* for a few years.'

'You've really got a thing for him, haven't you?'

'You mean you haven't? This whole trip's been a mess from start to finish. We did Tobinskiy, which is what we came for. But it's all been downhill from there. No real planning, no back-up, no fall-back plan for when the shit hit the fan, like it seems to have done. And now we're sneaking out like kids raiding a chicken coop – and after what?'

'We don't know if it failed. Gorelkin might have got the Jardine woman some other way. Anyway, when did you ever know an operation go perfectly as planned? It's why they use us, because we can adapt.'

'Adapt my arse...' Serkhov's head snapped up at the sound of an engine. It sounded closer and lighter than any before. 'What's that?'

'Probably a tender from the boat to pick us up.'

They both stood up, and it took a moment for both men to realise that the engine noise had come from the rear of the cottage, where they had left their car, not from the sea.

'Fuck!' Serkhov swore and pulled out his gun. 'This doesn't sound good.' He stepped across to the window and glanced out. When he turned to Votrukhin, he looked grim. 'Four men getting out of a car. They're armed with machine guns.'

SIXTY-ONE

Votrukhin joined Serkhov, pulling out his weapon. He peered out and shook his head. The sergeant wasn't exaggerating. It was no contest. Nowhere to go, nowhere to hide, and four men with fully automatic weapons. Enough fire power to blow this rotten building off its foundations.

'Whoever they are, they're not here to tell us job well done.' He paused, then did a double-take on the man in the lead, who was signalling his men to spread out, the way a good commander should. 'Mother of God, I know that man. His name's Brizsinsky, Breshevsky ... something like that. He was Spetsnaz. I heard he was in V Section.'

Serkhov looked relieved. 'That's good, isn't it? It means we're going home. Let the British try stopping us now.' He stepped towards the door, eager to be gone.

But Votrukhin wasn't moving. He grasped Serkhov's arm. 'Wait. You don't understand. V Section ran special penetration operations. Fast in, fast out. Really high-level stuff. If they've been sent here, it's not to pick us up.'

Serkhov frowned. 'What are you saying?'

'I heard V Section was closed down a few

368

years ago, but a few guys were kept on for special duties.' He nodded towards the outside. 'Including Brizsinsky or whatever the hell his name is. Nobody knows where they're based, and they work completely off the books. They're ghosts.'

'I never heard that. How come you know about them?'

'I'm an officer. We hear things.'

'What sort of special duties?' Serkhov's voice had dropped several notches.

'They're called cleaners. They make sure bad mistakes get buried.'

Serkhov stared at him for a few seconds as the implication set in. This wasn't something Votrukhin would joke about. 'Go fuck a goat. Doesn't look like there's going to be a boat after all, does it? Bastards.' He ejected the magazine, checking the load by feel, then clicked it back into place. '*Now* do you finally believe me? We've been stuffed.'

Votrukhin nodded. 'Yes. I believe you.' He turned and spat on the floor. 'God, I hate it when you're right.'

'Never mind. I had to be at least once.' He shook his head and spat on the same spot. 'You think we'll be heroes back home among the other guys, for what we did?'

'For knocking off Tobinskiy, you mean?' Votrukhin shook his head. 'No, my friend. Nobody will talk about that, ever. They might pretend to miss us when we don't turn up ... might even have a dinner at Tinkoff's in The Arbat with the proceeds of the sale. But that's about it.' He was referring to the alleged custom of selling off a fallen comrade's personal possessions if there was no family to consider. Neither Votrukhin nor Serkov had ever given time to such things as family. Not that either man had much to sell, in any case.

'I thought that sentimental shit was for officers only.'

'Not at all. It's just that the rest of you scum can't be bothered to celebrate our heroes.'

A few minutes passed, then Serkhov muttered, 'I would like to have been a hero. So people on the base could point me out to new recruits and say, "There goes Sergeant Leonid Serkhov. He's got the balls of a bull elephant." It would have been nice.'

'Are we talking about courage or size? There's a difference.'

'Sergeants can be heroes, too.'

'I guess. But not often, because they're mostly useless insubordinate bastards who prefer to get drunk. But it does happen.'

'Up yours, lieutenant. We sergeants are the backbone of any army, hadn't you heard?' Serkhov reached in his pocket and took out the pink plastic powder compact he'd taken from the Jardine woman. 'I won't be needing this anymore, will I? Do you think pink brings soldiers bad luck? Is that what went wrong?'

'No. But carrying that thing does make you look like a girl.'

Serkhov grinned. He bent and placed the compact on the plank where Votrukhin had been sitting. 'Maybe she'll get it back some day. The

370

Jardine woman.'

'Sure, why not?' Votrukhin slapped him on the arm and took a deep breath. 'Shall we do this, Leonid? Or should I call you Butch?'

'No, Fyodor. I'm Sundance. You're Butch.'

They walked to the door, guns held loosely by their sides, then opened it wide and stepped out into the night.

SIXTY-TWO

'It's over.' It was Ballatyne's voice echoing down the wire. He sounded tired. 'Two bodies were found on the shore near Canvey Island late last night. The descriptions match our two Russians.'

'What happened?' Harry felt an odd sense of relief. He'd done enough chasing and shooting recently; all he wanted now was for this to end.

'The locals heard a lot of gunfire coming from an abandoned fisherman's cottage. One was a former armourer and recognised automatic fire. He called in some of Crampton's pals. When they got there they found two dead and a lot of spent shells.'

'It wasn't your lot, then?'

'No. This was an execution; the two dead men got off a couple of rounds each, but if they hit anyone there were no signs of it. A couple of dog walkers further back down the road remember two cars going by at separate times, but it's a public road and popular with young couples. The cops are trawling any cameras in the area for footage, but they don't hold out much hope. They're writing it up as a gangland shooting, to keep the press happy.'

'It's a bit extreme, isn't it? Why would the Russians eliminate their own people?'

'Possibly to get rid of an embarrassing situation. If Gorelkin and his two hoods were operating off the books and without official sanction, no matter how high up the orders came from, nobody this side of the next ice age is going to say otherwise. We can't prove who they were, and Moscow will deny any knowledge until the vodka runs dry. In the end it'll be forgotten.'

'And Gorelkin?'

'Already gone. He was escorted onto a plane at Heathrow by two embassy security types late yesterday afternoon. He didn't look well.'

'You didn't stop him?'

'Why bother? He was here as a private citizen, and nobody wants to pursue a case of entering the country under false papers, which is all we'd get him on. We have to watch the pennies these days. In any case, my guess is he's going back to a far worse punishment than anything we could dish out. How's your neck?'

'My neck's fine. We were lucky ... they weren't trying to kill us, just put us off.' Harry was convinced that the ramming hadn't been accidental. The timing had been too perfectly executed,

372

when all their attention was on the car in front. It had taken skill, but even Bruce had agreed that it was possible, given the right training.

'You still think that?'

'I do. Any news about Paulton?'

'He's keeping his head down if he has any sense. There's now a charge out on him for suborning a member of the security services to gain information under the Official Secrets Act, and the murder of the same individual.'

Harry let it slide. There was something Ballatyne wasn't telling him; something to do with Paulton, he was certain. Maybe it would come out in time.

'And Deane?'

'Resigned. She's decided to pursue another line of deviousness elsewhere.'

'Did you have anything to do with that?'

'I couldn't possibly comment.'

Harry changed tack. 'I tried calling Clare. She's not answering. Do you have the address of the clinic where she's being treated?'

'I do, but I hear she left the clinic and has gone away with Balenkova. I think they're off somewhere hot for some rest and recuperation. Can't say I blame them, to be honest. Don't worry, Harry, I'm sure she'll call one day.'

Harry wasn't sure. Clare had no reason to call him. What had been between them was an incident in history, now over and done. She had a future to work on. All the same, he couldn't forget the words she had uttered in Vienna, about Paulton: 'If you don't get him, I will.'

SIXTY-THREE

The 20.00 hours Eurostar pulled out of St Pancras right on the button. George Paulton relaxed for the first time that day, after scanning the rest of the Business/Premier carriage. It was nearly deserted, as he'd hoped, with only a group of French business types further back, already fading fast towards sleep as conversation ceased and tiredness took over.

He watched the lights flickering by outside, and wondered how everything had gone so horribly wrong. By rights he should have been staying in London now, dining out wherever the mood took him, his freedom assured by order of the Home Secretary, his case made secure by pressure from the movers and shakers in the security departments, like Candida Deane.

But that was not to be. Deane had dropped off the radar, and no amount of digging had found her. The fact that she was refusing his calls meant one thing only: his value had dropped to nil in her eyes and she no longer wished to be associated with him. Instead, he was slinking out in the night to an uncertain future and with an even bigger price on his head than ever before.

But at least he was alive, which was a fate

better than Gorelkin could look forward to. If he knew the kind of masters the old spy faced back in Moscow, payment would be very short and sharp indeed.

Trying to play Gorelkin had been a huge mistake; he should never have responded to the Russian's call in the first place. The man had been born devious and it was in his DNA to keep his real cards behind his back. But the opportunity to buy himself back into the country had seemed too good to miss.

Now that was all in the past.

He fought to keep a lid on the rage that was bubbling away inside him. All jobs carried a tally, good and bad, and he had gained so little coming here; no redress with Tate, no settling of scores with Jardine ... and most of all, not even the pleasure of turning the tables on those in the security establishment who had turned their backs on him so easily and left him out in the cold.

His thoughts were disturbed by the connecting door at the end of the carriage behind him sliding open. Footsteps shuffled along the aisle, one set, maybe two. He settled instinctively deeper into his seat, reducing his profile, and became vaguely aware of two figures stopping at a set of four seats across from him. He watched in the reflection in the glass as they sat down across from each other, placing bags on the table between them. Two women, he noted, oddly dressed.

It took a moment for him to realise that they were covered from head to toe in black burkas, with only their eyes visible. They were speaking softly in French, the words muffled beneath the cloth, too soft to pick up. North African Muslims, he guessed, returning to Paris after a visit to London.

He ignored them and found himself drifting, his earlier anger now fading, deflected by the interruption. A good thing, he decided; agonising over what had not been accomplished was pointless; he'd learned that years ago. Now he had to face the future, wherever that might be. He had money enough, depending on where he finished up, but he would have to put his mind to one or two schemes he'd been considering in order to keep the funds coming in.

The train juddered, waking him with a jolt. He'd been dozing, his thoughts morphing into dreams, the images jumbled and confusing. The two women were still across the aisle, both intent on electronic readers. It reminded him that he should invest in a decent model soon; so much simpler than carrying around the laptop he had been using before this trip.

He put his head back and allowed himself to drift again, his mind sifting abstractly through the potential locations he had seen and considered over the past two years, locations where he could melt into the local fabric and be reasonably assured of safety and comfort; where he could at least be reasonably certain that neither Harry Tate nor any other vengeful hunters would ever find him.

He came awake again with a start. The sleep had

been deeper this time, his mouth gummy and dry, his eyes heavy, as if he'd been drugged. He was sure he'd felt some movement close by; another passenger passing in the aisle, perhaps, brushing against his shoulder. He shook his head and looked at the window. But all he saw was blackness and his own pale reflection. God, he looked old. Tired. He yawned and rubbed his head against the seat back, glancing guiltily at the two women across the aisle. But only one was still there, still reading.

He sighed and relaxed. That must have been it: her companion had stood up and stumbled against him with the movement of the train. He closed his eyes, relishing the arrival in Paris, and with it the feeling that, once again, he was beyond the reach of anyone who might wish him harm. Out beyond Paris was an open book, to be explored at leisure. Not quite the result he'd wanted, but not a disaster by any means.

He dozed. He wasn't sure for how long, but when he opened his eyes next, something had changed. He shook his head and blinked. Everything was dark. The lights had gone out. He started to turn towards the aisle when he became aware of someone close to him. Too close. He felt the proximity of a body and a fan of breath on his cheek.

'What...?'

'You should have changed the name you came in on, George.' It was a woman's voice, soft and lilting. 'That's sloppy tradecraft, using it all this time. I got all your train bookings and all Katya had to do was wait and watch.'

'Who the hell are you?' Paulton tried to push her away, but she'd got him pinned into the corner. And who was Katya? The name was familiar, but he couldn't recall.

'Somebody really doesn't like you, George. They told me where you were – even sent me a photo. You changed your appearance, but you got careless; Grosvenor House has got great CCTV. It got you and your new friends from Troparevskiy Park. The rest was easy. You're the last one left.'

Another touch, this time running across his leg, and a sharp pain brushed his inner thigh. Before he could cry out, he felt a rush of heat spreading down around his knee.

He wondered if he had wet himself, and felt an instinctive flush of shame.

'I think it's time you retired, George, don't you? Like Bellingham.' The woman patted him on the arm. 'Don't bother getting up. Oh, silly me – you probably can't now, anyway.'

Then she was gone and the lights came up. He blinked through the glare, saw her walking away from him, the burka flapping as black as a crow's wing. The connecting door to the next carriage opened and she stepped through. Her companion appeared just beyond her, a glow of light from the toilet cubicle falling across her head. Then she turned and both women stepped inside and closed the door.

Seconds later – at least, he thought it was seconds ... God, he felt so *tired* for some reason – they came out. Only this time, instead of falling across black cloth, the light fell on uncovered pale skin and hair. One woman was blonde, the other brunette. The clothes had changed, too, and they were now wearing jeans and sweatshirts, the anonymous dress of women all over the world.

Paulton struggled to focus, trying to make sense of what he was seeing. Had he fallen asleep and gone into some sort of fugue state? He didn't think so. *What the hell was happening to him?*

More movement. One of the women – the brunette – was walking back towards the connecting door. She stopped just the other side of the glass, but made no move to come through. She simply stood there. And smiled at him.

Paulton swallowed and tried to speak. But his vocal chords felt oddly disconnected. He could see her face clearly now, and for a second he failed to believe what his eyes were telling him. Then recognition came flooding in. *It couldn't be!*

Clare Jardine.

Something, he wasn't sure what, it wasn't something he could *feel*, some awful premonition, an association of ideas, a horrible knowledge, made him glance down at his lap. A dark shadow was spreading across his leg, which was starting to feel quite numb. When he concentrated, he saw it wasn't a shadow, but a bloody red flow that was glistening and pulsing and dripping to the carpet where it was forming a glossy, widening puddle.

He watched, somehow knowing that he was watching his life leaking out of him, but unable to do a thing about it. He lifted his eyes towards the connecting door, imploring.

But all he saw was the reflection of the carriage in the glass.